CYBORG VS. CYBORG

"You're good, very good," Sam told his opposite, having just parried a furious series of blows from the other's length of polysteel pipe. "But then, you should be, shouldn't you? I mean, you're me."

"Yeah, I'm you," the cyborg replied. "I'm better than you, though."

"How do you figure that?"

"Because I don't have feelings; you have feelings."

"You're right about that," Sam said, stepping forward and lashing out with a well-placed kick that knocked the cyborg back into a pile of empty oil drums. In an instant, he was standing over the evil machine that wore his face, trying his best to smash in its skull. . . .

Ace Books by Kenneth Von Gunden

The K-9 Corps Series

K-9 CORPS
UNDER FIRE
CRY WOLF
THE LAST RESORT

STARSPAWN
THE SOUNDING STILLNESS
THE PALE COMPANION

THE PALE COMPANION

KENNETH VON GUNDEN

ACE BOOKS, NEW YORK

This book is an Ace original edition,
and has never been previously published.

THE PALE COMPANION

An Ace Book / published by arrangement with
the author

PRINTING HISTORY
Ace edition / June 1994

ISBN: 0-441-00064-9

ACE®
Ace Books are published by The Berkley Publishing Group,
200 Madison Avenue, New York, NY 10016.
ACE and the "A" design are trademarks
belonging to Charter Communications, Inc.

PRINTED IN THE UNITED STATES OF AMERICA

10 9 8 7 6 5 4 3 2 1

Stir up the Athenian youth to merriments;
Awake the pert and nimble spirit of mirth:
Turn melancholy forth to funerals;
The pale companion is not for our pomp.

—***A Midsummer Night's Dream***
act I, scene 1

PART ONE

OLD BUSINESS

1

GALEN YEAGER WAS SWEPT TOWARD THE CUSTOMS RECEIVING area by the hivelike bustle that resulted from the commercial starliner *Independence* disgorging its three hundred fifty passengers. Since Galen had little patience for either bureaucracy or authority, it was not an encounter he was looking forward to.

"Good day, Citizen Harrison," the customs 'bot greeted Galen pleasantly as its visual circuits scanned first his passport and then his black hair, olive complexion, and brown eyes. "I am pleased to welcome you to Cousteau. Is this a first visit for you?"

"Yes, it is," Galen Yeager replied, the lie rolling easily off his tongue. More difficult for him was keeping his disdain for the 'bot out of his voice.

If the customs 'bot detected any hostility in Galen's voice, it did not show it. Of course, with its rudimentary face, "emotions" of any kind would have been difficult to discern.

"You are Terran born, Citizen Harrison?" the 'bot asked as all around them dozens of mechanical representatives of the Cousteauean government were simultaneously posing similar questions to travelers as harried as Galen, if not as resentful of the practice.

"Yes, I am." *It's on the passport, you worthless piece of junk!*

"All seems to be in order. Step up to the scanner, please," the 'bot told Galen, while the spindly artificial being's countenance assumed what was meant to pass for a smile.

Reluctantly, Galen moved forward and pressed his forehead against the edge of the scanner, blinking rapidly as he stared at the white dot which functioned to center and focus his gaze.

This is it, Galen thought nervously. It was one thing to darken your skin and change your hair and eye color; those were simple surface alternations that didn't affect one's official identity.

After what seemed an eternity but was probably only a second, the glow of a green light and a soft chiming indicated that the nerve-wracking experience was over and that he'd passed.

"Thank you, Citizen Harrison," the 'bot said, redundantly entering the identity confirmation in a small computer notepad it clutched. His mouth still as dry as Nasser's El Aurans globe-encircling desert, Galen thought gratefully, *It worked!*

It was theoretically impossible to fool a retinal scanner. The reason was simple: There was no known way to alter or disguise one's retinal pattern, a more reliable source of identification than fingerprints. If the scanner compared a subject's scan pattern to one identified in the computer records as belonging to a certain "Patrick Harrison" of Terra and they matched, then that person was indisputably Patrick Harrison.

The trick therefore, Galen observed, was not to attempt the impossible: to alter his retinal pattern. Rather, it was to falsify the records. And that is exactly what Rob MacKenzie, the Deputy Director of the Principate Secret Police, had done. Until the records were corrected and changed back, Galen Yeager *was* Patrick Harrison, businessman from Terra, because his retinal patterns said he was.

"You may pass, Citizen Harrison," the 'bot said in a pleasant baritone voice. "Enjoy your stay on Cousteau."

"Thank you," Galen said between gritted teeth.

Nodding at the elderly couple standing in line behind him, patiently awaiting their encounter with the customs 'bot, Galen waded through the crowd to the baggage retrieval area and began scanning the slow-moving luggage beltway for his bags.

"Some people actually *enjoy* traveling," he muttered to himself.

Galen prayed that his things hadn't been placed on the wrong ship. He would be thoroughly pissed off if his things ended up in New Nippon, Harriman, or Made It. He could always buy new clothing, but he had become attached to his Salinas 250-HF needle gun. A gift from Sam, the needle gun had served him well for the past year; he would dislike having to become accustomed to a new weapon.

Then he lightly smacked his forehead with the palm of his hand—a classically cliched gesture, but satisfying nonetheless. How could he have forgotten? His boss, Hashem Fedalf, had sent the small, steel-gray weapon ahead in the diplomatic pouch. He was to redeem it from the PrinSecPol resident headquarters located in the old Governor's House, now the Principate embassy.

No one, not even the ambassador, had been told who would be picking it up. The locals knew only that it belonged to a top operative whose identity was a highly guarded secret.

A highly guarded secret, mused Galen as he retrieved his luggage. That wasn't the half of it; no one here knew he was coming. He was too well known on Cousteau, having become a minor celebrity as a result of his exploits with the Whale Nation. Given his unwelcome infamy, and to lessen the chance someone might learn of his visit, Galen had made the trip alone. This time around, his partner Sam Houston wouldn't be by his side to help him. Sam had become his partner when Galen and the Voorhees Foundation had "rescued" him. Sam had been a cryogenic sleeper, a person frozen in hopes of a later revival. In truth, all such people were as dead as frozen carp. Galen had overseen the retrieval of Sam's faint memory and personality matrixes and the implantation of them into the body of an android.

That made Sam into Galen's secret weapon: an android with all the powers and abilities of his robotic brethren, but with the capability to kill human beings if necessary. *And working with me*, thought Galen, *it was all too often necessary.*

Actually, Galen reminded himself, *I'm* not *alone—I have access to Alfie when and if I need him.*

Since so much about Alfie seemed like magic, Galen had taken to thinking of the small crystalline object as his "familiar," using the term used to describe witches' and warlocks' spirit helpers.

Because Galen was too rational to ultimately believe that

Alfie was a supernatural being, he subscribed to Arthur C. Clarke's notion that any sufficiently advanced science or technology seemed like magic. Whoever or whatever made Alfie was, by that definition, clearly a technical magician of the first rank.

<*I'm thinking about you, Alfie,*> Galen transmitted.

<<*Yes, I know,*>> Alfie replied, the words forming in Galen's mind.

<*You haven't been "listening in" on me, have you?*> asked Galen.

<<*Of course not,*>> Alfie replied instantly with what passed for indignation in his "voice."

<*All right, then, I'm sorry for even suggesting it,*> Galen told his familiar. <*It's just that I'm touchy about leaving the door to my mind unlocked and having people walk in unannounced—or to know that there is someone listening to and watching everything I say or do.*>

<<*I understand,*>> replied Alfie—who didn't, really. But the alien intelligence accepted Galen's need for privacy of self. He never entered Galen's mind unless invited.

<*What I* don't *understand is how you can communicate with me instantly across light-years of space.*>

<<*I can show you, but you would not understand,*>> Alfie said.

<*Try me.*>

Immediately, Galen's mind was filled with odd, alien hieroglyphic shapes and designs. After several seconds of staring at them uncomprehendingly with his mind's eye, Galen said, <*All right—you win. I* don't *understand.*>

Never one to gloat, Alfie maintained a discreet silence.

<*Oh, well, I was just checking up on you, Alf. Now be a good little familiar and disappear.*>

<<*I am here when you need me.*>>

<*Goodbye.*>

Knowing that Alfie *was* there for him made Galen feel more secure. But Alfie was a noncorporeal presence at best; anything dirty or dangerous that needed to be done was Galen's to accomplish on his own. Alfie could advise and inform, but he couldn't participate.

His brief internal dialogue over, Galen went about his business. Not entirely pleased to see the relentless proliferation of the supposed benefits of progress, Galen stepped onto the spaceport's newly installed people movers. Nearly stumbling getting onto the moving belts, Galen was saved from an embarrassing fall by a Good Samaritan who reached out a hand to prevent him from toppling over his own luggage.

"Thanks," muttered Galen, his face reddening. Someone was unable to stop himself from uttering a short, barking laugh at Galen's expense. Galen swallowed and lowered his gaze, inspecting the tops of his shoes as the moving belts carried him out to the taxi and bus area.

In addition to allowing him to avoid eye contact with those around him, staring at his shoes permitted Galen to wonder why he had let himself to be talked into letting the field supply people to put lifts in his shoes. The few centimeters added to his height hardly seemed worth the effort, especially since he'd now called attention to himself by all but falling flat on his face.

The lifts in his shoes and the cosmetic changes to his hair and eye color were indignities he grudgingly suffered in order to return to Cousteau incognito. It was imperative that no one in authority know he had intervened in the planet's affairs once again. No one—especially Tey Varro—was to know he was back.

Tey. Galen swallowed. Beyond the obvious political motives, he had personal reasons not to see Tey again. He had put their relationship behind him. Seeing her would rip open a wound that was just beginning to heal.

Galen knew he had to accomplish his mission without his being detected by Tey or anyone else in the new government. It was for their own security that they know nothing of what he was doing on their newly independent planet. Galen and Sam—and Tey Varro, daughter of a Cousteauean politician—had helped to free the planet from the grasp of the Terran Principate. To those who preferred the old days, the time before independence, Tey Varro was a traitor, not a heroine.

Galen sighed. Picking up his bags and stepping off the moving belts without incident, he hailed an autocab.

* * *

Galen sipped his omo as he patiently awaited the return of the boy he had hired. The young Cousteauean's mission was simple: cross the street and gain admission to the Principate's embassy. Once inside the ornate building, he was to present a sealed envelope to the officer of the day. Unless there was some problem, the embassy (and PrinSecPol) employee would hand the youth a small package.

Galen smiled as the boy approached his table at the outside cafe—he'd gotten the package. Throwing down enough money to pay his tab, Galen stood up to meet his young go-between. He traded a ten-credit coin for the package the boy clutched, turned on his heel, and quickly and effortlessly melted into the early afternoon street crowd.

Turning a corner, Galen stepped up his pace and then ducked into a fabrics shop. Peering out the window, he waited until he saw a well-dressed man hurry past the storefront.

He permitted himself a self-satisfied smile. *You embassy people never were any good at tailing a subject.*

* * *

"I don't understand why it's necessary for someone from the Company to infiltrate Cousteau again," Galen was saying to Hashem Fedalf. "And, if it *is* necessary, why does it have to be me?"

"Who better than you?" asked Rob MacKenzie rhetorically. "You know the lay of the land, so to speak." When Fedalf made an incompletely stifled choking sound, MacKenzie realized he'd made a horribly vulgar pun about the beautiful Tey Varro. Fortunately for MacKenzie, Galen Yeager's limited sense of humor did not encompass puns.

"I'm also pretty conspicuous, considering my past," Galen said looking at the oddly red-faced Fedalf.

Taking a sip of the strong black coffee he was rarely without, Fedalf said without raising his eyes from the cup, "Following the shake-up of the Magistracy and the rest of the government in the wake of the Cousteau affair, our ranks have become rather thin. It seems the corruption ran deep."

"Meaning?"

"Meaning I have very few agents I would trust with my life—or yours, for that matter."

Galen looked down at his hand, flexed the fingers, and imagined himself pointing a needle gun at someone and pressing the firing stud. "I thought these kinds of assignments were behind me," he said finally in a low voice.

"There is no one else," MacKenzie said with a hint of exasperation in his voice.

"No, there *is* another," Fedalf said.

Startled, Galen looked up at Fedalf. The face of the director of the PrinSecPol revealed nothing. Galen shot MacKenzie a glance, turned his attention back to Fedalf, and then almost imperceptibly nodded at the door. Fedalf understood.

"Please leave us alone now, Rob," Fedalf told his deputy.

"But—"

"Please."

"I *do* have to clear up something with Chang in operations," MacKenzie said as he got up, crossed to the door, opened it, and exited.

Wasting no time, Galen said, "You mentioned another. You can't mean—"

"Yes, I can. I mean Sam."

"Sam doesn't work for you," Galen argued. "Not officially anyway. He's my partner."

"That's why he would gladly do this: to spare you."

"Damn you!" said Galen hotly. "You calculating bastard! You know that's the same reason why I'll say yes—to prevent him from having to act as a hired assassin in my stead."

Fedalf replenished the steaming dark liquid in his small cup, dropped in two sugar cubes, and stirred it all around. Taking a sip, he said over the cup's rim, "Neither of you has to do it, you know. Tey Varro's government *might* survive to the end of the year without our assistance," he said, playing his trump card.

Galen knew when he'd been beaten. "When do I leave?" he asked wearily.

"Tomorrow."

"That soon!"

"Secrets are difficult to keep, Galen, even for the 'secret' police. The sooner you leave, the better."

"Yes, sir."

II

Galen Yeager sat on the end of a remote Cousteauean pier, staring forlornly out to sea as within his mind and soul a violent psychological storm raged. The disk of the dying sun began to disappear as if the sea were swallowing it bit by bit and extinguishing the light. The sight paralleled Yeager's grim conviction that, as the sun was being devoured by the hungry sea, so too was his soul being eaten by the awful realization that his days as one of the Federation's most cruelly efficient assassins were not yet behind him. His quest for inner peace, it seemed, would have to be postponed.

Normally, he would have spoken about his feelings with Sam. Not only was Sam a good listener, he also understood Galen better than anyone else. *I'm doing it again,* Galen realized suddenly. *I'm forgetting about Alfie.* He thought about that for a moment. *No, that's not true. I'm not so much forgetting about Alfie as wondering if he can perform the same function as Sam in this sort of situation.*

Even though Sam was nominally an android, his human personality and mind made him a person through and through. The same could not be said about Alfie. Galen wanted Sam's very real shoulder to cry on, not Alfie's virtual one. Not yet, anyway. Someday, once he understood the friendly but totally alien intelligence better, he might turn to Alfie. But not now; not yet.

That pretty much was that. Now, as the sun dipped below the horizon, a last flash of yellow-white light visible, Yeager took out a happy stick and lit it, drawing the smoke deep into his lungs and sighing. When he'd smoked it down to a butt, he threw it into the sea.

Galen found the luxurious home he was looking for in an exclusive enclave of expensive houses located on the outskirts of Krow. He parked the rental vehicle he had picked up in the city, walked up to the door, and rang the bell.

"Yes, may I help you?" inquired a medium-sized domestic 'bot.

"I would like to speak to Yas Tanna."

"Citizen Tanna is quite busy right now," the 'bot informed Galen. "His duties as First Advisor to President Varro prevent him from seeing unannounced visitors or anyone who does not have an appointment. Do you have an appointment?" the supercilious 'bot asked disdainfully.

Galen smiled a deceptively friendly smile. "Actually, I don't. However, I believe that if you give this to Citizen Tanna"—he handed the 'bot a message cube—"he will see me immediately."

Turning the cube over in his "hand," the 'bot appeared dubious, but finally said, "You may enter. But wait here, please."

Stepping inside the door, Galen watched as the 'bot disappeared down a long entryway and around a corner. In less than a minute, it returned.

"First Advisor Tanna will see you," the 'bot said, unable to hide the disbelief in its voice. "Please follow me."

The 'bot showed Galen into a room all but dripping with rain-forest humidity. It contained a small pool in the floor, several utilitarian pieces of furniture, and a plaswood desk in one corner. Behind the desk, standing patiently, was Yas Tanna.

"Good day, Citizen Tanna," Galen said as the 'bot left the two of them alone.

"And just who the hell are you?" asked Tanna sharply. He stared down at the piece of plaspaper in his hand which the cube had disgorged. "It says here that you are someone who wishes to speak to me about my association with the late Nevin Feller's Shadow Legion."

"That is correct."

"I know nothing about Magistracy spy organizations."

"Then why did you agree to meet me?" Galen asked innocently.

"I wanted to see who you were and what you had to say for yourself before I sent for the police," said Tanna, his hard eyes glinting.

"Yas, Yas," Galen said, shaking his head. "We both know you are not about to do that."

"And why is that?" challenged Tanna.

"Because you do not want your connection to your planet's former colonial occupational forces to become common knowledge."

Tanna's right hand went involuntarily to his throat, and hc traced a finger across the markings there. "You seem somehow familiar to me. Do I know you?"

"I was very close to your president once," Galen said.

"Close to . . ." Tanna's eyes narrowed. "No! It's impossible! You . . . you can't be him."

"I can be and I am," Galen said.

"But you do not look the same. You are taller. You are different in a number of ways."

"It was necessary to change my appearance before making a return visit to Cousteau," Galen explained.

"I see."

You have to admire the guy, Galen thought. *He's awfully cool in the face of what must be a major shock.*

"Please don't touch anything," Galen warned Tanna when the Cousteauean glanced down at his desk. "I want this to remain a private meeting."

Drawing himself up to his full height, Tanna said, "What is it you want from me?"

Galen didn't answer Tanna directly. Instead, he said, "It was you who set Gar Varro up to be taken by the Legion, wasn't it? And, playing the other side of the fence, you also helped Suo Hann arrange Tey's kidnapping."

"That's not true," Tanna insisted. "Anyway, you have no evidence—no real proof—or you would not be here."

"Very good," said Galen, smiling grimly. "You are right about my not having the sort of evidence that would stand up in a court of law."

"Then what do you want? Are you here to blackmail me?"

"Blackmail you?" Galen seemed genuinely surprised. "Heavens, no. I am here to kill you."

Tanna's eyes widened in surprise as Galen's needle gun leapt into his hand when he contracted a muscle in his right wrist.

"NO!"

Galen pressed the firing stud and a ceramic shard blasted a small groove through the First Advisor's forehead, exiting out the back of his skull in a red mist. Gar Varro's onetime rival for the leadership of the Liberation Party fell to the floor without a sound.

Galen crossed over to Tanna's desk, pulled open the top drawer and withdrew the energy pistol he found there. The other drawers of the deceased Tanna's desk yielded very little. Galen then began a search for the safe that he knew had to be somewhere in the room. Galen's quest didn't take long at all—the safe was behind a picture on the wall.

"What an original hiding place, Yas," Galen said to Tanna's body.

Peering closely at the safe, Galen whistled through his teeth. No mere hundred-credit steel box, the safe was the nearest thing to an impenetrable "bank vault" in the galaxy. It was a Qumalii multidimensional security cube. He cupped his face in his hands and slowly drew his fingers down his face.

"Luck be a lady tonight," Galen whispered hopefully as he pulled out the piece of plaspaper with a series of numbers on it. He keyed them into the small numeric pad below the cube. Nothing. He tried several variations. Still nothing. "Sonofafuckingbitch!" he swore. "I should have known that it was too much to hope for to expect Tanna to use his own birthday for the combination."

<*Alfie,*> he called. <*Put down whatever you're doing and help out a frustrated safecracker.*>

<<*How may I assist you, Galen?*>>

<*Cousteauean citizen Yas Tanna was married once,*> Galen said. <*He had a son by his first wife.*>

<<*Yes?*>>

<*What is his son's birth date?*>

<<*Just a moment. I am accessing the Praetor's memory interfaces now.*>> Alfie said, referring to the massive computer that was the Principate's central nervous system.

<*Take your time,*> Galen told Alfie. <*Well, within reason, that is.*>

<<*I have it now,*>> Alfie said and provided Galen with the date.

Galen keyed in the numerals, held his breath, and the cube opened. "You are . . . er . . . *were* unoriginal, weren't you, Yas?"

<<*Success?*>> Alfie asked.

<*Yes,*> Galen told him. <*That did it, Alfie! Thank you very much.*>

<<*I am proud to have been of service to you, Galen.*>>

The cube yielded the names he was after and other priceless information; the bounty was more than Galen could have hoped for. "Thank you very much, Citizen Tanna," he said to the corpse on the floor.

Checking to make sure the energy pistol was fully charged, Galen rang for Tanna's robotic butler.

"Yes, sir?" the 'bot asked, opening the door and rolling into the room. "Sir, what is the matter? Are you injured?" the 'bot asked, seeing its master on the carpet of living moss.

"He's come down with a touch of death," Galen explained to the concerned 'bot, leveling the energy pistol. "Since you have seen me, I must terminate your functioning as well." Before the robot could protest, he burned a hole through the 'bot's abdomen, the site of the mechanical servant's brain.

Working quickly, Galen tapped into the house computer and erased all evidence of the events of the past twenty minutes. That accomplished, he left, satisfied with a job well done.

III

Tey Varro felt like she was drowning. Not in water, which was impossible, but in politics, bureaucracy, and special interests. Besides balancing the needs of the wealthy sea farm owners (*like myself*, she was forced to admit) and the small business owners and independent fishermen, she was faced with keeping Suo Hann's fervent supporters and the sullen remnants of the old leadership from each other's throats.

"I'd like to toss them all in Kubyshev prison and throw away the keys," Tey muttered.

"What was that you said, Tey?" questioned Lin Manna, a senior presidential advisor in the small room with her.

Aware that she was being indiscreet, Tey Varro replied, "Nothing, Lin, I was just thinking out loud."

"I was about to interrupt your thoughts in a moment, anyhow," Manna said to Tey. "Kei says she has an important message for you."

"Oh, from whom?" Tey asked.

"The message is from the . . . ah, from the 'Green House.' " Kei Dakki looked at Tey and asked, "Do you know what that means?"

Tey exchanged a look with Manna. "Yes."

"Oh." Kei shrugged. "It also says it's for your eyes only."

Tey Varro took the message cube containing the coded message, keyed it open, and quickly scanned its contents.

Uri Goldblum, an embassy functionary who had revealed himself to her as a disgruntled intelligence agent, was seeking a meeting with her at the "Green House," an anonymous two-story apartment building on the edge of Bandar.

Goldblum had introduced himself to Tey Varro at one of the many embassy functions she was required by protocol and common sense to attend. Getting her alone, he had confessed a growing dislike for his job and a desire to do what he could to provide helpful information to the new government.

Unwilling to accept Goldblum at face value at first, she was pleased by his requests for some "good faith money."

She found it easier to trust a person who sold secrets in exchange for hard cash. She'd had her fill of ideologues and their personal agendas.

Goldblum's message said it was urgent that he speak to Tey Varro. She crafted a response, telling him she would see him there that evening. She calculated that she had plenty of time to make her dinner engagement and still cross town and meet Goldblum at eight P.M.

She wondered what he had to tell her. He clearly thought the matter was important, since he'd asked for a face-to-face meeting. It also probably involved yet another attempt by the Magistracy to infiltrate and traduce Cousteau's democratic institutions.

Although the Magistracy had recognized Cousteau as a free world and withdrawn the battle cruisers which once enforced the Principate's will, Tey Varro recognized that their former colonial masters still had a massive, if largely unseen, presence on the planet. The Legion and the Shadow Legion still operated as before. *And why not?* Tey Varro asked herself. *They know we have no similar entities yet to challenge them.*

CAREFUL NOT TO LEAVE HIS HOTEL PREMATURELY, GALEN checked his watch and then stepped out into the street and headed toward the nearest of the few walkways on Cousteau.

With the agility that years of experience had provided him, Galen would have quickly hopscotched across the traveling belts from the three-kilometer-per-hour entry belt to the 100-KPM belt under normal conditions. But these weren't normal conditions: encumbered by his elevator shoes, he moved like a hundred-and-fifty-year-old man.

As he made his way across the progressively faster belts, he was vaguely aware of shadows and forms behind him. Good; they hadn't lost him this time.

When it was time to get off the walkway, Galen reversed his initial progression across the belts and was deposited just one block away from Tey Varro's headquarters.

Her offices were in a gleaming new four-story government building and Galen found yet another of the ubiquitous outdoor cafes. There seemed to be one in every block. Ordering a soft drink, he waited for Tey Varro to exit. He glanced at his watch. It wouldn't be long; he knew about her dinner engagement.

Finally! Galen thought when Tey Varro and her aide Kei Dakki emerged from the building. Watching dispassionately from across the street—he had already begun to prepare himself mentally for his evening's ordeal—he thought only, *What a handsome woman Tey is.*

Tey and her assistant got into an official vehicle that drew up to the curb less than fifteen seconds after they had come out of the front entrance. *Very good, very professional*, Galen noted. Security concerns dictated that a leader should not spend any more time exposed in a public place than necessary.

Once Tey's limousine had pulled away, Galen got up, crossed the street, and entered the building. Inside, he pressed a stud outside an unmarked door to announce himself and immediately placed his hand over the vision chip. "Yes?" a suspicious-sounding voice asked.

"Tell the lady of the house her laundry has arrived," Yeager said, using Uri Goldblum's emergency code, designed to gain the agent immediate access in an emergency.

"What color is the ticket, please?"

"Blue."

"Come in." The lock on the door clicked and the door swung open. Galen wasted no time. Ignoring the lift/drop tubes, he made his way up the stairs and was permitted to enter Tey Varro's office.

As he passed through the door, Galen whispered a key word to himself to induce a semihypnotic state of mind. Once inside, Galen nonchalantly shot the man who'd opened the door in the head and continued walking into the room.

Standing over a computer printout, Lin Manna was not immediately aware of Galen's presence or what he'd done. By the time Manna turned and saw both Galen and the dead man, his eyes widening in surprise, Galen already had the energy pistol leveled at his chest. Galen's bolt of energy burned a hole through Manna's chest and he fell to the floor without a sound.

Galen turned and killed the other two people in the room as quickly and efficiently as he had Lin Manna. All four of his victims were co-conspirators whose names he had found in Yas Tanna's security cube. They had intended a coup to topple Tey Varro and replace her with Yas Tanna.

A cursory search of the room provided Galen with an old-fashioned slug-thrower which he pocketed. With the odor of charred flesh in his nostrils, he left the room and closed the door behind him.

As he exited the building, Yeager crossed the street to where one of his "tails" sat in a vehicle trying not to look directly at him. Yeager stopped by the car and leaned in as if to ask directions. Instead, he aimed the laser gun at the startled man and burned a small hole through his forehead.

Knowing that another tail, pretending to read a newscube, had not clearly seen what happened when he leaned into the car to talk to the man's partner, Galen was able to get within a meter of the puzzled man before he pulled the vibroblade from inside his clothing and thrust it up and under the man's rib cage and into his heart.

Galen was wearing an extremely thin layer of a synthetic material on his hands embossed with Uri Goldblum's fingerprints, so he deliberately allowed the vibroblade to clatter to the street. Walking unhurriedly away, he disappeared around the corner before he heard the first sounds of alarm and discovery behind him.

Galen took the walkways across town to the Green House and made his way to the apartment Uri Goldblum used for his meetings with Tey Varro. He keyed in the entry code and the door swung open.

Goldblum, a dark and intense-looking man, had his feet up on his real-wood desk and was leafing through a hol-vee porno magazine when Yeager came into the room. Goldblum looked puzzled, then mildly alarmed. "Who the hell are you?"

"Manna sent me, Uri."

"Do you know me?" Goldblum asked.

"Yes—and you know me, too," Galen told him.

"I do?"

"I'm Galen Yeager."

"Galen Yeager? Galen Yeager?" Goldblum repeated Galen's name as if uttering the syllables aloud would help him to understand what was happening. "What the hell are you doing on Cousteau?"

"The Magistracy's dirty work, as usual," Galen explained. "I just iced Manna and several other of Tey Varro's associates. They were Yas Tanna's people. Yours too, I assume."

"Jesus Christ!" Goldblum's feet flew off the desk, and he sat bolt upright in his chair. "I was working him," he said wonderingly. "What the hell's going on? What's the Magistracy up to?"

"Oh, did I say the Magistracy?" Yeager said. "I'm sorry. I meant to say I'm doing Fedalf's dirty work."

"Listen, Yeager," Goldblum began. "I don't know what

games you're play—" He stopped when Yeager withdrew the slug-thrower from his pocket.

"You shouldn't have killed Tey Varro's people like that," Yeager said. "The others didn't appreciate it. And when they figured out your scheme, they realized that they had to get here before her to head off your planned assassination of her."

"You're crazy!"

"They're not in your league, Uri, but they did manage to get here in time to stop you before you could execute your plan to shoot President Varro."

"No, please—"

Galen raised the silenced slug-thrower and fired. The first shot caught Goldblum in the cheek, just below his left eye. Angered by his poor marksmanship, Galen fired again, and this time the slug pierced Goldblum's skull at the hairline and bored through to explode out the back in a pink shower of blood and bone fragments.

Galen wiped the gun clean and threw it on the floor beside Goldblum's body, into a pool of blood that was forming near his shattered head.

With one of Chang's electronic sniffers, he swept the room for bugs and found three—which he ground to bits beneath his heel. Satisfied with his efforts, he left the office, used the drop tube to reach the ground floor, and then exited.

Walking down the street, Galen uttered a three-syllable word which ended his trancelike state. Almost immediately he began to shiver violently and then to shake. A wave of nausea forced his last meal up his throat and out into the gutter. Several passersby uttered sounds of disgust and turned away from the unpleasant sight.

Perspiring heavily, Yeager leaned against a building, steadied himself, and then went on. He was a professional, and that was what professionals did; he went on.

Besides, all this wasn't over yet. There had been another name in Tanna's cube. Killing a former Consul would not be easy.

II

Anyone who had ever met Tegan Rian called him lizardlike. The stocky, brown-haired Rian was a fight promoter in

Smithville, one of the larger and least savory cities on Yeltsin. Actually, he was something more sinister than that; he was a Doro trainer and exhibitor. Although he had his own stable of fighting Doros, Rian oversaw the training and fighting of perhaps two dozen more.

Simply put, Rian was the owner of record for several rich, powerful, and anonymous Doro owners—people who enjoyed the "sport" but wished not to be connected with it publicly.

The wealthiest, most powerful client Rian represented was also the one with the strongest need and desire for anonymity: former Principate Consul Peter Zajicek. The onetime leader of the Magistracy had long been a Doro fancier and had even been seen publicly at Doro "fist offs"—often sniffing verboten joy dust.

That was before he joined the Magistracy, of course. Once he was in the limelight of power and responsibility, Zajicek recognized that continued attendance at the officially frowned-upon contests was out of the question. And now that he was in hiding, he needed a surrogate owner/trainer more than ever.

After the financially successful fist offs at his private ring held the night before, Tegan Rian counted the take and planned for the special high-stakes-betting bouts he was organizing for this evening. Everything had to be just so because Consul Zajicek himself was coming with a retinue of friends and sycophants—druggies, lezzos, Cally boys, and various suckers-up to the rich and powerful former Consul.

Rian spent as little money as possible on the upkeep of the Doros, even Consul Zajicek's, and the cages two floors beneath the already sunken exhibition hall where the fist offs took place emitted a vile odor of excrement and decaying food.

"Look at 'em," Rian said to his small janitor 'bot, busy giving the passageway outside the cages its once-weekly scrubbing. "Look at 'em—they're the best damn fighters in the whole city and they're all mine." Since the janitor 'bot's voice circuits had long since shorted out, the barrel-shaped little thing made no reply but continued to scrub the grime off the soiled plascrete.

Pleased at the prospect of making a lot of money this evening, Rian inspected his stable of fighters. Careful not to get too close to the front of the cages, Rian peered happily at each sullen Doro inside. Long used to such treatment, the Doros turned their backs on their master, and sucked on the fruit the 'bot had tossed in before beginning its cleaning routine.

"Yes, children, you're going to make me a lot of gravity tonight," Rian said to himself, using the slang word for money. Rian paused before one cage which bore the name KING KONG. "And how are you today, Kong?" he asked. In response, the Doro lunged at the bars and reached out, its hands seeking Rian.

The promoter just stepped back and raised an electric prod. "Get back, you big bastard!" he shouted. "Want to get your hands on me, eh? Like to tear me limb from limb? Well, you'll never get the chance." He thrust the prod at the frustrated Doro, driving the beast away from the front of the cage. "Save it for tonight, Kong—Consul Zajicek thinks his Mississippi Mauler can take you; we both know otherwise, but you'll be in for one helluva fight, though."

His inspection over, Rian took his time walking back to his crowded little office. Once there, he plopped heavily into his cuddle chair and took out a huge cigar and lit it. The air was immediately filled with acrid smoke, and Rian settled back to begin the serious business of blowing perfect smoke rings.

He was starting to link the rings together in the air when his human assistant Otto Huyck stuck his head into the office and announced, "Someone to see ya, Mr. Rian. You in?"

"Maybe. Who is it and what's he want?"

"Dunno for sure—he says his name's J. J. Coupling and that he wants to make you an offer you can't refuse."

Rian considered that; there was always a place in his heart for another rich sucker like Consul Zajicek. "This Coupling, he look like he got money?"

Otto pondered that for a second before replying, "Yeah, I'd say so: He's wearing pretty good-lookin' duds and he's sporting a star sapphire ring that'd choke a horseface."

"Let's not keep Mr. Coupling waiting, then, Otto my boy. Show him in."

"Ah, Mr. Rian, I presume?" asked Galen, dressed as flashily as his imagination could conceive. Galen had initially been reluctant to go out looking like an interplanetary pimp, but he saw Rian's eyes widen involuntarily at the sight of the ring he was wearing and had to admit that his decision had been a wise one.

"Yeah, that's me. What can I do ya for?" Rian asked, indicating a chair in front of his small desk.

Galen flicked away a piece of food on the chair—at least it looked like it had once been food—and sat down. "Actually, it's what we can do for each other," he told Rian.

Galen watched a big smile break through and spread across Rian's face. Since he himself was never at a loss for the money to buy the few things he desired, Galen was always surprised at the effect the mere mention of a possible financial windfall had on others.

"Yeah, well, I'm always open to suggestions," said Rian.

Galen looked carefully around the room, leaned closer to Rian—somehow managing not to flinch at the vile odor that wafted his way from the fight promoter's mouth—and said conspiratorially, "I understand a certain former Consul will be here for tonight's fist offs. Is that true?"

Rian's face darkened. "How'd you hear that?" he demanded.

"Oh, I have my ways," Galen responded. "Is it true?"

Rian now looked suspiciously around his own office. "Maybe yes, maybe no. What's your interest?"

Galen took out a huge roll of bills. "Ten thousand credits if his Doros all lose their contests."

"You wanna bet ten thousand credits on the other Doros?" asked Rian.

"You misunderstood me," said Galen. "The ten thousand is for *you*. I'm placing two hundred thousand on the other owners' Doros."

Rian felt faint. He stared greedily at the money—what he could do with ten grand! But there was Consul Zajicek . . . if he found out he'd be a dead man. "I . . . I . . . ah."

"Why don't we send your people away and discuss this matter in more detail?" suggested Galen.

"I guess it won't hurt to talk," agreed Rian. "Hey, Otto!" he shouted.

"Yeah?" said Otto, sticking his head through the door.

"Listen, you and the other boys go take a coffee break and don't come back for a half-hour, okay?"

"Sure, boss," said Otto, happy to oblige.

"And, Otto . . ."

"Yeah?"

"Lock the doors."

"Gotcha, boss."

"Now, then," said Rian after Otto had gone, "let's talk business."

"Well," said Galen, leaning forward, "here's what I have in mind." Seeing that the big moment had arrived, Galen took a device from inside his coat pocket. It looked like an ordinary pen but it was something else altogether. As Rian leaned expectantly forward, Galen discharged a spray of gas in his face. Rian looked startled, gasped, and slumped over his desk.

"Come on, Mr. Coupling," Galen chided himself, "get this over with."

Working quickly and efficiently, Galen undid the top of Rian's shirt and carefully felt for a place just beneath the unconscious man's collarbone. He marked it with a soft grease pencil and took out something that looked like a staple gun. Pressing it against the mark he'd made on Rian's skin, Galen pulled the trigger.

Putting the implanter away, Galen carefully removed the grease mark, sprayed Rian's chest with a "freeze tube" to make sure it didn't cause him pain, and rebuttoned Rian's shirt. He placed the promoter's arm on the desk in front of him and gently laid Rian's forehead on his outstretched arm, making it appear like he was sleeping.

That's it, Galen thought. *He's all set for his big night.*

* * *

Otto Huyck returned to find his employer dozing in his cuddle chair, his head on his desk. Since the sight was nothing out of the ordinary, Otto thought little of it and began to back out of the room. Suddenly, he froze.

Creeping back into the room, he stared at the pile of bills half hidden under one of Rian's arms. He could see a lot of zeros. *That's a lot of gravity*, he thought. Licking his lips, Otto stared at the money like a cobra studying a chicken.

After several minutes had passed—during which he saw himself throwing down a pair of dice surrounded by beautiful android prostitutes with glittering gold eyes—he thought better of succumbing to the lure of the plan forming in his head. He didn't have much of a life, but it *was* a life.

Stealing money off the top of Tegan Rian's desk was like looking for a shortcut to the morgue. Besides, maybe it was a test. Or a trap. He licked his lips—a test *and* a trap.

This time he backed completely out of the room.

* * *

It was another hour until the drugged Rian awoke, feeling groggy and confused. He looked around the office and then at a timepiece. He blinked, unable to accept the fact that nearly ninety minutes had elapsed since . . . since . . . since *what*? He couldn't remember what he'd been doing before he blacked out. He shook his head—he'd seen people do that on the holodramas—and tried to recall his actions.

"Otto!"

"Yeah, boss?"

"What was I doing about an hour or so ago?" he asked tentatively.

Otto looked confused. "You kiddin' me, boss?"

"Do I look like I'm kiddin'?"

"You was with that J. J. Coupling guy, remember? You told me and the boys to take a jumper to the rim worlds while you picked his pocket."

Suddenly Rian's eyes fell on the packet of bills lying on his desk and he barked, "Okay, then, that's all. Go back to whatever you were doing."

"Sure, boss."

Rian picked up the wad and thumbed it—about five thousand credits. "What in the hell?" he said aloud to no one in particular. Then he saw the envelope. Quickly, he tore it open and his eyes gulped down its contents: "Remember—bet it all on Kong." It was signed "Coupling."

Rian just scratched at the slight itch near his collarbone and looked dubiously at the money. "I gotta lay off the joy juice," he told himself.

* * *

Since the arrest of Consul Ramona Somoza on Made It, the other two members of the Magistracy had taken extraordinary security precautions. Before Peter Zajicek deigned to enter Rian's secret Doro ring, his agents—*his* people—thoroughly checked the area out, snooping about with electronic devices and specially trained dogs. Only when they were convinced that all was safe was the Consul himself allowed to enter, his entourage trailing along behind him like a depraved supply train.

While everyone else stayed up in the bleachers surrounding

the ring, Consul Zajicek accompanied Rian down to the holding pens, anxious to see his "champions" before the contests began.

"Aren't they magnificent, Tegan?" asked Peter Zajicek. "I enjoy seeing them this way, just before the bouts commence."

"They're in first-class shape tonight, Consul Zajicek," agreed Rian. "I think they'll give you plenty of entertainment."

"I certainly hope so," Zajicek said, motioning for several of his flunkies to approach him. He reached out and pulled an exotic-looking young woman wearing many intricate tattoos, but little else, tight against his body. Staring into the girl's almond eyes, he kissed her hard and slid his moist tongue down her throat.

Rian looked away as a young woman with a shaved skull sidled up to the embracing Consul and the tattooed woman and directed Zajicek's hand to her own body. The Consul's fingers insinuated themselves into the girl's minuscule panties and Rian found that he was unable to prevent himself from watching Zajicek's fingers moving around beneath the silk like a tarantula under a sheet. Feeling out of place, Rian mumbled something about having work to do, walked away, and lit a cigar.

From his vantage point across the street, Galen watched as the security people, leaving several members of their force inside, emerged to take up their posts surrounding the building. *Very professional*, thought Galen. *No one can get in or out unless Zajicek wants them to.*

Galen took out the device that controlled the small atomic charge he'd implanted in Rian's chest that afternoon. A joyless smile spread across his face as Galen poised a finger above the firing stud on the detonator and then pressed it.

After an excruciatingly long pause, the building housing the illegal Doro arena seemed to lift off its foundation and hang suspended in midair for just a moment. Then blinding shafts of light burned from the windows as if a sun had been contained inside. The building's sides erupted outward in a shower of fragments. Galen stepped back around the corner of the building facing the ruined one as the shock wave hit and a wave of hot air roiled past.

Galen did not wait for the sirens to start or the emergency crews to arrive; he left. As he walked away he remembered the sounds of the caged Doros he'd heard when he visited Rian that afternoon. Their agony was now over. And those who had ordered the assassination of Tey Varro were dead.

It was a good day's work.

* * *

It was still an hour to jump time, Galen Yeager noted, looking at his watch. Around him the other passengers in the lounge were talking among themselves, sniffing joy dust, reading, drinking, smoking or chewing synbacco or happy sticks, and otherwise doing what people do to take their minds off an unpleasant possibility—being lost in hyperspace.

Despite people's irrational fears, very few ships were lost on jumps into and out of hyperspace any longer since the discovery that ESPers could clear the hull of the dimensionless hypermatter that could and did hold some ill-fated ships in that nontime when they were jumping from one point in the galaxy to another.

Strange, Galen thought, *but the passengers on any starship always look* exactly *like the passengers on every other ship I've ever been on*: *the bored sales people*, *the young marrieds*, *the ultra-rich and ultra-bored planet hoppers*, *men and women in various uniforms*, *a permissive couple paying no attention to their loud bratty kids*, *a Neo-Christian nun, two girls with backpacks*, *and a young man with a musical instrument. Maybe I'm the only* real *person here and they're all from Central Casting*.

Galen shrugged and turned his attention back to the scholarly article he was studying on his holoreader about Westerns, a 20th-century "pop culture" form that was being rediscovered as popular entertainment. One paragraph in particular stood out:

> Although the hero's presence makes the fight possible—i.e., he insists on obstructing the evil one in some way—it is the latter who invariably attacks first. Were the hero ever to draw first, the story would no longer be a Western. And he must kill only in self-defense and never an unarmed man—the "hero" who kills the villain in cold blood (as in our modern melodramas) *cannot* be a true hero of mythic dimensions; he becomes indistinguishable from the villain.

Galen laughed dryly and turned off the 'reader. The tiny image always blurred a bit no matter what you did. Modern technology. He massaged his eyes with the heels of his palms, but the words still danced across his retinas like accusing phantoms: "he becomes indistinguishable from the villain."

Jesus, he thought, *we're* all *indistinguishable from the villain nowadays.*

A pause and then another part of his mind said: *No, Galen, as much as you'd like for it to be true, it isn't. That's the easy way out.*

Galen decided that the lounge was not the place to be at this particular moment. He really needed a place with the proper atmosphere. He went forward to talk to the Captain.

III

"Look again," Galen was saying to the Captain.

"No, I accept your credentials. You're who you say you are—a senior PrinSecPol officer with an A-prime security rating. It's . . . well, it's just that what you're requesting is very unusual. Unheard of, actually," the Captain explained.

"That may be," Galen conceded, "but I still wish to be in the forward observation deck with the screen open when we transit hyperspace. It's only a twelve-minute jump, subjective time."

"But no one but an ESPer or a 'scraper has done that and remained sane," the Captain persisted, the features of his ruggedly handsome face softened by concern.

"Maybe I'm insane now. Maybe what lies out there for me *is* sanity," said Galen.

The Captain shook his head sadly. "Do you really believe that?"

Galen looked away then back again, meeting the Captain's steady gaze. "I don't know what to believe anymore," he said truthfully.

"You have to sign something," the Captain said finally. "Come with me."

They left him in the forward observation deck—alone—just minutes before the scheduled jump. Galen could hear the sounds of things being made secure and the eerie echoes of distant voices shouting down emptying corridors.

There was no turbulence in hyperspace, no physical manifestations at all, yet objects had a way of behaving strangely if they weren't tied down.

The jump itself would take twelve minutes of body time although all timepieces on board the ship would register the passage of absolutely no time at all. If one were able to view the jump simultaneously from both the point of departure and the point where the ship entered normal space again, he would observe the ship leaving and arriving at the same nanosecond. The physicists had several theories to explain this "impossible" phenomenon; none seemed completed enough, however, to account for all the contradictory details.

The universe isn't just stranger than we think it is, marveled Galen, *it's stranger than we can* imagine *it to be!* He looked at his watch and saw that there was just over a minute left before the ship jumped. He stared out into deep space, noting the blinking serenity of distant stars.

Galen shrugged and glanced at the room he was in. Except for the rear observation deck, there was no other place where one could look out of a starship. For to gaze upon the yawning emptiness of hyperspace for more than a few minutes was said to be as deadly as gazing upon the writhing visage of the Gorgon Medusa.

Insanity, all the locked-room claustrophobia of incurable madness, was normally the penalty for looking at the forbidden: for looking into the bowels of hyperspace. That was why, Galen knew, the Captain had tried so hard to dissuade him.

The ship jumped.

Galen experienced a momentary feeling of nausea. An odd awareness, a rippling, passed through him, and he felt out of focus, blurred. Then everything was normal again. Except for one thing: The stars were gone.

In the stars' place was . . . nothing.

Rigid with anticipation, Galen sat for what seemed like an eternity. The blood pounding in his ears attested to the passage of time even though his watch said differently, lying to him by refusing to acknowledge even a second's passing.

Galen stared out into the void, waiting.

Galen was not a believer, not in the traditional sense. Even so, something had caused him to get the idea into his head that if he stared into the incomprehensible void of hyperspace he would see the ultimate—he would see the face of God. If not

God, then he would see whatever superior intelligence was at the center of being and the universe.

Neither happened.

What he finally saw was in its own way more horrifying than he could have anticipated.

He saw nothing. Not 99.99999 percent of nothing. Nothing. His examination of hyperspace yielded no deity to take away his burden of guilt or his pain.

"It's not fair! Something, show me *some thing*, anything!"

Galen rose with glacial slowness, as if it hurt his bones to rise, and confronted the vision screen, a supplicant whose petition seemed unlikely to be granted.

He raged and beat against the surface of the screen with his fists until they were bloody. "Show me something," he repeated dully as his blows grew weaker and less frequent. His hands left a smeared, red trail down the screen as he slumped to the floor.

Galen remembered the last thing the Captain had said to him before leaving him in the observation deck: "I don't know what you expect to see, but remember this—it will almost certainly be the thing you fear most."

"Goddamn you!" Galen screamed at the void. "How dare you deny me forgiveness!"

PART TWO

FAMILY TIES

GALEN YEAGER BIT HIS LOWER LIP IN CONCENTRATION. IT didn't help much, however. He couldn't seem to coax the proper notes out of his violin no matter how hard he tried. As thick and clumsy as a fat man's, his nonresponsive fingers felt like sausages. And Galen was no fat man.

Engrossed in attempting to force his fingers and his bow into some form of obeisance, Galen failed to notice his partner Sam Houston intently staring at him over the neck of the 'cello he caressed like a longtime lover. Sam's golden-hued irises grew larger with interest and concern as he focused on his partner's troubled expression.

"Dammit!" exploded Galen, finally pushed beyond the limits of his patience.

"Something the matter?" Sam asked mildly.

"Something the matter?" repeated Galen. "No, not if you think I'm doing justice to Mozart's music."

"That's not what I meant," Sam said in that same infuriatingly mild voice.

Galen's eyes flashed and he was about to make an intemperate remark when he noticed the concern creasing his friend's face. Just as quickly as it had arisen, the anger he felt ebbed. "It's the Foundation," he said after putting down his instrument and the horsehair bow.

"The Foundation?"

"Well, not really the Foundation, *per se*, but my family."

"Your family?"

"Must you repeat everything I say?" demanded Galen crossly.

"No, I mustn't," replied Sam in a deceptively innocent voice. Sam used it whenever he wanted to irritate Galen. He resorted to it now to take his friend's mind off his troubles and to transfer Galen's anger or frustration onto his shoulders.

"Good."

"Well?"

"Well, what?"

"Your family," Sam prompted.

<<*Tell him already, Galen!*>> pleaded Alfie.

"Ah, you're eavesdropping again," Sam said, turning his head to stare at the egg-shaped crystal, safe and secure in its foam-padded hemispherical container on the coffee table.

The "protective" container was a concession to Galen's sincere, albeit groundless, concern for Alfie's well-being. If forced to admit the truth, Galen would reluctantly agree that not even a moly-steel drill bit could scratch Alfie's surface.

<<*That is true,*>> Alfie agreed. <<*I was attending to your conversational exchanges.*>>

Galen shook his head. When Alfie had first joined them, he was unfailingly polite and grammatically correct—if a bit stiff. Now, after months of exposure to Sam's unique personality, the little alien entity was becoming a little too human at times.

Ignoring Alfie's comment, Sam pointed at his lips with both index fingers and slowly and exaggeratedly mouthed the words, "Your family."

"I give up," Galen said, sighing deeply. "I've been invited to join my family in a sort of combination family reunion-cum-shareholders meeting."

"In Texas?" Sam asked, using the name of the state instead of the city; he felt funny whenever he had to say "Houston."

"No, not Texas." Galen sighed again. "In Africa."

Sam was impressed. "Africa. You're really getting back to your roots, eh?"

Although the reference escaped Galen, Alfie chuckled appreciatively. Sam was teaching the little alien intelligence all the pop culture and history he could dredge up from his elusive memories.

Galen waved a hand. “Every two or three years or so, someone in the family decides that it is time to return to the fountainhead of the family fortune.” He frowned, vaguely aware of the alliterative nature of his last sentence.

<<*Is it time?*>> asked Alfie.

<*I guess so. It* has *been nearly four years since the last get-together.*>

<<*Galen,*>> Alfie reminded him, <<*you know you can speak out loud to me if you wish.*>>

“Yeah, I always forget.”

“So why are you so depressed?” Sam wanted to know. “Do you not get along with the members of your extended family?”

“It’s not that,” replied Galen. “It’s . . . well, it’s just that when I’m at one of those things I’m not me.”

Unable to resist the opening, Sam said, “That should make everyone grateful.”

“It does,” replied Galen, unperturbed by Sam’s jab. “You see, I become ‘little Galen.’ ”

“Little Galen?”

“Me, my cousins, all of us under forty, we revert to being kids again. In the eyes of our parents or our aunts and uncles, that’s what we are. We’ll always be kids to them.”

“I see,” said Sam, surprising Galen by adopting a sympathetic tone. He walked over and rubbed Alfie’s smooth surface. “I guess there *are* advantages to having no family, Alfie.” Cocking his head at Galen, Sam asked, “Are we taking Crystalman with us?”

“Crystalman?” asked Galen. Then he understood Sam was referring to Alfie. “No. I mean yes. Well, not really.”

“Which is it, Hamlet, yes or no?”

“Alfie is coming along in spirit only,” Galen said. “Since he can stay in contact with us wherever we go, it seems pointless to require his actual physical presence.”

“Hmm-m-m, good point,” acknowledged Sam. “What do you think about that, Alf? Do you object to mind-melding with us mere mortals?”

<<*Not at all, Dr. Floyd. As you know, I enjoy interacting with humans.*>>

“Heeheehee.” Sam giggled like a little boy.

"What's this 'I enjoy interacting with humans' crap?" Galen asked Sam. "And who's 'Dr. Floyd'?"

"Oh, I'm just having a little fun, Gale," Sam said between involuntary hoots of laughter. "I asked mineral-breath here to respond to me like that every once in a while."

<<*It tickles him,*>> explained Alfie—causing Sam to chortle again.

"Don't call me Gale," Galen snapped at Sam.

"Yassir, boss. We pore ole field hands sure am sorry we spoke outa turn to the massa."

"And don't start that stuff, either!"

<<*Hehhehheh.*>>

"Dammit!" exclaimed Galen. "You're corrupting Alfie now!"

<<*I am sorry, Galen,*>> Alfie said seriously. <<*Did I offend you?*>>

"No, you didn't offend me, Alfie," Galen quickly reassured his friend. "It's just that one maniac around here is enough." He glared at Sam.

"Boy, if you didn't have the Tin Woodman"—Sam pointed to his own chest and then at Alfie—"and the Scarecrow's brain here as friends, you'd have to advertise for best buddies."

Galen blinked as if he'd confronted something unpleasant. "Yes, you are absolutely correct, Sam," Galen said softly, realizing how stiff and humorless he was being. *As usual,* he told himself.

Sam closed his eyes as if in pain. *Sonofabitch! That's right, Sam, insult Galen by implying he has no friends and couldn't get any except by paying for them!*

"Shit, Galen, I'm sorry! I didn't—"

"I know you didn't, Sam," Galen said. "What hurts is how much truth there was in what you said. Even Alfie has his . . . his friends—the 'others' he speaks with when the two of us are otherwise engaged," he said, carefully putting quotation marks around the word "others."

Galen and Sam knew almost nothing about Alfie's mysterious "others." From what little he permitted them to learn, it seemed that the others were other-dimensional minds, vast alien intelligences that Alfie communicated with in ways neither Galen nor Sam could begin to understand. Once again, it was a case of Clarke's advanced science as magic. Since these "others" were beyond their comprehension, Sam and Galen soon gave up any hope of comprehending the relationship Alfie had with them.

All Galen and Sam knew, and this was from Alfie himself, was that Alfie would never betray Sam or Galen or allow these other beings to harm the two of them. Having no alternative, they accepted Alfie's assurances.

"Tell me, Alfie?" Galen asked. "Have you been speaking to the 'others'?"

<<*Yes. They have remarkable minds. I do so enjoy our exchange of ideas.*>>

"Sparkling conversationalists, eh?" said Sam.

Alfie sensed Houston's friendly sarcasm but only said, <<*Yes. They know things those who inhabit this universe cannot begin to imagine.*>>

"Uh-huh," Sam grunted. Practical and down-to-earth, Sam accepted Alfie's mindlink with other-dimensional intelligences with a certain degree of skepticism.

Galen tugged nervously at his earlobe. "I hope we don't bore you, Alfie," he said. "I don't know that we can compete with your . . . uh . . . friends. We're pretty dull folks."

<<*Even the members of your family, Galen?*>>

"Ha, he's got you there," laughed Sam.

"So, you're ready to meet my family, are you, Alfie?" Galen asked.

<<*I am always eager for new adventures, Galen,*>> Alfie replied seriously.

"Attaboy," said Sam.

"Thank you, Alfie," Galen replied. He held out his hand, and Sam passed over the crystalline egg. In much the same manner as he would pet a cat, Galen stroked Alfie's cool, smooth surface.

When a sense of pleasure emanated from the crystal in response to his touch and his words, Galen realized that Alfie drew as much comfort and support from his association with himself and Sam as the two of them did from him/it.

Watching Galen rubbing Alfie, Sam asked, "Do you two want to be alone?"

"Don't be jealous . . . Tin Woodman," Galen said, making Sam smile.

"Tell me, Crystalman," Sam said. "Does it feel good to get out of that box and stretch your legs?"

Instead of responding to Sam's tongue-in-cheek inquiry,

Alfie said matter-of-factly, *<<There is a call coming in via subspace for you, Galen.>>*

"Subspace?" Galen frowned. "Where's it coming from?"

<<From Cousteau.>>

"Uh-oh," Galen muttered. "Someone's put two and two together and come up with the correct answer."

Sam and Alfie had a private exchange, and Sam looked at Galen oddly. "What? What is it?" Galen asked nervously.

"Alfie says it's Tey Varro who is calling."

II

"Tey, dear, it's so good to see you again!" Galen gushed when her image blossomed in the center of the room. Then, suddenly remembering something, Galen corrected himself and said more formally, "I mean *President* Varro."

Tey laughed a musical laugh that made her bare breasts jiggle. Beads of sweat formed on Galen's brow. "Oh, Galen—you haven't changed a bit."

Galen's broad smile retreated a bit when he realized her words could be taken several ways. "Ah, yes. Well, neither have you, Tey."

She shook her head. "I'd like to think that's true," she told him. "But I think I've aged a hundred years in the last eleven months."

"It doesn't show," Galen told her.

And that was the truth, he realized. At the advanced age of thirty-one, Tey Varro was still as gorgeous as ever. Her olive skin glowed and her emerald eyes sparkled. Her hair was slightly different. Although still as black as the bottom of the sea, it was not as close-cropped as before. That made sense, Galen thought. Tey was a world leader now; she obviously had less time to spend in the water, where shorter hair was advantageous.

"Thank you, Galen." Tey's face adopted a more serious mien and she asked, "Tell me, Galen, have you been back to Cousteau recently? Returned here without my knowledge?"

"Back to Cousteau? Me? What are you talking about?"

"I'll take that as a yes," Tey said.

"Tey, I can assure you that—" Galen began.

"While you are clearly one of the best secret operatives in

the Principate, Galen Yeager," Tey said, "you never could lie to me. Not convincingly."

"I *haven't* been back to Cousteau," Galen insisted.

"Uh-huh." Tey was buying none of it.

"And even if I had, I couldn't tell you," he said weakly. "Now what is this about?"

"Okay, okay. I realize you can't speak freely." Tey glanced beyond the frame at something or someone—*Dya?* Galen wondered, remembering the tiny, barrel-shaped old woman who had helped raise Tey and her brother Bec. Without revealing what had drawn her gaze offscreen, Tey returned her attention to him.

"It seems that Yas Tanna, my father's old comrade and my vice-president, and a Legion spy named Uri Goldblum were planning to overthrow my government and install Tanna as the new leader of Cousteau. A leader who would be more sympathetic to Principate interests than I have proved to be."

"Really?" Galen winced to hear how phony he sounded.

"Please, Galen—don't even try pretending." When he just shrugged, Tey continued, "Something happened. The two factions screwed up, turned on each other, and both Tanna and Goldblum were very coldly and professionally killed"—Galen winced at that "coldly"—"along with several of my closest advisors. It turns out—no surprise, I guess—that they were in Tanna's pocket, too."

"Wow," Galen said, not even bothering to sound convincing.

"Yes, wow," agreed Tey. "The thing is, there seems to have been an unknown third party operating on Cousteau. It's highly probable that this third party was really the one who defused the situation by assassinating the plotters and making it appear they killed each other off."

"Gee," deadpanned Galen.

"I take it you aren't going to confess your involvement in all this?" Tey said, looking like she couldn't make up her mind whether she wanted to scold him or laugh.

It was Galen's turn to shrug. "What can I say? I haven't been to Cousteau since . . . Well, you know since when."

Tey nodded. "The records show that it couldn't have been you. They reveal that it was probably a man named Patrick Harrison."

"Well, there you go."

"The thing is, this Harrison person doesn't seem to exist outside the Praetor's data banks."

"Really? Curiouser and curiouser."

"It can't be said of you that you don't know how to keep a secret, can it, Galen?"

"Your father," he said, changing the subject. "How is he?"

Tey looked wistful. "He is . . . unchanged." She reconsidered that. "No, since his trip to Terra to see the specialists you generously provided, he has improved a little bit. I suppose I hoped for too much too soon. The doctors said he would get better—but very slowly and over a long period of time."

Galen nodded. "He *will* get better, Tey. He will. You'll see. One day you'll have the father you knew back with you."

"I hope so."

"You will, believe me." Galen prayed that he sounded more confident and truthful than he really felt. *Dammit! Why should she believe me when I don't even believe myself?*

Tey dropped any semblance of formality and official distance. "Thank you, Galen. Thank you for saving me and my world once more." There was sadness in her voice. "I can only imagine how hard it must have been for you to do what you had to do—to kill that way again. Thank you."

As Galen felt a lump rising in his throat, Tey stood up.

When she approached the holographic imager, Galen said, "Killing is what I do best, I'm afraid."

When it appeared that Tey's holographic image was about to walk right up to him, Galen began rising from his chair. More than anything, he wanted to embrace her, to hold her close once again.

Tey's nictitating eyelids covered her eyes, but not before Galen saw the tears forming in them. "Goodbye, Galen," she mouthed silently, then reached out and touched the offscreen controls. Tey abruptly disappeared in a spray of multicolored specks.

Galen settled back down into his chair. "Goodbye, Tey," he said softly to the now-empty air.

Galen remained motionless and silent for so long that Sam crept up to the door of the room and peeked in. Seeing Galen sitting in the semidarkened room caused Sam to shake his head sadly and back away noiselessly.

III

"Welcome to Africa," Galen said with a smirk as he gestured at the gleaming anywhereness of Johannesburg's air- and spaceport. Galen had traveled enough to know by now that the institutional nature of arrival lounges resisted all but the most insistent attempts to make them reflective of the planet or country that welcomed the incoming passengers.

"So this is it, huh?" said Sam Houston, beaming. "The Dark Continent."

"Uh . . . yeah," agreed Galen, finding it hard to reconcile Sam's words with their bland surroundings.

Sam's head swiveled as if on a gimbal as his hungry gaze took in everything. The busy airport was filled with the typical mob of people of all genders, races, shapes, and sizes. More exotic—and more in line with what Sam was expecting to see—were the dignified men and women clad in brightly colored robes.

But Sam's pleasure abated a bit when he saw that those in traditional garb were a distinct minority. And even they were carrying briefcases or wearing the blank-faced look of people communicating via microencephalonic telecomm devices.

"Internals?" Sam said, disappointed.

"They're business people," Galen told him. "They're only doing what business travelers like themselves always do wherever they are: using their implanted comlinks to send reports or to get the latest stock prices on the Afro-Arabian Exchange."

"But why are so many of them wearing Euro-American suits and dresses?"

"What did you expect?" snorted Galen. "A bunch of natives with bones in their noses clad in loincloths? I told you not to watch all those old sinnys on the hol-vee."

"Yeah, but—"

"In *my* family, you're a hopeless bohemian if you don't wear your old school tie."

Understanding flashed in Sam's eyes. "So *that's* why you tied that tourniquet around your neck. I thought it was to cut off even more of the blood flow to your brain."

"Very funny."

"Yeah, I must be—because everyone's looking at me," said

Sam self-consciously as he observed the number of boldly inquisitive stares being cast in his direction. Several attractive women had coolly appraised him, only to turn away in apparent alarm when they'd noticed his golden-irised eyes.

"I don't think they see very many androids in much of Africa."

"And why is that?" asked Sam, watching two small children pointing at him wide-eyed with wonder and pressing close to their mothers' sides.

"Since the Middle Ages people have been using the sword to impose their particular faiths on the continent. The Crusaders and the Saracens weren't the first or the last to do so. Later, the Europeans and the other empire builders who parceled up Africa for king and country, raped and pillaged Africa, robbing it of its natural resources."

"Takers," agreed Sam.

"They didn't just take, they gave," Galen said. "Since they bore the 'White Man's Burden' of bringing Christian values to the Dark Continent, as you yourself called it, they 'saved' the natives by doing their best to eradicate the indigenous religions."

"That's terrible!" exclaimed Sam.

"Terrible?" Galen shook his head. "From the natives' point of view, I suppose it was. But people like the missionaries saw themselves as bringing Jesus' message of sin and redemption to the unenlightened. They were saving the souls of these people. They believed they were doing a sacred thing."

"Jesus!" muttered Sam.

"Yes—and Mohammed and Buddha, too," Galen said. He smiled and continued, asking, "Is it any wonder, then, that many Africans turned back to the practice of their old holistic, animalistic, or totemistic religions in carefully thought-out acts of ethnic and spiritual self-defense?"

Although he wanted to say, "Wow, could you repeat that?" Sam just asked, "They worship animals, trees, and ghosts?"

Galen nodded. "A lot of people still believe that the very air that surrounds them is filled with animal, human, and demon spirits. Since artificial beings—robots, androids, and the like—are soulless, they are prime candidates to host an evil or mischievous spirit."

"Are you serious about this?" asked Sam. Then he thought, *Soulless?*

"Absolutely serious," said Galen with a small, satisfied smile.

"But . . . I mean, you were giving me grief for expecting Edgar Rice Burroughs natives and—"

"Who?"

"Never mind. He's before your time," explained Sam. "As I was saying, you were chiding me for—"

"There's a brave youngster," Galen interrupted again, this time to point out a small boy edging slowly toward Sam.

"Oh, for Pete's sake!" Sam said, exasperated by the sight. He leaned over slightly to put himself on the child's level and said, "Boo!" The boy uttered a high-pitched shriek of alarm and hurried back to the safety of his mother's arms.

<<*That was not nice, Samuel,*>> Alfie scolded.

<*That's telling him, Alfie,*> Galen replied on their internal link. He was nervous about speaking aloud to his disembodied familiar; he and Sam were suspicious enough already in the eyes of those around them.

"Hmmph," grumped Sam. "Are there at least some lions around here someplace? *They* shouldn't be afraid of me."

"Lions?" said Galen.

It was only when they left the climate-controlled comfort of the airport that Galen noticed Johannesburg's heat. Stepping out into the burning afternoon rays was like walking into a vast, brightly lit oven. "Is this more like what you were expecting?" he asked Sam.

"A little," Sam admitted, his sensors recording the severity of the heat. "But I won't be satisfied until I see a lion."

"Hmmm," mused Galen. "Let me try my lion call."

"Lion call?" Sam watched in wonder as Galen first moistened and then clasped his palms together; he began blowing between them, producing a noise that sounded suspiciously like lip farting.

Still producing the hideous sound, Galen studied Sam's face out of the corners of his eyes. Finally, he couldn't keep a straight face any longer.

"You bastard!" erupted Sam, finally catching on. "You were pulling my leg!"

"Me?" said Galen innocently. "That's impossible—you know I don't have a sense of humor." He headed toward the waiting line of cabs and autocabs, hailing one with a human driver.

"Hey—wait," said Sam.

4

GALEN POINTED THEIR RENTED ROVER SOUTHWEST ON THE Johannesburg–Kimberley–Cape Town E-Mag highway. Half surface vehicle and half variable-grav floater, the Rover had cost a small fortune to rent. Ever mindful of out-of-pocket expenses, Galen fretted about the cost until he remembered that he could submit the bill to the Soweto Corporation. That brought a smile to his face.

Staring at the increasingly rural and less inhabited countryside just off the magway, Sam was glad to leave the urban towers and city streets of Johannesburg behind. Nonetheless, he was growing curious where his partner was taking them. So far, Galen had been closemouthed about their destination. When he could contain his curiosity no longer, Sam asked, "Where are we going, Bwana?"

"To my grandmother's estate."

"In Soweto?"

"More or less," Galen replied. "It's just a bit south of the old South-Western Township."

"The what?"

Galen smiled. "Soweto is actually an acronym for South-Western Township. It stems from the time of apartheid, when the black population which worked in Johannesburg was not permitted to live there. Soweto was their own planned urban community."

"Blacks had to live in a separate area?" asked Sam incredulously. "Why?"

"Because they were *black* and not *white*."

"Yeah? I still don't get it."

"In those days South Africa was a white-ruled nation; blacks and 'coloreds' had no share of the power. They were not true citizens of the country."

"What happened?"

"What you might expect to happen when the majority of a country are denied their rights."

"Was it bloody and awful?" asked Sam.

"Actually, it wasn't. More and more of the ruling elite of the country looked around, took a deep breath, and accepted the inevitability of the numbers. While they didn't welcome the breakup of the country into smaller autonomous states, it averted all-out racial warfare. Eventually, just like the rest of Terra, the formerly segregated state achieved racial harmony through intermarriage, which blurred once-prominent racial characteristics."

Holding out his arm, Galen said, "Look at me. I'm living proof that so-called 'white people' are becoming more darkly pigmented, while many 'black people' are becoming progressively lighter."

Sam grinned. "That's wonderful."

"I agree," said Galen. "Racists, however, call it 'mongrelization.' "

Sam was silent for a long time before finally saying, "Okay, we're going to your family's estate, your grandmother's home. Why there instead of the corporate headquarters?"

"I told you," Galen said patiently. "This is a *family* get-together, not a stockholder's meeting. We'd be in Bern if we were going to the corporate headquarters' actual physical location."

"Oh," said Sam. Under the impression that Galen's family was gathering to conduct some serious business, Sam was now more than a little confused about what they were doing here.

As if reading Sam's mind, Galen said, "You have to understand how my family does things. The only reason there are *any* stockholder's meetings is to satisfy the requirements of being a publicly owned corporation. The family makes all the major decisions in private. We still control fifty-five percent of the stock."

"Can I ask a rude question?"

"That's never stopped you before."

"Just how rich are you?" Sam asked.

"That *is* a very rude question to ask anyone, but I'll answer it this one time," Galen allowed.

"Yeah?" said Sam expectantly.

"None of your business."

"Awww, you promised."

"Oh, all right. I usually have a book worth of between ten and fifteen million credits."

"Jesus H. Christ!"

Galen closed his eyes as if in supplication. "Try not to talk that way when we get there. Some of my family still belong to the Dutch Reformed Church. They're serious about not taking the name of the Savior in vain. My grandfather would have washed your mouth out with soap."

"I'll try to keep that in mind."

"As for my fortune, well . . ." Galen shrugged. "It's all 'paper profits' anyway, based on the current value of the stock. That's why the amount is so fluid." A look crossed his face as he remembered something. "Oh, and take away some of that as a result of my divorce from Adrianna."

* * *

They left the crowded magway for a smaller version of the road that continued for less than another twenty kilometers or so. When they left the guidance systems behind, Galen lowered the wheels and allowed the vehicle to settle onto them. After that, the roads deteriorated so rapidly that even the fat, all-terrain tires and stiff suspension of the Rover had difficulty handling the ruts and potholes.

"I sure hope I don't have any loose connections," Sam said, bracing his hand against the padded dash.

"Do you think I ought to switch back to the null-grav motors?" asked Galen. "I hate using them when I get a chance to drive like this."

"Only if you're satisfied that you've met the demands of your penance, my son," Sam said, the top of his head nearly bumping up against the Rover's roof.

"Penance?"

"Never mind," Sam sighed. "I'll quit. I wouldn't want you to have to pull out your pocket humor detector just for me."

When Galen complained that the Rover's climate controls were not working, Sam nodded and asked rhetorically, "It's damned hot inside here, isn't it?"

Galen turned and stared quizzically at his partner. "You're plastic and metal," he said as if Sam was unaware of that fact. "Look at you, for Chrissakes! You're not even perspiring. How can you complain about the heat?" Sam did look remarkably cool and collected.

"I am *aware* of the temperature, meat-boy," Sam replied. "I must confess, however, that it has little effect on me within a range of several hundred degrees in either direction."

"Uh-huh," Galen said, wiping his brow with a handkerchief. A part of him was actually glad for the air-conditioning malfunction; it meant that he would probably get a substantial rebate on the Rover's costs or maybe even a credit for a future rental.

"Even without my temperature sensors," said Sam, "I can literally see the heat." He pointed at a ten-meter-high wall of air shimmering in the distance.

Galen looked and said, "That's not hot air."

"Huh?"

"Turn up your hearing."

Sam did as Galen suggested and said, "You're right: I hear a high-pitching sounding, a sort of electronic keening."

A drop of perspiration fell from Galen's nose. "That's a force field."

Sam whistled. The shimmering air extended as far as his inhuman vision could see. "That is *some* force field installation."

Galen nodded. "We're almost home."

Galen allowed the Rover's inboard computer to take over while he dug out his Soweto Corporation credentials and mentally repeated the sequence of numbers that would allow him to pass through the fast-approaching guard post.

"Armed guards?" Sam said questioningly. "Out here?"

"Yes, even out here," Galen told him. "Almost anyone in my family would be a prime target for terrorists. Put the whole family together and we're damned near irresistible."

Galen slowly lowered the window on the driver's side of

the Rover and kept his hands where they could be seen and accounted for. As a security person approached the vehicle, Galen said *sotto voce*, "Don't get cute. This would be the wrong time to be a smartass."

"Good afternoon, Mr. Yeager," the mustachioed security man said, bending over slightly to peer inside the Rover.

<Hey, he knows your name.>

<I've never seen him before, but I would imagine that he has holos of all the family members expected for the meeting.>

<That makes sense.>

"Good afternoon," Galen replied pleasantly through slightly clenched teeth.

"And who is with you, sir?"

"This is my friend and partner, Sam Houston."

"Please step out of the vehicle so I can be sure that you are not a prisoner."

<I told you androids were rare in this neck of the woods,> Galen told Sam. "Ah, Sam is an android."

"I am aware of that, sir. Please step out of the vehicle and let me see your identification."

Galen opened his mouth to say something, thought better of it, opened the door, and climbed out. The security guard—it said "Sgt. Nwrani" on his name tag—examined the holocard Galen presented him.

"All seems in order," Nwrani said. He handed Galen a small cube. "Punch in the security code, please, Mr. Yeager." Galen did as he was asked. The results were apparently satisfactory, since the sergeant told Galen he could get back into the car and proceed.

"Whew, I'm glad that's over with," Galen said when they had left the checkpoint behind. "I felt all sweaty and guilty even though I had no real reason to."

"That's just a manifestation of your feelings about authority," Sam told him. "You're a cop who hates cops."

"I am not a cop. I am—"

"Hey!" shouted Sam. "Look! There they are!"

"There who is?" asked Galen, looking where Sam was pointing. "Oh, yeah—a pride."

Sam bounced up and down in his seat like a small boy. "Can we stop? Huh, Galen? Please!"

"All right," Galen said, a firm yet indulgent parent. "But no getting out of the Rover."

"Ahhh, jeez!"

II

"Here goes nothing," Galen said, pressing the bell. After perhaps twenty seconds, the door opened.

"Hello, Amman," Galen said to the dignified and impeccably turned-out butler who answered the door.

A smile lighting up his face, Amman Ropani responded by saying, "It is good to see you again, Master Galen. I presume this gentleman accompanying you is Master Samuel?"

"Just Sam will do," Sam told him, shifting his weight from one foot to another. "I'm nothing but a fancy robot, a proletarian worker."

"What!" exclaimed Galen.

"Robot means worker in Czech," Sam explained. He looked at Amman and shook his head sadly. "Education is so spotty these days, don't you think?"

Shaking his own head, Amman retorted, "Proletarian worker? Nonsense. I have been told that you are to be treated as a guest of the family."

"I am?" asked Sam, taken back by Amman's deference but also pleased by it.

"Please come in, gentlemen," Amman said as he stepped to one side to allow them to enter.

"Amman, you shiftless old sod!" cried a voice from down the long entry hall that stretched out behind the butler. "Who's there, for goodness sake?"

Turning his head but not his body, Amman said in a voice that carried down the hall without his having to shout, "It is Master Galen and his friend Sam."

"Oh, my *gawd*! It *is* cousin Galen!"

Sam watched in awe as a slim black woman dressed in a simple, if clearly expensive, white dress grabbed hold of Galen, planted a big kiss on his cheek, and hugged him to her.

Sam noticed that Amman slipped away discreetly while all this was going on. *He'd make a good surveillance person*, Sam thought approvingly.

"Hello, Elani," Galen said, intimidated by the emotional outburst directed at him by his cousin.

Sam winced, saddened by his friend's shyness and reserve.

Pulling back from the well-intentioned assault, Galen said, "Elani, I'd like to introduce you to my friend and partner, Sam Houston. Sam, this is my cousin Elani Landskroner."

"Sam . . . Houston?" she asked, tilting her head like a curious parrot. "Is his name really Sam Houston, Galen?" She spoke standard Prin'glish with a slight accent that Sam couldn't quite place.

"Yes, my-name-is-really-Sam-Houston," Sam said, affecting a toneless mechanical voice. "I-am-a-robot. Correction, I-am-an-android." He raised his left arm in a series of stiff, jerky movements, bringing his watch close to his face. "Oh-my. It-is-time-to-wind-my-works, owner-Galen."

When Elani looked at Sam in slack-jawed amazement, Galen said apologetically, "Sam is just kidding."

"I am?" Sam asked innocently. Then he relented. "Yes, Ms. Landskroner, I am. Kidding, that is."

Elani Landskroner's gaze switched back and forth between Galen's face and Sam's. "Yes, I see." She laughed a tiny, forced laugh. "Uh, come in, please."

"Thank you," Sam told her. "I can't wait to meet the rest of the family."

As he passed by his cousin, in pursuit of Sam, she grabbed his arm and hissed, "Galen, we need to talk. Are you sure you know what you're doing by bringing him here?"

"Later," Galen said, disengaging himself from her a second time in as many minutes. Her swift about-face made him wonder about the sincerity of her effusive greeting. He followed Sam down the long corridor toward the conversation and classical music being funneled toward them by the hall's shape.

"Wait up, partner," he said to Sam's back.

"Hurry up, then. I have people to meet."

"Christ, I hope bringing you along wasn't a mistake."

Sam laughed. "Too late to worry about that, Gale."

The room they entered was enormous, easily a hundred meters by forty or more. But what caught Sam's eye was not the room's size, but what it contained. A waterfall seemed to come out of nowhere at the far end; the resulting stream wound its way through the room, bridged at strategic points by lovely wooden arches. Shooting up toward the ceiling many meters overhead were slender-trunked trees, their broad branches seeking the sunlight streaming down through a transparent canopy.

The room was a multileveled wonder, with open areas filled with coffee tables, sofas and chairs, and other furniture. There were terraces containing a wealth of brilliantly colored flowers and other exotic plants.

"Is that a sloth?" Sam asked, peering at a tree limb high above their heads.

"Uh-huh," grunted Galen. "And that's a macaw, I think," he said, pointing out a large-beaked bird with vivid blue and purple plumage.

"This must be a bitch to vacuum," Sam said.

"I don't know," replied Galen, seriously. "I never had to do it." He gestured at the nearest clump of people. "Shall we?"

"Try and stop me."

One by one, Galen introduced Sam to everyone. Galen's aunts' side of the family was by far the easier for Sam to remember, despite their acquiring different names through marriage. The patriarch's sons and the sons of the sons tended to blur into one another because they all bore the Voorhees name.

Seeing someone standing alone by a quiet pool filled with large golden carp, Galen said, "There's my uncle Hans. Come on."

When his uncle saw them approaching, Galen smiled and waved. After his uncle made the usual so-glad-to-see-you-again small talk, Galen introduced Sam to him.

"Pleased to meet you, Sam," Hans Voorhees said, shifting his drink to his left hand and reaching out with his right.

"The pleasure is mine, Uncle Hans," Sam replied, shaking the proffered hand. Sam graciously allowed Galen's uncle to win the "manly handshake" competition. Had he wished to, Sam could have crushed the man's hand to a bloody pulp.

Galen's mouth turned up slightly at the corners in an almost-smile. Uncle Hans appeared a bit taken aback by an android calling him "Uncle."

"Ah, yes, thank you. Yes," Uncle Hans said. He stared dumbly at the glass of Scotch in his left hand as if surprised to see it there. He took a large sip.

"This is the first encounter I've had with Galen's family," Sam said pleasantly. "To meet virtually everyone in one fell swoop is almost overwhelming."

"Hmm-m-m, yes. Yes, indeed," replied Hans Voorhees. His eyes seemed to focus on someone or something across the room. "Ah, there is Mother." He paused a moment before adding unnecessarily, "She is Galen's grandmother."

"I see," said Sam as if that was news to him.

"If you two will excuse me, I must go and pay my respects." He hurried off.

"Someone might think his pants were on fire," said Sam dryly.

"Both he and Elani did seem about as comfortable with you as those youngsters we saw in the airport," agreed Galen, sipping his own Jack Daniel's and water. "I hope you don't have that effect on everyone here."

"Something tells me I don't," replied Sam, watching a thoroughly attractive young woman looking him up and down hungrily, the tip of her tongue just protruding from between her lips.

Galen followed Sam's gaze and remarked. "That must be my cousin Nelson's daughter; I hear she's the sort who finds the unknown stimulating. Should I tell her you're a fully functioning model?"

"No," Sam sighed. "I don't want to make trouble for you in the bosom of your family."

"That's a first," Galen snorted.

III

Galen loved his family; he really did. But it took less than fifteen minutes for him to realize why he didn't see them more often. He rediscovered what a long time spent away from them always made him forget: Spending time with them was maddening.

"The law is a very important undertaking, Galen," Kurt Voorhees said to Galen, driving home his point by jabbing a stiff forefinger into Galen's chest. Annoyed by this action, Galen looked down and observed that while Kurt's fingernail was perfectly manicured, it was also dirty. "And that is why we lawyers are paid so much. We deserve it. We perform a vital function for society."

"By creating 'busy work' for bureaucratic nonentities, Kurt?" Galen asked, gently pushing aside the offending digit.

Galen had long thought that his large, russet-haired, and thickly built cousin was more like a tree or other vegetative life form than a human being. As Kurt went on and on in his nasal monotone, Galen decided that being compelled by good manners to submit to his cousin's blowhard lecturing on any subject was akin to having large strips of flesh ripped from your body by red-hot tongs.

Like many on the Afrikaner side of the family, Kurt was relatively fair-skinned. As a result, his face and neck were leathery and cross-hatched with lines beneath the sort of ruddy sunburn look common to people with a northern European heritage. The sun wrought its worst on mad dogs and Englishmen—and Dutchmen, Germans, or anyone else from above the forty-eighth parallel.

Covertly eavesdropping on Galen's and Kurt Voorhees's conversation from across the room, Sam focused on their words, easily audible to his superior hearing. *<Why's your cousin Kurt so white?>* Sam asked Galen. *<For that matter, why are so many of your cousins on the Voorhees side so white? I thought you said your family was racially mixed.>*

<Oh, it's you again,> Galen replied good-naturedly. *<The answer to your question is simple: Although they themselves are half white and half black, most of my aunts and uncles married Caucasians. The cousins are changing that.>*

<Good for them.>

Oblivious to Sam and Galen's internal exchange, Kurt Voorhees was droning on. "What I do is essential for the workings of our international and interplanetary economies," he insisted. Then, out of the blue, and as nonchalantly as asking about the weather, he said, "Tell me, Galen, are you still a spy for the government?"

Before Galen could answer what was an impossible question—many in his family *knew* what Galen did, they just weren't supposed to *say* it out loud—Sam joined them and said, "Gee, cousin Kurt, could you ask that a little more loudly? I'm not sure everyone heard you, especially the listening devices hidden about the room."

Flustered, Kurt Voorhees reddened noticeably. "This is the Voorhees family, Mr. Houston. We have no secrets from each other. And as for there being any listening devices in this house, *sir*—that is impossible."

<Notice how he pronounced "sir" like he really wanted to

say "cur"?> Sam asked Galen before saying, "Impossible?"

"Impossible," Voorhees repeated, for emphasis. "Our security people are the finest. This room was examined and found to be free of bugs this afternoon."

"Oh, I see," Sam said, ignoring Galen's gestures to knock it off. "Then this transmitter I found over by the bar was supposed to be there, I take it?" He held out a minute black speck that was no larger than a flake of pepper.

After taking it from him and examining it, Galen concurred with Sam's judgment. "It's a bug all right."

"But our people—"

"Have probably been gotten to. Or at least one of them."

"This is intolerable!" Kurt Voorhees sputtered. "What if there are other such devices? We cannot—"

"Actually, there were two others," Sam informed him. "Don't worry: They are no longer in working order."

"Sam, what would I do without you?" Galen asked. He hadn't the heart to tell his friend that the bugs were probably planted at his grandmother's insistence.

"See, bringing me along *wasn't* a mistake, after all, was it?" Feeling smug, he walked away.

<*Say, Alfie . . .* >

<<*Yes, Sam?*>> came the other's voice.

<*Thanks for locating those bugs for me.*>

<<*It was my pleasure.*>>

<*There's just one other thing, Alf.*>

<<*Yes?*>>

<*Let's not tell Galen about this.*>

* * *

"Galen!" a familiar voice called to him. "Galen!"

Galen excused himself from the small group he was in and turned to greet his aunt Kitrina. "Hello, Aunt Kitrina," he said, as an imposing woman with dark eyes and medium-length black hair came toward him, arms opened wide.

"Galen, Galen!" she cried. "It is so good to see you."

Galen smiled at the pleased look that lit up her broad and homely face. "It's good to see you, too, Aunt Kitrina." That was no falsehood; since his childhood, Kitrina Tollersrud had been one of his favorites among his late mother's brothers and sisters. She was the oldest child and still fit and healthy at eighty-two. Galen couldn't help observe ruefully that, as she had aged, Aunt Kitrina had more and more come to resemble a man in women's clothing.

"Come now," Aunt Kitrina insisted. "It is about time you paid your respects to your grandmother."

"I haven't had much of an opportunity, so far," Galen said in a defensive tone.

It was true; his grandmother, as the matriarch of the Voorhees family, had been as surrounded by her offspring as any queen bee in a busy hive. And like the queen bee's attendants and caretakers—both drones and workers—they had swarmed around her bringing her food and drink and tending to her every need or wish.

"Please bring your friend along," his aunt commanded.

<Oh, Sam.>

<Yes, Master Galen?>

<Someone wants to meet you.>

<Is she pretty?>

<She was once; it's my grandmother.>

<Why do I suddenly wish I was still frozen?>

They headed for a distant corner of the large room. With Aunt Kitrina showing the way like Moses leading the Israelites, the assembled family members and their guests parted at the trio's approach as magically as the Red Sea. Just as magically, they flowed back together in an amorphous mass once they'd passed.

"I understand you have divorced Adrianna," his aunt asked with the directness of the old.

Please, thought Galen. *Anything but this*. "That's right, Aunt Kitrina."

She shook her head sadly. "I'm sorry to hear that. For you it is a personal tragedy; for our family enterprise, it is an unwelcome and expensive blow that comes at a most inopportune time."

"The family thinks the breakup of my marriage is bad for the corporation?" Galen asked.

"Of course," Kitrina Tollersrud said, and Galen felt like he was six years old again and she'd caught him with his hand in the cookie jar. "Like you, Adrianna is part of a powerful family enterprise. Your marriage provided a much needed connection to their wealth and influence. I can't imagine the divorce not leaving a residue of bitterness that will cost us all dearly."

"I see," said Galen. And he *did* see, finally. The corporation was all about business; and business was supposed to be about money, power, and influence, not about personal feelings. But since theirs was a family affair, anything that affected the family's financial welfare was a matter for concern—no matter how personal and private it might be on other levels.

"And so," Aunt Kitrina said, "that's why your grandmother invited her here today."

Galen's stomach did a flip-flop. "Ahhh . . . invited *who* here today, Aunt Kitrina?"

"Why, Adrianna, of course."

PART THREE

ALVES

5

"ADRIANNA?" GALEN SAID, LOOKING AROUND IN ALARM.

"What are you doing, Galen?" Aunt Kitrina asked. "If you're expecting to see Adrianna, I can tell you that she has not even arrived yet."

"Oh," Galen said, feeling foolish.

"Come along now, Mother is waiting."

"I get to meet your grandmother *and* your ex-wife!" Sam said to Galen. "This is my lucky day."

"Glad it's someone's," Galen replied sourly. Then he added, "By the way, although her legal name is Mugambi-Voorhees, we have simply called her Grandmother Mugambi since the death of Grandfather."

As they made their way through the crowded room, Sam saw a wrinkled old woman sitting on an ornate chair inlaid with ivory. <*Your grandmother?*> he asked.

<*No, that's Adrianna,*> Galen said crossly.

<*You're right—stupid question.*>

Sam thought that the chair made Galen's grandmother look like an aged Cleopatra reigning from the throne of the Ptolemys. He wasn't sure what he'd expected, but it wasn't this wizened old crone.

<*Just how old* is *your grandmother?*> Sam asked Galen.

<*Nearly one hundred and thirty.*>

<Is that all?>

Despite himself, Galen laughed. *<I know what you mean. She was over ninety when I was born.>*

<She certainly seems older.>

Any number of things conspired to make Ghannee Mugambi-Voorhees look less like a beloved family matriarch than an ancient unwrapped mummy: her white hair cropped close to her skull, the way the stubby and stained corncob pipe she kept putting between her lips seemed to emphasize the vertical wrinkles around her mouth, and her large, rheumy eyes. Sam studied her masklike face and decided that perhaps she was more respected—feared?—than loved.

"You've finally brought my grandson to me, have you, Kitrina?" Ghannee Mugambi-Voorhees asked in a querulous voice. Like many other members of the family, she spoke Principate English—Prin'glish—with a pronounced accent.

"Yes, Mother. Here is your grandson, Galen," Kitrina said, stepping aside so that Galen and Sam were front and center.

Facing his oldest living relative, Galen said stiffly, "Hello, Grandmother Mugambi."

She stared at him down her nose. "Look at you, child. You're still as rigid as a petrified python. I would have thought that Adrianna or this Fib woman you took up with might have loosened you up. I guess not."

"Fib?" Galen said incredulously, his facade of studied disinterest slipping for just an instant. Regaining control, he swallowed and pushed back his anger. *I allowed her get to me again!* he chided himself.

Unwilling to get into an argument with his grandmother in front of the other members of his family, Galen decided to ignore her use of the insulting word "Fib." His emotions once again veiled, he said, "Grandmother, I would like to introduce Sam Houston." When Sam nodded, Galen added, "Sam is my partner."

"He looks like a very pretty man, but I am told he is not a real man at all," Grandmother Mugambi observed, peering at Sam with watery eyes. "They say men such as he are soulless machines possessed by evil."

<Sam, please don't—>

<Don't worry, I'll be good,> Sam promised. *<But only if you protect my name.>*

<You've got a deal.>

"Sam is not a soulless machine, Grandmother," Galen said, biting his lip.

"Then there is a spirit that lives in him? He walks and talks because of black magic?"

<This is getting better and better,> Sam said, astonished that Galen's grandmother could hold such superstitious beliefs.

"There is no black magic involved, Grandmother," Galen said wearily. "Simply science." He shrugged and held his hands apart. "Some people say that science itself is a form of magic. If that is true, then Sam is the product of white magic, not black."

Aunt Kitrina broke her silence by saying, "And I hear Dr. Bussot is the magician." Sam raised an eyebrow at her mention of Bussot, but said nothing.

"I see," Grandmother Mugambi said dubiously, turning her attention back to Sam. "Don't you try to put the evil eye on me, machine-man," she warned, pointing the stem of her pipe at the bemused android.

"I won't," Sam promised soberly.

"Tell me, Galen-child, what for you come here with news for your old grandmother that you want to hurt the family?"

Caught off guard by her sudden switch of subjects, Galen stuttered, "I . . . I don't wish to hurt the family, Grandmother."

"Then why you divorce Adrianna, Galen-child?"

"I don't *love* her anymore, Grandmother."

Grandmother Mugambi snorted. "What l-o-v-e got to do with it?" she asked, drawing out the word.

"Didn't you love Grandfather?" Galen asked. He heard Aunt Kitrina's sharp intake of breath at the temerity of asking his grandmother such a question.

"We're not talking about your grandfather, child!" Ghannee Mugambi snapped. "Wc'rc talking about you and Adrianna and what's best for this family!"

"I'm sorry, Grandmother, but I can't stay married to someone just for the benefit of the family."

"Apparently not," sniffed Aunt Kitrina.

"Do you expect this machine-man to stay for our family meeting?" Grandmother Mugambi asked Galen, again pointing at Sam.

"And why shouldn't he?"

"Because he is an outsider," Aunt Kitrina told him. "The family's business is the family's business and no one else's."

"I'll wait outside with the other guests, Galen," Sam said.

<Are you sure?>

<It's for the best.>

"All right, Sam." Galen tilted his head and, looking askance at his grandmother, asked, "Are you satisfied now, Grandmother?"

"Yes, I am, child," she said, watching Sam make his way through the crowded room and toward the front of the house. "Yes, I am."

While Sam was trying to coax one of the sloths down from its perch high in a tree by tempting it with a piece of fruit, Galen sought out his Aunt Kitrina's only daughter and his favorite cousin.

"Hello, Ghannee," he said to the beautiful, slim young chocolate-complexioned woman intently watching several children trying to catch salamanders in one of the shallow pools.

Startled by the sound of his voice, she said, "Yes?" and turned to see who was calling her name.

"It's just me," Galen said, smiling.

"Galen!" she shrieked. A red-haired boy and a blonde girl, up to their elbows in the water, looked up at the sound of her exclamation. After staring slack-jawed at the two adults embracing, they shrugged and returned to their hunt.

"Let me look at you," Galen said, pulling back and holding her at arm's length. "I forgot how gorgeous you are."

Ghannee blushed—and Galen recalled how their darker cousins used to chide her about her how easy it was to know when she was flustered or embarrassed. "You have not changed much, either, cousin," she told him in that little-girl voice he remembered so well.

"Not on the outside, perhaps," he replied. "But I'm not the same as I was on the inside, in my heart and soul."

"Your soul is . . . different?" Ghannee asked, her eyes going wide with wonder.

Galen smiled and took her right hand in both of his, remembering that one had to watch his words with Ghannee; she took many expressions literally. A childhood disorder had left her mentally impaired. Only marginally, but enough to have caused her to remain perpetually childlike and innocent. It was her most endearing quality, Galen thought.

"Yes, but only because it was touched by love and tragedy during my stay on Cousteau," he explained.

"Love?" repeated Ghannee slowly. Then her eyes glowed and she smiled bashfully. "I am in love, cousin Galen."

"You are?" asked Galen, simultaneously astonished and delighted. "With whom?"

"With the man I am going to marry."

Galen saw that she was enjoying playing a little game. He smiled and played along. "And who might that be? Is he here? Am I going to get to meet him?"

"No, he is not here," Ghannee said solemnly. Then she giggled, covering her mouth with her hand. "But you are going to get to meet him."

"What are you talking about?" Galen demanded, mock seriously.

"You'll see," was all Ghannee would say.

Galen wasn't satisfied, but he knew once Ghannee made up her mind about something, she couldn't be budged.

* * *

"I simply do not accept that the Soweto Corporation's already limited and circumscribed mining operations on Archeon IV pose a serious threat to the indigenous life forms," said one of Galen's cousins, taking issue with a report filed by that planet's Corps of Engineers.

"I agree," said Richard Voorhees, another of the cousins. "This sounds to me like another attempt to hit us where it hurts until we buy our way out of the problem."

"I am almost certain that is exactly what the local population wants," Mahute Yaari, one of the cousins and a partner in the legal firm of Voorhees, Kandar, Crosley, and Yaari, which, not surprisingly, worked exclusively for the Soweto Corporation.

"What do you mean?" asked Galen.

"It's simple," Mahute Yaari said. "It appears that this threat to use the Corps against us may be nothing more than a bargaining ploy."

"A bargaining ploy?" repeated Richard Voorhees. "So what do they really want?"

"I think I can answer that," said Uncle Hans. "We've built a massive but temporary encampment at the primary mining site; it's a typical boom town. What I'm hearing is that the planetary government would like nothing more than to have us put up a more permanent facility, leaving the structures in place when the mining operations are over."

"They want the Soweto Corporation to build a small city and then simply hand it over to them?" asked Galen.

"I believe so," said Uncle Hans.

"Is it feasible?" asked cousin Richard.

"It is not only feasible," said Uncle Hans, "it is also a wise investment."

"For them or for us?" Galen asked.

"For us," Hans Voorhees replied.

"I agree," said Mahute Yaari. "The mines are producing an embarrassment of riches. The locals know it and they want their fair share." She looked at Uncle Hans and said, "So it looks like the Soweto Corporation will be building a town, eh, Uncle?"

"That is up to the family," Hans Voorhees said. "However, when we vote upon this and other matters at the close of the meeting, I am confident that the decision will be positive."

"Now, then," said Aunt Kitrina. "We have other matters we must turn our attentions to."

The meeting continued in that same vein, which was much the same as any other meeting Galen had attended: Should the family get into this or that line of commerce? Should they allow their financial interests in this or that company to continue or be terminated?

Boring, Galen thought. It was more of the same old same old. Things got a little more interesting when a lively discussion broke out after one of the cousins pointed out that unknown speculators were buying up thousands of shares of the stock available to the general public. Estimates put the total accumulation by outsiders at nearly sixteen percent. It was agreed that someone should look into the matter, but only after a strong denunciation of the plan by Aunt Kitrina. *That's odd*, thought Galen.

Things seemed to winding down when Amman the butler entered the room and slowly made his way over to Aunt Kitrina. He made a small noise to get her attention, then handed her a small message cube. She glanced at its contents and made a gesture of dismissal.

Mesmerized, Galen watched as Amman retraced his steps and his aunt looked at his grandmother. Her head had fallen forward onto her chest; she was fast asleep and snoring.

Aunt Kitrina approached the old woman and, after a moment's hesitation, gently reached out and shook her shoulder. Ghannee Mugambi's head snapped up and she pierced her daughter with a steely glance of annoyance. Kitrina said something that seemed to pacify the old woman.

When Ghannee Mugambi craned her head to allow her daughter to whisper something into her ear, Galen studiously made believe he wasn't watching. A lot of others did the same.

Ghannee Mugambi's eyes narrowed to slits and she pulled her daughter's head close to her mouth so she could whisper something back. Whatever it was, Aunt Kitrina's face registered no emotion. When she looked at her mother and shrugged, Ghannee Mugambi gestured as if to say, "It's in your hands, not mine."

Aunt Kitrina nodded almost imperceptibly toward the front of the house, and her mouth moved as she said something to her mother. Wishing he'd learned to read lips, Galen watched his grandmother's head bob forward and back several times. Having received her marching orders, Aunt Kitrina strode across the room, making her way toward the front.

<*Galen. Oh, Galen,*> came Sam's voice in his head.

<*What is it, Sam?*>

<*A simulacrum just showed up,*> Sam informed Galen.

<*A simulacrum? Here?*> Galen was caught off guard by Sam's information. Simulacra were incredibly expensive robotic surrogates. He wondered who was utilizing it.

<*What's its face look like?*>

<*I don't recognize him—it is a him—but whoever he is, he looks like he's used to giving orders and having them followed—pronto,*> Sam said.

<*Is he black?*>

<*Yeah, but light-skinned like the Voorhees clan,*> Sam said. <*There's more. As soon as this thing was in the door, it sent Amman in to relay the news of its arrival to your grandmother.*>

<*You said "like the Voorhees clan." Does the simulacrum's face look like a Voorhees?*>

<*No, for what that's worth,*> Sam said. <*He—it, this is damned confusing, isn't it?—does have a mustache.*>

<*A mustache?*>

<Yeah. It's really part of a beard, one of those little goatee jobs, kinda like the one Malcolm X wore.>

<Who?>

<Never mind,> sighed Sam. *<Do you know who this thing's user is?>*

<Not really, but I think I might be able to make an educated guess.>

<If he is who you think he is, tell me: Does he have a thing for android pleasure units?>

<I wouldn't know. Why do you ask?>

<Because he's giving me the full head-to-toe treatment. I feel I should blush.>

<I told you that you were special in this part of the world.>

<That may be so, but I'll bet that I'm not half as special as a simulacrum is around here. Hello!> Sam said brightly. *<Here comes your Aunt Kitrina. I wonder what she wants.>*

<She's going to tell him that my grandmother will receive him now,> Galen told him.

<Receive who?> he queried. Then, when Aunt Kitrina smiled at the simulacrum and gave it a big hug, Sam asked *<Who* is *this thing's user?>*

II

"Grandmother, I am pleased to present the simulacrum of Luis Jorge Alves." As the robot with Alves's face imposed upon it made a slight bow, Kitrina continued, "Mr. Alves, my mother Ghannee Mugambi-Voorhees." If Grandmother Mugambi was taken aback by being introduced to a humanoid robot with a human's face, she didn't show it. *Tough old bird,* Galen thought appreciatively.

Kitrina's words of introduction confirmed Galen's suspicions concerning the newcomer's identity: Luis Jorge Alves was a businessman who sought out troubled companies and acquired them when they were no longer able to defend themselves against him.

Depending on what the company was worth as a whole or as its component pieces, he either stripped it of its assets and abandoned it or sold it off division by division to the highest bidder. He had no interest in running failing or undervalued companies, simply in raiding them for what they could yield on the trading block.

Casually sipping his Jack Daniel's and water, Galen edged in closer and closer to his grandmother and the dangerous man who had come to pay his respects—albeit through a simulacrum. This unexpected visitor made Galen more than a little nervous. Depending upon Alves's intentions, he could be trouble for the family.

Grandmother Mugambi was shrewd and hardheaded—or at least she had been. There was always the danger that her advancing years were finally taking their toll upon her; perhaps she was no longer capable of outsmarting a young fox like Alves.

Shooing away a formally attired waiter who was anxious to take his drink and replenish it, Galen reconsidered his worries about Alves. *What's bothering me?* he asked himself. *Alves takes over troubled companies; troubled* public *companies. Even if he wanted to, he couldn't make a run on the Soweto Corporation.* Then he frowned. *Why did a bell just go off?* he asked himself.

Grandmother Mugambi opened her mouth to say something, closed it, then started over. "I was about to say I finally have the pleasure of meeting you," Galen heard Ghannee Mugambi say to Alves. As she devoured him with her rheumy eyes, she added, "But I am uncertain whether I am meeting Luis Jorge Alves or not."

"Forgive me for appearing to you in this way . . . Grandmother," Alves said, his own eyes riveted to hers. "I had planned to be there in person, but urgent matters arose that made that impossible."

"I see," replied Grandmother Mugambi.

Galen loved his grandmother, but the sight of her confronting the stick-figured simulacrum made him think of the wicked witch who lived in the gingerbread house and her habit of popping unwary little boys and girls into her oven and having them for supper. Maybe it was Alves who was in peril.

"I pray I am not being presumptuous in calling you Grandmother?"

"Perhaps a little bit," Ghannee Mugambi said, taken aback by Alves's bold demeanor. "Do not forget that you will not be a member of our family until you have married Kitrina's youngest."

Galen nearly choked on his drink—which certainly would have called attention to his eavesdropping. Still, it wouldn't have been much of a transgression, he decided, glancing about him. He was far from the only one straining to hear the words passing between his grandmother and this tall intruder.

As if suddenly aware of the interest in what was passing between the three of them, Kitrina said, "I suggest that we say what we have to say in private, Mother."

When both Grandmother Mugambi and Alves agreed, Kitrina indicated to the latter that he should assist her in helping her mother to her feet. When they had done that, they escorted her out of the room.

<Speak to me, partner,> Sam said to him. *<What's happening?>*

<I'm not sure,> Galen replied. *<But I think the family is about to welcome trouble into its midst.>*

<The simulacrum?>

<Luis Jorge Alves is its user's name,> Galen informed Sam. *<When he targets a possible acquisition, he clamps down like a Gila monster and doesn't let go until he's squeezed the life—and all the gravity—out of it.>*

<So don't let him in,> Sam suggested sensibly.

<He's going to marry Ghannee.>

<He's going to marry your grandmother?>

Even though Sam couldn't see him, Galen shook his head. *<My cousin, Ghannee. She's Aunt Kitrina's daughter.>*

<Oh,> said Sam, as if just now remembering something important. *<There's something I have to tell you. Your—>*

"Hello, Galen," said a soft, seductive, and familiar voice.

<—ex-wife is here.>

* * *

"Hello, Adrianna," Galen said, slowly turning around. When his eyes met hers, it was as if a laser bolt had struck him. There was no doubt that Adrianna still had the same power over him; even worse, he saw that she realized it as well.

"Are you surprised to see me here, darling Galen?"

"Nothing you do surprises me, Adrianna." That was certainly true.

"Tell me, have I changed since you saw me last, Galen?" she asked challengingly.

"Let me take a good look," he said. *I'll be damned if she's going to make me feel like a schoolboy every time we meet.*

His eyes began at the top and made a very slow descent. Her raven's-wing black hair flowed to the small of her back from a point just above her delicate ears, whose lobes were stylishly notched in the latest fashion. He gulped, and the thought suddenly occurred to him that he would like nothing better than to stick his tongue into one of those invitingly dark and moist canals.

Her high cheekbones were perfectly rouged to draw attention to them. Her neck was slender—like a swan's, he'd always told her, unable to improve on the classic cliche. Sighing to himself, he noted that her svelte torso always left him unprepared for the fullness of her high breasts.

Intelligent enough to realize the folly of depending solely upon her natural endowments, Adrianna took the necessary money and time required to clothe herself in the most stylish and tasteful of attire. Observing the primrose-yellow sheath that clung to her body in a perfect definition of the word "flattering," Galen was forced to acknowledge that her taste in clothes, at least clothes that showed her to best advantage, was still impeccable.

Her only jewelry, apart from a diamond-studded watch, was a deceivingly simple necklace of perfectly formed emeralds that complemented her large green eyes.

"Well?" she inquired after Galen's eyes had made the journey from top to bottom. "Am I just as you remembered?"

"More or less," he admitted.

She emitted a calculatedly coquettish laugh and said, "Oh, Galen, you haven't changed at all."

"I know you didn't mean that as a compliment," he said. "But thank you anyway."

"Aren't you going to ask me what I'm doing here?"

"You'll tell me soon enough," he replied. "Besides, once I knew you were here, it didn't take a Pseudo-Quantum-Gravity brainpack to figure out what brought you."

"Tell me, then."

"The divorce isn't final."

When she opened her mouth to protest this obviously incorrect statement, Galen shook his head and waved her to silence. "No, not *our* divorce; that's as final as death and taxes. I meant that you and the family aren't divorced quite yet. Your family and its fortune are still entangled with my family and its fortune. I would guess that you still control a large number of shares."

Adrianna smiled. "You can be a cold fish sometimes, Galen, but no one ever said you weren't smart."

"No one?" queried Sam, joining them. "Are you sure you've tested a large enough sampling to make such an absolute statement?"

"Aren't you supposed to be with the other guests?" Galen asked mildly.

"I thought the meeting was over since non-family members are being allowed in here," Sam said, staring meaningfully at Adrianna.

"It is, mostly," allowed Galen. "I still think we should find somewhere else to continue this conversation."

"Excuse me," said Adrianna, putting up her hand like a schoolchild attempting to attract the teacher's attention. "Who is this person, Galen?"

"Why, I'm Sam. Sam Houston," Sam said, putting out his hand. "Gorgeous dress," he added.

After looking dubiously at Sam's proffered hand, Adrianna grasped it and shook it, surprised at how warm and human it felt. "Sam Houston?" she repeated. "And just who or what are you, Mr. Houston?"

"Even though you know the answer, I'll make believe you don't and tell you," Sam responded. He leaned over conspiratorially and whispered, "I'm an android. Please don't tell anyone, especially not Grandmother Mugambi."

"Is this . . . this thing for real?" Adrianna asked in a voice that reminded Galen that his ex-wife's personality usually proved inferior to the packaging it came in; sooner or later, the steel beneath the lace became apparent.

"Be careful," warned Sam. "I think that's a trick question."

"Yes, Sam is for real," Galen said lamely, unable to come up with anything sharper.

"My hero," gushed Sam.

"We're wasting time," Galen said. "Why are you here, Adrianna?"

"As you yourself pointed out, I still have a vested interest in the dealings of the Voorhees family." She paused, looked at Sam, and then asked, "Must we speak in front of . . . ah . . . Mr. Houston?"

"Yes, we must."

"And why is that?"

"As I said, he's my partner."

Adrianna looked nonplused. "I thought you were joking when you said that a moment ago." She stared into his eyes. "No, I can see that you're not—you never could lie to me, Galen."

Galen closed his eyes for a moment. *That's what Tey told me*, he remembered. *I hope I can lie to* someonc, he thought ruefully. *Mr. Secret Agent Man!*

"Galen has told me he never lies to anyone," said Sam brightly. "I believe him because he tells me how handsome and wonderful I am."

"Can *you* lie, Sam?" Adrianna asked, knowing that the answer was presumably no.

"Me, lie? No, of course not."

"Sam just won't tell you all the truth if it endangers me or another human being," Galen was quick to point out.

"I see."

"Why have you come here today?" Galen asked his former wife. "I understand your ongoing financial interest in the Soweto Corporation, but you are permitted no voice in the family discussions and final voting."

"My family asked to me to attend to see if it was true," she told him.

"If what was true?"

"That Luis Jorge Alves was about to take over the Soweto Corporation."

"Hehhehheh." Galen laughed nervously. "Where did you get that idea?"

"From the presence here of his simulacrum."

"It appears he is about to marry into the family," Galen conceded. "But I cannot imagine that Grandmother Mugambi will permit him to play any real role in the family business. Marriage or not, he will still be an outsider—like yourself."

Adrianna waved a hand. "I understand all that about him not being a voting family member because he is not a grandchild of Piet Voorhees and Ghannee Mugambi." Her emerald eyes darkened. "That does not mean, however, that he will not use his wife to gain access to whatever information and company and family secrets it takes to eventually seize control of the Soweto Corporation. I repeat: *any* secrets," Adrianna said, giving Sam an oddly evaluative look.

"Christ!" said Galen, gulping his Jack Daniel's.

"DO YOU THINK ADRIANNA IS CORRECT?" SAM ASKED.

"About what?"

"You know what I'm talking about. Do you think she's right about this Alves guy?"

Galen shrugged. "That's hard to say. On the one hand, what she says about him is correct, as least as far as his reputation goes. But gossip is one thing, and the truth may be something else altogether."

"So you think Alves may actually be a Star Scout at heart?"

"I didn't say that!" snapped Galen crossly. "I just mean his reputation may be overhyped to provide him an edge in business negotiations. If you think your opponent is a shark, you act accordingly. People who might otherwise fight tooth and nail might consider it the better part of valor not to make an enemy of someone who'll supposedly stop at nothing."

"Makes sense," Sam said.

"I wonder if we're all making too much of his appearance here," mused Galen. "Would anyone, in this day and age, marry someone just to gain entry into her family? It's possible that this Gila monster just happened to do a very human thing: He fell in love with Ghannee."

"Why don't you ask him?" Sam said, lowering his voice.

"Huh?"

"Good day, gentlemen," said a Portuguese-accented baritone voice over Galen's shoulder. Galen turned to see the simulacrum that wore Luis Jorge Alves's face. He shivered. A robot with a human face imposed on it was an oddly unnerving sight.

"Well, speak of the devil," said Sam, shooting Galen a sly look.

<Sam!>

Alves's simulacrum laughed. "There is probably more truth to your friend's use of that old saying than I might wish to know."

"Your name *did* come up in our conversation," Galen admitted sheepishly.

"The curse of being famous," said Alves. The simulacrum's face broke into what was meant to be a smile. "Or perhaps I should say *infamous*."

Galen took advantage of this opportunity to look Alves's simulacrum over at close range. It wasn't remotely like meeting Alves in the flesh, but the simulacrum's face was supposedly an accurate representation of Alves's own. Although not all simulacra were so endowed, this one had a full head of jet-black hair combed straight back from its forehead just as Alves wore his own. Its eerily lifelike eyes were a rich mahogany and strangely penetrating. While Alves's long nose was not especially thin or thick, it flared slightly at his nostrils, spoiling an otherwise straight line.

The mustache and goatee Alves favored were neatly trimmed and served to focus attention on his mouth, which was small and sensual. If the simulacrum's face was a fair representation of Alves, he was a good-looking man, Galen conceded.

"Since there's no point in denying that we know who you are, and you seem to know who we are," began Galen, "I suppose we should do the socially acceptable thing and formally introduce ourselves."

When Alves bowed slightly, Galen continued. "Luis Jorge Alves, this handsome hunk is my friend and associate, Sam Houston."

"Pleased to meet you, Mr. Houston."

"Likewise," Sam replied.

"And you are Galen Yeager?" asked Alves.

"Little Galen," Sam said, making a face at Galen. When Alves's eyebrows rose, Sam explained, "Family joke."

"Yes, I'm Galen Yeager," Galen said, feeling slightly foolish.

"I've heard of your father, Orin Yeager, and your grandfather, Matthew Yeager, Mr. Yeager."

"Please, call me Galen."

"Thank you, Galen," Alves said. Turning to Sam, he said, "Pardon me for displaying an unseemly interest in something which is none of my business, Mr. Houston, but I cannot avoid observing that you are an android."

Galen saw the faint smile playing about the corners of Sam's mouth and warned, <*Sam!*>

<*Talk about the pot calling the kettle black,*> laughed Sam. Out loud he exclaimed, "Found out again!" allowing his face to fall. "What was it this time? My voice? My too-perfect features? My physical grace and dancer's coordination?"

"Try your eyes," muttered Galen.

"My eyes!" cried Sam melodramatically. "Of course, my cursed eyes!"

The simulacrum smiled a halfhearted smile that quickly gave way to a broad, forced one. "I must admit to never having met an android with quite your personality, Mr. Houston."

"There are so few good ones," agreed Sam.

"Sam is special," said Galen before he could stop himself.

"Special?" asked Alves.

<*Now you've done it, big mouth,*> Sam told him.

"Ah . . . yes," said Galen haltingly. His mind raced. "Sam has been especially modified for my needs."

"For your needs?" asked Alves skeptically. "What sort of special modifications does an android need to assist a dilettante scientist?" When he saw the sour expression on Galen's face, he added, "No insult intended."

"Dilcttantc?" mouthed Sam silently before saying aloud, "Galen special-ordered me with a larger brainpack and certain built-in molecular testing capabilities. I also come with a fish scaler, Swiss army knife, and tweezers."

"I see," said Alves. "And where does one have special modifications like this done?"

"The Voorhees Foundation," said Galen, again unable to disengage his mouth before he said too much. For the second time in as many minutes, he wanted to kick himself. Tiny beads of perspiration formed on his forehead.

<*Jesusfuckingchrist!*> Galen cursed. <*I'm sorry, Sam.*>

<Why don't you tell him the combination to the Qumalii security cube where the family jewels are kept while you're at it?> Sam asked sarcastically.

<I said I was sorry.>

"The Voorhees Foundation?" Alves said wonderingly.

"Tell me," said Sam, hoping to change the subject, "when are you and Ghannee getting married?"

"In several weeks," said Alves, clearly distracted by something.

"You gonna do it for real, or just send your simulacrum?"

"Jesus!" Galen swore under his breath.

He needn't have worried. Alves seemed not to have heard what Sam said. The simulacrum looked around, and then Alves said, "Would you two please excuse me? I need to speak to someone about something important before it slips my mind."

"Certainly," said Galen.

"Goodbye, then. It was good meeting you both."

"Thank you, the pleasure was ours," Galen said.

"Goodbye," Sam said to the simulacrum's retreating form. Then he turned to Galen and asked, "Well, what are you thinking?"

"Just cut my tongue out now!"

II

Although Galen wasn't seated with Adrianna at dinner—someone in the family, or, more likely, Amman, was discreet enough not to put them at the same table—he *was* seated with Sam on one side and one of his cousins' husbands on the other.

Galen observed both Sam and Alves's simulacrum to see how they behaved. The two artificials "ate" whatever was placed in front of them, which must have pleased his grandmother, but the other family members and guests kept shooting them both strange looks.

<I think the others would be more comfortable with my metal buddy and me if we were the Mad Hatter and the March Hare,> Sam said.

<This is one family reunion no one's going to forget,> agreed Galen.

Apart from the matter of attendance at the dinner, the meal was very pleasant and gracious. Amman and the cooks had outdone themselves. Galen picked at his salad, unwilling to risk filling up on greens and vegetables; as it was, the salad only served to whet his appetite for what was to come.

Once the salad bowls had been cleared away, several superb wines were poured; they were immediately followed by shrimp cocktails each graced by a half-dozen of the largest and tastiest shrimp—prawns, the others called them—that Galen could remember eating.

For those who were so inclined, and that was almost everyone, the shrimp cocktails were followed by a delicious seafood soup, made with the bounty of the Indian Ocean: fish, chunks of sweet-tasting lobster meat, scallops, cream and potatoes.

Among the main courses available to everyone were freshly steamed lobster, plain or stuffed with crab meat; sea bass grilled to perfection and topped with a perfectly flavored sauce; thick-cut steaks from the small but pampered herd of grain-fed cattle raised in a compound on the estate grounds; and several hot and spicy vegetarian dishes for those who wished to eat lower down the food chain.

For dessert, one had a choice of a bewildering array of cakes, glaces, sherbets, and fruits. Pleasantly satiated but not stuffed, Galen took pains to insure that he still had room for his favorite among Amman's specialties.

"What is that?" asked Tom Chernak, his cousin's husband, seated to his right, as Galen poised a forkful of culinary delight in front of his mouth, allowing the scent to titillate his nostrils.

"This? This is tiramisu," Galen replied.

"Tiramisu?"

"It's ladyfingers layered with coffee-flavored cream and chocolate shavings."

"It sounds delicious."

"Not half as delicious as it tastes," Galen informed him, taking his first bite. Then he looked on approvingly as one of the servers poured him a cup of deep, dark, steaming-hot coffee. He added a sugar cube and a little cream, stirred the contents of the cup with a spoon, and had his first sip.

"Christ, is this good," moaned Galen.

"I agree," said the man on his right. "The only thing missing is a good cigar." He looked around. "But smoking at the dinner table is a no-no; my wife tells me it's rude."

"It isn't rude to smoke in the game room," Galen said, nodding in that direction.

"The game room?"

"Besides having nice big ashtrays, it has as fine a poker table you'd ever want to see."

"Did I hear someone say poker?" came the simulacrum's voice from across the table and toward the head where Grandmother Mugambi sat as the family's leader.

"Do you play?" asked Galen.

"I play."

<*How's your poker game going?*> Sam asked him an hour or so later.

<*Same as always.*>

<*That bad?*> laughed Sam. <*And to think—you're not even playing a person, you're playing a mechanical man with a human face.*>

<*I'm playing a person all right,*> Galen snapped. <*Now bugger off!*>

Sam left, but not before admonishing him, <*You can't win if you play mad.*>

Sam's right, Galen conceded to himself. He felt a little wired, a little edgy. *Too much caffeine,* he decided. When one of the servers was poised to refill his coffee cup, he said, "No more of that hundred-kilometer brew. I'd like decaf from now on, please."

"Certainly, sir," said the server, returning almost immediately with a carafe of decaffeinated coffee.

"The coffee making you jumpy, Galen?" asked Herbert van der Park, a big, black cigar stuck into the corner of his mouth.

"A tad," Galen replied.

"Come on, you two," exhorted Tom Chernak. "You in or out on this one, Galen?"

"I'm in," Galen said, throwing a ten-credit coin into the pot in the center of the table. He picked up his cigar, sucked deeply on it, and, tilting his head back, blew a huge smoke ring toward the ceiling.

"It's to me?" asked Simon Voorhees. "Okay, I'm in, too," he said, throwing in a ten-credit piece of his own. "I want to see what cousin Alves is holding."

"He's not cousin Alves yet," Galen said matter-of-factly and with a neutral expression.

"That's right," agreed van der Park. "He has to marry Ghannee first."

"Sure," said the simulacrum, its voice deliberately light. "Pretend I'm not here."

"You aren't, not really," pointed out Chernak. "The simulacrum represents you, but it isn't you in the flesh."

"Well, that's true," admitted Alves. "But it's also true that a full house beats most other hands." The simulacrum laid down its hand, faceup.

Everyone else at the table groaned, including Galen. He looked at his hand. Aces and treys; good, but not good enough. He tossed his cards down in disgust, careful not to turn them over.

"So, what did you have, Galen?" asked Alves.

"Nothing," Galen replied. "Trash."

"Let's see," said Tom Chernak, reaching for Galen's hand.

"I said I had nothing," Galen said, reaching out and preventing Chernak from turning over the cards by grabbing his wrist. He smiled as he said it, but Chernak could feel the power in Galen's grip.

The simulacrum fixed Galen with its oddly human/inhuman eyes. The intensity of the absent Alves's stare was palpable; Galen returned it in equal measure. Finally, the simulacrum dropped its gaze.

"I'm doing about as well as I usually do, tonight," said Herbert van der Park, trying to lighten the suddenly changed and charged atmosphere.

"I like that, Galen," the simulacrum said as if van der Park had never spoken. "A man should never reveal his hand unless he has to."

"Is that a business principle of yours?"

"Why, no, just a rule of thumb for playing poker."

"Uh-huh," Galen said. Looking at Tom Chernak, he said, "It's your deal, I believe."

As Chernak shuffled and cut the cards, Galen caught Alves's eye again. The two clearly recognized something in each other, and the simulacrum acknowledged it with an almost imperceptible nod of its head.

When the server returned with more decaf coffee, Galen asked for a Jack Daniel's. He never drank when he played, but his poker playing was about finished for the night.

* * *

"Boy, it sure gets pitch black early in these parts," Sam said, looking through the parted curtains of his room at the surrounding compound.

"It seems like I've been up for hours," Galen said, sipping his drink. "I can't wait to get to bed." He opened his mouth wide in an enormous yawn.

"Bed?" queried Sam. "Don't tell me you're going to bed at this hour."

"Some of us aren't made out of polysteel and polymers."

"Shame," sniffed Sam.

"It was just a figure of speech," Galen said. "Besides, it doesn't make any difference to you what time I go to bed, does it? Since you never have to sleep, I presume you're going to stay up and speed-read a few dozen journals anyway. You don't need me around."

"I enjoy talking to you, Galen," Sam said seriously. "You're intelligent and you put up with my shenanigans. After today's meeting of the Voorhees clan, I'd thought we'd have a lot to talk about."

"Shenanigans?" Galen said, looking at Sam with real affection in his eyes. "I appreciate hearing that you think I'm okay, partner. I have to confess that I enjoy your company, too." He smiled. "Why else would I go along with your smart mouth and your *shenanigans*?"

Sam cleared his throat—another of the clever touches the android part of him was endowed with to make him seem more human—and said gruffly, "Let's not get sloppy about this, Gale."

"Don't call me Gale," Galen said mock-angrily.

"Good night, Galen," Sam said, clapping him on the shoulder and heading toward the door. He turned back momentarily to wag a finger at Galen and admonish him, "Don't drink too much."

"Good night, Sam."

III

Even though it was well after midnight, Galen tossed and turned in bed; only slightly more asleep than awake, his awareness was very near the surface of his consciousness. Throwing an arm across his eyes in response to the approaching thunderstorm whose flashes of lightning briefly turned the night into day, he was distantly aware of the series of thunderclaps that rolled across the veldt. Troubled by something, even in this semiconscious state, he reached for a nonexistent needle gun.

It wasn't the first blast in the compound that shattered Galen's rest, it was the chattering of an automatic slug-thrower. Acting instinctively, he tumbled off his bed's null-grav mattress and onto the floor. His reflexive actions were not a moment too soon—a line of heavy-caliber fire tore through the wall.

"Jumping Jesus!" he swore as he heard the plastic-jacketed slugs ripping through the bed's headboard and pummeling the pillows.

It was only then that he realized that the thunderstorm he'd heard earlier was probably an attack on the outer defensive posts.

Galen crawled across the floor on his hands and knees to the large, walk-in closet and closed the door behind him. The light came on automatically when the motion and body-heat detectors sensed his presence. With the closet wall protecting him—even from high-velocity penetrators—he stood up and grabbed a pair of trousers.

The concussive blast wave of an explosion that must have been outside his window battered the closet and he stumbled against the wall. "Maybe I'll just stay in here," he told himself, aware he'd never do that when there was a firefight going on.

Once he'd slipped into his pants, a T-shirt, and his shoes, he located the two holsters containing his energy pistol and his Salinas 250-HF needle gun. "Hi, guys," he muttered. "It's good to see you again."

Like a dandy deciding which smoking jacket to wear, Galen briefly mulled over his two choices. Deciding to go for raw power, he strapped his needle gun holster under his armpit as a backup and wrapped his fingers around the energy pistol.

Then he saw the old Swanscombe elephant gun leaning against the wall in one corner of the closet. His eyes lit up at the sight of it: Double-barreled and impossibly large-bored, a Swanscombe could stop the largest land mammal in its tracks.

Galen's grandfather had taught him how to handle a weapon similar to this one when he was deemed old enough and big enough to withstand the massive recoil. Staring at the elaborately carved stock, Galen realized this gun could be the very one his grandfather had used to teach him. Peering closely at the gun, he saw the words *Wyverncolla* inscribed on one of the barrels. "Dragonslayer," he whispered, running his fingers over the cold steel where the words had been cut into the barrel.

Exchanging the energy pistol for the old rifle, he removed two cartridges from a box he found on the floor, broke the gun at the breech, slid the shells into the twin barrels, and snapped the weapon shut. Then he stuffed the rest of the huge cartridges into his pocket and discarded the box.

After slipping a couple of extra energy packs into his pockets as well, Galen said, "Here goes nothing." Dropping to his knees, he crawled back out into the bedroom.

The blast that had rocked the room while he was taking stock of things in the closet had apparently blown in the window. As a result, the room's artificially chilled air was rushing over him to pour out of the gaping hole in the wall like an invisible river. Much of the furniture was splintered and smashed, and what was left of the 'phone by the bed hissed and spit, giving off a foul black smoke.

A sharp-edged light sliced through the opening where the window had been, and Galen could hear the high-pitched whining of Kessel repulse motors; that meant that the attackers had arrived in floaters. He risked a quick glance that revealed that they were combat floaters.

"Shit!" Galen swore. Since combat floaters were proscribed vehicles for anyone except legally recognized police and defense forces, whoever had authorized their use had a lot of money or clout. Probably both.

Suddenly the door burst open. Galen turned and aimed the Swanscombe at the intruder, his finger tightening across both triggers.

"Don't shoot, it ruins my shirts," said Sam, energy pistols

clasped in both hands like some old-time cowboy or pirate.

"I thought it might be you," Galen said. "That's why I didn't cock the hammers." He lowered the Swanscombe. "But I had to make sure."

"No problemo," replied Sam, joining Galen on the floor. He glanced around the ruined room and then at Galen. "You okay?"

"I think so," Galen said haltingly. He hadn't actually taken stock of his physical condition, which accounted for his hesitancy.

"Well, I'm peachy keen," Sam said. "The important thing now is to see about the rest of your family and to defend them and ourselves against whoever the hell's attacking this place."

"What kind of levels do you have?" asked Galen, meaning the charges in Sam's energy pistols. "I have a couple of reloads in my pants."

"Please, Galen," Sam said. "Don't hand me straight lines like that at a time like this, okay?" Then he relented. "I have full charges and a couple of reloads of my own." His eyes widened at Galen's antique rifle.

"What the hell is that thing?" asked Sam.

"An old Swanscombe," Galen informed him.

"Now that's what I call a gun," said Sam, whistling appreciatively. Glancing at what he carried in his hands, he said, "I can't raise the skin temperature of those attack floaters by more than a few degrees with my pistols, but you might actually be able to do something with that monstrosity. Feel up to giving it a try?"

"Sure," said Galen. He made his way over to the hole in the bedroom wall where the window used to be and peered outside. Seeing one of the battle floaters hovering outside the house like some gigantic dragonfly, he raised the rifle to his shoulder, cocked the hammers, pointed the gun in the general direction of the floater, and pulled both triggers simultaneously.

The world exploded. Or so it seemed to Galen.

The moon became as blood as a huge tongue of flame shot from the Swanscombe's twin barrels, and the air was rent by a thunderclap as loud as that which the book of Revelation prophesies will sound when the Lamb opens the sixth seal.

Galen was thrown back across the bedroom as if hurled by some unseen giant. Sam reached out and caught him an instant before he would have smashed against the far wall.

His ears ringing with the concussive explosion of gunpowder, Galen asked, "What happened? Did I hit it?"

Shaking his own head as if to clear it, Sam released Galen and crawled to the window. "Mother of mercy!" he hissed. Sam watched as the stricken floater, black smoke pouring from a manhole-cover-sized hole in its fuselage. shuddered convulsively and began corkscrewing toward the ground. It impacted like a watermelon stuffed full of fireworks, exploding in a giant fireball and throwing Sam back into the room, almost on top of Galen.

"Well?" asked Galen.

"I'd say you hit it," Sam said dryly.

7

TAKING INTO ACCOUNT WHAT HAPPENED TO ITS MATE, NEITHER Galen nor Sam was surprised that the second floater had disappeared. Had they considered the craft's pilot's options, they might also have figured out the logical place for it to go, aside from giving up the attack and withdrawing completely. In any event, it didn't take long for them learn where the floater had gone when they heard a loud thump on the roof of the house.

"What's up there?" asked Sam, pointing.

"Nothing much," said Galen. "There's an attic of sorts, as I recall. There's nothing in it except insulation." He stared down at the Swanscombe. "Apart from the occasional water buffalo head, that is."

When they heard the sound of heavy boots above them, Sam said, "Well, it sounds to me like there's something alive and unstuffed up there now. How do we get up there?"

"Follow me," Galen said, making his way to the door to his room and pushing it open. "There's a set of pull-down stairs down the hall."

"After you, great white hunter."

From the tenor of the excited shouts and curses from below them as they hurried down the hall in a crouch, it sounded to Galen as if the attack had so far failed to penetrate the house's elaborate state-of-the-art defenses. Should the attackers manage to get in, Galen told himself reassuringly, they would find themselves face-to-face with a large family well versed in the martial arts—trained in hand-to-hand combat and crack shots with just about any weapon one might put in their hands.

"Here it is," Galen said, hitting the release panel. The ladder steps obligingly swung down from the ceiling.

Moments after Galen mounted the ladder and began climbing the steep incline, he felt his legs seized in a powerful grip, and he was pulled from the steps. "Let Sammy go first," Sam said in a no-nonsense voice.

"Have it your way."

Tucking one energy pistol into his belt, Sam mounted the steps and paused at the trap door leading into the attic long enough to gesture at the hall lights. Galen got the message and said, "Lights off." When the hall was plunged into darkness, Galen whispered his thanks that the computer was still programmed to recognize and respond to his voice.

Now protected by darkness, unless the attackers had infrared goggles to match his own wide-spectrum eyesight, Sam gingerly lifted the trap door. Things happened very quickly from that point on: Sam propelled himself up and into the attic, and two bolts of energy flashed by Sam's head as he simultaneously fired at several shapes, lighting up the small and confined space with bright, jagged streaks of manmade lightning.

Tucking in his shoulder and rolling on the hard, dusty floor, Sam came up firing as rapidly as any action hero the hol-vee had to offer. Screams of pain and muffled curses were testament to his success.

"Hey!" shouted Galen as the fierce electromagnetic storm raged above him. He clambered up the steep steps in pursuit of his impulsive partner, ready to back him up as best he could. Not nearly as agile and quick-moving as Sam, Galen twice missed his footing and, the second time, his foot catching in the shoulder sling of his rifle, slid all the way back down.

"Sonofabitch!"

Galen's chagrin at being unable to join Sam was tempered by the sight of a bedroom door at the end of the hall opening. *If I'm lucky*, Galen thought, shouldering the Swanscombe and cocking the hammers, *they'll be family*.

They weren't.

Three heavily armed invaders stepped out into the hallway. *Goddamnit!* thought Galen. *They must have used a third floater to blast their way in through a bedroom window on that side of the building.*

Wearing moly-weave vests sporting hundreds of bristling wirelike protuberances—miniature lightning rods to catch and disperse the electromagnetic steams of energy emitted by all but the most powerful of energy rifles—the three attackers made no effort to beat Galen to the draw. Seeing that the man they encountered wore no body armor and carried only an old slug-thrower, the trio assumed the advantage was theirs.

Their assumption was more than flawed; it was fatal.

Bracing himself as best he could, Galen raised the Swanscombe and pulled the right barrel's trigger. Since it was confined by the hallway, the resulting blast of flame and sound was even more blinding and deafening than the double-barreled one that brought down the floater. The rifled bore of the Swanscombe spat its heavy-caliber slug straight and true, and the bullet punched through the first attacker and his companion immediately behind him as easily as a boy with a slingshot might blast a steel ball-bearing through a snowman. The remaining attacker, his face hidden behind a protective mask, seemed to go limp with fear.

"Sorry," Galen apologized with a shrug as he pulled the second trigger. The man's head and upper torso disappeared in a shower of gore.

"*Wyverncolla*," Galen said softly, staring at the awesome weapon he held in his hands.

* * *

Although Galen had no way of knowing what the now-repulsed attackers were after, he assumed that his grandmother had been their target. He realized that he had no evidence yet to direct him to that conclusion, but it provided a temporary logic for the assault.

The destruction on the ground floor of the house was less than Galen might have expected. Unlike the upper floors, the attackers were less successful in breaching the building's formidable defenses. Apparently, the plan had been to drop men on the upper balconies and come in through the windows. Galen and Sam, among others, had thwarted that line of attack.

Although the front door had been blown in and several invaders had made it inside, none had penetrated further than the long hallway. A line of bodies was strewn from the entryway all the way down the hall, ending just at the deceptive double doors leading to the central living room. The elaborately patterned doors were deceptive because of the moly-steel core that lay beneath the varnished wood; it would have taken more firepower than the invaders had at their command to breach this inner line of defense.

"Grandmother, are you all right?" Galen asked when he and Sam were finally ushered into her presence by a gun-toting Amman.

Ghannee Mugambi-Voorhees had ridden out the attack safely cocooned in the underground survival vault the family had constructed for just such an occurrence—all the while vehemently protesting being hustled down into the depths while there was fighting taking place. A tough old bird, she wanted to pick up a weapon and join the firefight herself.

"Of course I am all right," Ghannee Mugambi-Voorhees replied testily. "Although these mother hens will not allow me to defend myself"—she glared at Aunt Kitrina and several others—"I have my children and their children to protect me."

"Given the skill of this family, that's no small thing," Sam agreed with a smile.

"And what good were you during the attack, machine-man?" Grandmother Mugambi asked, looking askance at the energy pistol tucked into his belt. "They tell me you cannot harm a human being."

"Sam was a great help to me, Grandmother," Galen said, coming to his partner's defense. "It was he who shielded me from the invaders who attempted to gain entry through the attic," Galen lied. "While Sam distracted them and saved me from catching a laser bolt in the head, I was able to kill them all."

"It is true then what you do, Galen," observed Uncle Hans. "You are a . . ." He paused before choosing his words carefully. "You are a professional?"

"Maybe," admitted Galen. "But it appears to me that the so-called 'amateurs' in this family did all right by themselves."

"I should say so," agreed Herbert van der Park.

Galen shot him a look; he was covered in dried blood. "Are you all right?" he asked his cousin.

Van der Park's head bobbed up and down. "Yes, of course. Why do you ask?" Then he saw everyone staring at his tunic and looked down. "Oh," he said, "that's not my blood."

"Obviously," said Sam.

"Tell me," said Galen. "Is our esteemed guest unharmed?"

"Who?" asked Grandmother Mugambi.

"I think he means Alves," van der Park said.

"There was no possibility he could have been injured in the attack," said Uncle Hans.

"Oh, and why is that?" Galen asked.

"He is here only by simulacrum," said Uncle Hans.

Christ! thought Galen. "We *know* that, Uncle Hans," he told the older man patiently. "It's the simulacrum we're talking about."

"Oh. Well, that was destroyed in the attack."

"It's lucky he wasn't here in person, then," said Herbert van der Park.

"Yeah," agreed Galen. "Lucky."

II

Sam was beside himself. "You mean to tell me," he was saying to Galen. "You mean to tell me that after a week—"

"Five days," corrected Galen.

"All right, five days," conceded Sam. "After five days there's been no progress in finding out, officially or unofficially, who tried to break into the compound and murder your whole family in their beds?"

"That's right," said Galen.

Sam's jaw dropped. "What about the local authorities? Are they satisfied with such an inconclusive result?"

"If the family is satisfied, they are satisfied," replied Galen, gingerly testing the rich, aromatic Kenyan coffee in his mug; he put it down when he found it was still too hot to drink. He shook his head at his grandmother's insistence on retaining human servants. A robot chef would have seen that his coffee was set down in front of him at precisely the temperature he preferred.

"Why in the name of the crocodile god is the family satisfied with such a piss-poor investigation?" demanded Sam.

Galen shrugged. "The family has a lot of enemies. Whoever set this attack up was a pro. None of the dead men could be traced to any gang, any rival corporation or company; they were all apparently free-lancers hired for this one job. What was left of the floater that I brought down was devoid of identifying marks or any other information."

"So that's it?"

"Until we find something concrete to go on."

"What now?"

When Galen smiled mysteriously, Sam's eyes narrowed and he asked, "What do you have up your sleeve now?"

"You've been bugging me to go on a safari before we go back to NorAm, haven't you?"

"You mean . . . ?"

"Pack your gear, Stanley—we're heading into the Heart of Darkness."

Sam raised his eyes to the sky. "Thank you, Jesus!"

* * *

The small jeep that Galen had borrowed from his grandmother's fleet of vehicles hit a small mound of dirt and bounced into the air, flying across the rough-surfaced bush veldt for ten meters or so until it landed hard and bounced like a rubber ball. Galen fought to keep control and did so—just barely.

When a clump of low trees appeared in front of him, he spun the wheel hard to avoid colliding with them. Despite himself, he laughed out loud. Although he would never admit it to Sam, he was having a ball.

<Where are you, partner?>

<I'm coming, I'm coming,> Galen beamed back. *<This little pony is no match for you or those cheetahs.>*

Suddenly the jeep topped a small rise and Galen caught sight of Sam racing through the bush veldt, his normally perfectly coiffed hair blowing in the wind. Just ahead of Sam, running all out, were two thoroughly spooked and confused cheetahs.

<I've got you again, buddy,> Galen told him, lifting his foot from the accelerator and preparing himself for the jolt

he knew was coming when the jeep's suspension bottomed out at the foot of the hill. The jeep smashed down, leapt up and slightly sideways, and Galen stomped down hard on the pedal, spraying red and brown dirt from the wheels. He had to push the jeep as hard as he could just to stay in contact with Sam and the cheetahs.

<I think they're tiring,> Sam observed.

<I'm not surprised,> Galen replied. *<Cheetahs are built for speed, but only over short distances.>*

<Think I should break this off?>

<Unless you want to run the poor beggars to death,> Galen advised him. *<The park authorities might frown on that.>*

<It wouldn't make me feel good, either,> said Sam. *<I'm pulling up now.>*

Since hurdling blindly over a rise and smashing headlong into Sam's polysteel and viviplastic body could severely damage the jeep, Galen eased up on the accelerator. No longer bouncing and jouncing across the veldt like crazy, the jeep settled down to a reasonable speed and Galen marveled at the difference a few kilometers per hour could make. *Well, fifty or sixty kilometers per hour*, he amended.

Galen soon spotted Sam loping toward him across the veldt at a sure and easy pace. He turned the wheel slightly and the jeep crossed in front of Sam, circled around, and pulled up alongside.

"Going my way?" asked Sam. Although a light sheen of fake perspiration made his face glow, his chest wasn't rising and falling. Other than for verisimilitude, there was no reason for him to appear out of breath, since his body didn't require oxygen.

"Maybe. Got any good stories?"

"The farmer's daughter and the traveling condom salesman?"

"That'll do," said Galen, stopping. "Hop in."

"I've never seen so many animals," Sam marveled, gesturing at the herd of zebra scattering ahead of them. "Giraffes, wildebeests, monkeys, and even the odd ostrich or two."

"I told you Kruger National Park had it all."

"It does," agreed Sam. "It's terrific to see all these animals in such a concentrated area."

"What do you want to see next?"

"You know," Sam said.

"All right. Lions it is." Galen checked the jeep's compass and the stun settings on his energy rifle before heading for a nearby water hole.

Sam glanced at the energy rifle and then at Galen. "Wish you had your old dragonslayer instead of that peashooter?"

"It's only a peashooter if you compare it to my Swanscombe," Galen replied. "But to answer your question, sure. The Swanscombe can stop anything on two or four legs."

"Or anything that flies."

Galen nodded agreement. "But the thing about a gun is—if you have it, you might use it. Since all the animals in the park are protected, that's a no-no. As far as the park authorities are concerned—and I agree with them, by the way—there are more than enough people. It's the wild animals that are in short supply. We're expendable, but they aren't."

"Sounds reasonable to me."

Galen yawned. He was tired already. The long day had begun when Galen climbed out of bed in the before-dawn darkness and found Sam out on the veranda, staring thoughtfully into the gloom.

"I love this time of day," Galen had said to the pensive Sam.

Without taking his eyes off the horizon, Sam replied, "You surprise me, partner. I thought you were a late sleeper."

"Normally, I am," Galen agreed. "But you have to get an early start to appreciate the bush veldt. By noon, the sun will be pounding down like a jackhammer. If we move out briskly, we'll have five or six hours before the sun burns off the morning coolness." He jerked his thumb toward the darkness-draped veldt and added, "The animals know that, too. If you want to see them up close and personal, it's best to try to catch them before they seek shelter from the midday blast furnace."

"What are we waiting for?" Sam had asked.

"My breakfast."

"Oh."

III

"Look over there," Galen said, putting down his self-adjusting binoculars and pointing. "Down there near the water hole."

Sam looked. "Yes, I see them."

"They're a good-sized pride," Galen said. "I can't get over how many lionesses and cubs there are."

"I'd estimate about twenty," said Sam. "That sound right?"

Galen quickly did a head count. "I think you're correct."

"Where are the males?" wondered Sam. "I don't see any manes."

"It's probably an all-lioness pride. Males don't do much for a pride except father cubs," Galen explained. "And a male will kill any cub he encounters that isn't his offspring. Since the lionesses do all the hunting, they don't really require a male around—certainly not a pride of this size."

Sam seemed confused by Galen's words. "They need a tough old male to lead them, don't they?" he asked. "A 'king of the jungle' to keep everyone in line."

"Maybe a pack of wild dogs," said Galen, shaking his head, "But not lions. They're all pretty much equal except when they're feeding at a kill; that's when you don't want to get between them and their food—it's every lioness for herself."

"Oh."

Galen heard the high-pitched whine of mosquitoes and saw a small cloud of them descend on Sam with the intention of drilling for blood. Unfortunately for them, Sam's skin was impervious to their persistent attempts to plunge home their feeding tubes. He waved a hand at them to drive them away, saying, "Sorry, girls, try the next guy."

"Hey, the next guy is me," protested Galen.

"You've got your repellent on, haven't you?"

"I'm well protected," Galen said.

"Good," said Sam. Then he asked casually, "What are you using, tiny holos of your Aunt Kitrina taped all over your body?"

"That's not nice!" Galen said. Then, picturing his aunt's homely face in his mind's eye, he laughed despite himself.

"Your aunt's daughter, this Ghannee, she doesn't look anything like her mother, does she?" Sam asked. For some reason, he hadn't met her at the family meeting and she'd left to be with Alves immediately after the attack.

"No, she doesn't," Galen admitted.

"Good for Alves," Sam said.

"Anyway, I want to get back to lions—not mosquitoes, aunts, or their daughters," said Galen, shading his eyes as he looked at the somnambulant lions.

"Do ants have daughters?" Sam wondered, half to himself.

"Huh?"

"Nothing," Sam said. Then he sneaked a peek at Galen and saw him staring out across the bush veldt, a wistful smile on his face.

"Centicred for your thoughts," Sam said.

Galen rested his chin on his forearm, watching the roly-poly cubs chasing each other around their mothers, waddling about on stubby legs that often went out from under them. "I was just thinking how much I missed all this," he said. "I grew up in the greater Boswash section of NorAm, but I spent my vacations here under the watchful eye of my aunts and uncles. I had forgotten how beautiful it all is."

"That it is, pard," Sam agreed. "That it is."

Galen slowly got to his feet. If the pride noticed, they paid him no attention. "Well, you've seen the lions. Now what?"

"Yes, I've seen the lions," Sam said. "But only from a distance."

"What's that supposed to mean?"

"Figure it out, Einstein," Sam said. "You have three guesses—and the first two don't count!"

"Don't tell me you want to get closer."

"I want to get closer."

"But that's . . ." Galen's voice trailed away.

"Dangerous?" finished Sam. "Not for me."

Galen tried to think of reasons to say no. While it was true that if Sam got too close to one of the cubs a lioness might try to take a bite out of him, it was also true that she'd find his polysilicon skin as impervious to her teeth and claws as it was to the frustrated mosquitoes' proboscises.

"Well?"

"Go ahead," Galen said reluctantly. "Just don't scare the bejesus out of these guys like you did those poor cheetahs."

"Right you are, guv," said Sam, saluting.

By the time Galen had returned from getting an icy self-cooled can of Dutch beer out of the jeep, Sam had managed to work himself to within thirty meters of the nearest lion.

That was the easy part, Galen knew. Getting closer without spooking the protective lionesses would be much more difficult.

As Galen sipped his beer, he scratched an ear and sighed. He felt like a parent who'd taken his child to the beach. While he sat up here and drank his beer, his son was playing in the sand down by the water's edge. It was dangerous, but only if his son went into the water.

<*Hey, you're doing pretty damn good,*> Galen said, watching Sam patiently lifting one foot, slowly moving it, and then putting it back down and repeating the laborious process with the other foot. His snail's approach took time, but Sam had been able to edge ever closer to the pride without arousing the suspicions of any of the watchful lionesses.

<*Thanks. I think I must have a smattering of Daniel Boone's genes in me,*> Sam said, adding, <*And don't ask me who Daniel Boone is, please.*>

<*Give me* some *credit, Sam. Everyone knows about Daniel Boone,*> Galen replied. In reality, he had no idea who Daniel Boone was. He figured a little white lie once in a while wouldn't hurt anyone. Besides, he rationalized, he was sick and tired of coming up short every time Sam mentioned someone from the history cubes.

One of the dozing lionesses lifted her head and snorted, blowing a blast of air out her nostrils that produced a half-challenging, half-inquisitive "Whuuf?" Rising to her feet, she ambled toward Sam, who lowered himself down onto a rock and impersonated a statue.

Trailed by two cubs, all head and feet, the lioness approached the absolutely motionless Sam, halting her advance less than just a meter from him. Sam watched her nostrils working as she tried to capture his scent. Gingerly, she reached out with one massive paw and patted at him, unsure what to make of him.

<*Good thing you don't smell like the huge hunk of meat you're supposed to emulate,*> said Galen, amused by Sam's situation.

<*Yeah,*> agreed Sam. <*Wonder what she* does *make of me, though?*>

<*We'll see, won't we?*>

The lioness put her face centimeters from Sam and, panting in the late-morning heat, stared at him with intelligent yellow eyes. Her breath, like that of any meat-eating predator, was vile and odoriferous. Rasping in and out of her throat, it sounded like a small handsaw being worked through a slab of wood.

When the cubs waddled fearlessly up to Sam, the lioness growled and nudged them back, pushing them down on their little lion butts. They immediately got up back up and resumed stalking Sam's boots. Pulling at his laces, the cubs drew the lioness's attention to the fact that Sam's footwear was made of leather.

Butting her two cubs away with her massive head, the lioness licked Sam's boots several times, decided she liked that, and then, carefully biting one boot, began gnawing at it with her incisors.

<I'll be calling you Stumpy soon,> teased Galen, sounding more confident than he felt. *Sam, you idiot. Why did I let you talk me into this?*

Sam tried to pull his foot away from the lioness—gently—but she reached out with one huge paw, her claws extended, and pulled it back. *<Oh, no,>* Sam moaned when a second lioness showed up in case the first had discovered something good to eat.

While Sam was trying to decide what to do next, the rest of the pride suddenly turned their heads toward the brushy undergrowth that lay just meters beyond the water hole.

Galen put his binoculars to his eyes and looked, too.

"Uh-oh," he said, alarmed.

THE REASON FOR THE LIONS' CONCERN IMMEDIATELY BECAME apparent as a huge bull elephant, four cows, and two young ones emerged from the bush.

The lioness suddenly lost all interest in Sam's boot and roared at her cubs, urging them in the opposite direction from the elephants.

Although the rest of the pride pretended at first not to be alarmed by the sudden arrival of the elephants, their air of unconcern was quickly dropped when the bull began to approach the pride's resting place, swinging his massive head and his equally massive tusks from side to side.

The lions quickly scrambled to their feet. Deciding that discretion was the better part of valor, the pride moved away at a deliberate pace. If there was any animal willing and able to challenge the authority of the lions, Galen thought, it was an African bull elephant.

Sam, on the other hand, proved not to be as smart as the wise lionesses who led their cubs to safety.

<Sam, get the hell out of there!>

<Don't worry, dadder. I'll be okay. I'll just sit here quietly like I did when the furball was inspecting me to see if I might be edible.>

<Dammit, Sam!> Galen told him. *<Elephants are different.>*

<Different? Yeah, how?>

<Elephants are smart.> Galen said. *<Even worse, although they're normally gentle giants, elephants can be* mean.>

<So what do you want me to do, Sabu?>

<Back away from there,> Galen advised. *<Do it slowly, but get your metal butt out of there.>*

Sam followed Galen's advice and slowly backed away, careful not to make any arm movements. Things were going fine until Sam's foot came down on the tail of one of the lion cubs that had somehow gotten left behind when the rest of the pride beat its retreat.

The surprised and frightened cub screeched loudly and Sam, startled and unbalanced, waved his arms like a human semaphore and crashed to the ground. Its ears laid flat against its skull, the cub shot across the veldt like a tawny rocket.

"Sam, don't move!" Galen shouted.

Too late.

The bull elephant trumpeted angrily and thundered over to Sam, who was struggling to his feet. Enraged at this funny-looking creature that threatened its family, the elephant knocked Sam back to the ground with its breast, and then gored him through the chest with one of its huge tusks.

"Sam!" screamed Galen helplessly.

The enraged elephant wrapped its muscular trunk around Sam's body, picked him up as easily as a shopper picking up a loaf of bread. The bull flailed him against a tree like the elephant was beating it with a stick—*whack, whack, whack.*

Satisfied with the results of this action, the bull elephant then hurled Sam to the ground and kneeled on him like an old man with arthritis getting down to pray before an altar.

The elephant, its tiny eyes red with fury, rose up slowly and stomped on him several times. Then, one massive foot pinning him to the ground, it used its muscular trunk to pull him apart like a piece of taffy. That accomplished, it hurled his legs into the tall grass.

Satisfied with its handiwork, the elephant thundered off at express train speed, its family following in the bulldozer-wide path of destruction it left through the vegetation.

"Sam!" cried Galen. "Ohmygod, Sam!" Sick to his stomach, Galen approached what was left of his friend.

Sam's upper body, its thoracic protective plate and polysteel ribs crushed by the elephant's rampage, lay on the flattened bush grasses, various fluids draining into the absorbent soil.

"Hi, partner," Sam said when Galen approached what was left of him.

"Jesus, you're a mess!"

Galen sighed with relief when he saw that Sam's skull, his head, was intact; his brain, cocooned inside a marvelously elaborate and ingeniously constructed "egg carton," might well have sustained trauma, but it appeared he hadn't suffered a life-threatening encephalonic injury. Sam was fortunate: A true android could get another Pseudo-Quantum-Gravity AI pack; Sam's brain was organic and all too human.

"Does it hurt?" asked a concerned Galen.

"Only when I laugh," Sam replied, "and that's not a problem with you around." He seemed oblivious to the thick brownish liquid dribbling from a corner of his mouth. He looked down at his ruined body and asked, "Wasn't I taller when I got here?"

"You've been truncated," Galen said.

"Hey, you made a pun!" Sam said, laughing appreciatively. Then he flinched and added, "If it's any consolation, you were right about elephants."

"You *must* be seriously injured if you're giving me credit for being right about something."

"I have to confess I debated not acknowledging your warning," Sam said. "I was torn."

"Christ!" exclaimed Galen. Shaking his head, he turned away.

"Hey, where are you going?"

"To find your legs."

"Good idea. I'm going to give Alfie a call."

"Break the news to him gently," Galen said, over his shoulder. "The little guy likes you."

"I'll tell him I've been to see the elephant."

"That's one way of putting it."

II

Galen was normally pleased to be back in Texas. He just wished this trip was the result of more pleasant circumstances.

"How is Sam doing, Henri?" Galen asked, shivering. The air-conditioning, its levels set by people who wanted nothing to do with Houston's normally oppressive heat and humidity, was giving him chills.

"Just fine, Mr. Yeager," Dr. Bussot assured him.

"Galen," said Galen with a wave of his hand. Determined to know the truth rather than be humored, he asked, "Is he really doing 'just fine'?"

As a member of the Voorhees family and a stockholder in the Soweto Corporation, Galen was one of the few people in NorAm who could go to the top and talk face-to-face with the director of the Voorhees Foundation.

"Really," Bussot repeated. "There are some small problem areas, to be sure, but nothing major to worry about."

"I can worry about anything," said Galen with a half-smile. "For one thing, aren't you afraid Sam will catch his death of cold?"

Dr. Bussot shot him a curious look before he realized that Galen was pulling his leg. "Computer, what is the current assigned temperature?"

"Eighteen degrees."

"No wonder I can see my breath," muttered Galen.

"Make it twenty degrees, please," Bussot ordered. "I like it cool," he explained to the shivering Galen.

"Thank you for changing it for me," Galen said. "I know Sam was frozen once; I don't think his rehabilitation need go back that far, however."

"I agree."

"Returning to what you were saying," Galen resumed. "Just what sort of 'problem areas' are you talking about?"

"Sam is a very complex biotechnological integration. On one hand, he is an android, an artificial being. On the other hand, his cellular -regenerated organic brain has been imprinted with the remnants of his human mind."

"I *know* what Sam is," Galen said in a tone that suggested Dr. Bussot was patronizing him.

Bussot shook his head. "I am sorry if I am lecturing, but you must understand that Sam is unique in many ways. He was the Foundation's first and the most fully realized attempt to commingle man and machine in this manner. Our subsequent attempts have fallen short of the success we have achieved with Sam."

"What does that have to do with Sam's recovery?"

"Since we have had difficulty duplicating our original breakthrough, producing nothing but failures, we must be very careful when we put Sam back together again."

Distracted by his fears for Sam's recovery, Galen didn't think to ask what sort of failures the doctor was referring to. Instead, he was puzzled by Bussot's words concerning Sam. "His brain wasn't injured, was it?"

"No, it was not," Dr. Bussot confirmed. "We are merely being very conservative with our only triumph. I would be most annoyed if anything were to go wrong."

"That makes two of us, Doctor," Galen said. "Three if you count Sam." When Bussot nodded, Galen asked, "May I see him now?"

"Of course. Follow me, please."

Galen hated hospitals. He had to admit, however, that the Foundation's biomechanical research laboratories were not true hospitals. Even so, they had that stereotypical hospital look and smell. Apart from coming here to monitor Sam's "awakening," the last time he'd been in a true hospital was when his father died. That was already more years ago than seemed possible, he realized with a jolt.

While the Foundation's administrative and operational offices were housed in a twelve-story-high, granite-faced building that dominated Voorhees Square, the research labs were hidden underground. Galen knew that it was here, many levels beneath Houston's streets, that the Foundation conducted highly secret experiments and oversaw long-running experiments in gene technology and bimolecular engineering.

Galen knew of no other facility on Terra that could have produced Sam. Half android and half human, Sam Houston was the result of everything the Foundation knew about mind and personality retrieval, about the interface between the manmade and the natural, and about the integration of artificial and human intelligence.

And speaking of Sam . . .

"Come in, Galen," Sam said in response to Galen's discreet knock on his room's door.

"How'd you know it was me?" Galen asked as the door hissed shut behind him.

"Nobody else knows I'm here apart from Alfie and you."

"Alfie?" Galen knew his familiar had been doing a lot of hibernating—for want of a better word—lately. He was surprised to hear that Sam and he had "visited."

"Yeah, Alfie. But to answer your question—I knew it was you because Dr. Bussot and the others don't bother with niceties like knocking."

"You're a patient now; you haven't any rights, certainly not to privacy," Galen told him. "Even so, you're looking well."

Sam was sitting up—or being propped up—in a long hospital bed covered with slate-gray sheets that had presumably once been white. The top sheet was pulled up to his neck, and his arms were outside, resting on top of the sheet and by his sides.

Sam shook his head at Galen's observation. "It doesn't take much to fool the brain," Sam told him. "First, fool the eye."

"What do you mean?"

"I mean here I am in bed, the covers pulled up over me, right."

"Right."

"Wrong," said Sam. He reached down and pulled the sheet away from his chest—except his chest wasn't there, just a series of what looked like polysteel barrel staves. They weren't even part of Sam; they were attached to the bed. "Where's the rest of me?"

"Jesus!" gasped Galen. "Where *is* the rest of you?"

"In the shop," Sam told him. He looked down at what was left of himself. "I don't much exist below my shoulders and arms." He smiled. "But you can see that for yourself."

"But . . . why?" sputtered Galen.

"So far, my meat patty of a brain is having compatibility problems with the bimolecular neuroprocessor in my spinal cord. The processor is supposed to act the part of a traffic director, but it's waving everyone into the intersection at the same time. As you might expect, this causes a certain amount of electroneural gridlock. It's sort of what it must be like in your nervous system every day."

"Yeah, well . . . *What?*"

"Just seeing if you were paying attention, pard," laughed Sam.

"Uh-huh," grunted Galen. Then he did a double take and asked, "Hey, where'd these come from?" He pointed at a tasteful, and presumably expensive, flower arrangement.

"They're from . . . Well, read the card for yourself." Galen did and Sam advised him, "Please don't move your lips; it's embarrassing even if we are the only ones in here."

Galen glanced around the room, bathed in *faux* sunshine, and said, "What makes you think we're alone?"

"Huh?"

"This card is from Fedalf and MacKenzie," Galen said.

"So?"

"So it's *not* just me and Alfie who know you're in residence. How'd they know you were here? I didn't tell them. Did you?"

Pulling the sheet up over his mostly missing body, Sam said, "C'mon, Galen. It's Fedalf you're talking about—the head of the PrinSecPol. If an albino bear shits in the Black Forest, he knows about it. He's got contacts everywhere."

"I know. That's what worries me."

"What are you talking about?"

"If Fedalf knows you're here, if he knows how to find you, who's to say someone else can't track you down?"

"Who in this quadrant of the big milky would *want* to track me down?" Sam asked.

"You have a point there," Galen conceded. "Still, the point *I* was making was that, knowing Fedalf, it wouldn't surprise me to discover that he's bugged your room."

Sam pointed a finger at his head and made a circular gesture. Then he shook his head sadly and said, "You need a vacation, Mr. Paranoid. You were—"

"Don't shake your head like that," admonished Galen. "Something could fall off."

"As I was saying, you were in Africa a week—a whole week—but it wasn't enough to make you forget who you are and what you do. You need to stop thinking like a secret operative."

In an argumentative mood, Galen countered by saying, "Going back to my Grandmother Mugambi's is hardly the best way for me to try to forget who I am. And being attacked by a horde of homicidal invaders also does nothing for one's peace of mind."

"That's right," agreed Sam. "You're confirming my point. You need a respite from all this."

"Assuming that's true," said Galen, "I suppose I'm going to have that opportunity now. You'll be in here for some time to come."

Sam looked down at himself. "Yeah, you're right. It doesn't look as if I'm going to be able to go asteroid walking for a week or two yet."

"A chest, hips, legs, and feet do seem to be the minimum requirement." Galen smiled down at his friend. "You take care of yourself, partner."

"I will if you promise to ask Dr. Bussot to send me some attractive nurses. That squarenut who looks like a refugee from a Frankenstein sinny just doesn't cut it."

"What do you want, a pleasure android in a nurse's uniform?"

"That'd be nice."

Galen raised the sheet and pointed at Sam's nonexistent body. "And just what do you think you could do about it? It looks to me like you're a little lacking in the goodies department."

"Sure, you've got all the equipment; you can make fun of my shortcomings."

"If it's any consolation, I get laid about as often as the Pope," Galen confided.

"Yeah, but it's quality versus quantity."

"Goodbye, Sam."

"He's going now, Hashem!" Sam said loudly. "Who knows?" he said to Galen. "You may be right about Mr. Mystery Novel listening in."

Looking around, Galen surprised both Sam and himself by saying, "I hope so. For some reason, I hope so."

III

Galen looked around the apartment he kept near the Foundation, aware of how empty it seemed without Sam. It finally was brought home to him how much he missed his wisecracking friend and partner. To make matters worse, he knew that he couldn't find refuge in talking to Alfie, his familiar. Alfie had been inaccessible for long periods of time lately, communing with his other-dimensional friends.

He went over to the liquor cabinet and poured himself a drink. "A boy's best friend is his bottle," he said aloud. As soon as the words left his mouth, he regretted uttering them.

Listen to me—I sound like some self-pitying fool, acting like he hasn't a friend in the world. Like without Sam's company or access to Alfie I'm doomed to sit around by myself with nothing to do but drink myself into a stupor.

He took a sip of the bourbon, glanced around the apartment, and laughed sourly. *Christ! Who am I trying to kid? I* don't *have any friends, do I? I've been too much the loner to be "one of the guys."*

He sat down, got up again, paced a bit, then decided to listen to a little music. "Put some Yu Jing on," he ordered the apartment computer, deciding he was in the mood for the Sino-European melodies the late 21st-century composer was famous for.

"Do you wish to be more specific?" the computer asked.

"The 'Coming of Spring Suite' will do."

Immediately, the lush, sweeping melodies floated out into the room from the hidden speakers. "That's better," Galen said, refilling his glass and sitting down. He wiggled, trying to get comfortable.

"Goddamn sofa," he muttered. He remembered that his ex-wife had picked it out. No surprise there; she had selected all of the apartment's furnishings. She had insisted on it, saying that she was the one with "good taste."

"Christ!" he said, moving around the couch in an ultimately fruitless search for a spot that didn't feel like there were rocks inside the cushions. The reason Adrianna had decided this was *the* couch—and love seat and matching chair—for them was that it was compatible with the carpet and the overall color scheme.

Galen moved over to the love seat. Deciding it was marginally more comfortable than the sofa, he put down his glass, settled back and closed his eyes, hoping to escape into the music. He was just beginning to relax when . . .

"Pardon me, sir," said the apartment computer.

"This had better be good," Galen said, not opening his eyes.

"There is someone at the door," the computer announced. "The appropriate building entry codes were successfully entered, and the correct codes to the front door are being programmed into the lock right now."

Galen eyes opened. "Who is it?" It was a stupid question, he realized; there was only one person it could be.

"It is Adrianna Palmieri-Yeager."

* * *

"Guess I should have changed those codes," Galen said to his ex-wife once she'd entered.

"That's a warm and caring welcome."

"Hey, I'm a warm and caring sort of rutter," Galen told her. "Or I was before I found out you were sleeping with the starting five members of the Toronto Null-Gee Basketball team."

"Don't be ridiculous, Galen, it was only the center, and it was only one time."

"Thanks, I feel better about it now."

"Men," she said, shaking her head and putting her bag down.

"I see you still know your way around," Galen told her after she'd hung up her wrap and made herself a drink at the wet bar.

"I never forget things like that," she said, sipping her white wine.

A small domestic 'bot trundled out from the utility closet and chirped, "Good evening. May I take madam's things?"

"You're too late," Adrianna told the diminutive 'bot. "Madam's already hung up her 'things.' "

"Yes, go away," Galen said to the 'bot.

"I can—"

"GO AWAY!" Galen roared. The 'bot chirped in alarm and hurried from the room as fast as its treads could transport it.

Adrianna tried unsuccessfully to smother a giggle; it escaped and was followed by another and then she burst out laughing.

"What's so . . . ha-ha . . ." Galen couldn't stop himself from laughing too.

Suddenly, he sobered up and said, "I guess this is the first time we've been together since the divorce. Alone, that is," he added.

"You're right. We can't really count our meeting at your grandmother's house, can we?"

"No." Galen glanced at an easy chair. "Please, have a seat."

"Thank you," she said, ignoring the chair and sitting down beside him on the love seat.

"That's fine; sit there if you wish," Galen said.

"Do I make you uncomfortable, Galen?" she asked. He

could feel her warm breath on his face. The love seat was too small for him to retreat.

"Uncomfortable? Um, no." Then he confessed, "A little nervous, maybe."

"Why do I make you nervous, Galen? I'm the same old me I ever was," she purred, leaning against him.

"I rest my case."

She laughed and put down her glass. "Oh, Galen, I miss you so much."

"You do?" he said, puzzled. "Then why did we fight all the time?"

"I don't know," she admitted. "Perhaps it was because we had so little in common."

"Nothing in common is more like it."

"Oh, no, Galen," she said, moving closer to him, her hand settling on his thigh. "There was always one thing that was good for us both."

"Let me guess," he said. "Was it—"

"Shut up and kiss me, you fool," she said, her lips finding his. She kissed him hard and long; she kissed him until he kissed her back. "It's about time, dear," she said, pulling back briefly to look into his blue-gray eyes.

With his heart pounding, she undid several of his shirt buttons and slid her hand inside. Her fingers played with the sparse curly hair on his chest, then inscribed a circle around his nipples.

"This is wrong," he protested.

"How can something that feels so good—or so 'bad'—be wrong?"

"We're divorced, remember?"

"Heavens!" she said, her eyes widening in mock horror.

"Yeah, you're right—that's a pretty stupid thing to say."

"Words always get in the way, Galen. You don't need words to show me how you still feel about me, do you?"

He had no answer to that except to crush her against him and smother her with kisses. He bit the lobe of one ear, then nuzzled her neck and buried his face in her hair. Together, they toppled over slowly onto the thick carpet, and she thrust her tongue into his ear. That drove him mad with desire.

She pulled away and stood up. "Let me get out of these things."

"Hurry."

She stepped out of her clothes and said, "Well?"

She was still stunning. Her body was lithe and supple; she wasn't angular and bony like so many women who starved themselves to please other women, instead of men. She had a womanly fullness of body that promised that her creamy flesh would be smooth and silky to the touch.

Galen smiled when he saw that the erect nipples that bobbed atop her full, high breasts were rouged. She had remembered how much he liked that. His gaze fell and his eyes greedily saw how her small waist swelled at her hips, and the triangle of her pubic hair shimmered moistly.

As she watched him studying her, the pupils of her green eyes grew large with lust. "Well?" she asked again.

"Words fail me."

She leaned forward to him as he sat on the edge of the sofa, offering her full yet firm breasts to him. Her eyelids fluttered as he drew her closer and gently encircled the tips of her breasts with his mouth. He felt the rose-petal-hued nipples stiffening between his lips. She moaned and reached down between his legs. "Take me, Galen, take me."

He pulled her down again.

Galen watched as Adrianna got up, strolled into the bedroom, found a robe, and returned. But instead of coming directly back to their place in front of the fireplace, she went to where she'd put her bag.

"What are you looking for, Adrianna?" he asked as she dug around in its interior. Galen wondered how any woman could ever find anything in her bag, convinced that purses and bags had to be larger inside than outside.

"You'll see soon enough," she said without looking up. While she continued her search, he admired her back. There was no part of a woman's body he did not like—lips, breasts, legs, neck—but he particularly admired a nicely sculpted back, with the muscles around the spinal cord delineating the natural bifurcation.

"Here they are," she said, standing up. She examined whatever it was she'd extracted from her bottomless bag, and padded softly toward him. Sitting up, his back against the abandoned love seat, Galen watched Adrianna's progress across the room with a certain degree of prurient interest.

Correctly interpreting his avid stare, Adrianna said, "Oh,

no—not again. Not now. It's time to talk business."

"Business?" repeated Galen, wilting.

"Business," Adrianna insisted firmly.

"If that's the case," Galen said, getting up, "then *I* need to get a robe, too. I'm constitutionally unable to talk business in my birthday suit."

"Get my slippers while you're in there," Adrianna said. "I forgot them when I got my robe."

When Galen returned from the bedroom, knotting his robe's belt at the waist, he handed Adrianna her slippers, then went to the bar to refresh their drinks.

"Shoot," he said, plopping back down on the love seat.

"These are from your cousin," she said, handing him a message cube and a sealed envelope.

He turned the cube over in his hands, then looked at Adrianna and asked, "Which cousin?"

"Herbert van der Park, although I believe that whatever is in there represents the concerns of several of your other cousins as well."

"And the envelope?"

"You're to open it first," Adrianna said. "In my presence."

"All right," Galen said. He had no problem with that; he was dying of curiosity.

After examining the envelope carefully to see if it had been tampered with, more for show than for any realistic hope of finding evidence that someone had opened it and resealed it, he slit it open with a souvenir letter opener he'd bought at LunaWorld.

He unfolded the letter inside and perused the skimpy contents. Feeling Adrianna's interested stare on him, he looked up and said, "Do you mind?" She laughed softly and walked over to the window.

"Make the window transparent, please, computer," she said, yawning. The apartment CPU did as she requested, and she stared out at the lights of Houston.

Galen returned to reading the letter. It wasn't long, just a single handwritten page. He scanned it quickly, looked up at Adrianna standing at the window, and then read it again.

"Okay," he said.

Adrianna turned toward him, cocked her head, and asked, "Are you sure?"

"I'm sure."

She crossed the room and sat down across from him. "Well?"

"Do you know what this note says?"

She nodded. "Yes, I was there when Herbert wrote it."

"I see." He glanced down at the handwritten note. He recognized his cousin's crabbed writing. He wasn't sure how he recognized it until he remembered that it was Herbert who had sent him a personal note specifically reminding him about the family business meeting.

Adrianna sat back, crossing her legs. "Unless I'm wrong, it says that I'm 'okay' and that you can share with me whatever's in the cube. But it's up to you."

"You don't know what's in the cube?" he asked.

"I have my suspicions, but no, not really. Not the specifics."

"And what do you suspect is in it?" He tensed slightly, certain he knew what she would say.

"I think it's about Alves."

He nodded.

"Are you going to read the contents of the message cube now?" Adrianna asked him.

"I suppose I should," he said slowly.

"You sound reluctant. Why?"

"I feel like Adam just before he took a bite out of the apple. As soon as I read the cube, I'll no longer be able to claim innocence. I suppose I'd like to savor my ignorance for just a little while longer." He grimaced, expecting her to laugh at him.

Instead, Adrianna just nodded and said, "I understand."

After taking another sip of his drink, he tapped in a short series of numbers, then pressed his thumb against a postage-stamp-sized glowing square. The cube opened.

PART FOUR

REBIRTH

HE SAT SPLAY-LEGGED INSIDE THE PLACE THE BIG ONES PUT him when they left him alone. He stared at the boxy things on his feet. There was something about them that continually caught his eye. It was the smiley face on them. He knew about smiley faces. Smiley faces were one of the first things he learned to recognize. These smiley faces were different somehow from the ones that periodically appeared above him and then zoomed down at him, growing larger and larger until they were all he could see.

He had no words for any of this, of course. He didn't know the boxy objects on his feet were shoes and the smiley face was Mickey Mouse, or that his feet were his feet. He did know that the wiggly things the big ones grabbed and kissed and tickled and made funny noises about were a part of him. When he was not as big as he was now, he liked to stick the wiggly things into his mouth.

But more and more, they were covered by soft things; sometimes by soft things that went inside those funny little boxes. And it was also getting harder to reach them and put them in his mouth.

He was still contemplating the smiley faces when he heard the bad sounds begin. Again.

"Why can't you come home after work like everyone else

instead of hanging around some cheap bar?"

"What do I have to come home to, bitch? Just a dirty house and kid who needs to be changed. At least I don't sneak my drinks when there's no one around but the brat."

"You bastard! And don't shout so loudly, you'll wake the baby. I don't want him to hear us fighting again, goddamnit."

"The baby, the baby—it's always the damned baby! And so what if he hears us? He's just a baby. He doesn't know what's going on. He can't understand a word we're saying."

"We don't know that; nobody does. I don't want him to hear his father acting like an asshole."

"You rotten little whore!" the loud, deep, bad sound roared.

There was another sound and then he heard crying. He recognized crying; the warm smiley face who took away his hunger did it all the time.

"I can't take any more, Tom. I'm sick and tired of you treating me like a punching bag. I'm leaving and I'm taking our son with me."

"The hell you are!"

That bad sound again. And again. And again. There was more crying, too. He squirmed and made little sounds of his own, hoping the bad sound would stop.

This time, though, there was a new sound—the loudest he'd ever heard. It was followed by more of the bad noise, but not as loud this time.

"You . . . you shot me, you dumb bitch."

"Tom! I . . ."

More bad noises. Then it was quiet. It was quiet for a long time.

The fuzzy thing with the cool, wet part it liked to press against him until the big ones made it go away began to make soft sad sounds; then it quieted.

He slept. When he woke up he felt uncomfortable; where was the good-smelling smiley face to make him feel better again? And he was hungry. He cried.

The fuzzy thing began to cry, too. Then it made that loud noise that frightened him. It kept on making the loud noise. No one did bad things to the funny thing to make it stop. It made the noise again and again. He cried for food; where was the smiley face?

A new loud noise.

"Jesus Christ!"

"Ohmygod! I told you I thought something was funny when the dog wouldn't shut up. I tried calling but I only got the machine."

"Looks like they've been dead for a day or two, all right. Where's the kid?"

"I don't know, I—Jesus, you don't think the dog . . . ?"

"No, in here."

The three big ones stared down at him; they weren't smiling.

Sam felt someone's gaze on him. He opened his eyes to find Dr. Bussot standing beside his bed, looking down at him with kindly concern in his eyes.

"Good morning," said Dr. Bussot.

"Good morning?" repeated Sam, puzzled. "Was I . . . ?"

"Sleeping? Yes, or as close to it as you ever get, I suppose."

"Oh."

"Tell me, did I . . ." His voice faded as he now sensed that there was more of him than there had been for a while. He was whole again.

Dr. Bussot smiled and pulled the top sheet off. "How do you like your new body?"

Staring down at his unclothed body, his new legs nearly reaching the foot of the hospital bed, Sam said, "It looks pretty much the same as my old body, Doctor." Not wanting to disappoint Dr. Bussot, he continued, "It does seem a wonderful thing, however."

He wiggled his toes. *Where are the smiley faces?* he wondered. *Smiley faces? Where'd that come from?*

"While there are only superficial surface differences in the appearance of your new self, the improvements are quite extensive."

"Yeah?" said Sam, forgetting, for the moment, the odd question that appeared, unbidden, in his mind.

"Your garveridium and molecular steel leg and arm bones are much stronger than your old polysteel ones; your skin is not only more lifelike, if such a thing is possible, it is simultaneously more flexible and less likely to be damaged by anything short of a fusion torch."

"Gee," said an impressed Sam, gingerly pressing a fingertip against the pink flesh of his stomach.

"Can you feel it?" asked Dr. Bussot.

"No. Yes. I mean—"

"Good," laughed the doctor. "When you touch yourself like that, both your fingertip and the surface of the skin across your stomach sense what their human counterparts would sense: nothing; that is, both sense skin—self—and nothing else."

"I think you're right," agreed Sam. "But how do you *know* that?"

"We've used some medication to make you . . . ah, sleep at night."

"I was asleep when you came in?"

"Yes," Bussot confirmed. "It's during this 'downtime' that we've been running diagnostics and comp-sims on you. The stimulus/sensory readings conform to normal human brain patterns and computer maps of expected electroneural activity."

"Oh." Sam sounded so odd that Dr. Bussot asked what was the matter.

"I suspected I was 'off line,' so to speak, but I still possessed a rudimentary awareness."

"You did?" said Dr. Bussot. "Normally, I would say that is impossible, but we've learned never to say anything so definite when it comes to your skills."

"I wouldn't call them skills, necessarily."

"What *would* you call this activity?"

"Dreaming."

* * *

When Galen Yeager was shown into his office, Hashem Fedalf reluctantly closed the leatherbound copy of *The Murders in the Rue Morgue* he was reading, returned it to the safety of one of the climate-controlled display cases that held his most precious acquisitions, and stripped off the white gloves he was wearing.

"Hands cold?" Galen chided.

"You're infuriatingly oblivious to the cultural treasures of the past, Galen," Fedalf replied, picking up his coffee cup.

"You're right." But I haven't time for one-tenth of the cultural treasures of the present, much less the past," Galen countered.

"You should make time."

A gleam in his eye, Galen pursed his lips and then leaned toward at the seated Fedalf and asked, "And how is it that the director of the Principate Secret Police has so much free time on his hands?"

"It is a well-known fact that nose-to-the-grindstone workaholics actually accomplish much less than those of us who maintain a healthy attitude toward our duties," sniffed Fedalf. He gestured at the chair in front of his desk. "Please sit down; you know I don't like anyone hulking above me."

It was a measure of Fedalf's respect for Galen and his abilities that he allowed his agent such license to verbally fence with him. Since Galen had solved—or at least been a part of the solution of—the Cousteauean crisis, Fedalf had developed an ever greater regard for the younger man's unusual talents and unorthodox, if effective, approach to his job.

"How is Mr. Houston, by the way?" Fedalf asked.

Amused by Fedalf's sudden formality, Galen replied, "Sam is fine. He thanks you for the flowers and the note, although he was surprised that you knew where to send them."

"But not you?"

"No."

"Ah." Fedalf sipped his coffee and then said, "You said you had something to discuss with me. I got the idea that while you implied it was personal, it could turn out to be something rather more than that."

" 'Something rather more than that'?" said Galen. "You've been reading too many British mysteries again, Hashem."

Fedalf smiled and went on. "I can think of no other operative who has the ability to so thoroughly intertwine his private and professional life as you, Galen."

Galen looked down at the floor, slightly abashed. "I know. I don't understand it, but I become a part of the process somehow. It just happens."

"Being a member of such a prominent family might have something to do with it," Fedalf observed sagely.

Galen's head snapped up, and he shot the director a sharp look. "My family? What have you heard?"

Fedalf seemed genuinely surprised by Galen's reaction. "Why, nothing. Nothing at all, apart from what you reported about the attack on your family's estate in Africa. I assumed that you'd found something out, something you wished to discuss with me."

"Oh," said Galen, relaxing a bit. He grinned sheepishly. "Actually, what I wish to discuss with you does concern my family. It has nothing to do with the attack, however."

"Then feel free to say what's on your mind," Fedalf told him. "As the director of the PrinSecPol, I am always interested in learning more about the Soweto Corporation's affairs."

"This is for your ears only."

"Of course; that's why we're alone."

"Don't patronize me, Hashem," Galen said wearily.

Fedalf stared at him for a moment. "You're right," he said finally. "All recording devices off," he said in a loud, clear voice.

"All recording devices off," replied the computer.

"Satisfied?"

Galen didn't reply immediately. Instead, he mentally crossed his fingers and called, *<Alfie?>*

<<Yes, Galen?>>

<Good, you're there. Tell me, Alfie, are there any recording devices still operating in this room?>

<<There is an audio-only device in the beverage dispenser in front of Hashem Fedalf.>>

<Thank you, Alfie.>

<<You're welcome, Galen.>>

"May I?" said Galen picking up the coffee carafe.

"Of course. Help yourself."

"I had something else in mind," said Galen, getting up. He went to the door and, after it hissed open, placed the carafe in the hallway outside. Several passersby shot him startled looks and were careful to give both Galen and the carafe a wide berth.

When Galen returned and sat down again, Fedalf looked at him with an expression of mild annoyance on his face. "Why did you do that?"

Galen just wiggled an index finger at the director.

"You're right," conceded Fedalf. "Forgive me, but I had to try."

"I understand," replied Galen. And he did. Fedalf was just playing out his role as head of the PrinSecPol. Galen couldn't expect him to give up his old tricks any more than he could expect a scorpion not to attempt to sting him; it was just his nature.

"Do you wish to begin now?"

"Yes," said Galen. When he saw Fedalf staring wistfully into his cup, he asked, "Is anything the matter?"

"No," said Fedalf. He looked down at his cup again and added, "It's just that I wished I'd gotten a refill while the carafe was still here."

Galen laughed, shaking his head. Then he became serious again and began. "I received a message from . . . ah, people in my family."

"From family members? Who?"

"From . . ." Galen paused, deciding to censor himself. His mouth had been wagging like a duck's ass lately, and there was no real need for him to name his cousins.

"I can appreciate your reluctance," Fedalf said. "You'd rather not say who it is, even to me."

"Yes," Galen said, grateful that Fedalf understood. "Anyway, I received a message which indicated that its senders have developed a mistrust of Luis Jorge Alves's motives."

"What is it they fear?"

"That Alves will attempt a takeover of the Soweto Corporation."

Fedalf, who'd been leaning forward, now settled back in his chair. After a few moments, he asked, "Is that possible? I thought that the Voorhees family held a majority of the stock."

"What if someone were to acquire the proxies of several family members?"

"Could Alves do that?" asked Fedalf. "Who would sign over his or her voting rights to him?"

"The cousins fear that my Aunt Kitrina has made some sort of pact with him to do just that," Galen said. "The fact that Alves is preparing to marry her daughter, my cousin Ghannee, offers one motive for her decision—if she really is intending to support his takeover of the corporation.

"Aunt Kitrina has substantial holdings. Ghannee, on the other hand, like myself and the other cousins, controls a much smaller proportion of the outstanding stock; she, like us, has only a limited voice in saying how the corporation should be run."

"Even given her . . . ah . . ." Fedalf paused, unsure how to tactfully bring up the matter of Ghannee's diminished mental capacity.

When she was eleven, Ghannee had been treated for a routine viral infection with a not-so-routine experimental drug.

Inadequately tested before being put on the market, the drug turned out to have a devastating effect on the brain. The brains of recipients of the so-called miracle drug were affected in ways that were still not fully understood. Although Ghannee's condition was recognized and treated, the damage done was irreversible. Although she was a normal young woman in many ways, she had never progressed beyond a childlike personality that was as endearing as it was frustrating.

Galen shrugged. "Aunt Kitrina has strong feelings about medicine now; she's successfully fended off attempts by Corporation doctors to examine Ghannee to see if she's capable of making informed legal judgments."

"I see. With her vote and Aunt Kitrina's, can Alves amass a majority share of the stocks, or at least the voting power?"

"I don't know," Galen replied truthfully.

"I guess I'm asking, is it possible? Theoretically?"

"Theoretically, anything is possible," Galen said grimly.

* * *

"Come on," the physiotherapist 'bot said to Sam. "You can do it."

"I can't." Sam clung to the cool polysteel rails, his hands griping them tightly.

"You *can*," the 'bot insisted. "But you have to try. You don't have to do it all at once. Take it one step at a time."

"You sound like a self-help holo," Sam said.

"There's a lot of truth in self-help holos," the 'bot replied, a smile crossing its elementary visage.

"But what if I fall on my face?"

"Oh, goodness, you're right! Since you're made of porcelain, you'll break into a million pieces!"

Sam looked sharply at the mechanical physiotherapist's broad features, unsure how to interpret the minimalist expression it wore. Then he smiled. "You're good, very good," he said, realizing that the 'bot had decided that he would respond more to goading than pleading.

"May I interpret that response to mean that you are willing to try?" the 'bot asked.

"Yeah, yeah," agreed Sam. "You can read my answer that way."

"I am gratified to hear that. However, there seems to be a

dichotomy between your expressed intent and your action—or should we say inaction?"

"Jesus Christ on a bicycle!" exclaimed Sam. "Give me a moment, willya?"

Gripping the rails tightly, Sam slowly slid his right foot along the floor. Grimacing, he leaned forward, putting much of his weight on the rails, and dragged the other foot up to the first. "There," he said proudly.

"Very good," the 'bot said, clapping two of its four hands.

"Thank you," said Sam, bowing slightly.

"A fine performance. Now for an encore."

"Encore? An encore, you flaming hunk of junk!"

"Temper, temper," chided the 'bot. Then, in an irritatingly baby-talk voice, it asked, "Is Sammy all tired out from his big walk?"

"You said take it one step at a time," he snapped back. "Now you expect me to climb Mount Gagarin!"

"Maybe the first time was just a fluke," the 'bot said, putting one hand to a rudimentary chin and studying Sam and the twin rails the human/android clung to like a child clutching his mother's hand.

"A fluke!"

"There is a very easy way to prove me wrong," the 'bot said. "Just do it again."

Mumbling something about a household disintegrator beam under his breath, Sam repeated his earlier two-step. Again, he grasped the rails so tightly he nearly left an indentation in them.

"Satisfied?"

"I don't know," the 'bot replied.

"You don't know?" repeated Sam unbelievingly. "What's not to know?"

"You *look* like you're walking," the 'bot admitted, "but are you *really* walking?"

"What else would you call it?"

"You see," the 'bot explained, "I'm not sure if you're walking so much as swinging yourself along with the aid of those rails."

"The rails have nothing to do with it," Sam insisted. "I'm walking, I tell you."

"Can you at least stand without the rails?" the 'bot said, going on as if it hadn't heard him.

"Of course," Sam said, letting go of the rails and holding his hands out in front of him.

"Oh, good," the 'bot said. "Then you won't miss the rails if you're not using them, will you?"

"Huh?" said Sam, not comprehending.

The 'bot did something that caused the rails to withdraw into the floor. "There," it said. "That's better."

"Hey!" said Sam, teetering back and forth like a silent film comedian whose shoes have been nailed to the floor. He began to lean dangerously forward. He lost his balance momentarily and took a step forward to regain it. He took another and another. Before he knew it, he was walking.

"I'm walking," he announced proudly.

"Yes, I believe you are," the 'bot agreed. "Can you make it over to where I am?"

"I can try." Sam staggered across the floor toward the 'bot, arms outstretched like Frankenstein's Monster. The 'bot retreated slightly as Sam got closer. Finally, it ceased its backward advance and allowed Sam to reach it. Lunging, Sam grabbed hold of the 'bot like a drunken sailor embracing a street lamp.

"You made it," the 'bot said, holding onto Sam's outstretched arms.

"I did, didn't I?" Sam said, proud of himself.

"Stay here while I go and set up the tightrope."

"The tightrope?" Sam asked, blanching.

"Just kidding," said the 'bot.

10

<<*THERE IS A CODED SUBSPACE TRANSMISSION COMING IN.*>>

<*Thank you, Alfie,*> Galen said. <*Could you prepare everything for me, please?*>

<<*Certainly.*>>

While Alfie received the incoming signal and stripped it of its encryption, Galen made ready. Having Alfie do all the work was a luxury that spoiled him for the times when the familiar wasn't around.

Clutching a big glass of ice water in his hand, Galen was ready when Alfie announced, <<*Here it comes.*>>

A holographic projection of Tey Varro appeared in the center of the living room. "Hello, Galen," the image said. "It's good to see you again." From the background, it was clear to Galen that she was transmitting from her presidential office.

"Hello, Tey," Galen replied. "It's good to see you, too."

She stared at the glass in his hand, her eyes widening in surprise. "Is that water?"

"Huh? Oh, yeah, water."

"And you're drinking it?"

"Come on, you make it sound like I can't do without a drink," he said uncomfortably.

"I'm sorry," Tey told him. "I was just shocked to see you drinking something other than bourbon for a change."

"I need a clear head about me," Galen told her.

"And why is that?" she asked.

"I'd rather not say over the—"

"Didn't Alfie tell you this is a coded transmission?"

"Well, yes, but—"

"Then we can talk," she insisted. "No buts about it."

"Go ahead, then," he shrugged. "You called me; it's your decicred."

"How's Sam?"

"You used a coded transmission to call me to ask about Sam?"

"How is he?" she repeated in a no-nonsense voice.

"He's fine. I mean, I think he is. He was getting ready to try walking for the first time since his . . . ah, accident." Galen took a sip of water; it was refreshing. *Hm-m-m,* he thought, *I ought to try this more often.*

"Has anyone else been asking about Sam?"

"Sure," he replied, answering her question too quickly to realize that there might be more to it. "Hashem Fedalf and Rob MacKenzie sent their best wishes—and some flowers."

"Maybe you'd better go back to whiskey," Tey snorted.

"What?"

"I'm not talking about Fedalf, MacKenzie, or any of your mutual friends," she said forcefully. "I'm talking about others."

"Others?"

"Strangers."

Galen shook his head. "No, I can't recall anyone else asking about Sam. Why do you ask?"

"Because there have been several people poking around Cousteau. They've been inquiring after the two of you, but they seem more interested in Sam than you."

"People? Can you be a little more specific?"

"I can, but it doesn't make any sense," she told him.

"Tell me and maybe I can figure it out."

"Of the four people we've run identity checks on, three have turned out to be fully licensed and bonded private investigators, the sort of people you hire to do a search through the public and private records to see what they can come up with on a prospective spouse." She made a face to indicate how distasteful she found the whole subject. "You know what I mean; looking under the carpet for dirt and in the closet for naughty secrets."

"And the fourth?"

Tey frowned. "She's the one who doesn't add up. Number four is a hard-edged corporate type, a blonde who doesn't fit the profile of the others."

"She's not a private investigator?"

"That's what's so funny about her."

"Yeah?"

"She works for the Soweto Corporation."

"Jesus!" He gulped his water, thinking it was booze; he didn't notice the difference.

"Galen," she said, staring earnestly at him. "I want you to be careful."

"I'm always careful."

She shook her head. "Promise me you'll be careful."

He stared at her image for a long time before replying, "Okay, I promise I'll be careful."

"Good."

* * *

"Hello, Sam," an armed security guard called out to him as the android ran past him down an improbably long corridor toward a distant right-branching turn. Like the four levels above it, this level of the Voorhees Foundation, known as Sub-Five, was a huge hexagon whose corridors each ended in a sixty-degree turn to the right—if you were going in the direction Sam was traveling.

"Hi," Sam grunted as he swept past the security man standing guard at one of the corridors that ran from each of the outer perimeter junctures in toward the core, slicing the underground facility into pie-shaped wedges. Seen from above, each floor would have looked remarkably like an eight-spoked wheel.

This was Sam's third time around; each circuit he made had been run faster than the last. Sam had no intention of admitting to Dr. Bussot and the others he was as good as new—better than new, actually—until he had proven to himself that he was everything they said he was.

A minute or so passed. With the corridors devoid of personnel on this pre-dawn Saturday morning, they were eerily silent, allowing the security guard to hear Sam's footsteps approaching long before he could see him.

From a tiny speck down the corridor, Sam grew larger and larger. "Hi, Sam."

Sam nodded as he flew by, his arms beginning to pump and his knees coming up higher and higher. Then he was gone down the corridor, growing smaller and smaller until he turned the far corner.

Sam was quickly back. Again the guard called out a greeting; again Sam grunted an acknowledgement. Then again. And again. The guard began timing how long it took Sam to travel the six sides of the hexagon. He looked at his watch and whistled. Sam was going faster than any human could hope to duplicate.

And still he kept accelerating.

* * *

"And how's the mother of the bride today?" Galen asked his Aunt Kitrina when he saw her standing outside the church. Combined with her height—she was tall and imposing in her gown, and with her strong features flattered by more makeup than Galen could recall her ever wearing—Aunt Kitrina looked remarkably like a broad-shouldered transvestite. Not the type who passed for a woman, but the type that everyone immediately recognized as really a man.

"I am very nervous," she admitted, leaning over so that Galen could give her the obligatory peck on the cheek.

"You look beautiful," Galen told her, having performed his osculatory duty.

"Thank you, Galen. I don't believe a word of it, but thank you, nonetheless."

"Where is everyone else?"

"Inside the church," Kitrina told him. "It will be time soon."

"What are you doing out here, then?" Galen queried.

"It is stifling inside," she said. "I just had to get some fresh air or I feared I would faint." She fanned herself with one of the small folding fans the church provided on the back of each pew along with the hymnals.

"Have you come alone?" Aunt Kitrina asked him.

Galen nodded. "Yeah, usually I have Sam to talk to, but with him in the shop, I'm forced to attend by myself."

"Ah, yes, your friend is being repaired," Aunt Kitrina said. "I wouldn't worry. He's in good hands. Dr. Bussot and the rest of the Foundation staff are miracle workers."

Frowning slightly, Galen nodded his agreement. Then he

tugged on an earlobe and said, "If we're the last two, I suppose we should go inside. They can start without me, but it wouldn't do if the mother of the bride was late."

Looking over his shoulder, Aunt Kitrina told him, "We are no longer the last two, nephew. More than that, you now have someone to sit with."

Galen turned and saw Adrianna getting out of a limousine.

"I thought you didn't like to attend weddings," whispered Adrianna.

"Only when it's my own," Galen whispered back.

"You prick!" hissed Adrianna, punching him on the arm.

"Don't forget where you are," Galen reminded her.

I'd better not forget, either, Galen reminded himself. Since the organist, a florid-faced fat woman wearing a hat that looked like a bird cage that had collided with a rosebush, hadn't begun any of the processionals yet, he still had time to count heads in the church.

Galen was surprised at how few members of his family were in attendance. He'd arrived late, but he did catch the eye of Herbert van der Park and a few of the cousins. Although the look that van der Park shot him spoke volumes, it was the little nod that he directed toward him when Galen acknowledged his cousin that told Galen that they would have a lot to talk about at the reception.

He glanced over at Adrianna, beautiful as always in a salmon-pink dress that had been designed by one of Terra's top couturiers, probably for a sum of money larger than most people earned in a year. "Hol-Shop?" he asked in a low voice.

"What?"

"Your dress—the Hol-Vee Shopping Channel?"

"Shall I send you the bill and allow you to see for yourself?" she whispered back.

"Ah, no," he said. "Actually, it's lovely."

"For a dress from HVSC, you mean?"

Galen smiled, then noticed several people from the bride's side of the aisle gawking at the two of them so intently he began to wonder if his fly was undone.

Actually, it wasn't hard to figure out what it was about the two of them that attracted the attention of other members of his family; it was Adrianna sitting with him, of course. He had followed his Aunt Kitrina's advice and asked her if he could be her escort, realizing what a stir it would cause.

"Aren't you afraid you'll start tongues wagging all over again?" she'd asked. "The aunts probably just stopped talking about our divorce."

"I'll take that chance," he'd told her. "Half the aunts think I'm a pretend scientist, and the other half think I'm a ruthless killer."

"Think how shocked they'd be if they realized that both assumptions were true," Adrianna jabbed.

"That would pretty much put an end to the Christmas cards," Galen agreed.

"Galen!" Adrianna exclaimed. "Are you developing a sense of humor?"

"Maybe," he admitted. "Someone has to fill in for Sam while he's flat on his back and out of the action."

Now, as the organist struck up the first processional, Galen sneaked a look at his watch and saw that it was just one P.M. He wondered what was happening back in Houston where it was approximately five A.M. Most people would still be in bed, Galen realized, but then most people needed to sleep. Not Sam.

Galen leaned to the right and then to the left, shifting his position on the hard surface of the pew. At least Sam wasn't compelled by family ties to attend the wedding of a man he only met once and who might be planning to try to usurp his inheritance.

Lucky bastard, Galen thought.

II

The security guard nodded at Sam as he flashed by. At least the man thought he'd nodded at Sam; it was difficult to tell from the blurred streak that rocketed past his position if it was still the android. The guard wondered just how much faster, if any, Sam could go. He scratched his head, taking into account the fact that the sixty-degree turn Sam had to make at the end of each corridor *had* to be one constant which would limit Sam's ability to continue accelerating.

If the cocky android wasn't careful, the guard reasoned, he

might find himself losing control at the end of a corridor and smashing into the wall with a devastating impact. That might prove to be every bit as deadly as being stomped by an elephant.

The guard's mental arithmetic came to a sudden halt when plascrete and polysteel beams erupted into the hallway halfway down the corridor.

As stunned and shocked as he was by this occurrence, the guard didn't need the wailing of the siren or the calm feminine voice of the computer announcing, "There has been a security breach," to realize that they were under attack.

A gigantic form thrust itself into the corridor like a stubby crocodile crawling into a tunnel just barely large enough to contain it. The guard was forced to avert his eyes from the star-bright glare of the fusion torch that burned and disintegrated everything ahead of the massive mining machine.

The human attackers inside the civilian mining machine formally known as a Caterpillar FME-3A, but called a John Henry by everyone else, had used it to gain entrance to the underground labyrinth that contained the Minotaur they had come to capture: the android known as Sam Houston.

Moments before the John Henry had burst out into the corridor, Sam's ultra-sensitive hearing had detected it tunneling through the soft subsurface soil. Although he had no point of reference for the sound, he knew it meant trouble and he skidded to a halt before he ran himself smack into the middle of a situation he didn't understand.

A weapon, he thought. *I've got to get a weapon*. But where? The security guards carried weapons, but they were only limited-power energy pistols. An energy pistol was useless against a John Henry, and little more than an irritant against a mercenary in battle armor. *That's funny*, Sam thought. *Why'd I assume the attackers are mercenaries?*

The answer came quickly enough: because the attackers at Galen's family's compound had proved to be mercenaries. Sam didn't know why he immediately assumed there was a connection between both incidents, but he did.

The security guard knew none of this; his only insight was that he was doomed—a walking, talking dead man. Blinking against the glare, his sight still not fully returned, he readied his weapon and awaited the brief confrontation that would end in his death.

"I'm sorry I won't see you again, Martha," he whispered. "Kiss the kids and tell them dadder loves them."

"Tell them yourself," said a shape that loomed up from nowhere and pinned his arms against his sides. Pressure was applied to his carotid artery until he blacked out. Now as limp as the corpse he had expected to be, the security guard was dragged down one of the eight perimeter-to-core corridors and into an unused room. His attacker quickly and efficiently stripped him of his uniform.

The mercenaries emerging from the John Henry moved cautiously, yet with the awareness that they were more than a match for the poorly armed security people they anticipated encountering. After consulting their maps, the mercenaries split into several groups. Most exited from the left hatch of the John Henry and proceeded toward the core. The rest investigated other corridors on this level.

A trio of mercenaries had hardly proceeded more than a hundred meters down the John Henry–ruptured corridor before they saw the first defender. So confident were they of their superiority in armament and protective covering that they laughed when they observed him draw his energy pistol and fire at them. As they expected, there was little observable result; the defender's weapon was useless against their moly-weave vests and arm-and-leg armor.

One of the three emerging out of the glare leveled an energy rifle and fired. "That's one less guard to worry about," he said to his companions in accented Prin'glish. "Let's take care of the others and then find the android."

"Should we do anything with the body, Delta-one?" asked a second mercenary, a female.

"Leave it," the one she had questioned told her. "We make messes, we don't clean 'em up."

The three mercenaries had barely advanced five meters before the dead man rose up and seized the woman from behind.

"Jesus, he's alive!" she shrieked. "Tomás! Hari! Help me!"

Her attacker wrapped his arms around her, ripping her hand from the rifle and replacing it with his own. Concentrating his fire on the Achilles' heel of their armor—the vulnerable opening between their helmets and vest—the guard used the woman's weapon to blow off her companions' heads.

Having dispatched the female mercenary's cohorts, her attacker let go of the rifle and grasped her jaw. A single, swift yank to the right snapped her neck. He allowed the rag-doll body to slide to the floor.

"I'm sorry, but you three killed me first," Sam said, looking down at the dead mercenaries. He turned one of the bodies over with the toe of the security guard's boot—which he'd "borrowed" along with the man's uniform, since the running shoes he'd been wearing would have given him away if he hadn't taken the guard's shoes.

"It's time to change clothes again, and you're about my size, Hari," he said to the headless dead man. He needed the mercenary's clothes since the energy-rifle bolt that had struck Sam had burned away most of the guard's shirt, making it highly unlikely he could successfully reprise his security guard ruse.

Attired in the dead mercenary's clothes, vest, and armor, Sam now had his pick of the three weapons. Although he'd already used the woman's rifle, he immediately rejected it as not powerful enough for his needs. Delta-one, the man the dead woman had called Tomás, had carried the weapon he decided to take. A typical leader's weapon—*a typical* male *leader's weapon*, Sam corrected—it was a powerful laser pulse rifle with as many extras as a Swiss army knife.

"Yes, this'll suit me just fine, Tomás," he told the dead man. "Muchas gracias, amigo," he said, clipping a half-dozen hand grenades onto his moly-weave vest.

"Hm-m-m," he mused. "Can't leave a mess like this for just anyone to stumble over."

He found an unlocked door and dragged the bodies inside the room. The motion-activated lighting revealed a closet door. Inside he found and activated a janitor 'bot.

"Awaiting orders, sir."

"There's a bloody mess outside in the corridor," he told the 'bot. "Please go and clean it up." While the 'bot cheerfully carried out Sam's instructions, he stowed the bodies in the closet, throwing a tarp over them. Sam knew the three mercenaries would be found sooner or later, but concealing the bodies would gain him some valuable time.

Hearing voices coming down the corridor, he decided it was time to move on.

"Goodbye, sir," the 'bot called out cheerfully.

"Goodbye," Sam said as he half-walked, half-ran down the corridor.

Coming toward him were several heavily armed mercenaries

going in the opposite direction. Rather than avert his face, which might have made them wonder what he had to hide, Sam strode confidently toward the three rough-looking mercs, muttering under his breath, "It's always me who gets the dirty jobs. I didn't forget it. Why do I have to go back and get the goddamned . . ." The others laughed and kept moving.

Sam unslung his purloined energy rifle, pointed it at the backs of the unsuspecting mercenaries, and muttered, "Whatever you're getting paid, it isn't enough." With that, he shot them dead.

"Oh, hello again," the little janitor 'bot greeted Sam.

"I have another job for you," Sam said.

"Oh, good," the 'bot said brightly. "I am so pleased to serve you."

"Um, *yeah*," Sam said, grabbing the legs of the dead mercenaries. As he dragged them toward their hiding place, he said, "Make sure you get all the blood up."

"Sir . . . *please*," the 'bot said, its voice full of reproach.

"It's always a thrill to meet someone who loves his work," Sam muttered under his breath.

The bodies safely stowed with the first three, Sam now approached the quiescent John Henry. Unmoving, the massive mining machine resembled Captain Nemo's fabulous *Nautilus*, left abandoned momentarily on the sea floor while the crew attended an undersea funeral.

Could it actually be as vulnerable as Verne's deserted *Nautilus*? Sam wondered. There was only one way to find out.

Sam found a hatch that someone had halfheartedly tried to close. He pushed it open and, taking a deep breath—unnecessary physically, but satisfying psychologically—he entered.

Although Galen had used a John Henry to assist in his jailhouse rescue of Gar Varro on Cousteau, Sam had been flying a battle floater overhead at the time. Consequently, this was his first time inside one of the huge mining machines.

Undeniably impressive on the outside, it was a rather mundane plasmetal and steel tube on the inside. He found himself in a long bay. Although it was now empty, it was clear from the detritus on the floor that this was where the mercenaries had come from. Old news, he realized; he had known where they'd come from.

A tall blond Terillian youth came out of a cabin in the rear of the John Henry, shot him a cursory glance, plopped down on a seat, and began rummaging through a duffel bag. Still digging around in search of whatever it was he was looking for, he looked up at Sam and asked conversationally, "Do you think we'll find that damned android any time soon?"

"Probably sooner than you think," said Sam, sitting down one seat away from the young mercenary. Reaching under his vest, Sam asked, "You have any idea why we're looking for this guy, anyway? I mean, you can *buy* a goddamned android for a lot less than this operation costs."

"Money is supposed to be no object to the person who hired us," the young blond said.

"What's his name again?"

"Huh?" the young man said, looking up with a curious expression on his face. "Why'd you ask that? Who are—"

Sam pulled the vibroblade out and thrust it into the young man's heart in one economical motion. The surprised youth grunted once and then slumped over.

"Shit," Sam said softly. He disliked all this killing. It was necessary, but he disliked it all the same. *This kid just happened to find himself in the wrong place at the wrong time.* A cruel thing, fate.

A search of the Terillian youth's body yielded a perfectly balanced throwing knife. Sam admired its utilitarian beauty; it was just the sort of thing he'd expect a Terillian mercenary to have in his possession. He slipped the knife inside his vest and got up, a heaviness to his actions, and walked forward to the pilot's cabin. The John Henry's operator, a slightly pudgy brunette bent over a clipcube, was too engrossed in making entries to look up. That was probably for the best, Sam reasoned. She was spared seeing the vibroblade coming.

Sam reached for a grenade, planning on wedging it under the controls, but stopped. The obvious thing to do seemed to be the destruction of the John Henry, but Sam couldn't bring himself to do it. Instead, he popped open a control panel and removed a key component. He smiled; the John Henry wasn't going anywhere without the small cube he pocketed.

"Oh, shit!" His smile disappeared when he realized he was faced with having to conceal two more dead bodies.

11

SAM DECIDED WHAT TO DO NEXT AFTER EAVESDROPPING ON the radio transmissions between the various invading mercenaries. *First rule of battlefield communications*, he thought. *Don't communicate unless you absolutely have to*.

The invaders blithely radioed their current positions, their expected positions, and any and all information they had at their disposal. It was via this voluble chatter that Sam learned they were rapidly securing the rest of this floor.

The radio traffic was revealing as hell. Although it was clear that the invaders strongly suspected that he was still on this level, there was a certain amount of disagreement. Some of the mercs, relying on what they would do in a similar situation, argued that he had certainly made his way to the next level.

There was a puzzled tone to the radio exchanges when it came to Sam's disabling of the John Henry. What bothered the mercenaries about that particular act of sabotage was why Sam didn't just destroy it.

"I don't get it," a voice that identified itself as Beta-two said. "Why didn't this tin man blow up the John Henry when he had the chance?"

"Maybe he's planning to use it to escape," an unidentified voice said.

"What's he waiting for, then?"

Maybe the thing can't drive a John Henry," came the response from another unidentified voice.

"We were told this guy could do just about anything," said Beta-two. Sam could hear the puzzlement in the merc's voice. "He could have gotten out. Why the hell didn't he?"

Good question, Sam thought. Even as he was disabling the John Henry, the same question had occurred to him: Why was he doing it? It hadn't taken long for him to discover the answer—he didn't want to escape. Not right away; not until he'd made them pay for attacking the Foundation. *The foundation of my new life*, Sam thought. *And that's no pun, either.*

So far absent from the radio chatter was any mention of the deaths he'd caused. Either the mercenaries hadn't discovered the bodies yet and didn't know he'd killed some of their number, or they had been told not to discuss it. Even if his first three victims hadn't been found yet, Sam knew, there was the matter of the John Henry. What did they think happened to the people left on board?

He shook his head. There was so much he didn't know; so much he could only speculate about. And then there was the question of what he should do next, where he should go. For the moment, if the radio communications were to be believed, they thought he'd made his way to the next level up.

Sam hadn't done so, of course, but he found it hard to resist following that plan of action. Going toward the surface would be the first step in a journey that would take him to Dr. Bussot's suite of offices. No matter how much he owed to Galen for initiating the project, it was Dr. Bussot who had made it happen. It was Dr. Bussot who had taken what little of him had remained in the lifeless shell of his former body and transferred his personality to a new brain. He had to make sure nothing happened to the doctor; he owed him his life.

Sam found his way into one of the supply areas and quickly located the small freight elevator that serviced it. Deciding that calling for the elevator might not be the smartest thing to do, right up there with shooting off a flare to pinpoint his location, Sam pried open the elevator doors and looked up. The elevator car appeared to be at least several levels above him and unmoving. He reconsidered his decision not to call for the car. Smiling, he closed the doors and pressed the glowing down button.

The elevator arrived in seconds and the doors opened. No one. Lowering his gun, he stepped inside and told the elevator, "Sub-level four, please." Then he popped open the emergency hatch in the car's ceiling and pulled himself through the opening before the doors closed.

As the elevator ascended to the next level, he clutched his energy rifle and waited. The car stopped and its doors opened. "Shit," he heard, "there's no one in here."

"Let's take it down," he heard another voice say. "Someone sent it up from the bottom level. He might not have gotten far."

Sam walked to the edge of the car's roof and transferred to the side of the elevator shaft. He waited until the elevator car dropped away beneath him before he began his climb.

After climbing up to sub-level three, he pried open the doors and risked darting his head out and back. Nothing.

Feeling more sanguine about things, he was about to ask the computer a question about the layout of this level when something stopped him. *What if they've compromised the computer?* he asked himself. *It could be like one of those old sinnys where the good guy talks to someone on a phone, someone he thinks is a friend, but the camera reveals that it's a shape-shifting alien imitating his now-dead friend's voice* He laughed, the sound echoing down the empty corridors. "What an imagination, D'Artagnan!"

"Attention, attention," the computer's voice announced, coming from the hidden speakers in the corridor. "The android Sam Houston is now on sub-level three."

* * *

<*Alfie, oh, Alfie . . . ?*> Sam projected.

<<*Yes, Sam?*>> asked Alfie's "voice" inside Sam's brain.

<*Boy, am I glad you're taking calls today, Alf!*> Sam exclaimed gratefully.

<<*What may I do for you, Sam?*>>

<*I know you're a wiz at electronics, even by long distance,*> Sam began. <*So I'd like you to help me to short-circuit a computer if you can.*>

<<*I do not understand.*>>

Sam explained that the Foundation's computer was tracking him, and asked what Alfie could do to help him make himself invisible to the computer. <*Either that or knock it off line.*>

<<*Do the other life forms know where you are?*>>

<*They may know, because of the computer, but they haven't arrived here. Not yet.*>

<<*Then you must immediately get as far away from your current position as you can.*>>

<*Roger Wilco.*> Sam stuck his head outside the room he'd taken refuge in and glanced up and down the corridor. Nothing. He leapt out into the corridor and ran as fast as he could, made a left at the first juncture he came to, and dashed through a series of interconnected rooms.

That should do it, he thought. He was probably a few hundred meters from his starting point. <*Okay,*> he told Alfie.

<<*Good,*>> Alfie replied.

<*Now what?*> Sam asked.

<<*Now you must find and address a computer interface,*>> Alfie told him. <<*That should not be difficult.*>>

It wasn't. Sam tried several doors until he came to one that was locked. Assuming that people didn't lock a door unless there was something important inside, he forced it open and discovered himself in a small operating room containing a computer-assisted dissection table. Pleased by his success, he popped open the table's computer access cover. <*I'm ready for the next step.*>

<<*Then please open the small compartment at the rear of your skull.*>>

<*Left side?*>

<<*That is correct.*>>

Sam did as he was told, parting his hair and pulling back a flap of his synthetic skin. Opening his skull revealed just a portion of the complex series of electronic components and connections that surrounded the protective shell which enclosed his brain.

Using Sam's sensitive fingertips to "see" the conduits leading into Sam's brains, Alfie said, <<*I am searching for the left-side power and informational relays. Ah, there they are.*>>

<*Everything okay?*> Sam asked.

<<*Yes,*>> Alfie told him. <<*You must now connect with the computer via your power relay.*>>

<*You do it,*> Sam said. <*I'm yours.*>

Alfie took control of Sam's functioning and quickly spliced the android into the computer's electroneural pathways. <<*As soon as I download a schematic of the Voorhees Foundation's above- and below-ground levels into one of your Mishuru moly-mem chips, you are going to take a brief rest, Sam,*>> Alfie told him.

Before Sam could reply, Alfie had completed the download and directed a complete shutdown of his logic and memory functions. A nanosecond later Alfie directed a tsunami of disjoined AI language into the Foundation computer's net, overwhelming it by the sheer intensity and volume of the flow. That was just the first blow of a one-two knockout combination; immediately following the AI transmission, Alfie sent an enormous power spike pulsing through the hapless computer.

Alfie broke the connection between Sam and the computer before restoring Sam's systems to normal and initiating a revival sequence.

Sam opened his eyes. <*Auntie Em?*>

<<*It is just Alfie.*>>

<*That's okay, don't apologize,*> Sam said. Then he blinked and asked, <*What happened to the lights?*>

<<*The computer is no longer functioning normally,*>> Alfie told him. <<*I anticipate that its self-repairing diagnostic tools will be called on line by its emergency programming and that it will be able to restore minimal functioning within several minutes to a quarter of an hour. Its higher functions will most likely not be restored for at least thirty minutes to an hour. Does that provide you with sufficient time?*>>

<*If I'm not outa here in twenty minutes, I'm not getting out,*> Sam said.

<<*Is that all, then?*>>

<*It is. Thank you, Alfie.*>

<<*You are welcome. Goodbye.*>>

"Now it's just me and the boys in the moly-weave vests," Sam said. He clutched his energy rifle and headed out into the corridor. "Ready or not—here I come."

II

"Sonofabitch!" someone swore on the helm-com.

"Follow standard hostile area communications protocols, Charlie-two," a disgusted voice responded.

It's a little late for that, isn't it? Sam thought, listening to every word the invaders were exchanging.

"Sorry, Green Leader," Charlie-two replied. "It's just charlie unit has found delta unit. They're dead; all three of them are dead. That bastard killed them; blew their fuckin' heads off!"

"Is that possible, Green Leader?" the voice of Beta-two asked. "I thought the target was an android, a blondie eyes."

"That's correct, Beta-two," Green Leader responded.

"Then he should be incapable of violence against humans. I can understand him blowing the computer's mind, but he shouldn't be able to hurt anyone."

"Tell that to delta unit," Charlie-two said.

"This changes things," admitted Green Leader. "But not much; we still have to bring this thing back in one piece."

That's good to know, Sam thought.

"Yes, Green Leader," said Charlie-one, "but he doesn't have to return the favor."

"We know that the computer was tracking him on level three when it was sabotaged," Green Leader said. "If we pull everyone up to level four, seal off all the stairs, lift/drop tubes, and elevators, then we have him trapped below us."

"We can take our time zeroing in on him," agreed Beta-two.

"Negative on that," Green Leader replied. "We have a limited time frame. We should be acting to accomplish objective two of this mission."

Objective two? Sam thought.

"I just thought of something," said Beta-two. "If he ambushed a unit, he might have taken some of their equipment."

"Is anything missing, Charlie-two?" asked Green Leader.

"A weapon, some grenades, and body armor."

"What about a helmet?"

"That too, sir."

"I'm ordering double zee status immediately," said Green Leader.

"Yes, sir," Beta-one said. The helmet radios fell silent and remained that way.

"That's all she wrote," murmured Sam.

The mercs had gone to their internals, just as he and Galen would have done in a similar situation. He wondered why they hadn't been on internals from the beginning. This operation smacked more and more of one put together hastily. But why?

Something else puzzled him: What was "objective two"? Maybe it was their second target if they failed to get their hands on him—something they seemed to want to achieve very badly. But what if, as things were working out, they *didn't* get him? Sam doubted that they had an unlimited period of time to accomplish their mission.

Unless they had planned things down so perfectly that nothing could go wrong—which was possible, if highly unlikely—someone or something would leak the information that an armed intrusion into the Voorhees Foundation's underground laboratories was taking place. Even if the police and the private security forces had been paid to ensure that they looked the other way for an hour, they would have to become involved at the point when what was going on could no longer be kept secret.

If he acted now . . .

Making up his mind, Sam moved out smartly.

"Hey, this elevator's coming up!" exclaimed one of the mercenaries standing guard on Sub-Four.

"Get ready," one of his two companions said.

The third man was already reporting what was happening to their superior officer.

"I copy, Gold Leader," he said.

"Shit!" grumbled the first mercenary. "Don't kill it, he says."

"Don't worry," said the man who'd informed Gold Leader what was going on. "We can blow this thing to bits. We just gotta be careful not to damage the brain."

"Which one? Some of 'em got a second one in their abdomen area."

"Shut up, the doors are opening," the first mercenary said. "Just blast him chest high."

When the elevator's doors hissed open, thick clouds of acrid smoke poured out of the opening. Unable to see who or what might be inside, the three mercenaries opened fire nonetheless, sweeping the interior of the elevator with streams of laser energy.

"Think that's got him?" the second mercenary asked as they stopped firing.

Before either of the others could answer, two small and round objects came bouncing out of the elevator.

"Grenades!"

The two grenades exploded in a blinding flash of flame and fragments. Although the three mercenaries' moly-weave vests stopped most of the shrapnel, their primary function was to turn away bolts of laser energy. The fragments of metal that struck the three men in the neck and groin areas were sufficient to badly injure or kill them outright.

As the smoke from the gas grenade that Sam had set off just before the elevator had begun its ascent started to dissipate, he opened the small hatch in its roof and jumped down inside the car. A glance was all it took to confirm that the mercenaries outside the elevator's doors were dead or incapacitated.

"Time to move on," he said in a low voice.

III

"What are you doing?" Galen whispered.

"What's it look like, you fool?" asked Adrianna. "I'm crying."

"Why?" Galen asked, genuinely puzzled. "Ghannee's my cousin, not yours."

"That doesn't matter," explained Adrianna, dabbing her cheeks with a tissue. "It's a wedding; I always cry at weddings."

"Oh," said Galen skeptically. "She *is* beautiful," he observed. "I'm so happy her problem did not prevent her finding a husband."

She dug an elbow into his ribs. "Men," she said. "You're even worse than most," she told him. "It's times like these that remind me why I called you that name that upset you so."

Galen grimaced. "Ouch!" he said. Angered one time too many by his seemingly cold exterior, Adrianna had nicknamed him "Sushi." Ever dense, it had taken Galen a little while to catch on that she was calling him a cold fish.

"You have to remember I have German-Dutch blood in me; hugging and kissy-face stuff isn't in my genes."

Adrianna snorted derisively, then, looking toward the front of the church, said, "Here comes the big moment."

"Huh?" Then Galen saw that she meant it was time for the exchanging of vows and rings. Adrianna began to sniffle again.

It seemed to Galen that it took forever for he and Adrianna to reach the head of the receiving line; but reach it they did, finally.

"Hello, Galen," the bride said to him, smiling.

"Hello, Ghannee," he told her, hugging her and then giving her a warmer and more intimate kiss than one usually gave to a cousin.

"Hey, what happened to those cold German-Dutch genes?" asked Adrianna.

"I make exceptions," Galen said, not taking his eyes from his beautiful cousin's face. Had he been forced to, Galen reflected, he would have admitted that Ghannee and he had been unusually close during their early teenage years. She was one of the cousins with whom he had played lighthearted games of sexual investigation and experimentation. Aunt Kitrina had come close to catching them in the act several times, and the memory of those near misses helped forge a strong bond between the two cousins.

If Alves only knew what we did as children, Galen thought. Then a second, more unsettling, thought occurred to him. *What if he* does *know? What if Ghannee told him? That would certainly provide one explanation for his animosity toward me.*

"You look gorgeous, Ghannee," he said, putting aside his fears. "Or should I call you Ghannee Tollersrud-Alves?"

"Call me whatever you wish to, Galen," she laughed. Then she looked at Adrianna's smiling face and asked half-mockingly, half-seriously, "Tell me, Adrianna—does this mean you and Galen are reconsidering your divorce?"

When Adrianna just shrugged and smiled an enigmatic smile, Galen jumped in quickly to say, "No, it doesn't." Both women laughed. Galen reflected ruefully that while Ghannee's powers of reasoning were not what they should be, she was far from unintelligent or unperceptive.

Women! Galen thought, moving forward to shake Alves's hand. "Congratulations, Luis," he said. "You realize, don't you, that this is one transaction where you're really getting the better of the deal?"

"I can't agree with you more, cousin Galen," Alves said, accepting Galen's hand and pumping it up and down. "Thank you very much." *He can't be that much of a bad guy if he loves Ghannee*, Galen grudgingly admitted to himself.

"I am pleased that we finally get a chance to meet each other—in person, that is," Galen said, looking Alves in the eye.

Alves was black but light-skinned like Ghannee and many in the Voorhees clan. Not only was he ruggedly handsome in a way that Galen knew appealed to women, he was also taller than Galen. *Maybe a hundred and ninety centimeters*, Galen estimated.

"Where is your friend Sam?" asked Alves. "I made certain that he was added to the guest list."

"Sam could not be here today," Galen replied. "He had an unfortunate encounter with an elephant."

"Ah, yes," said Alves. "Kitrina said something about him being in Texas for . . ." He laughed. "Excuse me, but I think the word she used was repairs."

"Really?" said Galen, more as a conversational response than a real question. He glanced to his left and saw that the bride and groom had a great many more people to greet, and said, "I don't want to hold up the line. Let me just congratulate you again on your good fortune finding such a wonderful woman as Ghannee. She is . . . very special. Take good care of her."

"I will. Thank you very much, Galen."

After Adrianna exchanged pleasantries with Alves, Galen led her outside to the steps of the church. "What is it?" she asked him.

"Tell me," he said conversationally. "Are you thinking of sending a get-well card to Sam?"

"To that machine?" she asked. "No, I wasn't planning on it."

"Not even for my sake?"

"Well, I will send one if you want me to that badly," she said. "Where must I send it to?"

"Don't you know?" asked Galen, careful not to impart any discernible inflection to his words.

She gave him a look. "Of course I don't know. You haven't permitted anyone to know where he was taken after the accident."

"Oh, yeah," said Galen. "That's right. I forgot." He glanced back at his Aunt Kitrina standing beside Ghannee and Alves. "No one knows where he is."

* * *

With the building's blueprints in his supplemental memory, Sam knew the edge was now his—and he intended to make the most of it. He quickly found an advantage of his insider's knowledge that he could make immediate use of. He discovered that each pie-shaped section had several small polyglas conduits that carried fiber-optic wiring. Because the vertical tubes had to be large enough to permit the passage of diagnostic and repair drones and 'bots, they were just large enough for Sam to squeeze inside and climb up or down.

Working his way down to Sub-Five, he shivered with anticipation. If he was able to exploit his new found mobility as successfully as he hoped, he would sow confusion among the mercenaries—not to mention fear and dread.

They seek him here, they seek him there, those Frenchies seek him everywhere—that damned elusive Pimpernel. Sam had no idea of the origin of that bit of doggerel, which had leapt unbidden into his mind, but it seemed appropriate, wherever it had come from.

He pushed out against an access panel and emerged in a small, unlit room. His infrared vision confirmed that he was in a place where the repair 'bots retreated to whenever they weren't in service. Rummaging around, he found a meter-long polysteel bar which was apparently a replacement part for something or other. Whatever its actual function, it made a pretty good weapon, he decided, swinging it back and forth experimentally.

When the single repair 'bot occupying a corner took note of his presence and began to power up, Sam said, "Oh, no, you don't; power off, please." The 'bot's service lights dimmed and it returned to its quiescent state. "That's better," Sam said, checking the charge on his energy rifle.

He opened the door and slowly stuck his head out, like a two-hundred-year-old tortoise cautiously peering out of his shell. He glanced to the right.

Nothing that way.

He turned his head and looked around to the left.

"That's him!" someone shouted and all three mercenaries pointed their weapons his way.

Sam pulled his head back into the little room a lot faster than he'd stuck it out. Immediately, the door began to splinter about a meter up from the floor.

"Slug-thrower," Sam noted. "Good, I can use one of those."

Taking a figurative deep breath, he stuck the polysteel bar into his belt, readied his energy rifle, kicked open the door, and leapt out into the corridor.

12

PANDEMONIUM.

With both sides firing as rapidly as they could, laying down an incredible level of intersecting energy beams and plasteel-jacketed slugs, it seemed nothing could live. But the moly-weave vest of the mercenaries did their job admirably. Sam's vest wasn't strictly required for his safety, but he saw no reason to get shot up any more than necessary.

One of Sam's laser bolts found an unprotected area on a mercenary's leg, and the wounded man bellowed in pain and fell backwards as his leg collapsed under him. When his head rolled back and exposed his vulnerable neck, another of Sam's hard-and-high laser fastballs struck the wounded mercenary's Adam's apple. The tightly focused beam flashed up through his skull, and the top of his helmet burst open and out in a shower of brain and blood.

Sam withdrew the Terillian throwing knife from his vest, balanced it carefully, and then his hand flashed forward in a blur. Plunging in to the hilt, the knife struck one of the mercenaries in his left armpit, its long blade piercing his heart and killing him instantly.

Sam was dimly aware of several high-velocity slugs finding openings between his own moly-weave vest and limb armor. Unlike the flesh-and-blood mercenaries, however, his polysilicon skin was impermeable to such an assault. It would take more than the mercenaries' standard-issue weaponry to cripple Sam.

When the four surviving mercenaries began retreating from their furious firefight, falling back in the face of his ferocious onslaught, Sam responded by doing something that astonished them. He threw down his energy rifle.

With a bloodcurdling yell that would have made Pickett's infantry hoot, holler, and stamp their feet in appreciation, Sam charged headlong at the mercenaries.

All but turned to stone by Sam's war cry, the men dropped their weapons and turned to run. Sam overtook them in an instant, and all five combatants tumbled headfirst to the floor. One of the men, landing atop the fallen android, pulled out an energy pistol and tried to stick the barrel in Sam's ear. Sam jerked his head as the man fired and the pencil-thin stream of energy seared the side of Sam's face, burning a decicred-sized hole through his helmet.

Sam threw the man off, stumbled to his feet, and then seized the hapless mercenary in much the same way the bull elephant had taken hold of him. A stream of coherent energy from the man's gun sparked and flashed as it played over Sam's molyweave vest, but to no effect. Sam flung the man against the wall with tremendous force; the mercenary slid down the wall to end up in a rag-doll position he could never have emulated if his bones were not broken.

Another mercenary had found Sam's vibroblade and, crawling across the floor until he reached him, tried to thrust it into Sam's leg while the android picked up the metal bar. Although he sensed it as a tickling sensation, Sam's skin turned away the blade. In response, he whirled and smashed the heavy polysteel bar down on his attacker.

With a succession of punishingly powerful blows, Sam methodically brought the heavy polysteel bar down on the two mercenaries. The inhuman strength behind Sam's swings of the bar shattered the helmet of one of the men, killing him instantly.

Turning on the lone surviving mercenary, Sam became an unthinking, unfeeling avenger. Hearing the screams of the soft smiley face echoing endlessly through his mind, he cried out, "I'll save you, Mother!"

He was blinded by a red haze of hate and anger at the one

who made the loud sounds. Wanting to make the bad sounds stop forever, Sam smashed the bar down, fruitlessly trying to kill someone long dead. He swung again and again, again and again, again and again.

Again and again, again and— *Enough!* a part of Sam's mind cried out to the raging demon in him that drove him to batter the dead man who was a surrogate for someone beyond the possibility of revenge.

Blood.

There was blood on his face; Sam could feel it running down his cheeks in rivulets. Dropping the bloodied metal bar, he touched his face with his fingers. He looked down at his fingertips, and what he saw surprised and shocked him. What he had imagined was the blood of the dead mercenaries was really tears. His own tears.

He laughed bitterly at that, then cried. And then the wonder of it all came home full force to him. *You've done a brilliant job, Dr. Bussot. Maybe too brilliant.*

If Sam still harbored any doubts concerning whether or not he was fully human, they had been dispelled by the combination of blood and tears. *Blood and tears—how much more human than that can you get*?

* * *

"Well?" asked Data Leader, charged with the task of finding and collecting the information their employer was after.

Listening intently to the multiband chatter going on around them, Data-one looked up and said, "Nothing yet." He thought for a moment and amended his original answer. "Let me qualify that. Nothing yet, *but* there's a certain amount of low-level questioning going on between the various layers of local law enforcement."

"What does that mean?" asked Data Leader, toying with the straps of the helmet she had removed for comfort.

"Blue jackets is blue jackets," explained Data-one. "Even when they're in the dark, some of them can *feel* that something is happening, something they think they ought to know about."

"You sound like a kiss-ass police buff," sneered Data-two.

"No, but I was a blue jacket once," admitted Data-one. "I know how cops think."

"And what are they thinking?" asked Data Leader, running her fingers through her dirty-blonde brush cut.

"Five will get you ten that the folks in blue are suspicious. They know something's going on at One Voorhees Square—they can taste it—but so far they're willing to obey orders and keep their distance. That won't last, however. Sooner or later someone will come nosing around."

"Why?" asked Data-two."

"Because he's a blue jacket."

"As long as the ban on using slug-throwers and grenades above ground holds, we should be okay," opined Data Leader. Turning her attention back to their prisoner, she said, "Well, Doctor, even though it appears that our presence here is still secret, I'd like to get you out." She looked over in the corner at Bussot's two personal assistants, unconscious courtesy of a electroneural hosing by a stun gun. "The others will be fine here."

Dr. Henri Bussot, his hands bound and his mouth gagged, stared back angrily. There was no mistaking the hatred that burned in his eyes.

"Look at him," marveled Data-two. "He'd like to stick a vibroblade between your ribs, Data Leader."

Ignoring her subordinate's comment, Data Leader's eyes narrowed and she said, "I'd like to get you out of here—but we can't leave until you tell me where the records are kept." She motioned to Data-three, and the young Terillian mercenary removed the doctor's gag. "That's better," Data Leader said. "Now then, Doctor, it would be better for us all if you told me what I wish to know."

"What records?" asked Dr. Bussot.

"Don't be coy, Doctor," Data Leader said. "You know what records I'm speaking of."

"I'm not being coy."

"Have it your way." Data Leader sat on the edge of Dr. Bussot's magnificent karkka-wood desk, one leg swinging freely. "I'll go along with your little game if it makes you feel better, Doctor. I'm talking about the records pertaining to a certain android." When Bussot stiffened, the mercenary leader smiled and continued, "See, you *do* know what I'm talking about. I didn't even have to use Mr. Houston's name."

"They're not here," Bussot told her. "Not any longer.

Mr. Houston, as you called him, is special."

"Special?" laughed Data-two.

"Yes, special," snapped the doctor. "But he is not the sort of experiment who exists entirely within the bounds of proper medical research—at least according to small-minded Principate bureaucrats who believe it is better to say no to most proposed research rather than yes." He looked down at his bonds. "Untie me, please."

"Perhaps later," Data Leader said. "Please continue. I find all this fascinating."

Bussot snorted but did as the mercenary said. "For the sake of a scientific and financial opportunity that no self-respecting scientist could resist, I compromised the Foundation by pursuing a proscribed line of research." He glanced at his sleeping assistants. "My people and I could all be arrested and prosecuted if the records pertaining to Mr. Houston's genesis happened to find their way into the wrong hands. Since we are not stupid, the records were all destroyed after he became operational."

"Destroyed?"

"At Mr . . . . ah, at the authorizing agent's request," Bussot said.

Data Leader shook her head from side. "I don't think so," she said finally. "Even if you made a show of destroying your notes and records, you wouldn't—couldn't—do that with something so wonderful as this android, no matter how great the risk of detection and prosecution." She nodded at Data-two.

Data-two took a step or two closer to Bussot, striking his palm with a round object he clutched in his other hand.

"Where is the information, Doctor?" Data Leader persisted.

When Bussot remained silent, Data-two asked, "You know what this is, Doc?"

"No," he admitted.

"You must not watch much hol-vee," Data-two said. "This is a nerve baton."

Bussot gulped. "A nerve baton?"

"Yeah," Data-two told him, admiring the thing's stark utilitarian design. "A coupla minutes of being tickled with this black beauty and you'll talk fast enough." He laughed and then confessed to Dr. Bussot what was amusing him so much. "Shit, you'll tell us stuff you wouldn't admit to St. Peter even if it was to get you through the gate and a seat at the head table." He laughed out loud at his own cleverness.

"This is all so melodramatic, Dr. Bussot," Data Leader insisted. "I would much prefer that you tell me of your own free will where to find the information I'm after. Could you do that for me . . . please?" Data Leader smiled and spread her hands palms up, beseeching him to talk.

"I . . . ah—" He was interrupted by a sudden outbreak of sporadic gunfire and the muffled thump of a grenade going off.

<*This is Data Leader. What the hell's going on out there? There is supposed to be no fighting on the upper levels!*>

<*You had best tell that to the android . . . sir,*> an unidentified voice responded. <*And you won't have long to wait—he's coming your way.*>

"Coming this way?" said Data-three, his voice tinged with a mixture of awe and fear.

Hearing only the external exchanges, a confused Dr. Bussot asked, "What's coming this way?"

"Your metal—"

The door was blown into the room by an explosion, striking Data-three and knocking him backwards and against the opposite wall.

Too stunned by the suddenness of the explosion to express either fear or exhilaration, Bussot reacted only when he looked on helplessly as a signed Dolan Terranova watercolor tumbled from the wall, its frame shattering when it hit the floor. "My God! That's a priceless piece of art!"

Sam Houston stepped out of the roiling cloud of dust and smoke, an energy rifle in one hand and the plasteel bar in the other. When Data-one lunged at him, Sam clubbed him down with the bar. Equipped with wide-angle peripheral vision, Sam turned toward a half-perceived movement the same instant Data-two crossed the one and a half meters separating them and thrust the barrel of the energy rifle against his side.

There was a flash, then a second and a third. Looking more annoyed than anything else, Sam dropped the polysteel bar, reached down, grabbed the barrel of his would-be assassin's rifle, yanked it from the astonished mercenary's hands, and swatted him away with it.

Sam turned back to see Data Leader pushing Bussot toward the door, glancing back with a face contorted by fear. "Going somewhere?" Sam asked, grabbing hold of the mercenary leader's shoulder with his hand.

"Argh!" Data Leader shouted in pain as Sam's powerful fingers dug into her flesh, breaking her collarbone. She fell to one knee and looked up in time to see Dr. Bussot bringing his manacled fists down upon the back of her unprotected head and knocking her into cloud-cuckooland.

"My God, I did it; I hit someone," stammered Dr. Bussot.

"You certainly did."

"Sam!" exclaimed Dr. Bussot, as if just becoming aware of the other's presence.

"Its good to see you again, Doctor," Sam said pleasantly. "Come, we must be going."

"But what about Margot and Keena, my assistants?" he asked, gesturing at the two unconscious women.

"They'll be safer here than with us," Sam told him.

"They will?" asked Bussot nervously. "Where are you taking me?"

"You'll see," Sam said enigmatically. "And besides, before we can actually go anywhere, you have to borrow some protective gear from these folks." Without further ado, he snapped the polysteel chain linking the manacles' wrist-encircling restraints and then twisted open the locked rings themselves.

"Here," Sam said, bending over and unfastening Data Leader's moly-weave vest. "She's about your size, Dr. Bussot."

"Yes, thank you," said the doctor, slipping into the vest and taking the helmet Sam offered him. He looked at it, unsure what to do next.

"Put it on," commanded Sam. "She didn't, and look what happened to her."

"Yes, you're quite right." Bussot pulled the helmet on. Sam shook his head; never had he seen anyone so ill suited to the military look as Dr. Bussot.

"It's time we got out of here," Sam told the doctor.

"Where are we going, Sam?" Bussot asked, picking up the fallen artwork and carefully laying it on a flat surface where it wouldn't get bent or stepped on.

"Down."

"Down?"

"Yes," Sam said. "But first we have get to the jumping-off point." He hefted the polysteel bar, sighed, gave it a kiss, and then tossed it into the corner of the room; hand-to-hand combat would be too risky with the doctor in tow. To take the bar's place, he picked up two energy rifles, handling them as if they were constructed of balsa wood.

"Now what?" asked the doctor, watching Sam searching the bodies on the floor.

"I was looking for these," Sam said, handing Bussot two energy pistols. "You probably won't do much damage with them, but they'll be useful in forcing the mercenaries to keep their heads down."

"Oh."

"Now I'm ready. How about you?" he asked.

"Ready," affirmed Bussot, although he had no idea what he was saying he was ready for.

"Good. Keep behind me."

Sam stuck his head out the door, glanced right, then stepped out. "C'mon," he insisted, "you have to stay with me." Bussot gulped and stepped out into the corridor; he immediately took refuge behind Sam's body.

Several bolts of energy struck Sam's moly-weave vest and were absorbed and then dissipated by its remarkable composition. Firing his own weapons, Sam smiled and began striding down the corridor.

"Shoot," he commanded Dr. Bussot.

"At whom?" the doctor asked. "I can't see anyone."

"Just stick the guns around my torso and fire. You don't have to aim to be effective."

"All right," the doctor said, doing as Sam had instructed.

The mercenaries fell back as the duo approached. Ignoring the multiple hits he took, Sam was able to force his way to the lift/drop tubes.

"He's gonna use a drop tube," someone shouted, and that information was passed to those below. When and if Sam and Bussot dropped toward a lower level, the mercenaries would be lying in wait to open fire on them.

Sam knew this, too. That was why he had decided upon a mode of descent that he hoped would prevent their ambushers from getting off a good shot at the two of them.

"Put your arms around me," Sam told the doctor, firing the odd bolt or two to keep the mercenaries who'd followed him to this upper level from getting any closer.

"I beg your pardon?" Bussot said.

"I said put your arms around me," Sam repeated.

The doctor reluctantly did as Sam instructed, facing the android and wrapping his arms around him. Still rapid-firing the energy rifles, Sam carried the doctor to a drop tube.

When Bussot saw what was happening, he said, "Ohmygod!" and closed his eyes.

"That's a good idea," said Sam, stepping into the drop tube, which was barely large enough to accommodate the two of them.

With a combined weight of nearly two hundred and fifty kilos, they hurtled down the tube in an instant.

"Jesus!" exclaimed an awed mercenary.

II

"You still can't dance, can you, Galen?" marveled Adrianna as the two of them waltzed to the music of the human band.

"Sorry," Galen apologized, which pleased Adrianna until she realized there hadn't been a gram of sincerity in his voice. "I keep intending to make an appointment with an android dance studio to learn the latest steps, but you know how it is."

"The latest steps?" snorted Adrianna. "What you're murdering is just a simple waltz step. It doesn't get much more basic than that."

"Sure, but—"

"Ouch!"

"I always warned you to buy shoes with plasteel toe guards," Galen told her.

"Oh, yeah? Well, you can—"

"Wait a minute." Galen almost came to a complete stop but had his wits about him enough to keep moving.

"What is it?"

"Remember you told me that you saw Alves slipping away about five minutes ago?"

"What about it?"

"He's back," Galen said, turning Adrianna around so that she could see the head table.

"So?" she asked, before she caught sight of Alves.

"So he looks like someone who's just been handed some very bad news."

"I wonder what it could be," mused Adrianna.

"Sam," said Galen with sudden conviction.

"Sam?" she wrinkled up her nose. "Sam's hidden away in your mystery hospital."

"Yeah, my 'mystery hospital,' " Galen said. "What a big fucking genius I am."

"What are you going on about?"

He looked her in the eye. "Come on, you know me and the family, so take a wild guess where I might hide Sam away while he's being repaired."

Her eyes widened. "The Foundation? In Houston?"

"Bingo," nodded Galen.

"If I can figure that out . . ." began Adrianna.

"Then so can someone else who knows a little about me," finished Galen. "I'm so fucking unimaginative at times it makes me want to throw up!"

"But who are you talking about?" She gasped. "You can't mean Alves."

"Oh, yes, I can. Alves or Aunt Kitrina—or even someone in the game we're not even aware of."

"But if Alves—or whoever," she said when he frowned, indicating he wasn't ready to pin all his suspicions on Alves just yet, "knows where Sam is, why's he so angry?"

"You don't really know Sam, do you?" asked Galen.

* * *

Even forewarned that Sam and the doctor were hurtling down the polyglas tube, the mercenaries had about as much chance of successfully hitting them as a Star Scout would have pinning a fly to a wall with his knife from ten meters away. The two were a blur that rocketed past too quickly for would-be ambushers to do anything other than sigh.

"Jesus and Mohammed!" cursed Henri Bussot. "We're going to die!"

"O ye of little faith," intoned Sam, dismayed that the doctor lacked confidence in his abilities in light of all that Bussot knew about Sam's reconstruction.

When it seemed certain that they were doomed to smash into the plascrete floor of the bottom level, Sam extended his legs and, using his boots to provide the necessary friction, began to check their descent.

"Hey, these are pretty good 'brake shoes,' don't you think?" Sam asked as his actions first slowed them, then stopped them completely.

"I don't believe we're still alive—or that you made that horrible pun," Bussot said, shaking.

"Yes, we're alive," confirmed Sam, squeezing past Bussot to exit first in case someone with an energy rifle was waiting for them; fortunately, the corridor was empty. "If we don't get to the John Henry as quickly as we can, however, we're going to lose this ephemeral advantage." He grinned and added, "I almost said 'transitory advantage,' but I was afraid you'd accuse me of forcing further *pun*-ishment on you."

"For the first time, I fully appreciate your uniqueness, Mr. Houston," the doctor said. "There cannot be another being like you in the galaxy."

"I should hope not," Sam said, pushing Bussot down the corridor toward the abandoned John Henry; without the part he had pilfered, it was just a hunk of inert metal and plastic.

Bussot seemed awed by the massive mining machine. "This thing, is *this* the John Henry you mentioned?"

"The very same."

"John Henry?" Bussot said, rolling the unfamiliar words around. "Why is it called a John Henry?"

"John Henry, so they say, was a steel-driving man."

"Yes . . . ?" Bussot clearly expected to hear more.

Sam shook his head. "Forget about it; we haven't the time."

Sam pulled a hatchway open and used his infrared vision to make sure no one was lurking inside. Satisfied that the John Henry was really and truly deserted, he stepped inside and waved for Bussot to join him. Then he sealed the hatch.

"Now what?"

"Now I return this to where I found it," Sam said, pulling back a flap of skin and removing a centimeter-square ceramic cube from its hiding lace inside his abdomen.

While Bussot watched, Sam did exactly that. "And before you can ask 'Now what?' again," he said, "it's time we ate some serious dirt." Looking at Bussot's bewildered face, he told him, "That means put your behind in one of these command chairs and strap yourself in; I'm about to fire up the fusion torch and make like Mighty Mole."

"Oh, um, right," said Bussot, sitting down and following Sam's directions.

Sam looked at the array of controls, said, "Eeny-meeny-miney-moe," and shoved a green lever forward. He smiled beautifully when the John Henry began to move forward.

Cracking his fingers—"Nice touch, Doc," he told Bussot—Sam thrust his hands into the John Henry's waldoes, spinning it expertly on its wheels and then plunging it back into the perfectly circular tunnel its torch had eaten through the earth on its arrival at this subterranean level of the Voorhees Foundation.

"Here's hoping this thing gets us back to Kansas, eh, Professor Marvel?" Sam said brightly.

"Whatever you say," Bussot replied, burying his head in his hands.

13

GALEN SHIVERED AS A BLAST OF COLD AIR FROM THE VENT under the window blew over him. Although Rome was suffering through a heat wave, you wouldn't know it from their over-air-conditioned room.

"Can someone turn that down?" Galen asked.

"You're the closest to it," Mahute Yaari told him. "You do it."

"You're right," Galen said getting up.

As soon as he had adjusted the flow of cool air, the door to the hotel suite opened, and Galen Yeager, Adrianna Palmieri-Yeager, Mahute Yaari, and Richard Voorhees all looked up. They relaxed when Herbert van der Park entered.

The mixture of anticipation and apprehension on their faces told Galen that he had the right to insist that they rent a hotel room far from Johannesburg for their meeting. There had been objections, especially from Mahute, who wanted to have the meeting immediately following the reception, but everyone had finally acquiesced.

"Well, they're gone," van der Park told the others as he closed the door behind him and made sure it was bolted and chained.

"Who's gone?" asked Mahute, leaning forward on the edge of the chair on which she was seated. Sending an unmistakable indication of her heightened psychoemotional energy, the living crystal in her right cheek increased the intensity of its glow.

"Mr. and Mrs. Luis Jorge Alves," Galen said. "Right?" He stared at the luminescent beryl crystal below Mahute's ear. While deciding that the expensive ornament's crimson glow perfectly complemented her creamy cocoa-colored complexion, Galen wondered how a partner in a prestigious law firm was permitted to be so avant garde. *I guess "partner" is the operative word*, he mused.

"That's correct, cousin," van der Park said. "The word is that Ghannee and Alves are on their way to a resort planet in some remote corner of the quadrant."

"To Forever?" asked Richard Voorhees, naming about one of the more popular honeymoon destinations for newlyweds.

"Can you see someone as socially conscious as Luis Jorge Alves taking his new bride to such a mundane place, the first choice of the proletariat?" laughed Adrianna. "No, I'm certain wherever it is, it's damned expensive and very, very exclusive."

Herbert smiled. "I'm sure of that. But like I said, no one knows for sure where the two lovebirds are headed."

"We needn't be so catty about our cousin's marriage," said Richard Voorhees. "Ghannee seems madly, blindly in love with Alves."

"And I understand that Luis Alves is said to feel the same way about her," Mahute added.

Richard Voorhees nodded, pleased that someone agreed with him. He was a big man, with long arms and legs, and immense hands; sitting on a sofa, his knees were almost level with his eyes. Staring at his long, dour face, Galen was reminded of photographs taken of the American president Abraham Lincoln before he grew his famous beard. Dimly recalling how Lincoln was mocked and ridiculed for his physical proportions, Galen wondered if Richard's expression of social delicacy was a way of unconsciously compensating for his size.

"Our cousin's marriage is one of the reasons we've gone to the trouble of coming together in this rented room," Mahute Yaari told Voorhees. "To discuss what that may mean for the family and the corporation, and to explore a host of unpleasant possibilities."

"I suppose you're right," Richard Voorhees admitted.

Wasting little time, Galen motioned Herbert to a chair and said, "Let's get down to what's directly behind this meeting: Our fear that Luis Alves is attempting a takeover of the Soweto Corporation."

"I think it's more than a fear, Galen," said Mahute Yaari.

"Yes," agreed Adrianna. "It's practically a certainty."

"You both say that with authority," Galen told her. "What's behind your assurance?"

Adrianna looked to Mahute, who said, "This, for starters." She dropped an aspirin-sized datachip into a small holo projector and turned the machine on. A multicolored graph appeared in the air above the small circular table around which they had arranged themselves. They stared up at the graph, its glow reflected in their faces.

"As these figures reveal," Yaari said, "trading in the Soweto Corporation's public shares has been unusually active for the past eighteen months. Beginning in December"—she pointed to a bold red line—"the stock began edging upwards as anonymous investors began accumulating larger and larger amounts of the outstanding shares."

Yaari reached up into the holo image and her finger traced a barely discernible arc. "The curve is almost imperceptible from December to this point here."

"In July?" asked Galen.

"Yes. Then it begins to rise more sharply as keen-eyed brokers and investors begin to notice the upward tick the per-share value is taking."

She was right, Galen realized with a start. Once you knew what to look for, the gentle gradient was clearly there for anyone to see.

"What's that bump in October?" Richard asked.

"That's when our phantom buyers threw caution to the winds and snapped up nearly five percent of the outstanding shares in a single day." She allowed herself a small smile of satisfaction. "That act of hubris may have been their undoing; it called unwanted attention to their previously low-profile buys."

"How did they accomplish such a massive onetime acquisition?" Galen wanted to know.

"Remember when the investment firm of Borghasi, Smathers, and Kort collapsed?" she asked.

"Vaguely," responded Galen, his brow wrinkling. "Now I

remember," he said, snapping his fingers."Aunt Kitrina left a message for me while I was on Cousteau; something about the family needing my proxy to buy back some shares coming on the market." He frowned. "I never heard anything more about it."

"I had nearly the same experience," mused Herbert.

"There's that name again," Adrianna said.

"Aunt Kitrina?" asked Galen. "You think that could have been when she and Alves lay down in bed together?"

"Don't be vulgar, Galen," Herbert said primly.

"Sorry," Galen apologized.

"*If* she's mixed up in this, that would be a likely starting point," Adrianna said.

"I agree," Mahute said. "That's when Mr. X's accumulated investment in the corporation passed the twenty-percent level and our own inhouse counselors and analysts could finally see the ominous pattern that had begun to emerge."

Galen tugged on one ear. He was dying for a drink. "I thought Uncle Hans or someone else at the family meeting put the total outsider accumulation at only sixteen percent."

"That's correct," confirmed Mahute. "But that was our best estimate at the time. We failed to connect the buyers—or buyer—of the investment fund's shares with the slow and steady institutional purchaser of the other shares."

"What does all this mean?" asked Richard Voorhees.

"Maybe nothing," said Yaari. "Maybe it's all a coincidence."

"But you don't think so?" Galen pressed.

Yaari looked at Herbert van der Park, who promptly got up and poured himself a cup of coffee. Returning to the couch and taking his seat, he said, "By herself, Ghannee Tollersrud-Alves controls a mere one-half percent of the family-owned shares. So Alves didn't really gain all that much leverage by marrying her."

"Maybe, maybe not," Yaari said. "You're not taking Aunt Kitrina's stock into account. Counting only her own shares, Kitrina Tollersrud controls another two and a half percent directly. But there's a good chance she possesses the proxies for even more."

"More?" questioned Adrianna.

"It's possible that she can influence how Uncle Hans votes, and perhaps one or two other children might throw in with her if she gives them a good enough reason."

"Or several billion of them," said Adrianna sourly.

"And then there's Grandmother Mugambi, of course," Galen said quietly. He licked his lips; they were as dry as his throat.

"What about Grandmother Mugambi?" asked Richard.

"I think what Galen means is that our grandmother has lived for over one and a quarter centuries. She is a very old woman whose health, mental as well as physical, is declining."

As the others exchanged knowing looks, Herbert continued. "We've all seen evidence of the growing influence Aunt Kitrina seems to have had upon her recent decisions."

As much as it pained him to take Aunt Kitrina's side, Galen felt he had no choice but to point out the sacrifice his aunt had willingly borne on behalf of them all. "When no one else wanted to be burdened with taking care of Grandmother Mugambi, Aunt Kitrina was the one who stepped forward," he reminded everyone. "It's probably impossible to overestimate the value of her contribution to the family; a contribution Aunt Kitrina has been making for a number of years."

"Galen's point is well taken," Herbert conceded. "I reiterate, however, that Aunt Kitrina's position of caretaker gives her an awful lot of power over the matriarch of the family. I believe this is something she has only recently realized herself."

"Okay, okay," said Richard Voorhees, his hands covering his kneecaps like enormous five-limbed arthropods. "So Aunt Kitrina might have some influence over Grandmother, and her daughter Ghannee has just married Luis Alves, right? Must that mean that they are co-conspirators whose goal is to take over the Soweto Corporation?" His long, earnest face wore an expression of bewilderment.

Adrianna was also bewildered. "If you have such difficulty believing that scenario," she asked, "then why are you here? Surely you have suspected something, or else you wouldn't have expressed similar fears to cousin Herbert."

Way to go, Adrianna! thought Galen. "Yes," he said. "Your being here seems to reveal a certain uneasiness about the prospect of Alves joining the family, however peripherally."

For a moment, Voorhees was at a loss for words. Finally, he said, "I admit that I was putting the pieces of the puzzle together, but I could not bring myself to accept the picture that was emerging." He smiled wanly. "I suppose I hoped that when we got together, the result would be a debunking of my doubts. I thought we would be able to explain it all away and then have a good laugh at our unfounded fears."

"You no longer feel that way?" asked Mahute Yaari.

Voorhees blinked. "No, I do not."

II

"Where are we?" asked Henri Bussot, looking around the luxurious bungalow located in eastern Pennsylvania, just outside Boswash's expensive blue zone.

"This is one of Galen's safe houses," Sam informed him.

"Safe houses?"

"You don't want to know," Sam said. Then he rubbed his chin. "Although, after all this, I suppose you'll know more about Galen Yeager than anyone else but me." He smiled grimly, adding, "That's a curse, not a blessing."

"I agree—if my experiences of the past twenty-four hours are any indication."

"Would you like something to drink?" Sam asked. "If you were Galen, I would already be pouring you a stiff Jack Daniel's and water."

"A glass of water would be heavenly," Bussot said, not realizing how thirsty he was until Sam had mentioned having a drink. Sam nodded and went into the kitchen, got a glass, and filled it from the built-in water cooler.

"Thank you," Bussot said, accepting the glass and taking several healthy swallows. "Tell me, Sam," he asked, glancing at him out of the corner of his eye, uncertain how the android would react to his question, "does Yeager see you primarily as a servant?"

"A servant?" repeated Sam, surprised. "No, of course not." Then he looked at Bussot's half-empty water glass. "You mean, because I told you that I often make Galen a drink, that you think he treats me like a domestic 'bot?"

Sitting down on a green cuddle chair, Bussot finished the rest of his water before asking, "It's not an outrageous assumption, is it?"

Sam thought about that. "I suppose not." He frowned. "But Galen is my friend; if I make him a drink and bring it to him, it's because I *want* to do things for him, not because I'm at his beck and call. Not because I owe it to him."

"*Do* you owe it to him?"

"If you put it that way, hell, yes!" Sam said a little more vehemently than he intended. "I mean, he's the one who initiated my rebirth," he said more levelly. "No offense. I realize that I also owe nearly as much to you and the Foundation, but it was Galen's desire to have a friend and partner that rescued me from an icy grave."

"Yes, you're right, of course," Bussot said. Veering off in another direction, he inquired, "How are you doing, Sam?"

"Me?" said Sam, surprised by Bussot's question. "I'm doing fine; why?"

"Go find a mirror and take a look at yourself," Bussot explained. "You're a mess."

Sam walked toward one of the lodge's bedrooms, unfastening his shirt on the way. He stared into the full-length Hylof nonreversal mirror on the closet door. "Jesus H. Nixon!" Sam exclaimed when he saw the burn marks and discolored patches on his torso and arms. When he dropped his trousers, he discovered that his legs hadn't been spared either.

"Christ," he sighed. "I was so pretty; fresh out of the box. Now look at me!"

Coming up behind him and staring into the mirror over his shoulder, Bussot said, "It's not as bad as after Africa, but you're going to need more work."

"But where and how?" Sam asked. "We can't go back to the Foundation, not now."

Bussot put his hand on Sam's shoulder. "Perhaps Galen can think of something."

"Galen?" Sam's face brightened. "Yeah, Galen'll know what to do."

Actually, after a moment's thought, Sam knew what to do."

* * *

Less than twenty-four hours later, riding Fedalf's personal elevator down to the underground level where Sam was being guarded, Galen mused about the location of clandestine laboratories.

"Centicred for your thoughts, Galen," Fedalf said, pulling on his thick mustache.

"I was just wondering why experimental labs and research facilities always seem to be underground."

"Seems obvious," Mackenzie said. "Security. It's pretty damned difficult to break into an underground facility."

"Unless you have access to a John Henry," Galen countered.

"Indeed," laughed Fedalf dryly. "The raid on the Voorhees Foundation will give nightmares to those in charge of this building's defenses."

If Galen saw anything funny in the situation, he didn't show it. "You *have* done something in response to that attack, haven't you?"

"We have encircled the building with . . ." MacKenzie's explanation faltered when Fedalf put his finger to his lips.

"We have taken precautions," was all Fedalf would say. "There is no 'need to know' on your part, Galen."

The elevator doors hissed open and they exited in the middle of a corridor. Since PrinSecPol headquarters were more modest than the Voorhees Foundation, this subsurface medical level was proportionally less impressive than the floor that had housed Sam in that facility. Even so, just being here gave Galen an odd sense of deja vu.

Galen didn't know what he expected to see when they entered Sam's room, but it wasn't the sight of Sam and Dr. Bussot seated at a small table, a chessboard between them. Bussot looked up, startled at their unannounced entry.

"See," Sam told him triumphantly. "Isn't it annoying when visitors just walk in on you like that?"

"Try to hold down your enthusiasm at seeing us," Galen said to Sam. "Displaying too much excitement might be bad for you."

Sam and Bussot exchanged a private look, and then Sam got up and wrapped his arms around Galen. "It's good to see you, partner," he said, embracing his friend.

"Um, yes," agreed Galen, coloring slightly. It was Fedalf and MacKenzie's turn to exchange looks of amusement at Galen's German-Dutch reticence. Fedalf had long found it amusing that Sam, a supposed android, was more emotionally demonstrative than his fully human partner.

After hugging Sam in return, and patting him clumsily on the back, Galen broke their embrace, stepped back a meter or so and said, "Let me look at you." He examined his friend from top to bottom, looking for changes; he couldn't find any. "I remember how disheveled and . . . *singed* . . . you seemed when you called me from the safe house, but I can't see any of that now." He shook his head. "You look great—as usual."

"Thanks to Dr. Bussot and director Fedalf's people," Sam told him.

"I hope you're not getting to be an open secret," Galen said, looking meaningfully at Fedalf and MacKenzie.

"I agree," said Bussot. "Just prior to the time Sam . . . uh, rescued me from the people who attacked the Foundation, I was explaining to the young woman interrogating me that he is more than unique, he's illegal. Robots, cyborgs, and androids with the capability to harm human beings have been outlawed since the robot wars."

"Then I would have to arrest you," Fedalf said. "That is, if I knew the truth about Sam."

"And you don't?" asked Sam with a smile.

"Haven't heard a word," Fedalf replied, returning Sam's smile.

"Well," said Galen, "someone has."

"Someone?" asked Rob MacKenzie.

Galen looked at Sam, who nodded. "Luis Jorge Alves."

"Alves?" sputtered MacKenzie.

"Alves," Galen repeated. He noticed that Fedalf didn't seem especially surprised. "May I assume from your lack of reaction that you already are in possession of this information, Hashem?"

"I had my suspicions after the attack upon your family's African home."

When MacKenzie's face registered an expression of disgust, Fedalf said quietly, "I'm sorry, Rob, but you should know by now that I keep my own counsel." It was as much apology as Fedalf was prepared to offer.

"What happens next?" Galen asked.

"I have already authorized a probe into the affairs of the Alves Group's activities," Fedalf said. "I will ask my people to intensify their efforts; it is important that the PrinSecPol learn all it can concerning Alves's interest in Sam and in the Soweto Corporation."

Sam walked back to the chessboard, moved a piece, and announced, "Checkmate in six moves."

PART FIVE

WHO'S THERE?

14

IF THE INVADERS OF THE VOORHEES FOUNDATION HAD HAD enough time to pressure Henri Bussot, they might have forced him to reveal the location of the Foundation's top-secret file storage facility. Unfortunately for them, they hadn't had enough time, and it was this failure that led to their recruitment of biomechanical systems engineer Dr. Everett Hanks.

Ready for a *very* dry Tanqueray martini, Everett Hanks arrived home to a strangely quiet house. When there was no reply to his cry of "Carla, I'm home," he muttered, "What the hell?" Rarely had he ever found the place this silent.

"Carla, I'm home," he said more loudly, taking off his jacket and throwing it on the couch; he'd hang it up after he'd had his drink. There was still no answer.

He walked into the family room; finding the hol-vee dark and silent was almost as big a shock as finding the room empty. He looked at his watch and scratched his head. Normally, Everett Jr. and Heather would be watching *The Kargo Kids*, a teen-oriented, wish-fulfillment show about a brother and sister who had stowed away on a starship. A typical plot usually ended with the two sickening cute and cloying leads coming to the rescue of idiotic adults.

Heading for the kitchen, he backtracked through the living room and—

"Jesus!"

"Good evening, Dr. Hanks," said a skeletal form sitting motionless in one of the big easy chairs. Although the simulacrum was formally dressed in a suit and tie, the effect was more horrific than if the robot had worn no clothing at all; its sticklike construction made it appear more a badly desiccated body than the image of a human being. Since its inhuman occupant lacked the body heat to activate the chair's cuddling function, it refused to snuggle up to the simulacrum's cold form.

"What are you, and what are you doing here?" Hanks demanded.

"I am a simulacrum," the spindly thing said in a strangely metallic voice that Hanks guessed must be electronically distorted.

"I can see that. What's going on? Where are my wife and kids?" It was only after his eyes grew accustomed to the dim lighting of the living room that he could see the simulacrum's face clearly. Or rather, its lack of a face. The simulacrum presented only the crudest representation of eyes, nose, and mouth. In a previous century, people would have said that the robot bore an amazing resemblance to a children's plaything known as "Mr. Potato Head." If Hanks noticed the resemblance, he didn't find it amusing.

"They are not here," it informed him. "They are safe, however."

"Why is this happening to me and my family?" he stammered. "I'm not a rich man. I may have some investments I can liquidate, but the money doesn't add up to much."

"It is not your money that we are interested in, Dr. Hanks," the simulacrum told him.

"What then?" he asked. He spread his hands. "I have nothing that anyone could want."

"That is not true, Dr. Hanks. You have something that we want very badly."

"What, for Chrissakes?"

"The records pertaining to your participation in the creation of the artificial human known as Sam Houston," the simulacrum said pleasantly. "That and your own expertise in bringing such a cyborg to life."

Everett Hanks's jaw dropped. "My work at the Foundation?" Suddenly, things began to make sense to him.

He recovered his equilibrium sufficiently to tell the

simulacrum, "That's impossible. The facilities and records are closely guarded. I'd never be able to gain access to information that well protected, especially after the break-in." That was not really true. Actually, getting into the archives would be difficult, but not impossible.

As if reading his mind, the simulacrum told him, "We have the utmost confidence in your abilities, Dr. Hanks."

"I'm not some kind of secret agent," he argued. "I can't do this; I'm not the right man for a job like this."

"Of course you are. The very fact that you are not a professional is your greatest strength." The simulacrum's rudimentary eyes seemed to harden. "If you wish to see your wife and children alive again, you will do as you are told."

Hanks slumped against the sofa, defeated.

The simulacrum smiled—or attempted to. Hideous and more than a little grotesque, the simulacrum's grinning-corpse smile chilled Hanks to the bone. In that instant, he knew the simulacrum was correct: He would do anything the kidnappers of his family demanded.

* * *

As the *faux* orchestra playing with them contributed its many instruments to the program's smoothly blended mixture of violin and 'cello sounds, Galen lost himself completely in his playing, coaxing sweet and luscious notes from the violin tucked under his chin. Seemingly inspired, Galen's fingering was dexterous and close to perfect; his bow work could not have been better.

Sam, himself drawing vibrant and full-bodied notes from his 'cello, had never heard Galen play with such a light yet confident touch. As they made their way through Shostakovich's First Violin Concerto, adapted by Galen's music computer to allow Sam's 'cello a larger role than the composer had originally intended, Sam was saddened to observe that the piece would end all too soon.

When the last note died away, Sam jumped up and said, "Bravo! That was fantastic! Don't deny that you've been practicing on the sly."

"Thanks, Sam," Galen said, carefully replacing his Karensky in its velvet-lined case and closing it. He pulled out a handkerchief and dabbed at his forehead, wiping away beads of perspiration. "Since we've had little to do these last few weeks, I felt I should use my time constructively."

"It *has* been a long time since anything noteworthy has transpired on the Alves front, hasn't it?"

"Yeah," Galen grunted. "Too long."

"How's Dr. Frankenstein doing?"

Galen cringed. "Leave the poor man alone," he said, bothered by Sam's flippant attitude toward Bussot and unaware that Sam was using that tone to disguise his concern for his co-creator. "He has enough problems."

"I thought you said that the corporation's PR people did a good job of hushing up the attack at the Foundation; is he in trouble with the authorities?"

"Not at all," Galen told him. "I filled bushel baskets full of money and spread it around judiciously. People quickly came to the conclusion that it was an insignificant incident."

When Sam guffawed, Galen decided to explain further. "This is a big city. Office buildings are broken into all the time. There are gangs that specialize in stuff like that."

"I imagine that it also didn't hurt that no one working at the Foundation was killed or seriously injured, and the damage suffered by the building and its interior was played down."

"You're right," said Galen. "That made it palatable for the local politicos to look the other way."

"Like you said, it helps to have deep pockets," Sam agreed. "But you still haven't answered my question about Dr. Bussot. If he's not in hot water with the police, what's the problem?"

"In two words: Aunt Kitrina."

"What's old hatchet-face been up to lately?"

"She's used her influence over Grandmother Mugambi to pressure Bussot to reveal what the attackers were after."

Seeing the sour expression on Galen's face, Sam asked, "What else?"

"Our fears about her and Alves seem to have come true with a vengeance. Kitrina's sudden interest in what's been going on at the Foundation is just another indicator that our worries are more than paranoid delusions. Clearly, my aunt is using her position to attempt to force Henri to hand over the very information Alves's mercenaries couldn't find the hard way."

"You said it yourself." Sam frowned. " 'The hard way.' Why didn't she and Alves try that *before* the attack?"

"I don't know," admitted Galen. "Hashem and I have asked ourselves that very same question. It would make sense to try to get the information in a less costly and visible manner." Sam nodded. "But then, nothing much about that raid seems all that rational," Galen finished. "I suspect it reflected a bit of panic on Alves's part."

"What's been the good doctor's response to Kitrina's demands for information?"

"He's been stonewalling her," Galen said. "No matter how hard she presses, and she can press very hard indeed, he won't admit to a thing. And unless Aunt Kitrina is prepared to reveal her association with Alves, she can't take her case to the rest of the family."

"Hmmph." Recalling that the PrinSecPol head had sent Galen a coded message earlier in the day, Sam now asked, "Did Fedalf's latest cryptex communique to you contain anything new?"

"Nothing we didn't already know. It's an open secret now that Alves has been behind the stockpiling of the Soweto Corporation's publicly traded shares."

Sam clapped his hands in appreciation. "You made a pun, son—I'm proud of you."

"Stockpiling?" asked Galen. "Well, I try my best; I have a great teacher."

"Ah, shucks," said Sam, shoving his hands into his pockets and digging the toe of his boot into the carpet.

"Herbert, Mahute, Richard, Adrianna, and some of the other cousins are trying their damnedest to buy up as many outstanding shares as they can, hoping to dry up the market before Alves's stake in the company reaches a critical level."

"Adrianna?"

"Yeah. She's become her family's representative in all this."

"Will their efforts be enough?"

"I don't know; the wild card in this deck is how much voting power the shares Aunt Kitrina controls gives to Alves." He made a face.

"What?"

"You know the funny thing about all this?" he asked. Without waiting for Sam's response, he said, "We're all a lot richer because of Alves's manipulations; the stock has risen quite a bit over the past month or so." Then, remembering the beginning of their conversation, he added, "See—not much going on."

"It's quiet, Bwana, too quiet," Sam agreed.

"I can't help thinking that it's the lull before the storm. Alves hasn't gone to all this trouble to just give up and stop dead in the water."

"Uh-huh," agreed Sam. "I have just one question. How long can you keep these cliches coming? I mean, 'lull before the storm' and 'dead in the water' are great. Do you have more?"

"Probably," said Galen agreeably. "After all," he said, a twinkle in his eye, "it ain't over until the fat lady sings."

II

"Why, hello, Dr. Hanks," the archive's day-duty guard said, staring up at the holo provided by the security camera.

"Hello . . . ah, Patricia," Hanks replied after dredging her name up from his memory.

"Now c'mon, Dr. Hanks," she told him. "Remember, I asked you to call me Pat."

"All right . . . Pat."

She smiled, then looked down at the desk in front of her. "That's funny, Dr. Hanks—"

"Everett," he told her. "I can't have you calling me Dr. Hanks when I'm calling you Pat." He licked his lips; engaging in this sort of banter was difficult enough for him normally, but it was excruciating under these circumstances.

"Thank you, Everett," she said. "As I started to say, though, I don't have you listed on my daily access sheet."

"No, you wouldn't have me there," he confirmed. "Dr. Bussot and I decided we needed some material at the last minute." He made a face. "I'm sorry, but anyone we work with can tell you how absentminded the two of us are, especially when you put Henri and me together."

"Uh-huh," she said, sounding noncommittal. He began to sweat, convinced that she could see through his obvious ploy.

"I have a priority password, however," he told her. "And you can always call Dr. Bussot and confirm what I've just told you. I don't imagine he'd be *too* angry about being interrupted in the middle of our current experiment." *Christ!* he thought. *That's so fucking transparent! There's no way she's gonna buy it.*

She stared at his shimmering holo image for a long time before finally saying, "Um, I suppose if you have today's password . . ."

Hanks's shoulders slumped in relief. "Antarctica," he said.

"Step up to the retinal scanner, Everett," the guard said.

"Thank you, Pat," Hanks said.

Less than thirty seconds later the massive molecular-steel door swung open and he entered the archives.

* * *

Hashem Fedalf's salary as head of the PrinSecPol was two hundred thousand credits a year. While hardly a pittance, neither was it an outrageous sum of money for a man in his position. While a number of his colleagues found it difficult to support their families in the city and in high style on that income, Fedalf, a confirmed bachelor, had no such problems.

Because of his otherwise spartan needs, Fedalf had more than enough money to support his few indulgences, such as collecting rare books—mysteries in particular. Tonight, after a long soak in a hot bathtub, he was going to read the first two chapters of a Dick Francis novel his antiquarian bookseller had bought at an auction. The book, a novel titled *Bolt*, had cost Fedalf's bookseller four hundred prin-creds. The dealer then marked up it to six hundred prin-creds, which Fedalf gladly paid since the book was in excellent condition.

Fedalf shivered in anticipation. *Two chapters and only two chapters*, he reminded himself. What he wanted to do was to sit down and devour the mystery in one sitting; reading a chapter or two a night, however, would prolong his pleasure. For a week or so, he would have something to look forward to when he arrived home at his otherwise empty apartment.

While the tub was filling with hot water, he went out to his small but tastefully furnished living room-cum-dining area and removed the book from its vacuum cube and caressed its dust jacket. The intact dust jacket was one reason the book was especially valuable. He ran his fingers across the smooth and glossy heavy paper.

After sniffing it once or twice, he put the book down without opening it. It was too early; that would come later. Not wanting to overfill the tub, he hurried back into the bathroom.

* * *

Like many people in his line of work—Fedalf had once been an agent for the PrinSecPol himself, many years earlier—Hashem Fedalf possessed a touch of the Ability. What few psi powers he had were weak and of little use to him normally; only occasionally did they come in handy.

This was one of those occasions.

Fedalf had just finished dressing when the hair stood up on the back of his neck. He stared at his face in the dresser mirror, one part of his mind noting that his expression was that of a man frozen by uncertainty. The cause of his confusion was a startlingly vivid premonition that someone had entered his apartment.

Were it not for his self-awareness concerning his trace of the Ability, he might have dismissed his warning out of hand. After all, he reasoned, there shouldn't—*couldn't*—be anyone there because of the two agents standing guard in the building's lobby.

There shouldn't, couldn't, be anyone out there; but there was. He could sense him.

Fedalf spotted his compact energy pistol on the small stand beside his bed. He crossed the distance between it and himself in an instant, picking up the weapon and checking its charge. He smiled grimly; if whoever was outside his bedroom door was expecting to catch him unawares, he was in for a rude shock.

The energy pistol in his right hand, he approached the door, took a deep breath, and pressed the glowing entry patch. The door slid open with a soft hiss.

Fedalf wasn't sure what to expect. One possibility was that there would be no one there at all. Another was that the person would turn out to be Rob MacKenzie or Galen Yeager, having decided, unwisely, to visit him unannounced.

What he did not expect was who *was* outside the door.

"Mohammed's cat!" he exclaimed, pointing and firing the energy pistol almost reflexively.

III

"Things have gone too far," Kitrina Tollersrud told Luis Jorge Alves. "My family means too much to me to allow this destructive conflict to continue."

Alves's simulacrum stood with its back to his mother-in-law, staring out the window at the streets of Johannesburg, its plasmetal hands clasped behind its back in a parody of human posturing. Their meeting was taking place in an expensively furnished conference room on the sixty-third floor of a building Alves leased in Johannesburg.

Finally, the simulacrum turned to face her. "It is a little late to be concerned about the Voorhees family fortunes, don't you think, Mother Tollersrud? The proper time to express your misgivings would have been before my people raided your family compound."

"Don't call me Mother Tollersrud!" she snapped. "Not when you're using that . . . that *thing* to stand in for you." Too old-fashioned to be comfortable with such devices, Kitrina realized that the simulacrum made her uneasy. It was unnatural to see something so lifeless and inhuman wearing the face of her son-in-law.

There was another of those inexplicably long pauses before the simulacrum replied, "I have already explained to you that the demands of my business require that I be elsewhere."

"Well, the demands of *my* business require that you be here in person." She looked at the simulacrum's face, unable to read its pinched features.

"That's not true, Mother Tollersrud," he said patiently. "I am working hard to resolve our mutual problems."

"Where are you?"

"That is something I would rather not reveal at this time," Alves said.

"Where is my daughter?" Kitrina demanded.

"Would you like to see her?" the simulacrum asked.

"Yes, of course," Kitrina said. "I have not spoken with her since the honeymoon."

"Then come with me," the simulacrum said after a few moments.

"Where?" she asked suspiciously. She waited for the simulacrum to voice Alves's response.

"To see Ghannee," the simulacrum told her.

"She's here?"

The simulacrum with Alves's face shook its head from side to side. "No, of course not. But there's a communications console in the next room. Ghannee is waiting to speak to you."

"Take me to this phone, then," Kitrina said firmly.

The simulacrum got up and opened a door connecting the conference room with another office. "After you, Mother Tollersrud," the simulacrum said, holding the door open for her.

"Thank you," Kitrina said tight-lipped, walking stiffly into the next room.

The simulacrum, a smile twisting its rudimentary face, followed her in and closed the door.

IV

"What is it now, Doctor?" Alves asked wearily. He was growing tired of hearing about Hanks's difficulties. That was his style—give someone a job to do and leave him alone until that person had finished it. Except that Hanks didn't get it; he wanted to keep Alves informed about every little glitch, every little bump in the road that slowed him down.

"Come and see for yourself," Hanks's holographic image said to him.

"I would rather not, Doctor," Alves said.

"But . . ."

"What is the problem?" Alves asked patiently.

"The sleepers' personality matrixes are proving to be many times more unstable than was the case with Sam Houston," Hanks's image told him.

"Unstable?" Alves frowned. "What do you mean, unstable? You're not telling me that they're untrainable, are you?"

"I think a full personality overlay *is* possible," Hanks said carefully.

"Then what's the problem?"

"I'm not sure how long the overlay will remain in place. It may be months, weeks, or as little a period of time as days," Hanks told him. "When it erodes and the original personality reasserts itself, the effects could be disastrous."

"Disastrous? How so?"

"Before I answer that, let me ask you one more time—are these subjects *truly* cryo-sleepers?"

"For the umpteenth time, yes, Dr. Hanks, they are," Alves lied.

Hanks's chest rose and fell. "Then something is wrong. Something is causing the personality matrixes of ordinary people to react in unpredictable ways. When and if the overlay fails or proves insufficiently strong to contain their original personalities, these cyborgs could be walking time bombs; they could be Frankenstein Monsters."

"Aren't you being just a little melodramatic, Dr. Hanks?" asked Alves sourly.

"Maybe, maybe not. I hope so."

15

THE LASER BOLT THAT HASHEM FEDALF FIRED STRUCK HIS mirror image in the chest. The phony Fedalf seemed surprised by the sudden assault.

Hashem Fedalf—the real Hashem Fedalf—stared first at the small, sharp-edged hole he'd burned through his doppelganger's shirt and then at his brown eyes. "Your irises—they're not yellow."

"Neither are yours," the cyborg with Fedalf's face and voice replied, reaching out to grab the energy pistol Fedalf clutched. With its inhuman quickness, the cyborg would have successfully seized the pistol ninety-nine times out of a hundred. Because Fedalf had already begun to step back and withdraw the pistol, however, the cyborg's hand closed on empty air.

When Fedalf tried to slam the door shut, hurtling it toward the other's face, the cyborg stopped it with his hand. "Not so fast," it said, confident of its abilities.

Fedalf foresaw in an instant (the Ability again?) that although the cyborg might kill him, it wanted to play with him first like a cat toying with a mouse. It wanted him to marvel at its superhuman strength and agility, its quickness and invulnerability. Above all else, it wanted him to feel fear.

"Shoot!" he shouted over the cyborg's shoulder.

While the cyborg had superhuman physical abilities, it had an all-too-human mind and fell for the oldest trick in the book. When it realized that there was no one coming to Fedalf's rescue, it turned back toward the PrinSecPol director—and took a full-intensity blast of energy in its face.

The cyborg's eyes, more delicate than its polycarbon skin, were a remarkable blend of petropolymer silicates; they were also unexpectedly vulnerable to the pistol's stream of coherent energy.

"My eyes! My eyes!" the cyborg screamed as they melted and ran down his cheeks.

Fedalf tried to push past the stricken cyborg, but it stuck out a leg and tripped him up. He stumbled forward a few steps before flying headfirst toward the carpet. Long past his prime as a field agent, Fedalf nonetheless managed to first catch himself on his hands and then roll to one side.

"You bastard!" the cyborg shrieked. "I'll tear you limb from limb."

"Gotta catch me first," gasped Fedalf, climbing onto his knees and then his feet.

"Keep talking," the cyborg said, lurching toward the sound of his voice like the blinded Cyclops Polyphemus trying to locate Odysseus and his men.

Fedalf shut up.

"That's okay, too," the cyborg told him when it realized the other was not going to give away his position by speaking. "I may not be able to see you, but I can hear you even if you don't say a word." The cyborg smiled; an eerie sight. Fedalf shivered to see this mirror image of himself grinning evilly. "I hear you breathing, little man."

The cyborg was telling the truth, Fedalf realized. Like Sam, this thing had preternaturally keen hearing. Holding his breath, Fedalf reached out and gently pressed first the glowing manual control square and then the power square on his apartment music system. The room was instantly filled with multidirectional music waves.

"Power off!" the cyborg said sharply in Fedalf's voice. Nothing. "Gotta hand it to you, you clever bastard," the cyborg muttered softly. "That's a smart move." It was even smarter than the cyborg was willing to admit; the would-be assassin didn't know Fedalf's apartment well enough to know where the manual/auto square was located.

"Doesn't matter in the long run, however," the cyborg told him, making grasping motions with its outstretched arms. "Sooner or later I'll find you and that'll be the end."

Padding gently around the deep carpet in his stocking feet, Fedalf was able to avoid the cyborg's groping movements, but he knew the cyborg had spoken the truth—sooner or later it *would* find him and choke the life out of him.

Fedalf's eyes swept the room, urgently searching for a weapon. He still had the energy pistol, but he'd already found the cyborg's one and only chink in its armor; or had he? If the thing had another Achilles' heel, he had to find it—and fast.

He finally saw the meter-high fertility statue a friend had given him. The figure of a steatopygous female was made of solid Nile Valley granite. If he could reach it, he might be able to use its weight and mass against the cyborg.

Fedalf was in the middle of a cautious step toward the statue when his leg bones cracked; it wasn't a very loud pop, but it was loud enough.

"Gotcha!" the cyborg exulted, immediately making a half-turn and lunging toward the sound.

Fedalf again threw himself headlong through the air, landing on one shoulder and executing a laudable head tuck and roll for a man whose bones creaked like a old wooden floorboards. He crashed through the spindly bric-a-brac room divider that housed the stone fertility totem.

Everything collapsed in a heap and the falling statue grazed the side of his head, narrowly missing crushing his skull. Somehow the cyborg had anticipated his direction, however, and it reached out and caught him by the ankle.

"Going somewhere?" it asked, its grip tightening. Although the thing's viselike fingers hurt like hell, Fedalf screamed louder than the pain actually warranted while his right hand frantically scrabbled across the carpet like a frightened land crab. He found the statue a second before the cyborg began pulling him back for the *coup de grace*.

"Come to dadder," the cyborg said, relishing the thought of pulling Fedalf's head off like one might pull the petals off a daisy.

"All right," agreed Fedalf, twisting slightly as he hefted the heavy statue and brought it down with as much force as he could muster on the cyborg's head. It wasn't an especially powerful blow, given the awkwardness of the position from which it was delivered, but it got immediate results.

A strangled sound escaped from the cyborg as the shock wave from the heavy object's impact rattled its brain. Fedalf struck the prone cyborg two more quick blows, then dropped the statue, crawled to his feet, and ran toward the door.

Like an indestructible villain in a cheap horror sinny, the cyborg shook off Fedalf's attack and found and picked up the fallen statue. It hurled it toward the door, catching the retreating Fedalf squarely between his shoulders.

"Argh!" he cried as the wind was knocked out of him and he was sent crashing into the closed door. He scrabbled away from the door on his hands and knees, the area between his shoulder blades burning with pain.

"You're good, you sonofabitch," the cyborg told him. "But it's time I ended this farce."

Sensing that another close encounter with the cyborg could well be his last, Fedalf opted to try a bold maneuver. He picked up the energy pistol and fired a single bolt of energy at the large polyglas picture window, shattering it into a thousand pieces. The shards blew out over the street and seemed to hang suspended in the air like glittering ice crystals before beginning their fall one hundred and three stories to the street below.

Gritting his teeth, Fedalf stuck the energy pistol in his belt and took a circuitous route to the gaping hole in the wall where the window used to be. Ignoring the shards of polyglas, he lowered himself over the edge, and in seconds he had found a small ledge to support his toes. He hadn't been rock climbing for years, but he quickly summoned up the old skills again.

Allah be praised for muscle memory, he thought.

All he had to do now was make it down two levels to a series of ledges and outcroppings where the building widened out. From there he hoped to be able to find a window to break through to safety.

"Where the hell are you?" wondered the cyborg, standing at the ruined window. He heard Fedalf's breath rasping raggedly in and out of his throat as his fingers and toes sought holds.

"I'll be damned," the cyborg said, its voice filled with wonder. "Climbing down the side of the building like a human fly, eh? Well, two can play that game."

The cyborg got down onto its hands and knees and slowly felt its way to the edge. It leaned out slightly and, its sightless sockets an unnerving sight, "looked" down toward Fedalf. "I'm coming," it told him.

Fedalf stopped his descent, wedged his toes in firmly, got the best hold he could with his left hand, and took out the energy pistol. "Say 'cheese,' " he told the cyborg.

"Why?" it asked, or began to.

When its mouth was opened as wide as it was likely to be—on the *w-h* of *w-h-y*—Fedalf fired a single bolt between its open lips, burning a pencil-sized hole through the unprotected roof of its mouth and into its brain.

It pitched forward soundlessly and fell past Fedalf, tumbling toward the street far below. He stuck the pistol back into his belt, pressed his cheek against the cool plascrete, and sobbed once in relief. Then he began to climb down the remaining six meters between him and safety.

II

"This is it?" asked Galen, staring down at the broken body.

"That's it," confirmed Hashem Fedalf, gingerly holding a cold compress against the side of his face as Rob MacKenzie filled a second one with ice.

Sam's gaze shifted from Fedalf's face to the cyborg's and back again. "You know," he mused, putting his hand to his chin, "I'm not sure this thing doesn't look better than you do, even after falling hundreds of meters and landing on its head."

"Sam's right," agreed Galen, wincing when Fedalf moved the compress, revealing an ugly purple bruise the size of a golf ball that had all but closed his right eye. "You don't look like the winner."

"I look a lot better than I would have if that thing had managed to pull off its assassination attempt." He laughed a bitter laugh. "It was dumb luck on my part that I escaped with my life. If this thing had carried out its mission successfully, not only would I be dead now, but you'd be talking to a cyborg impostor."

"I don't understand why its plan included assassinating you," Galen said. "How could it expect to kill you and then pretend to be you without having access to what's inside your head?"

"I was as surprised as you that this thing's primary mission seemed to be to kill me," said Fedalf. "So I asked Dr. Bussot that very same question." He gently replaced the compress with a cold one handed him by MacKenzie. "Ouch!" he exclaimed. Then the cold worked its magic and he sighed.

"Dr. Bussot . . . ?" prompted Sam.

"Yes, Dr. Bussot," said Fedalf. "According to the doctor, one of his top people from the cryo-sleeper project disappeared recently." He frowned as if trying to remember the name.

"Everett Hanks," prompted MacKenzie.

"Right," agreed Fedalf. "It seems that Hanks's family has disappeared, too. Most likely that's the reason he's cooperating with Alves."

"Wonderful," muttered Sam.

"Oh, it gets better," Fedalf informed him with a bitter smile. "Dr. Hanks also took copies of most of the research files with him."

"Jesus H. Christ!" cursed Galen.

"When it rains, it pours," said Sam, drawing an annoyed look from Galen.

"If what Dr. Bussot tells me about this man is correct, not only does he have all the relevant data to duplicate the success of the project that produced Sam, he has the expertise and skill needed to lead the team that could do it."

"What's all this have to do with this cyborg's attempt to rip your head off?" Sam wondered.

"I'm getting to that," said Fedalf. Still holding the compress to his head, he got up and poured himself a cup of his sweet, black coffee and took a sip. It seemed to restore him a bit, and he sat back down again. "It appears that the same medical technologies that made it possible to retrieve Sam's core personality from his frozen corpse . . ." He made a face and murmured, "Ah, sorry, Sam."

"S'all right," Sam shrugged. Talk like this didn't especially bother him.

"Those same techniques can be used to extract the memories from someone living—or from the brain of someone who's been dead for less than seventy-two hours."

"They needed your head, not you," said Rob MacKenzie grimly.

"It seems that way, doesn't it?"

"You said this thing took an almost gleeful pleasure in its attempts to kill you?" questioned Galen.

"That's right."

That had Galen stumped. He looked evaluatively at Sam; Sam just stared back blankly. "Sam is a human in an android's body," Galen began. "And that's all that he is."

"What are you getting at?" asked MacKenzie.

"Sam's a person inside a machine," Galen reiterated, "but he's not a murderer and he's not nuts."

Sam was going to say something smart, thought better of it, and just said, "No, I'm not."

"And you think these new cyborgs might be both?" asked MacKenzie.

"I don't know," admitted Galen. "But this Hanks guy must be under a lot of pressure to produce carbon copies of Sam as quickly as possible. Maybe he's being forced to cut corners. And maybe, just maybe, he's creating cyborgs that aren't as stable as they should be. The one that tried killing you doesn't sound like it was especially sane. Was it?"

"No," Fedalf said.

MacKenzie whistled. "An insane cyborg? That's a frightening thought."

"What do we do now?" wondered Sam.

"You and Galen must stop Alves and Hanks before they can produce more of these things," Fedalf told him.

"I was afraid you were going to say that," lamented Galen.

"Finding Alves's facilities isn't going to be easy," Sam said, scratching his nose thoughtfully. Then he saw the look that passed between Hashem Fedalf and his deputy. "What did I say?"

"We know where Alves's laboratories and manufacturing facilities are," admitted MacKenzie. "Or at least we think we do."

"You do?" Sam said, surprised.

"Where are they?" asked Galen.

Fedalf sipped his coffee, letting the suspense build. "On Empyrea," he finally said matter of factly.

"Empyrea," said Sam, frowning. "Alves is in heaven?"

"What?" Galen had no idea what Sam was talking about.

"Empyrea," began Sam patiently. "It's an old term the ancients used for the highest heaven."

"That's correct," Fedalf said.

"The highest heaven?" repeated Galen frowning. If he could only remember his classics courses . . .

Fedalf smiled appreciatively, as if he'd heard something that made him laugh. "Those who know nothing about Empyrea—and that's just about everyone—don't get the joke contained in its name. Rather than give the planet a a more appropriate name like Acheron or Orcus, the people who found it thought it amusing to bestow its heavenly name on it."

"Why?" asked Sam. "What *is* the joke?"

"The joke is that it is a hellish place," Fedalf told him. "Empyrea is a nasty, brutish, and foul world. Heavy rains fall constantly on a surface dominated by the cones of thousands of active and inactive volcanoes. The populace, meager as it may be, is constantly being bombarded by noxious fumes caused by the interaction of the water and the devil's cauldron of plasma and molten rock that bubbles and spits inside each lava chimney."

"You say the place is lousy with volcanoes?" Galen asked.

"That's right," said Fedalf.

"Then the name Empyrea isn't a total joke name," he said, beginning to remember his ancient mythology. "It's supposed to contain the pure element of fire. Volcanoes would fill that bill."

"Sounds delightful," Sam said. "Why does it exist?"

Fedalf looked at Rob MacKenzie, who picked up the cue. "Not unreasonably, most planets and their governments object to the presence of potentially unsafe factories and manufacturing plants in their midst, polluting the air and water and creating unpleasant or downright dangerous by-products. None of us wants such things near us, yet we demand the products they produce. Empyrea was picked to be the home of these unwanted factories."

"So all the godawful pollution-creating, chemical-spilling industries in the galaxy are located on Empyrea?" asked Galen.

"Not all of them," replied Fedalf mildly.

"Needing someplace where they could house such facilities, a consortium of corporations—many of them well-known companies, I might add—got together and convinced the Magistracy to allow Empyrea to be turned into an industrial hellhole where anything goes. Its surface is covered by massive facilities which produce everything from microscopic machined parts to the hulls of starships."

"I like that word 'convinced,' " Galen said. "It sounds so much better than 'bribed.' "

Fedalf shrugged. "One would be naive not to accept that such things are permitted to occur."

"How come you two know so much about this place?" Sam asked suspiciously.

"While I may accept that Empyrea prospers because the powers that be pretend it does not exist," Fedalf replied evenly, "that does not mean I do not keep an eye on what happens there."

"And what is happening there?" queried Galen.

"There is labor unrest," Fedalf told him, his face clouded.

"Labor unrest?"

"Someone has to work in the factories," Fedalf said.

"Don't Empyrea's mills and foundries use robots?" Sam asked.

"Many do," Fedalf said. "But people, genetically altered to suit their environment, are often more cost-effective."

MacKenzie again took over. "Empyrea was originally populated by men and women whose bodies had been altered by genetic engineering to better withstand the planet's severe gravity."

"Hi-gravs!" exclaimed Sam.

"Yes," agreed MacKenzie. "Empyrea's workforce consists of squat and powerful people compelled to labor under hellish conditions which are illegal everywhere else."

"You can be bred to withstand heavy gravity," observed Galen, "but I didn't think the geneticists were also turning people into sheep."

MacKenzie shook his head at that. "If the Empyreans are content with their lot in life, it's because they know nothing else."

Fedalf explained further. "There is no contact between Empyrea and its nearest neighbors—no regularly scheduled flights, no trade or social intercourse, and, most importantly, no opportunity for potentially disruptive ideas to find a fertile breeding place."

"I like this Alves guy less and less," Sam said.

Nodding, Fedalf said, "Even with all these safeguards, a nascent movement toward independence began about five years ago. A small group of workers, displaced after their factory was deemed too out-of-date to warrant rejuvenation, began a campaign to force the puppet government to permit corporations other than those owned by the consortium to construct factories and laboratories on Empyrea." He smiled grimly. "Not unexpectedly, their actions have so far met with little success."

There was silence while everyone withdrew into his own thoughts. Galen stared at the floor for a long time; finally, he looked up and said, "You're telling me that the punch line to this unfunny joke is that Alves's corporations are among those evading scrutiny for their actions by operating plants on Empyrea."

"That's correct," said Fedalf.

Galen looked at Sam, who nodded yes. "So," Galen asked, "when do Sam and I leave?"

* * *

The small yacht that Fedalf provided, called *Intrepid*, was a beauty, Galen decided. If he got out of this alive, he just might get himself a similar model. Then he remembered Fedalf's telling him just how much this thing had cost: nine million credits. That relatively immodest figure puzzled Galen until he reminded himself that the yacht had to meet two rigid specifications. First, it had to have hyperspace capability; secondly, and almost as importantly, it had to be small.

"The smaller the better," Sam had told him.

"And why is that?" Galen had demanded.

"Fedalf wants people to think you're just another hunk of iron-rich rock traveling around the galaxy," Sam had explained, without really explaining anything.

"A rock?"

"The better to get by Empyrea's defenses."

So, here we are, thought Galen. *Pretending to be a lifeless rock.*

"How's the autopilot doing?" Galen asked Sam.

Before Sam could respond, the computer's feminine voice said, "We are proceeding without incident toward our destination in the Lorassian sector. We will be exiting hyperspace in five-point-three-two minutes, nearly three million kilometers from Empyrea and hidden from the planet's view by its closest satellite."

"And what's the weather forecast for Elysium, the largest city?" asked Sam, giving Galen a wink.

The perplexed computer paused for several seconds, which was unusual, then asked, "I beg your pardon?"

"Never mind," Galen said. Looking at Sam, he told him, "You shouldn't do things like that to the poor bubblebrain; it isn't used to people like you."

"Oh, all right," sighed Sam.

After sneaking several quick glances at Galen's face, Sam looked at him strangely and said, "Ah, I want to tell you something, partner."

"Shoot."

"We've been in our share of tight places; we've faced some long odds, but never any quite as long as this. There's a fair chance that we might not make it this time," he said somberly, catching Galen by surprise. "And if that proves to be the case, I just want to thank you for everything."

"Sam, I—"

"I love you like a brother, Galen."

Galen stared at a bulkhead, a lump in his throat. "I . . . ah . . ." He shook his head. "Shit," he said softly. "I . . ."

Sam put his hand on his shoulder. "I know."

16

ONCE THEY HAD EMERGED FROM HYPERSPACE, HIDDEN FROM the reach of radar and particle beam scans by their position behind Empyrea's largest moon, Galen composed himself and then lay down on an acceleration couch to begin his breathing exercises. This was step one in their plan to reach Empyrea's surface undetected.

"Slowly, slowly," cautioned Sam, watching Galen's progress. Meanwhile, he began taking the ship's nonessential functions off line.

Galen just nodded, not wanting to interrupt the pattern he was trying to establish. Following Sam's advice, he breathed in slowly, held it, and then slowly exhaled and repeated. He tried to make his mind blank; it wasn't easy under the circumstances.

Sam now knelt down beside the couch and began whispering a soft, reassuring litany into Galen's ear: "You feel relaxed and comfortable. You can sense your muscles relaxing; all the tension and stiffness is leaving your body and you are totally relaxed."

Sam continued in this vein until Galen's breathing fell into a consistent rhythmic pattern. "Now that you are completely relaxed and ready for the next step," Sam said in a soothing voice just above the level of a whisper, "I will ask you to repeat the trigger phrase. As soon as you say the words, you will remember and follow your earlier programming. Is that clear?"

"Yesss." Galen felt oddly detached from his body, from reality. It was a comfortable, if strange, feeling.

"Very good," Sam said. "Listen carefully: The phrase is 'rogue elephant ears.' "

"Rogue elephant ears," Galen said thickly. Immediately, his half-opened eyes closed and the slight hiss of his breath ceased.

The three-word phrase had triggered a self-induced state of suspended animation. His body was functioning at the lowest level needed to sustain his life signs. His heart beat twice a minute, and not even Sam's keen eyes could register the minute rise and fall of his chest.

After Sam strapped Galen's apparently lifeless body tightly to the acceleration couch, he gave his friend a last look and then continued his task of shutting down *Intrepid*'s electrical system, including the artificial gravity.

With only minimal power to drive the ship, he maneuvered it around the immense bulk of the looming satellite and urged it toward the even larger planet just several million kilometers away. He activated a preset program that produced an almost phantom burst from the maneuvering jets. This modest nudge was the impetus that started *Intrepid* tumbling gently toward Empyrea. A second, slightly longer, burst completed the process.

Satisfied with the orbital trajectory that he calculated on his own inner mission computer, Sam now shut down the yacht's systems completely.

Intrepid was now indistinguishable from the dozens of inert hunks of space debris drifting toward Empyrea with one exception: its size. That was the wild card that could cause the whole plan to collapse: If Empyrea's planetary defenses were overly zealous, *Intrepid* still might face annihilation by the shield cannons orbiting just above the atmospheric orbit.

Their only chance, the consideration that Galen and Sam had pinned their hopes of survival on, was that, after calculating the object's trajectory, the defensive computers would note that it was headed for the middle of the Great Western Sea and transmit a signal for the cannons to withhold their fire. It was an immense risk.

Galen was lucky, Sam thought. If he awakened, he would know they had made it. If he didn't . . . well, he didn't. Sam crossed his fingers and watched as Empyrea loomed larger and larger in the viewscreen; their chances of not being shot out of the sky improved with each kilometer closer they came.

<*Alfie, are you there?*> Sam called.

Without hesitation, Alfie replied <<*Yes, Dr. Floyd, I am here.*>>

That made Sam laugh out loud; a sign, he realized, of the tension he was feeling. <*Dammit, Alfie, it's good to hear your "voice" again.*>

<<*It is good to speak with you again, too, Sam.*>>

<*Alf, I . . .* > Suddenly, Sam felt a bit self-conscious and ashamed. Alfie *did* sound pleased to hear from him.

<<*What is it, Sam?*>>

<*I was about to ask you about my calculations, wondering if you'd go over them for me to see if there was any mistakes.*>

<<*Yes?*>>

<*Alf, I hate to think I only call you when I have something for you to do. I'm a bit red-faced over my selfish relationship with you of late.*>

<<*Please do not concern yourself with such recriminations,*>> Alf responded. <<*I am conformed to your brain patterns. It pleases me to do things for you and Galen. It is my purpose, the reason I was created.*>>

Sam was touched by Alfie's declaration of friendship. <*Ah, well then,*> he said gruffly, <*since you enjoy it so much, could you please check my calculations?*>

<<*Certainly . . . Dr. Floyd.*>>

"Thanks, Alfie," Sam whispered.

Many hours later, and still well over a million kilometers from the planet's surface, Sam felt the first tentative touch of Empyrea's gravity tugging at them. Hour by hour, kilometer by kilometer, the heavy planet's gravity continued to pull them toward the Great Western Sea's storm-tossed waves, invisible gravitons reeling in *Intrepid* like some high-flying kite.

Because the long fall seemed to take forever, Sam passed the time by endlessly manipulating and recalculating the numbers. Everything seemed to be okay.

As the final minutes of the spacecraft's descent toward the ocean surface ticked off, Sam began a low-level repowering of the ship's navicomputer and other systems.

Finally, just thirty seconds from impact, Sam activated the specially strengthened shields and the Kessel anti-grav repulse generators and prepared himself for what was to come. It was in those final seconds and last few meters that the repulse generators played a critical role in shedding some of *Intrepid*'s momentum. Were it not for this last-second braking maneuver, the ship would have plunged into the ocean at a fatally high speed.

Even though he had been anticipating this moment for many hours, Sam was still surprised by the explosive nature of the actual impact. The ship's plunge into the sea caused a final deceleration that was shockingly wrenching. Sam blacked out momentarily as thousands of metric tons of seawater converted into steam and vented high into the overcast sky. Then, almost immediately, the ship was plunging toward the cold depths below.

In seconds it was over. The roiling surface of the sea began to calm, and an observer would shortly be hard pressed to point to the place where the falling object had entered the water.

The ruthless and unforgiving sea, ever alive, ever moving, seemed to have claimed yet another victim.

* * *

Sam had fully restored *Intrepid*'s systems by the time he spoke the wake-up phrase to Galen. He watched as his friend's chest began to rise and fall and his eyes fluttered. Finally, Galen's eyes opened and he looked like someone waking up from a long, drugged sleep. He blinked rapidly and turned his head from side to side. "Where am I?" he asked.

"On the bottom of the Great Western Sea," Sam informed him. "And in one piece, as you can see."

"I feel wonderful!" Galen exclaimed, stretching his arms and working his shoulders to get rid of the kinks. "I should try to do that every so often."

"Sure," sniffed Sam. "You get to sleep while I have to sit up worrying about whether or not we're going to be blown out of the sky by Empyrea's defenses."

"It's a dirty job, but someone had to do it," Galen told him.

"You *are* in a good mood, aren't you?" observed Sam.

"I told you I was," grinned Galen. "I feel as light as a feather."

"Really?" asked Sam, a half-smile playing around his lips. "Artificial gravity off," he commanded the computer.

"Artificial gravity off," the computer replied.

Suddenly, Galen didn't feel so light anymore. "Lordy!" he said, taking several steps forward.

"Still feel as light as a feather, Peter Pan—or should I say Tinkerbell?"

"Who put lead in my shoes?" moaned Galen. "I feel like I weigh a hundred and fifty kilos."

"One-point-six-two gravity, compared to Terran standard, will do that to a person," Sam told him.

"How's it affect you?"

"I can handle it."

"I can handle it, too," Galen said. "I was just wondering if you feel the difference."

"Of course I feel the difference," snapped Sam. He immediately regretted his outburst. "I'm sorry," he added.

"Hey, you had to fly this crate in," Galen told him. "I'd be surprised if you aren't feeling a little tense." He smiled. "You're allowed."

Unsure how to respond, Sam just said, "Ah, let's see about maneuvering this thing onto dry land."

"Sure," agreed Galen. "Where are we?"

Sam showed him the holo projection. "We're right here," he said, "about seven thousand kilometers from this irregularly shaped continent. It's pretty much where I hoped we'd splash down."

"That's Alves's continent, so to speak?"

"Yep. That's where his factories and labs are located."

"Think it's safe to fly?"

"I had planned to," Sam said, "staying low over the water. But I'm having second thoughts." He grasped his left elbow with his right hand, a sure sign he was having an internal debate with himself, and said, "It'll be a little slower and take us a bit longer, but I'd feel safer if we made like the *Nautilus* and traveled just *under* the surface."

"You think there are spy satellites that would pick us up?"

"I don't know," admitted Sam. "I'd just feel better playing it safe."

"You got us this far, partner," Galen said. "I'm with you."

"Good," Sam said. Then he gave the holo a long look. "I think we'll have all the danger we can handle when we reach our destination."

Galen just nodded.

"Hot damn!" marveled Galen when he saw the pile of armaments Sam had piled up by the hatch. "Are we ready for bear or what?" The arsenal included shrapnel guns, energy rifles, grenades, rocket-propelled grenade launchers, moly-weave vests, and fusion torches. The latter weren't usually considered weapons, but they could be used as such.

"Fedalf *did* give us everything we asked for, didn't he?" asked Sam. "It's more than enough for us two gaffs," he observed, using a popular hol-vee term.

"And what makes you think Fedalf sent along all this for us?" asked Galen.

"You mean it's like a duel?" queried Sam. "We bring along the weapons and Luis Alves gets to pick out some for himself?"

Galen shook his head. "Nope. It's simpler than that—Fedalf wants us to give some of this stuff to the rebels." He looked through the pile. "I think they'll like these grenades."

"The rebels?"

"Yeah. Remember, Hashem told us that some of Alves's workers, fired for insubordination and other activities at odds with being wage slaves, have gone underground. They're conducting a determined, if so far ineffective, war of attrition against Alvco Industries, the sole occupant of this island continent."

"Excuse me for seeking clarification of the obvious, but I take it that Alvco Industries is Alves and confederates?"

"Correct." Galen stared at the huge pile of weapons and ammunition. "Just looking at all this makes my back hurt already."

"I'll take the really heavy stuff," Sam said. "But I can only carry so much."

"I have an idea."

"Let's hear it."

"Why don't we unload it all and hide it nearby?" Galen said. "When we meet up with the resistance, we can tell them where it's hidden."

Sam nodded. "Good idea. That way we don't have to worry about the ship; we can activate the cloaking device and leave it in sentry mode."

"C'mon," Galen said. "Let's start moving this stuff outside."

The rain was heavy and steady, falling without a break from dark, brooding skies. The cloud cover made it seem like perpetual twilight. For that reason, Galen wasn't sure if the drab appearance of the few trees and other vegetation he could see was a result of the rain and the poor visibility or their natural coloration. It had to be the dim light, he decided; even on Empyrea, plants required chlorophyll in order to produce carbohydrates through photosynthesis. They were green, he was sure; he just couldn't distinguish much color under such gray lighting.

After a single trip outside with an ammunition case in each hand, Galen began to weary. Deciding that he preferred to face Sam's razzing rather than make many such trips through the hatch and down the ramp, Galen commandeered the ship's maintenance 'bot and put it to work carrying out cargo.

"I see you've decided to play the role of the Sorcerer's Apprentice," Sam chided him.

"Listen, Darwin," Galen said, blinking as a gust of wind blew rain in his face. "Why do you think we humans crawled out of the primeval slime and ooze and fought our way up the evolutionary ladder until we possessed large brains? To create machines that can do the dirty work for us, that's why."

Sam shook his head and went back inside for another load, reappearing almost as quickly as he'd disappeared.

After watching him trundle down the ramp, deposit his burden, and head back inside, Galen began to feel like a slacker. "Remember, one of us is only flesh and blood," he muttered and followed Sam inside. He returned carrying an energy rifle; only one, but it showed he was willing to share the work. Sam smiled at him and they continued.

"Um, Gale . . . ?" said Sam.

"Yeah, what is it? And don't call me Gale." Numbed and soaked by the constant downpour, Galen wasn't in the mood for kidding around. Although the raincoat he wore was effective, rain still managed to find a way to get inside the coat's collar and run down his back. His hat was marginally better, but the heavy rain striking the top and brim felt more like individual pebbles of marble-sized hail than fat drops of water.

"I don't think we have to bother with hiding the weapons we brought."

"Huh?" Then Galen saw what Sam was staring at. "Oh, yeah, I see what you mean." They had visitors. Four men, as wide as they were tall, had emerged from the gloom and stood watching them. Galen swiped his sleeve across his eyes and saw that the beards all four wore contributed to their intimidating aura.

Feeling the heavy rain drumming on his own head gear, he observed that their visitors wore old-fashioned-looking hats. "Are those fedoras they're wearing?" he asked Sam *sotto voce*.

"Yeah. The same as Indiana Jones wears." Without turning his head, Sam added, "Don't make any sudden moves."

"Right, like I'm gonna reach inside my raincoat and my moly-weave vest for a vibroblade and show these guys who's the boss," he said. "Besides, in this gravity, I *can't* make any sudden moves."

Sam sensed that they were surrounded, but he didn't see anyone other than the four squat men who approached them slowly. Not fearfully, simply deliberately. All four sported long, stringy beards that made them looked like characters in a hist-holo—mountain men or frontier scouts, maybe. Galen guessed that none of them was taller than a hundred and fifty centimeters; they were barrels with arms and legs.

"Good afternoon," Galen said, a smile fixed to his face. Their visitors each carried a weathered energy rifle; some had battered barrels while the stocks of others were discolored and chipped. Although Galen had never seen models that old, they looked like they still worked just fine, thank you very much.

"And who might you two be?"

"Well, we might be Alves's people," stated Sam, and Galen's eyes looked toward heaven for succor. "But we're not. We're Galen Yeager and Sam Houston." He smiled broadly. "I'm Sam."

"You've got those blondie eyes," said one of the sturdily built men, rain water streaming off his hat and down the front of his rain coat. His beard was a dark brown. "You an android?"

"Sort of," Sam replied.

"Sort of?" said another of the men. "Sort of? Are you or aren't you?"

"Well, yes and no."

"Sam is part man and part machine," Galen explained. "He looks like an android, but he's really a cyborg."

"Yeah?" said the first man to speak. He spat out a thick glob of synbacco juice. A little dribbed down into his reddish beard, and Galen's stomach turned over. Pointing his energy rifle right between Galen's eyes, he said, "This thing might not do anything to blondie-eyes, but it sure as hell will burn a hole through your head if you don't answer my next question to my complete satisfaction."

"Hehhehhheh." Galen laughed mirthlessly. "And just what is your next question?"

"Who sent you?"

"Hashem Fedalf," Galen said without hesitation.

"You're one of his boys?" the brown-bearded man said dubiously.

"That's right," replied Galen, looking at the unusually silent Sam.

"Fedalf still like to read them old-time Western novels and drink that funny Pakistani tea?"

Galen was surprised that these men knew enough about Fedalf to pose such a trick question. "He reads old mysteries and drinks cup after cup of some kind of godawful black coffee that he puts too much sugar into."

When the first man lowered his weapon, Galen muttered, "Thank you."

Brown-beard said, "Okay, he knows Fedalf. That doesn't mean he's one of his agents."

"Thomas, why are you giving these boys such a hard time?" asked the third member of the party, a burly man who'd remained silent to this point. "It's clear they're not with Alvco." He stole a glance at the stockpile of weapons, glistening in the constant rain. "Besides, they brought us such fine toys." He looked at the others, cocking his head inquisitively.

"All right," the one he'd called Thomas muttered. "Let's pick up this stuff and find someplace we can talk; someplace a little more private."

"And out of the rain," suggested Sam, speaking up finally. "I sure wouldn't want to rust in place."

The first man to speak to them, the red-bearded one, clapped Sam heartily on the shoulder and almost sent the human-android reeling forward into the mud. "I like this . . . this 'cyborg.' "

"Thanks," Sam said.

"Call the others, Stephen," Thomas said.

Red-beard was apparently Stephen. He slung his energy rifle over his shoulder, put his fingers into his mouth and blew. The piercing whistle brought a dozen men and women from the line of trees where they had remained, watching. Galen felt like an adult surrounded by a crowd of bearded, muscular children. With little ado, the newcomers picked up the weapons and they moved out.

"Does it always rain like this?" asked Galen, making conversation.

"No," replied Stephen. "Sometimes it comes down pretty hard; can't do a thing when that happens. Just stay inside and read. Maybe get drunk." Several others roared their approval and Galen decided that if he lived on this hellish planet, he would make getting drunk a priority, too. The reading part didn't make an impression on him.

"Tell me," asked Sam. "Is it far to Alvco's central facilities?"

"About two hundred kilometers, give or take a few," answered Thomas.

"Good," said Galen, already feeling the effects of the high gravity.

"You don't like our planet much, do you?" asked one of the original four, the one Galen had been calling "the second brown-bearded man."

"No, I don't," admitted Galen.

"Ha!" roared Stephen. "Our visitor is honest, Brant."

"Aye," agreed Brant. Looking up at Galen, he said, "We were all born here; we've known nowhere else. Still, there aren't many of us that wouldn't give anything to leave this evil place." He thought about that. "It's not that it's so evil, I suppose. It's just that a man or a woman has to have a job. He has to feed his family."

"What if the factories weren't here?" asked Sam. "Actually, I guess I mean what if the factories remained here, but in different hands?"

"Different hands?"

"In yours. Would you stay if the planet belonged to people like yourselves?"

While their escorts exchanged curious glances, Galen told Sam, *<Looks like you've given them something to think about.>*

<I think you're right, partner.>

Finally, Stephen spoke. "We have been waging a futile war of attrition against the owners for so long, it seems that it never occurred to us to ask ourselves what we might do if we actually won."

"Well, ask yourselves," Galen said.

"You're right," admitted Brant. "We must prepare for the unexpected—for freedom and democracy."

"Don't be foolish," snapped Thomas. "The Principate will do everything in its power to keep Empyrea in the hands of the ruling elite. Nothing will—or even can—change."

"Perhaps," said Galen. "But the old Magistracy fell because of a scandal involving Cousteau and the Whale Society. If you should somehow find a way to seize control of Empyrea, I don't think the current members of the Magistracy would dare intervene."

"Words!" hissed Thomas. "Why should we believe such empty words?"

"Actions speak louder than words," Sam told Thomas. "And Galen and I are here at the direction of the head of the PrinSecPol. Not everyone in the Principate is evil or wishes to see injustice and exploitation go unpunished."

This was too much for Stephen. "I do not agree with everything Thomas says," he said to Sam, "but it is hard to reconcile your rhetoric with the reality."

"And what is the reality?"

"There are only two of you."

"True enough," conceded Galen. Then he glanced at the silent majority surrounding them. "And how many are you?"

"What do you mean?" asked Stephen, confused by the question.

"How many of you are willing to go with us to Alvco's facilities?"

Stephen scratched his beard. He looked at his friends and fellow rebels, rain flying from his hat as his head swiveled this way and that.

"Well?" asked Sam.

"About a hundred, maybe more."

Sam and Galen exchanged somber looks that slowly transformed into grins; now they understood why Fedalf had provided so many weapons.

"Give me liberty or give me death!" proclaimed Sam.

"Let the revolution begin," Galen said.

17

"AT LEAST IT ISN'T RAINING DOWN HERE," GALEN SAID, grateful for small favors. His eyes were gradually becoming accustomed to the dimly lighted mineshafts that the displaced workers called home.

"That's right," agreed Sam. "Of course, being closer to the planet's core means the gravity is higher."

"Uh-huh," muttered Galen. "A few hundred meters makes a really *big* difference." He stared down the tunnel at an approaching ball of light.

"What are you two light-worlders complaining about now?" asked Brant, his face illuminated by the feeble glow of the small xylon sphere he carried.

"We miss the rain," said Sam.

That made Brant chuckle. "Come with me," he said. "It has been agreed to that you should be allowed to see how we live."

"Good," said Galen. He and Sam followed the stocky Brant in near darkness; his body, almost as wide as the tunnel at this point, did a good job of cutting off most of the xylon sphere's heatless illumination.

"Have you lived down here long?" asked Sam.

"For nearly three years now," replied Brant over his shoulder.

"And Alves's goons haven't found you in all that time?" asked an impressed Galen.

"Our sentinels are aware that permitting a patrol to pass unnoticed and unopposed would be the end of us," Brant said. "Their vigilance has so far allowed us to remain undiscovered."

"Impressive," said Sam.

"Besides," continued Brant, "they tend to leave us alone; those of us who live so far from the main works, that is."

Two things began to happen almost imperceptibly: The tunnel grew higher and wider, and the level of illumination gradually increased. What had once been a mining tunnel suddenly turned into an underground street intersected at numerous points by similarly broad and passable streets.

"This is amazing," said an awed Galen.

"What you see is the result of three years of nonstop work," Brant informed them. "After all, this is our home."

Galen noticed a series of plaswood doors facing out down each of the side tunnels. <*That must be where they live!*> exclaimed Galen.

<*I think you're right,*> agreed Sam.

"Where are you taking us?" queried Galen.

"To meet Alys and my two children," Brant informed his guests.

"To meet your family?" Galen was caught flat-footed by Brant's words. On one level he understood that the rebels were ordinary working men and women, but to come face-to-face with the reality of their families was unexpected. He resisted giving abstract figures actual faces and names, terrified that they would come back to haunt him if he was responsible for the deaths of their husbands or wives.

Brant stopped in front of a green door built into the tunnel wall; to the left was a blue door, and to the right a red one. "Come in, please," he told them, opening the unlocked door.

They followed him inside, entering a room whose walls, ceiling, and floor were constructed of large slabs of thin plascrete. A few rudimentary chairs and tables were the only pieces of furniture in the room. A single opening in the wall at the rear of the room served as the door into whatever room or rooms lay behind this outer one.

It was through this opening that two chunky children and an apple-faced woman materialized. Galen smiled at the sight of such small and round individuals. "Dadder, Dadder," shouted both children, smaller replicas of Brant and his wife. They rushed forward to hug him, but stopped short when they saw Galen and Sam.

"Don't be alarmed, Branton and Alyssa. These men are friends; everything is all right." Branton clung to his father's leg, and Alyssa retreated to the safety of her mother's arms.

"Alys," Brant said, indicating Sam and Galen. "These two men have been sent by the PrinSecPol to help us."

"To help us?" she asked in a high-pitched voice.

"Yes, dear."

"Come in, won't you, gentlemen?" she said, smiling for the first time. "May I offer you something to eat?"

"That sounds wonderful, ma'am," Sam responded politely.

"I would like nothing better," Galen agreed. When she went back through the opening, the children went with her.

"Please, have a seat," offered Brant, indicating two of the three rickety-looking chairs.

"Thanks," chorused Galen and Sam. Galen lowered himself gingerly, as if afraid he would cause the chair to collapse. Then he saw Brant dropping down onto onc no less fragile-looking than his own, and beamed to Sam, <*I wasn't sure these chairs could take our weight.*> He paused a second to allow that to sink in. <*Ridiculous notion, isn't it?*>

Shooting the broad-beamed Brant a look, Sam replied, <*You're right. As cobbled together as these chairs appear, they have to be sturdy enough to support these rather substantial folks.*>

Alys returned, the children each bearing a small metal plate with a large slice of unknown meat on them and two green squares which Galen assumed were some kind of vegetable. As Galen gratefully accepted his plate, he looked at the rapt expressions on the children's faces as they stared at the food on the two plates. *Christ!* he thought, stunned. *This is their supper!*

Catching Sam's eye, Galen said, "Um, you know, Sam is an android; he usually eats to blend in. Since this isn't one of those occasions, there's no need for him to go through the motions." He looked at the metal platter, steam rising from the food on it and tickling his nostrils, and handed it back to Alys. "Thank you very much, but I've brought my own food along."

"Oh, no, you must eat," protested Brant.

"I shouldn't," said Galen. "Since we hadn't had much time to prepare, I didn't receive every booster injection that I was scheduled for. It's dangerous for me to be exposed to any more alien bacteria than is absolutely necessary."

"Well, if you're sure . . ." said Alys.

"Absolutely," Galen said.

"Children, take this to the back," Alys said. She gave them each a warm smile before adding, "And you may eat it there."

"Thank you, Mommer," said Alyssa.

<*I'm proud of you for recognizing that we were about to blithely eat what might have been all the food they have for today,*> Sam told Galen. He thought about that. <*Maybe for more than one day*>

<*There's only one thing bothering me now,*> Galen replied.

<*Yeah, what's that?*>

<*I lied about having other food,*> Galen said, his stomach growling.

* * *

Brant, Thomas, and the others had decided that they should split up into four groups of approximately twenty-five raiders each. Still a bit spooked by meeting Brant's wife and children, and afraid to fight beside someone whose death he might be responsible for, Galen insisted that he and Sam accompany Stephen's people.

Stephen's group consisted of more than two dozen heavily armed men and women willing to risk their lives to free the hellish planet they called home.

"We must walk for one full day," Stephen told them as they made their way across the countryside, moving in groups of three and four, and taking care not to expose themselves more than necessary.

"And then what?" asked Galen.

"Then we will be in range of the daily patrols," he told him.

"What kind of private army are we up against?" Sam wanted to know. "Or are they people at all?" When he saw Galen's questioning look, he added, "After hearing both Hashem Fedalf and your people speak of Alves and his allies, it wouldn't surprise me if his proscribed activities extended to using illegal robotic weapons."

"Robotic weapons?" asked Stephen.

"Massive android warriors with P-Q-G brains, the sort of robot killers outlawed since the Robot Wars."

"There are no such beings on Empyrea," said Stephen. "At least none that I know about. While there are occasional self-guided tanks and other mechanicals, our main foes are the Dims and the werewolves."

"The what?" asked Sam, unwilling to believe he'd heard what he thought he'd heard.

"The Dims and the werewolves," Stephen repeated patiently.

"Let's start with the Dims," said Galen. "You can explain about the werewolves later."

Stephen didn't understand what was causing his two new friends to act so strangely. "The Dims are people like us, except . . . ah . . . except that they are not of woman born."

"Wanna run that by me again?" said Galen.

"Most Empyreans were born and bred for this planet," said Stephen. "We are as human as you, if shorter and stronger because of our planet's high gravity. The Dims, however, are more than genetically altered human beings. They are born from embryos brought to term in nutrient tanks; after they emerge, they are raised in nurseries by robotic caretakers."

"That's inhuman!" exclaimed Galen.

Stephen nodded. "Because they are denied even minimal human contact, not only do they not develop intellectually, they grow up lacking warmth and feelings."

"What's the purpose of this cruelty?" asked Sam.

"They are Alves's 'private army,' as you put it earlier," Stephen told them. "The Dims' education consists of training in warfare and little else. Knowing nothing else, they are incredibly loyal to their masters, much like trained dogs."

"Whoopee," said Galen flatly. "Something else Hashem forgot to tell us about."

Sam shook his head. "I don't think Fedalf knows about these Dims." He looked at Galen. "I think you could fill an encyclopedia cube with what Fedalf doesn't know about Empyrea."

"No wonder he's willing to take a risk to allow us to put Alves out of business," Galen agreed. "Alves and the others have been permitted to run amok here while the Magistracy and the rest of the government turned a blind eye to their activities. But they're getting out of control, pushing too hard against the boundaries. The people in power are starting to get a little nervous."

"Could be," Sam said, nodding. "Could be."

Out of the corner of one eye, Galen saw Stephen looking at him. "Yes, Stephen, what is it?"

"Do you wish to hear about the werewolves now?"

"Not especially," Galen admitted. "Why don't you give us the basics?"

"All right," agreed Stephen.

Before Stephen could begin, Sam asked, "They're not *really* werewolves, are they?"

"No, they are not men who turn into wolves when the moon is full," the rebel leader said. "They are Spencer's World wolves whose genetic makeup has been altered to include DNA from both humans and Doros."

"What an odd combination," Galen mused.

"Perhaps," Stephen said. "But they are effective killing machines. Most effective."

II

Their small group had courted disaster more than once by the time they were within thirty kilometers of Alves's heavily guarded and fortified industrial complex. Each step closer to their destination brought with it an increased risk of confronting Alves's ubiquitous security forces. The most frightening moments had come during the long, dark night. At one point, while all but Sam and the sentries slept like dead men, a free-ranging hunter tank had passed within meters of their position.

Still more asleep than awake, Galen had sat up and begun to mutter a question when Sam pressed his hand over his mouth. Startled, Galen quickly realized something was wrong. Although his hearing was no match for Sam's, even his ears could detect the high-pitched whining of the tank's motors.

When it had passed, Stephen came over and said to the two of them, "That was close." Galen couldn't see his face in the unremitting gloom, but he did catch a flash of white teeth. With a diet consisting of little more than gruel, with few sweets to rot their teeth, the rebels didn't require the services of dentists.

"What *was* that?" Galen asked.

"Just a cat crawler." When that didn't seem to satisfy Galen, Stephen added, "It's a sort of tank."

"Oh," said Galen. "It was just a cat crawler. That's a load off my mind."

"They're solitary scouts," explained Stephen, oblivious to Galen's sarcasm. "Since they usually hunt by themselves, there's no need to worry about a second one bringing up the rear."

As daylight began to force the night to retreat and the rebels roused themselves from their sleeping bags, Sam stopped what he was doing and asked, "What's that?"

"What's what?" Stephen wanted to know, automatically unslinging his energy rifle and checking its charge.

"I dunno," Sam told him, turning his head this way and that, one hand behind his ear. "It sounded like . . . like . . ." He frowned. "I'm not sure."

"Do you still hear it?"

"No."

While Galen and Sam packed up their own gear, Stephen consulted with several others. He returned to the two Terrans and told them, "We won't bother with breakfast right now. I think it's best if we move away from here. We can stop and eat something once the sun is fully up."

"Sounds reasonable," Galen said. "Lay on, Macduff."

"And damn'd be him that first cries, 'Hold, enough!' " responded Stephen, his white teeth showing in a broad smile.

<They're certainly not dummies, are they?> said Sam.

<No, they're not,> agreed Galen. *<They don't have much in the way of material goods, living the way they do, but they have a few old-fashioned holoreaders that they use.>*

<Clearly they have some Shakespeare.>

<They do. I saw any number of book chips in Stephen's home.>

<That explains their vocabulary, doesn't it?>

<I thought they'd be . . . well, kinda dim,> Galen confessed.

<No,> replied Sam. *<We haven't met them yet.>*

Ten minutes later, they were standing at the lip of a wide ravine, its bottom covered with giant boulders and smaller, sharper-edged rocks. "We going down there?" Galen asked Stephen.

"It snakes much of the way to Alves's compound. It provides good cover from the air, and it's relatively level."

"Yeah, good cover for us—*and* for just about anyone or anything that might be lurking down there," muttered one of the burly men standing nearby.

"There is that," Stephen agreed.

"Once more unto the breach," sighed Galen.

Stephen smiled, but said nothing. He led the way down the steep slope onto the ravine's floor.

After walking less than a kilometer, Galen cursed their choice of roadways; where the ground wasn't so rough and rock-strewn that it hurt one's feet and posed the threat of a turned ankle, it was marshy and mucky and pulled at a person's boots.

"This is one helluva good news/bad news journey," Galen griped to Sam.

"What's the good news?" Sam asked, playing along.

"I'm gonna be in the best shape I've ever been in in my life."

"And the bad news?"

"That's only if it doesn't kill me."

Galen thought it remarkable that the floor of the ravine was not only carpeted in places with clumps of weeds and wild grasses, but also dotted with scrubby bushes. Whenever it rained heavily—Galen smirked at that, wondering what constituted "heavy" rain on Empyrea—the ravine almost surely became a raging riverbed. Presumably, the floodwaters would uproot and wash away the larger vegetation.

When Galen mentioned this to one of the Empyreans, a steely-eyed man a few centimeters taller than the others, he grunted and said, "Things grow fast here." Galen nodded and waited for more; none was forthcoming. With just the taciturn man's four-word response to go on, he guessed that the bushes established themselves between flash floods, thrived for days or weeks, and then perished when the heavier rains came.

His curiosity piqued, Galen approached one of the more unusual-looking bushes. "What kind of bush is this?" he wondered aloud.

"Blast you!" shouted the hard-eyed man, reaching out and grabbing him by the elbow and yanking him backwards just as one of the flowers on the bush clacked angrily at him.

"What the hell!"

"That's a snapper bush, Terran," the burly Empyrean told him. "Get too close and it'll take off a finger or two."

Careful not to "get too close," Galen leaned forward and examined the bush's innocent-looking "flowers." Now that he knew what to look for, he could see a beak inside, not unlike the mouth of a giant squid.

"Nice flora they have here," Sam said, joining him.

"This is a place worth studying in detail," Galen replied. "It's too bad the outlaw corporations have prevented it being opened up for study and research."

"They'd probably be heartbroken if they realized the size of the monkey wrench they've thrown into the wheels of science," Sam replied with a straight face.

"Sam, sometimes you're the—"

Without warning, several huge shapes appeared from around a bend in the ravine and rushed at the men caught in a vulnerable location.

"Werewolves!" someone shouted, and sporadic firing immediately broke out.

For an instant, Galen—and even Sam—stood slack-jawed as a pack of large, monstrous lupine shapes loomed out of nowhere.

"Jumping Jesus!" Galen cursed as two huge gray-and-brown-furred creatures poured over and around the rocks to attack them, one of them bowling over the man in front of Galen and ripping and tearing at the bearded man in a frenzy. In the blink of an eye, it tore out the shrieking man's throat.

The second werewolf was determined to make Galen the next victim. Just as resolved not to end up like the doomed Empyrean, Galen pointed his energy rifle and fired, the bolt from his rifle catching the animal in mid-leap. It yelped once as its body flew past him. Just to be on the safe side, Galen turned and pumped another bolt into the creature's body.

Sam also shot a werewolf out of the air, and was preparing to find another target when the rifle was yanked from his grasp and his left arm was seized by a powerful set of jaws. The growling, snarling werewolf began twisting its head and shoulders violently in an attempt to tear Sam's arm from its socket. When, to the werewolf's surprise, that didn't work, it crouched down and yanked hard on Sam's arm, catching him off balance and pulling him down on top of it.

Tiring of this game, Sam began landing a series of powerful blows against the animal's skull and muzzle. His fist connected solidly, but the werewolf just shook it all off. Even as he grappled with the large creature, Sam marveled at its strength and durability. Powerfully built, its muscles made even harder and smoother by Empyrea's high gravity, the wolflike creature was a formidable foe.

"All right, all right!" Sam said between clenched teeth. It was time to free himself. With his left still held in the werewolf's powerful jaws, Sam's right hand found a grapefruit-sized rock and he crashed it against the werewolf's skull, stunning it sufficiently for him to free his arm and seize the creature's throat in a death grip of his own. Slowly and surely, he used his inhuman strength to choke the life out of the werewolf. Finally, it went limp and he threw its body aside.

While Sam and the werewolf were rolling around on the hard ground in a *danse de mort*, Galen and the others faced werewolf problems of their own.

Galen was about to burn a hole through the chest of one of the attacking pack when one of the burly rebels stepped into the line of fire. "Shit!" he swore, and turned to find another target of opportunity.

Seeing movement out of the corner of one eye, he turned and fired in one motion. As rapidly and fluidly as he moved, the werewolf was quicker yet. The white-hot bolts of energy he directed its way missed it completely, striking the stagnant water on the ravine floor and sending up clouds of steam. He kept firing into the steam, acting as if he had an inexhaustible store of energy to draw from.

For a second, he couldn't see anything. Then the werewolf's head and shoulders materialized out of the steam, and Galen pressed the firing stud on his energy rifle. Nothing. He tried again, and the result was the same. "Uh-oh," he said as the werewolf bunched itself and leapt at him.

Sam tried to intercept the gray-brown mass of fur flying through the air, but he was a step late. He still managed to get a shoulder into its flank as its front paws struck Galen full in the chest and sent him flying backwards. All three of them tumbled to the ground and rolled across the sharp stones until they thudded to a halt at the side of the ravine.

His face in the dirt, Sam rolled over just in time to see the wall of the ravine crumble. He shielded his face and head with his arms seconds before he was covered by a small avalanche of rocks and soil. Cursing, he struggled to unearth himself.

Galen felt the werewolf's hot breath on his face as he tried to stiff-arm it and keep it from his throat.

Even though Galen's arm wasn't made of viviplastic like Sam's, he forced it between the monster's jaws and reached for his vibroblade. He pulled it out and slashed out wildly at the werewolf tearing at his arm.

Galen plunged the vibroblade home. The werewolf whined in pain and jerked away. Shaking its head angrily, it attacked again, its teeth seeking the soft skin of Galen's throat. Throwing his bleeding left arm protectively across his face and neck, Galen waved the vibroblade back and forth, catching the werewolf on the chest and muzzle.

Hot blood spattered him as the vibroblade found the werewolf's neck and opened up a gaping wound. Risking a quick look over his arm, Galen guided the tip of the vibroblade into the werewolf's chest, plunging it into the creature's heart and killing it.

Sam finally managed to push off the last boulder pinning him down and got to his feet. He looked around quickly to make sure that there were no other werewolves at loose in their midst. There were none; while he and Galen had fended off those that had attacked them, the others had been killed by the rest of their party.

"Are you all right?" Sam asked, pulling the limp body of the werewolf off Galen.

"I think so," Galen said weakly. Overcome by exhaustion, he could barely move his arms to check them for wounds; in addition to his arm, which was bad, but not as bad as he feared, he found a dozen or so bite marks and places where the werewolf's fangs had ripped and torn his skin.

"Is it over?" asked Galen, covered in blood.

Before Sam could reply, Stephen, himself bloodied and frazzled-looking, appeared to say, "I see you two survived the werewolf attack."

"What about the others?" Sam wanted to know. As he waited for Stephen's reply, he pulled a first-aid kit from one of the packs.

"We lost three members of our small community," Stephen said, swallowing hard. "All things considered, we seemed to have more than held our own against the werewolves."

"Yeah," Galen said, nodding his head. With his right hand holding his left arm by the wrist, he blocked out the pain, stared at one of the werewolf bodies and asked, "What did you say was in their genetic mix in addition to wolf genes?"

"They contain human and Doro genes."

"Doros?" said Sam, spraying Galen's wounds with an antiseptic quick-heal solution. "That explains their longish body and almost primatelike front limbs. But most Doros are gentle creatures until they are forced to fight."

"Don't forget that Stephen said they also have human genes," Galen told him. "We're the most dangerous animals in the galaxy."

"God help us," muttered Sam.

"What is it?" asked Stephen.

"I was just thinking that the people responsible for these genetic monsters are the same criminals whose greed and blindness is driving them to create a horde of mentally unstable cyborgs."

"Gee," Galen said, his voice heavy with sarcasm. "It doesn't sound like a good thing when you put it like that."

Sam stared openmouthed at Galen. Finally, he said, "I think I liked things better when you *didn't* have a sense of humor."

18

THE DEAD WERE BURIED IN MAKESHIFT GRAVES, TO BE exhumed and reinterred under more appropriate and solemn circumstances later. Their grim task complete, they moved on.

As the Class-M sun began to wane, they found themselves at the base of a long-extinct volcano. Years of incessant rain had worn down the ancient cone to the point where it resembled a gigantic pie plate. Once it had been a mighty mountain of fire; now it was little more than a rock-filled depression two kilometers from rim to rim, surrounded by sloping walls less than a hundred meters high.

"We are close, very close," Stephen said. "This tired old volcano marks the periphery of Alves's compound."

"What's that odor?" asked Sam.

"Odor?" repeated Galen. Then he caught the rancid scent as the wind changed and carried it to the group. His nose wrinkled and his eyes began to water. "It smells like a combination of rotten eggs, dead skunk, and chemical spill!"

"That's the river Jordan," Stephen informed them.

"That's right," Sam told Galen. "While you were . . . ah, resting your eyes on board the ship, I was studying the lay of the land. The Jordan is a muddy, sluggish river that makes its way through Alves's site and then to the ocean."

"Calling this stream of chemical sludge the Jordan is another example of the slap-your-thigh cleverness of these people," Galen noted sourly. "Alves probably has a cat named 'Dog.' "

Not knowing what Galen was referring to, Stephen simply shrugged. "We are fortunate that the river is here," the Empyrean told them.

"And why is that?" asked Sam.

"We might still be walking if we were forced to trek to the very center of the Alvco complex. The factories are located where they are in order to take advantage of the opportunity to dump most of their industrial waste into the river."

"Which obligingly carries it out to sea," Galen said, shaking his head. He thought of the pristine oceans girdling Cousteau and wondered what they'd look like if polluters like Alves ever got their hands on that world. *Thank God for the Whale Society!*

<Dumping waste into the rivers and the oceans is a crime against nature!> Galen fumed to Sam.

<What Alves and the others like him have done to this planet is a crime, period,> Sam said.

As soon as it occurred to Galen that it hadn't rained for almost an hour, a steady drizzle began to fall. A nearby vent released clouds of sulfurous steam and smoke.

"I thought you said this was an ancient volcano," Galen said to Stephen as he squinted because of the throbbing in his arm. He swallowed another pain pill.

"It is."

"It seems active to me," Galen noted. "At least active enough to crack open the ground and emit scalding hot steam."

"This old cone is not active in the sense of being capable of spitting up lava or semimolten rocks, but the ground under and around it is still seismically volatile."

"If Lucifer shows up, tell him I want to compliment him on the wonderful job he's done with this planet," Sam remarked to one of the rebels, a ruddy-complexioned man named William.

"Some day, God willing, Empyrea will be worthy of its name," William replied, spitting a glob of synbacco into a small puddle.

"Good shot," Sam observed. Scanning the area around him, noting the snapper bushes and the fetid steam escaping from cracks in the ground, he added, "I suppose everyone loves his home."

"Quiet!" someone warned in a low yet penetrating voice.

"What is it?" Galen whispered.

"It's a Dim patrol," a mountainous blond man said, pulling a wicked-looking knife from its sheath in his boot.

Galen gulped at the thirty-centimeter-long polysteel blade; polished and gleaming, it had blood gutters running the length of the shaft. All around him, others unsheathed their own knives and flattened themselves against the low, almost level slope of the volcano.

Seeing no alternative, Galen and Sam also dropped down into the mud. <*I just love lowering my face into a puddle,*> Galen told his partner sourly.

<*Sure hope it isn't the one that William hawked his synbacco goober into,*> replied Sam wickedly.

<*What?*>

When Sam didn't answer, Galen raised his face from the mud just enough to see four massive shapes clutching rifles coming in their direction, wending their way around the volcano. They maintained five or six meters between them to frustrate any attempt to take them all out with one grenade or a single burst from a slug-thrower.

Thankful that the mud clinging to his face provided an effective camouflage, Galen charted the Dims' approach; it appeared to be fifty-fifty that the unwelcome visitors would walk right on by the hidden rebels, passing within meters of their position.

One of the scouts, his eyes sweeping the muddy ground ahead, seemed to pause when his gaze reached Galen. With the man staring him full in the face, Galen froze. Then, after an eternity, the man's incessant gaze moved on.

Galen swallowed hard. *He didn't see me! He looked right at me, but the mud kept him from seeing me.*

Just when it seemed to Galen that you could cut the tension with one of the Empyreans' nasty-looking knives, the situation erupted. After almost stepping on a rebel, one of the Dims shouted a warning. Instantly, the Empyrean leapt up and plunged the blade of his knife into the Dim's throat. That triggered a short-lived confrontation that ended with the other Dims being dispatched almost as quickly and efficiently as the first.

Almost.

It took several Empyreans to overpower one of the four scouts because he was unusually huge and bull-like. The brief struggle that ended in the man's death unnerved Galen. He had killed many times, but the shock of such a sudden and unexpected outburst of brutal violence made him sick to his stomach and he turned away from the bodies of men who just seconds earlier were animated and alive.

Chiding himself for his squeamishness—the scouts would have probably not given his death and the death of his companions a second thought—Galen forced himself to examine the powerfully built body of the Dim who had resisted so strongly.

Even in death, the Dim—*Awful appellation*, Galen thought—was imposing. It was impossible not to admire the dead man's physique. The human form, in all its permutations, was a wondrous thing, he decided.

"My God. I thought you people were a piece of work. These guys are something else altogether."

" 'Tiny' here could've squeezed your head like a pimple," Sam commented thoughtfully, looking at the mountainous dead man's bulging and rock-hard biceps.

Sam's matter-of-fact assessment broke the somber mood Galen had allowed himself to fall into, and he shot his cyborg partner a give-me-a-break look. "Thanks. I needed that."

"Any time."

"Come," said Stephen. "The way in is not far away now."

Stephen was as good as his word; after continuing their circumnavigation of the volcano for several more kilometers, they finally reached a location one hundred and eighty degrees from their starting point.

"Here we are," one of the men said, and the others put down their weapons and ammunition for a moment's respite.

Galen needed no urging to collapse in a heap. "All my blood's in my lower legs and feet," he complained, lying flat on his back on the wet vegetation and crunchy ash.

"Try this," suggested Sam, lifting up Galen's legs and resting his feet on a pack.

"Thanks," Galen said. After emitting small moans of pleasure at having his swollen legs and ankles elevated, Galen asked, "So what happens now?"

"We wait for the other three groups to show up."

"We're the first?" Galen said. "Do we win anything?"

"A rest."

"Yes, here we are," Sam said to Stephen as he expertly massaged Galen's aching calves. "But where is here?"

"Look up there," Stephen told him, pointing up the volcano's increasingly steep slope with a nod of his head.

"What? I don't see anything."

"Look more carefully."

"I am, but I don't . . . oh."

"You see it, then?" queried Stephen.

"Yes."

"See what?" asked Galen, awkwardly twisting and looking over his shoulder.

"There's an entrance into the volcano," Sam told him.

"Yes, into the mine," Stephen elucidated.

"Where is it?"

"You'll see it when we get there," Sam told him. Then he turned to Stephen. "You called it a mine entrance."

"That's what it is. Years ago, this volcano's subterranean lava chutes were pulverized and the minerals extracted. There wasn't much to find, and what there was was soon exhausted. But the glassy tubes that carried the molten rock still go this way and that."

"Like an abandoned subway system," Sam said thoughtfully.

Watching Sam rubbing his throbbing calves, Galen asked, "Do you mean to say that one of these old lava chutes will take us right inside the heart of Alves's compound?"

"Neither the original flows nor the subsequent mine tunnels went all the way," Stephen said.

"Oh." Galen felt a twinge of disappointment.

Unable to contain the smile that spread across his face, Stephen immediately added, "We had to extend a number of them ourselves to make them reach into the compound."

When Galen remarked, "You must have stolen a John Henry," Stephen threw back his head and roared. "Did I say something funny?" Galen asked Sam. Sam just shrugged.

Stephen looked around for a second, spied a huge rock, and approached it and picked it up, a loud grunt escaping his lips. He carried the boulder for several paces before putting it down again. "There's your John Henry, Terran!" he roared.

<Ask him to arm-wrestle,> Sam said. *<His muscles are probably momentarily depleted of oxygen; I'll bet you can take him easy.>*

<Kiss my ass!>

<It was merely a suggestion.>

II

"Where are we?" Galen asked when they were within a few meters of the tunnel's end.

"If our calculations are correct, we should come out inside an abandoned factory," Brant said. His group had shown up outside the mineshaft entrance within thirty minutes of Stephen's group's arrival. The other two groups had each run into two Dim patrols; both had won their firefights, but they had lost a total of eight men and women.

"Abandoned?"

"It happens all the time," Brant told him as they watched Stephen and several of the larger and stronger men using picks and shovels to dig through the ceiling. "Alves's industrial complex is like a living organism—a self-repairing living organism. When a plant is obsolete, it is temporarily abandoned. Eventually, it is either refitted with new machines or torn down completely and rebuilt from the ground up."

"Oh."

"Get back," Brant ordered. "It looks like they're about to break through."

"Break through" was an optimistic way of putting it, Galen thought. The diggers had struck plascrete. Although they had dug through the dirt, it still remained for them to penetrate the factory's thick floor.

For the final several meters, the rebels turned to one of their weathered fusion torches. The torch sliced through the plascrete like it was . . . well, butter. Two men and a woman had lost their lives in the raid that had liberated the fusion torch. Remembering the torch's high cost, several of the Empyreans had sighed sorrowfully when they saw the torches Galen and Sam had brought with them.

"I think we've done it," Stephen said, coming back to where they waited.

"We're through?" asked Galen.

"It appears that way," Stephen confirmed. "But before we can enter the factory, someone has to go up and take a look around. We don't want any nasty surprises."

"I'll go," said Sam.

"Are you sure?" asked Brant.

"Yeah, are you sure?" echoed Galen.

"I'm sure."

"Well, don't just stick your head up," Galen advised him. "That's your Achilles' heel. Pull yourself completely through. That way, if there *is* someone waiting, he's more likely to hit your torso, not your square head."

"Yes, dadder."

"You cost a fortune each time we have to rebuild you," Galen said gruffly.

"Thanks." Turning to Stephen, Sam said, "I don't want to drag this out, so I'm going over the top. If I don't make it, see that Fifi in Paris gets my medals."

"Huh?"

"Just go already," Galen said.

* * *

Alves scanned the report his top Terran operative had sent him. Now a highly successful private investigator, the woman had once been a detective on the Boswash force and possessed a remarkable talent for penetrating business or governmental hierarchies, ingratiating herself, and then sucking them dry of top-secret intelligence.

Once she had confirmed that the purloined data was legitimate, she consulted her list of clients and promptly sold the information to whoever valued it highly enough to pay her substantial asking fee. The buyers or their motives didn't concern her; she did business with individuals, corporations, and governments. All she asked was that they meet her price.

Reading through the report, Alves marveled at her uncanny ability to predict which of her clients to approach with the fruits of her industrial spying. Take himself, for instance: How did she know that he would pay almost anything to get his hands on the facts in this filecube?

Her report had cost him a small fortune, but it was worth it. He'd had it for several weeks now, but he never tired of getting it out and skimming through its contents like a child who discovers his Christmas presents hidden in the attic and unwraps and rewraps them several times to play with what he's getting.

Alves clutched the filecube and stared at its label, shaking his head at his good fortune. The label said, "Complete Biographical Information: John Patrick O'Brian."

"John Patrick O'Brian," Alves said contentedly. "A.K.A. Sam Houston."

A chime sounded softly and Alves put the filecube in a safe place. Then he activated the viewer. "What is it?" he asked the holographic image of Joab Lykens, his director of security.

"There appears to be a break-in at one of the B sector buildings. From the readings we're getting from the motion and body-heat sensors, the intrusion consists of a large number of people."

"Don't tell me its those damned rebels again!"

"I'm afraid it is," Lykens said.

"I thought I told you not to tell me that!" shouted Alves. Then he laughed, a high-pitched squeal tinged with hysteria.

"I'm sorry, sir," Lykens said. Alves's odd response was shocking, but less so than it might have been. Alves's behavior was becoming more and more erratic, Lykens noted. In a year, he'd gone from rich eccentric to borderline psychotic; perhaps not even borderline.

"B sector is awfully close to our core facilities, including the research and development labs," mused Alves, regaining his composure and slipping back behind his mask of sanity.

"Yes, sir."

Alves held up a finger. "One: How'd they get in?" A second finger joined the first and he intoned, "Two: How'd they get as far as they did without being detected?"

Lykens shuffled forward a step and straightened his spine, making him appear taller. "I refer you to my last report, sir," he said carefully. "If you recall, I advocated finding and destroying the network of abandoned mine tunnels that surrounds and at times penetrates this complex."

Alves chose to ignore Lykens's disrespectful tone of reproach—for now. "You think they used the abandoned mineshafts?"

"This whole quadrant is honeycombed by those old tunnels; I can't think of any other way they could have gotten past the perimeter defenses unnoticed, much less suddenly appeared deep inside the grounds."

"How many of them are there?"

"That's hard to say," Lykens admitted. "If the reports are to be believed, there may be nearly a hundred."

"A hundred!"

"This is no hit-and-run raid, sir," Lykens confirmed. "They're here in strength."

Alves considered that. "Actually, I think it's for the best."

"Sir?"

"Unless you and your people are overpaid and underskilled, even a hundred of these rebels should be no match for our defenses. We'll decimate their ranks; after today, the threat from these genetic freaks will be vastly reduced."

"Yes, sir," replied Lykens. There was nothing else he could say.

"Then I'll leave you to deal with this matter."

"Yes, sir, thank you, sir."

Alves broke the connection, but continued staring at the now-vacant area where the image had floated. He leaned back in his swivel chair, interlacing his fingers behind his head, then nervously swung the chair to one side and then the other. Something was bothering him, but what?

He laughed silently. That was a joke! Clearly, the break-in was out of the ordinary. Such bold and presumably suicidal behavior wasn't typical of the rabble that opposed him. Although they liked to call themselves rebels, they had never tried an attack like this, much less in such force. Normally, they were content to ambush the occasional Dim patrol, or entrap and destroy a cat crawler.

He thought about that word, "suicidal." Would the vermin that opposed him *really* waste their lives in a presumably doomed attempt to disrupt his operations? Why would they take such a risk? Why now?

This idle speculation was getting him nowhere, he decided. Swinging back to face his communications console, he keyed in a short combination of numbers. The holographic image of a man in a white lab coat, his back to the holocam, materialized in the space where Lykens's image had previously appeared.

"Yes?" the white-jacketed man asked, turning around.

"Good evening, Dr. Hanks," Alves said pleasantly.

"What is it this time?" Hanks responded wearily.

Ignoring the other's lack of enthusiasm, Alves asked, "Tell me, Doctor, how are our creations doing?"

"They should be ready in a week," Hanks told him, rubbing his red-rimmed eyes with the backs of his fists.

Alves shook his head. "A week. You are so predictable, Dr. Hanks. No matter how many times I ask you when something might reasonably be expected to be functional, you always answer by saying a week."

"Okay, two weeks, then."

"Very funny, Doctor." Alves smiled; it was a patently phony smile with less warmth than a four-watt night-light.

"All right, a week," agreed Hanks. "If it doesn't matter to you that they're not ready yet, it certainly doesn't bother me."

"What about my mother-in-law?" Alves leaned forward expectantly.

"Just a moment."

Hanks exited the holographic projection, disappearing not only from Alves's sight, but from the laboratory itself.

"Doctor? Doctor Hanks?" There was no response.

After what seemed an eternity to Alves, but was probably actually only a few minutes, Hanks walked back into the image.

"Sorry about taking so long," Hanks apologized.

"I hope you had a good reason to keep me waiting, Doctor." Alves's voice was icy.

"That's for you to decide," Hanks replied, unfazed by Alves's demeanor.

"I'm not very good at playing games, Doctor," Alves said. "I don't have the patience for—"

There was a discreet but clearly audible rap on Alves's office door. "I believe that's for you," Hanks informed him.

"Who . . . ?"

When Hanks didn't reply, Alves got up and warily approached the closed door. Licking his lips, he reached out with his right hand. Tentatively, he touched the glowing admittance square. The door hissed open.

"Hello, Luis," the visitor said.

"I . . . ah . . ."

"What is the matter?"

"Give me a minute to gather my wits," Alves said, more stunned by his visitor's visage than he thought he would be.

"You were dead the last time I saw you; I felt for your pulse myself."

"Well, I'm not dead now, am I?" the cyborg asked. Then it threw back its head and emitted a raucous, braying laugh.

III

"Straight ahead!" Sam shouted, turning to fire several short bursts from the shrapnel gun he carried.

"We're right behind you," Galen shouted back, glancing at the men and women following them. No one appeared prepared to question Sam's objective, a low, nondescript, windowless building that had no value except as a stepping stone to their ultimate goal.

Alves's headquarters building was the massive plasteel and plascrete building a kilometer or so ahead of their position. Because of the open space between them and the towering six-story structure, they couldn't simply head straight there. Since crossing such a distance in one unbroken line would likely be suicidal, Sam's plan for them was to jump from one building to another like a frog leaping from one lily pad to the next.

They reached their destination without encountering any resistance. That bothered Sam. "I don't like this," he told Galen and Stephen as they climbed a short flight of steps to a loading dock. "That was too easy."

"You think they're waiting for us inside?" asked Thomas, scratching his brown beard.

"Maybe, maybe not." Sam shrugged and said, "Who knows, perhaps they're going to allow us to reach Alves's inner sanctum before they unleash their big guns."

"Do you really believe that?" asked Galen.

"No."

"Neither do I," said Thomas.

"C'mon," Galen said. "It's getting dark. Let's get this over with."

"Here goes nothing," Sam said, pushing the unlocked door open with the barrel of his shrapnel gun. The inside of the building was cloaked in gloom. Sam had hardly taken two steps inside when he heard high-pitched cries.

"Don't sho—" he began as a slug-thrower exploded over his right shoulder, its owner firing blindly into the darkness.

Immediately, an amorphous and pointillistic mass hurled through the air at them, resolving itself at the last minute into individual black and blue-black shapes that darted and stuttered like a school of frightened fish.

"Tarns! They're just tarns," someone shouted.

There was an outpouring of embarrassed laughter as the trigger-happy rebels realized the source of the mysterious squeaking was a cluster of flying mammals analogous to Terran bats.

The hot orange-blue gases that had flamed from the barrels of the slug-throwers had no effect on Sam, but they had momentarily destroyed the night vision of those rebels caught looking that way.

"Shit!" cursed Brant, bright orange dots dancing before his eyes.

"My sentiments exactly," Galen said, blinking.

"Wait here while I take a look," Sam said, hefting the shrapnel gun and striding deeper into the gloom.

Heedless of his words, a dozen rebels whose vision hadn't been impaired followed him inside. "I thought I said to wait outside," Sam said a bit more loudly than he intended.

"Brant is my leader, not you, Terran," one of the Empyreans retorted.

True enough, Sam admitted to himself. "Be careful, then."

Using infrared vision, Sam scanned the open core of the deserted warehouse. Nothing. His ears strained to pick up the scrape of a boot or the rustle of a moly-weave vest against cloth. Nothing.

Hearing a squeaking, scrabbling noise, he turned and fired in one fluid motion, a few shards of shrapnel blasting out of the barrel mouth of his gun. The cylinder spun for several seconds, finally slowing down and stopping.

"Good job," said one of the rebels with him, mocking the result of his unleashing his considerable firepower. "Looks like you blew that rat right into vermin heaven." He spat a large glob of synbacco juice between his teeth onto the dusty floor.

The man was right: Sam had blasted a large brown-and-black rodent to bits. He castigated himself for his itchy trigger finger; the victim of his shoot-first, identify-later compulsion could easily have been an innocent factory worker.

"I'll tell the others they can come in," the man who'd spat said, shouldering his energy rifle.

Sam was about to reply when something caught his attention. Straining to pick up the slightest whisper, his sharp ears had finally located a sound. "Wait," he said, looking up at a second-level walkway that circumnavigated the entire interior. His eyes now caught a flicker of movement.

"What is it?" asked the man, quickly unshouldering his rifle.

Sam's eyes widened as he identified the source of the sound. "Sentry guns!" he shouted.

Too late.

Four .50-caliber sentry guns, one on each side of the building's second story interior square, opened up, firing a furious fusillade of plasteel-jacketed slugs.

* * *

Sam's superhuman reflexes and speed saved him; fewer than a half-dozen slugs impacted his moly-weave vest before he made it to the relative safety beneath one of the walkways that encircled the warehouse's interior. Following his lead, two of the rebels joined him seconds later.

The others were not as lucky: Caught flat-footed out in the open, each was pummeled by scores of slugs. Although their moly-weave vests turned away many of the slugs, some got through and dealt them crippling wounds on their arms and legs. Three of the Empyrean rebels were killed almost instantly, their unprotected heads blown off by the plasteel-jacketed slugs.

"You two concentrate your fire on that fucking gun!" Sam shouted, pointing the barrel of his shrapnel gun at the walkway directly opposite their position.

While the others obediently pumped bolt after bolt of laser energy at the sentry gun, Sam balanced the shrapnel gun on his hip and began firing short bursts of metal bits at it. The barrel of the automatic weapon swung back and forth several more times before the stream of rough-edged metal pebbles smashed it to bits.

While Sam and his two companions were silencing that gun, several of the rebels threw down their weapons and rushed inside to the aid of their stricken comrades, dragging them to the safety of the entrance.

"What'll we do now?" queried one of the two Empyreans with Sam, removing his rifle's exhausted energy pack and slapping in a new one.

"We can't stay here all day," Sam replied, his words all but drowned out by the angry chatter of the sentry gun above their heads.

"We got one of them," the second rebel said, shaking with fear. Swallowing hard and composing himself, he added, "Now we have to get the other two."

That's the definition of courage, Sam thought, giving the other man an appreciative look. *To be scared to death and still do what needs to be done.*

"I agree," Sam said. "But how?" The answer was apparent the moment he glanced around and saw a ladder leading to the second level. "Ah, the stairway to heaven."

"What's the plan?"

"I'll lead, you follow."

"Sounds like a reasonable arrangement to me," the Empyrean said, a crooked grin creasing his face.

After reloading the voracious shrapnel gun, Sam mounted the ladder and began climbing up, the planet's heavy gravity more a nuisance than a deterrent.

Counting *One-two-three-go*, he clambered through the opening and onto the walkway. Immediately, the sentry gun on that section swiveled toward him. It was less than two meters away and he could hear its internal mechanisms adjusting to this nearer target.

"Oh, no, you don't!" With catlike reflexes, Sam hurled himself at the gun. He struck the still-warm barrel with his shoulder, knocking the tripod over. Wrestling with the seemingly alive gun like a hol-vee jungle hero wrestling with a thrashing crocodile, Sam wrapped his arms around its stock and barrel and, stumbling to his feet, lifted the one-hundred-and-twenty-five-kilo weapon completely into the air.

The captured gun, equipped with a basic yet semiautonomous AI mindpack, squirmed and thrashed in his arms, emitting a pitched squeal of frustration. It continued firing, disgorging a steady stream of slugs. Taking advantage of the gun's dogmatic programming, Sam directed its firepower against its mechanical comrades.

The sentry gun's incessant flow of plasteel-jacketed slugs smashed and battered the other sentry guns, knocking the barrels this way and that, piercing and ruining their circular ammunition drums. In less than a minute, the other two guns fell silent.

Sam now put the sentry gun's barrel across his knee and used his inhuman strength to bend the barrel into an acceptable approximation of a "v." Then he threw the still-protesting gun down to the floor of the warehouse. It bounced several times, emitted a thin, piercing shriek of protest, then fell silent.

"You can come on in," he called down to the others waiting by the entrance. "It's okay now."

19

"PLEASE, LUIS," GHANNEE BEGGED HIM, "I WANT TO GO HOME."

"This *is* your home," replied Alves, aware of the stupidity of the words even as they left his mouth. "For now," he added lamely.

"This is no home, this is a hellhole!" she retorted.

"I know, I know," he said, coming over to her and taking her by the shoulders. "Even with Terran-standard gravity in our living quarters, this ugly edifice is a poor excuse for a domicile, even if it is just for a few weeks more."

"A week here is like a month anywhere else."

"You're right." He pulled her to him, burying his face in her fragrant hair for a moment before drawing back and regarding her somber face. He kissed her. She responded feebly at first, then kissed him back.

"That's better," he said, meaning it. Ghannee was the one thing in his life that meant something to him that he hadn't bought with his money. Nothing before or since had surprised him as much as his realization that he loved her.

"I still want to go home," she insisted.

"Of course you do," he agreed. Stepping back and holding her by her hands, he looked into her large brown eyes and asked, "Would staying here a little while longer be more bearable for you if you had a visitor?"

"A visitor?" she repeated. "Who?" She thought for a moment. "Adrianna!" she said, letting go of his hands and clapping her hands excitedly.

"No, it is not Adrianna." He did not laugh at her; she disliked that enormously.

"Who, then?"

"Your mother."

"Mother is here?"

"Yes," he told her, enjoying her childish pleasure at the news. He pressed a square on his communications console, activating the voice function only. "You may bring Mother Tollersrud to me, Doctor."

Still enthralled by the news that she was to see her mother, Ghannee nonetheless was bothered by one thing. "Why is the doctor coming with her?"

"She suffered a minor spell of hypersickness on the journey here," Alves lied smoothly. "I've asked Doctor Hanks to look after her while she's here; it's a simple precaution."

"Oh."

Ghannee waited impatiently. Finally, the door hissed open and her mother walked in, followed by Dr. Hanks. "Mama!" Ghannee rushed to embrace her mother.

"Ghannee, Ghannee," the cyborg said as the young woman wrapped her arms around what she thought was her mother and hugged her joyfully.

"Oh, I've missed you so much, Mama!"

"And I you, dear," the cyborg said, patting Ghannee maternally on the back. "But you are a married woman now, and I did not wish to interfere." The cyborg smiled and, glancing over Ghannee's shoulder, gave Alves a sly wink.

"My God!" Alves said under his breath. He shot Hanks a what-the-hell look. The doctor just shrugged and shoved his hands into the pockets of his stained lab coat.

"Just let me hold you and smell you and touch you and everything," Ghannee said happily.

"Of course, Ghannee."

"Mama, I . . ." Ghannee's voice trailed away. She looked at her mother's hand, still clutched tightly in her own. She frowned and looked again. Then she stared into her mother's face.

"What is it, dear?" The cyborg's homely face was creased by maternal concern.

All the color drained from Ghannee's face as she stared at

her mother's features, her eyes darting from her nose to her eyes, to her hair and back to her eyes. "Who are you?" she asked finally, her voice barely audible.

"Whatever do you mean, daughter?" asked the cyborg, taking a step toward the young woman.

"Stay away from me!" shouted Ghannee. "Keep away!"

"Ghannee, what is this nonsense?" Alves asked.

Turning to look at him, she hissed, "What have you done with my mother?"

"Don't be foolish, dear," the cyborg told her, beginning to show flashes of impatience. "I am your mother."

"No, you are not!"

"Yes, I am!" the cyborg insisted, its voice rising.

"I want my mother!" Ghannee demanded of Alves.

The cyborg, angered by the failure of its imposture, grabbed her by the arm and spun her around forcefully. "I am your mother, child!"

"No, no, no!" cried Ghannee, pounding the cyborg on its chest.

"Wicked child!" shrieked the cyborg, slapping Ghannee across the face with the flat of its open hand. "I told you, I *am* your mother!"

"Mother Tollersrud . . ." Alves said, confused and angered by the cyborg's illogical behavior. He put out a hand to restrain the false Kitrina.

Pushing Alves away, the cyborg told Ghannee, "I'll teach you to deny your mother," and began battering Ghannee with its fists. As the violence and intensity of its blows began to increase, Ghannee tried futilely to ward them off.

"Stop this immediately!" a horrified Hanks ordered his creation, but to no avail. He joined Alves in attempting to force it to quit its vicious attack upon Ghannee, but the cyborg shoved both of them backwards, sending them into the wall.

Now totally enraged, the cyborg struck Ghannee with increasingly powerful and deadly blows. Neither Alves nor Hanks could make the out-of-control creature cease its deadly pummeling.

"Stop this! Ghannee!" Alves cried, again attempting to pull the cyborg away from Ghannee; again the cyborg forced him back.

Screaming inhumanly, "I am your mother! I am your mother!" the cyborg continued its assault upon Ghannee until she was battered and bloody, her face unrecognizable.

"I *am* your mother," it ranted. "I am your *mother*."

Its homicidal outburst having run its course, the cyborg laughed hysterically and rushed from the room.

"My God!" Alves said, staring at the battered corpse of his bride. Alves howled like an animal and pressed his fists against his temples as if to obliterate the scene before by crushing his own skull.

Unable to look at Ghannee's body any longer, he transferred his gaze to Hanks. "This is all your doing! You are an incompetent quack!"

"I told you I needed more time!" Hanks said, shaken by the dreadful incident. "I will not accept the responsibility for what happened. The cyborg must be captured and destroyed. They must all be destroyed before they can harm anyone else."

A chime sounded softly on Alves's desk. Gulping down mouthfuls of air and composing himself, he went to it and pressed a glowing square. "Yes?" he asked the image of his security chief.

"This building has just been penetrated by intruders. I lack confidence in our ability to defend ourselves against so many well-armed invaders."

"Thank God!" Hanks said. "It's time someone put a stop to this insanity!"

Alves opened a desk drawer, withdrew a needle gun and fired at the surprised Hanks, a ceramic shard passing through the doctor's left arm. Acting instinctively, which saved his life, Hanks threw a syringe at Alves. When Alves ducked, Hanks ran from the room.

Alves sighed, then tossed the needle gun aside.

Falling to his knees and cradling Ghannee's head in his arms, Alves stroked her hair and lamented, "Oh, Ghannee, everything's gone wrong!"

II

The Empyreans had hardly entered the main facility before they ran right into a contingent of Dims who immediately opened fire on them. Returning their fire, Galen told himself with grim satisfaction that if there was a bright side to the slam-bang confrontation, it was knowing that they were better armed than their opponents.

"C'mon," the black-bearded Mark shouted. "Hunkering down in one place only gives them time to bring up reinforcements." The others understood Mark's meaning: The situation was ripe for a full frontal assault. One of the Empyreans, a woman with flowing blonde hair, popped the pins on two grenades and hurled them in the direction of the Dims. The resulting explosion threw the Dims off balance.

"Let's go," shouted Sam, charging toward the line of massive defenders to attract their fire to him. As his moly-weave vest sparked and hissed, the rebels took advantage of the distraction to successfully cross the open space between them and the Dims.

Shouting curses and whooping and hollering, the Empyreans overran the Dim position and a fast and furious hand-to-hand firefight erupted when the two lines of combatants intermingled.

While the Dims had size and strength in their favor, the rebels both outnumbered and outgunned them. It wasn't all guns, however. Bright shards of light flashed off the wicked blades of the knives that some of the Empyreans resorted to in the close quarters.

Finding a vulnerable opening just above the other's moly-weave vest, a squat Empyrean drove his knife into the shoulder of a hulking Dim. It was perfectly aimed and struck, but the attacker couldn't withdraw it to strike again. Seemingly unaffected by the wound, the Dim patiently pulled the other to him and, placing his hands on either side of the man's head, crushed his skull as efficiently as any hydraulic press.

A gigantic defender near Sam slipped on some blood and fell down. As he got to his knees, Sam shifted the shrapnel gun to his left hand and rocketed a short, powerful right into the center of the man's face, flattening his already broad nose and sending him toppling over backwards. "Nighty-night," Sam said to the unconscious giant.

Feeling like a dwarfish spectator at a clash of titans, Galen studiously avoided the give-and-take of the infighting and coolly targeted and picked off individual soldiers with well-placed head shots. Once they became aware of his deadly actions, the Dims were not disposed to allow Galen to continue his leisurely decimation of their numbers.

The Dim who had so cruelly crushed the knife-wielding attacker waded through the roiling mass of bodies toward Galen. He swept the energy rifle from Galen's hands and effortlessly lifted him completely off the floor.

"Jesus!" Galen shouted, more in surprise than fear—although pants-wetting fright wasn't far behind once he recognized the perilousness of his situation.

Hearing Galen's cry, Sam whirled to see the Dim contemplating the smaller man's skull like a melon he was considering purchasing. Sam raised his shrapnel gun and then lowered it; with Galen in such close proximity to the Dim, he couldn't fire without obliterating Galen along with the giant holding him like a small child.

Clutching Galen by the front of his moly-weave vest with his left hand, the Dim slowly and deliberately placed his enormous right hand over the top of Galen's skull, completely covering it.

The Dim looked at Galen and smiled.

Galen smiled back.

Still smiling, Galen swung his fist as hard as he could, striking the knife still embedded in the Dim's chest.

The Dim shrieked in agony and let go of Galen. As soon as Galen hit the floor and rolled away, Sam leveled his weapon and the shrapnel gun spat several controlled bursts. The marble-sized pellets pounded the Dim's enormous moly-weave vest before obliterating the Dim from the jaw up.

Galen said, "Christ!" as he was spattered by teeth, blood, and brains. Now several centimeters shorter than he had been, the Dim slowly collapsed, folding accordionlike to the floor.

Observing that the brief encounter between the rebels and the Dims had just about played itself out, Sam checked on Galen's condition. "You okay?" he asked the prostrate Galen.

"I'm just taking a little rest," Galen said, wiping gore from his face with his sleeve. "You guys go on without me; I'll catch up later."

"All right," Sam said amicably. "You can guard our tails, protecting against any Dims who might try a rear attack."

Galen sat up quickly, the heavy gravity draining blood from his head and causing him to feel light-headed. "Did I hear someone say we're moving on? Don't leave without me."

"The corridor takes a turn to the right up ahead," one of the

Empyreans noted. "I wonder what's around the corner?"

Sam smiled grimly. "Trouble."

Actually, what was around the next corner were more Dims and several Pseudo-Quantum-Gravity-brained robots. The Dims were at the far end of the corridor. Halfway down the long corridor, patiently waiting for the invaders to venture into their killing zone, the robots guarded a side corridor. To Sam's way of thinking, the Dims were redundant; after all, who could get by killer 'bots?

"P-Q-G 'bots?" Galen said. "Is there no illegitimate activity *not* being perpetrated in this cesspool?"

"Slavery?" Sam asked innocently.

"You're forgetting Hanks and his wife and kids."

"Oh, right."

"What shall we do?" Mark asked Stephen. "We've never faced killer 'bots before."

"There's a first time for everything," Sam said helpfully, the sound of his voice causing the two Empyrean rebel leaders to eye him like two hungry cats appraising a mouse. "Uh-oh," Sam said to no one in particular, "it looks like I'm about to volunteer to walk into the lions' den again."

"You're the only one of us who has a chance of reaching the end of that corridor alive," Galen reminded him.

"Okay," Sam said, accepting the inevitable. "Let's get all our dominoes in a row, shall we? That means get the people with the rocket launchers, the shrapnel guns, and the fusion torches up here."

"Then what?" asked Brant.

"Then you avenge my death." When everyone blinked at that, Sam explained, "Just kidding." When no one cracked a smile, he added, "Sheesh, don't take everything I say so seriously."

"This *is* very serious," Galen told him.

"For you," Sam said. "If anything happens to me, you're the one who'll have to break the news to my folks."

"I do not understand anything you two are saying," Mark told them, tugging on an earlobe in confusion.

"Don't worry," Sam told him. "When Empyrea is free, Galen will see that the government inoculates everyone with a sense of humor."

"Me, too?" Galen asked.

"You especially."

Sam exchanged his shrapnel gun for a fusion torch, paused to think for a second, then asked for the three rocket launchers as well. They were smart weapons, so he held them around the corner and allowed them to load the robots into memory as targets. He handed two of the rocket launchers back, keeping one for himself.

"You're going now?" Brant asked pointedly.

Sam sighed, then grasped and shook the hands of Galen, Mark, Thomas, Brant, and Stephen. "Once more unto the breach, dear friends, once more," he said.

"Give us the best part," Galen prompted.

Sam nodded and intoned, "Be copy now to men of grosser blood, and teach them how to war. And you, good yeoman, whose limbs were made in England, show us here the mettle of your pasture; let us swear that you are worth your breeding; which I doubt not; for there is none of you so mean and base, that hath not noble lustre in your eyes. I see you stand like greyhounds in the slips, straining upon the start. The game's afoot: Follow your spirit, and upon this charge cry 'God for Harry, England, and Saint George!' "

Without waiting for a response, Sam raised the fusion torch high, like a standard, and rushed around the corner.

* * *

Sam was convinced he was going to be killed. Pledging to take as many of the killer robots with him as he could, however, he vowed to remain among the living for as long as possible.

No sooner had he turned the corner and entered the corridor off which lurked three—or perhaps as many as four or five—of the killer 'bots, he ignited the fusion torch. That got the robots' attention, and two of the giant killing machines thudded out into the corridor.

"Halt, cyborg," ordered one of the still-distant robots, stepping further into the center of the corridor. The robot's right arm ended in a chaingun, a gatling gun configuration which utilized a large rotary drum to feed it a thousand rounds a minute.

At the far end of the half-kilometer-long corridor, several of the Dims, laughing and pointing, began firing their energy rifles and semiautomatic slug-throwers. It was a clever move, Sam thought; the robots were impervious to the Dims' firepower, so the human defenders didn't have to worry about their fusillade knocking out their mechanical allies when the 'bots got in the way.

Sam shrugged off the small-arms fire directed at him by the confident Dims and readied the launcher. "The one on the right," Sam told the two smart rockets the launcher contained. That said, he fired both as quickly as he could. There was no need to aim, since the rockets had been assigned their target.

As soon as two rockets left the twin barrels of the launcher, Sam threw it aside. Even as the rockets were punching one-two into the target robot's torso, Sam began a headlong rush.

The impacted robot blew up in a deafening explosion that ignited the walls and sent smoke and hot gases curling down both ends of the corridor. Ignoring the acrid black smoke, Sam accelerated rapidly, his legs pumping like pistons, until he was all but flying down the corridor.

The surviving robot seemed befuddled by Sam's laser-fast assault, acting as if it had been programmed to wait for him to comply with its earlier demand that he stop and surrender. Sam continued accelerating, ignoring the hits his moly-weave vest was absorbing and bounding off the walls like a jackrabbit on amphetamines.

By the time the twelve-meter-tall robot realized Sam wasn't going to halt, it was impossible for it to effectively track the rapidly moving, zigzagging Sam. The 'bot opened fire, its chaingun arm spewing forth a stream of heavy-caliber slugs.

When he was just a few meters from the robot, Sam flung himself into the air. Flashing by the 'bot, he swung the fusion torch in an arc, and the sun-core-hot fusion stream sliced through the robot's molecular-steel torso like a hot poker through jelly, instantly destroying its P-Q-G mindpack.

Sam was already beyond the halved robot when its top portion toppled backwards off the bottom, its chaingun still firing. The unexpected flood of heavy-caliber slugs from the chaingun caught the Dims at the end of the corridor by surprise, and the gun's hideously efficient killing capabilities turned half of them into a bloody pulp in the blink of an eye.

Sam hit the floor, allowed himself to take a headfirst tumble and land flat on his back, and then dug in his heels to brake his forward momentum; with all that he still slid nearly twenty meters down the corridor before coming to a stop.

Sam barely had time to find a niche in the wall where he secreted himself before the other robots strode out into the center of the corridor looking for blood. Fortunately for Sam, Galen and the rebels chose that instant to surge into the corridor, firing their weapons at the bunched robots.

A rebel-launched rocket struck one of the robots square in the back, the molecular-steel-tipped warhead penetrating a good ten centimeters into the 'bots chest cavity before self-destructing in a satisfying burst of flame and plasmetal.

The two remaining robots seemed demoralized by their unexpected vulnerability; their resistance, while still lethal, was neither as coordinated nor as vigorous as it might have been.

Wielding their fusion torches like light-sabers, the rebels cut the molecular-steel legs out from underneath the two robots. Then, in a display of mindless fury and determination that stunncd Galcn and Sam, thc powcrful hcavy-worldcrs pullcd the robots to pieces with their bare hands—albeit hacking at them with the fusion torches when necessary.

"Mother of mercy!" Galen exclaimed to Sam, coming over to the place where his partner had hidden himself from harm's way.

"At the very least."

Galen asked, "You okay?"

"I'm fit as a fiddle and ready for love."

"I'll take that as a yes."

"Do me a favor, willya, Gale," Sam said, watching the carnage down the corridor.

"What?" Galen asked suspiciously.

"Don't ever let me piss any of those guys off!"

"Deal."

III

Having conquered the robots, the Empyreans again split into several groups to make sure the building's perimeter was secure. That done, Galen, Sam, and the leadership conferred on how best to proceed. As they closed the circle on the core of the six-story building's ground floor, it seemed more and more probable that their quarry's lair was somewhere above them.

There were still surprises and traps for the unwary, however. Exploring the labyrinthlike inner corridors, one group of raiders found a seemingly empty room. They were about to investigate when they decided that discretion was the better part of valor; rolling an empty drum into the center of room, they watched in bemused satisfaction as two hidden sentry guns chattered to life and peppered the decoy with a hail of slugs. They relayed their discovery to the others, and it served as a warning against impulsive or foolhardy acts.

"I presume our next step is to find a way up," Stephen said.

"I'm not so sure," Galen said, surprising everyone.

"Come again?" Sam wasn't sure he'd heard his partner correctly.

"When Fedalf took me to see you at . . ." He paused, looking at the others watching and listening intently. Shrugging, he continued, "At the subterranean laboratories, I joked about such places always being underground, like at the Foundation."

"I'm with you so far."

"A secret underground facility *does* seem to be a cliche, but, dammit, it also seems the logical location for such a lab. I mean, cliches and stereotypes aren't spun out of fairy gold; they have to come from somewhere."

"You think there is a similar facility here?" asked Brant.

"I do."

"So where is it?" demanded Sam. "We've been all over this place."

"I have an idea," Galen said cryptically.

"This *is* the room guarded by the sentry guns, Cloris?" Galen, wanting to be absolutely sure, asked her a second time.

"Yes, of course," the blonde Empyrean said, a hint of exasperation in her voice. "You can see the perforated container near the far wall."

"Good." Galen looked around; where *was* Sam?

"Sorry," Sam apologized, arriving with four stubby maintenance 'bots in tow. "Am I late?"

"No more than usual." Galen looked at the battered and grimy 'bots Sam had collected. "Jeez, these fellows have certainly seen better days."

"What are those worker 'bots for?" asked Cloris.

"They're better than empty barrels," Galen explained. "They have wheels."

"Oh," said Cloris, instantly grasping the essence of Galen's plan.

"Do they know what to do?" Galen asked Sam.

"They're not smart weapons, but they're prepared to do their bit for God and Country."

"And Harry and Saint George," Stephen added.

"Okay," said Galen. "One at a time." He tapped one of the garbage-can-shaped 'bots on its "head" and said, "Go into the room and move around in circles. Whatever happens, keep moving as long as you are able."

So primitive that it lacked speech circuits, the little 'bot just chirped and wheeled into the room. The sentry guns immediately opened up and Galen, looking through the door at the 'bot's progress, flinched each time it took a hit. After one prolonged volley, the 'bot ground to a halt, its control mechanisms destroyed by gunfire.

"Next," said Galen, and the second 'bot wheeled in to meet its doom. Turning away from the door, Galen looked at Sam and asked, "Why do I feel so bad about this?"

"I understand," Sam told him. "But you have to tell yourself that these little guys are no more alive—truly alive—than the sentry guns blasting them to bits."

The barrage of gunfire slowed and then stopped. Sighing, Galen sent in the third 'bot. This time, however, the firing was not nearly as intense and began to grow more and more ragged and sporadic. Finally, it ceased altogether.

Galen sneaked a look inside. The third sacrificial 'bot was still functional; just barely, but it was moving. He gave the thumbs-up sign to Sam. "It worked."

"Let me check it out," Sam said, readying his shrapnel gun and moving toward the doorway.

"We'll wait out here," Brant told him.

"Be careful."

"Yes, Gale."

"Don't call me . . ." Galen stopped; Sam had already slipped inside the long, rectangular room.

"C'mon in," Sam called out to them. "I think I found something."

The "something" that Sam found was a section of wall that

slid back to reveal a short corridor containing both an elevator and stairs going one way: down.

"I don't like this," Galen said, eying the narrow stairwell suspiciously.

"Okay, let's go," Sam said, pretending to leave.

"Not that," said Galen. "Well, yes, *that*, but what I meant was I don't like the fact that this stairwell funnels us into a tight bunch. If more than a handful of us venture down there, we're all nicely packed four abreast."

"Ah, the old World War One machine gun theory."

Galen's forehead wrinkled. "What?"

"Those empty sentry guns are essentially .50-caliber machine guns on tripods, right?" Sam asked.

"Yeah."

"Well, when the killing power of the newly invented machine gun was contemplated, so-called experts calculated that if a column of soldiers packed four or five abreast were to march straight into the line of fire, a single machine gun could wipe out thousands and thousands of them in a day, a hundred thousand or more in a week, or even millions if you kept them coming." He paused to allow that to sink in. "There was only one catch."

"And that was?"

Sam grinned slyly. "How to convince the soldiers to line up and walk lemminglike into the machine gun's maw."

The Empyreans guffawed at that, and Sam made a little bow of acknowledgment.

"Why does that story not make me feel better about descending those stairs?" Galen asked rhetorically.

Sam just shook his head. "Where's that old 'Once more unto the breach' spirit?"

"Blow it out your ass!" Galen snapped, causing the Empyreans to laugh even harder.

"Cheer up, Galen," Thomas said, clapping him on the shoulder. "We all have to die sometime. And besides"—he looked around at his comrades—"you're lucky to still be alive after what we've encountered so far. You have to figure we're going to have to cross the real river Jordan sooner or later."

"All right, all right," Galen said, weary of arguing. "But no more than ten or fifteen of us are going down those stairs."

"Why?"

"That's a high enough number to sacrifice. If we don't make

it, the others can withdraw, pack this place full of explosives, and blow it from the outside."

"All right," said Brant amiably. He stepped forward. "I'm going."

"No, you're not," Galen told him.

"And why not?"

"Because," Galen said evasively.

"You have to have a better reason than that," Stephen said.

"I . . . I met his family," Galen confessed.

"I thank you for that," Brant responded, "but most of us here have families. I'm going."

"Me, too!" chorused the rest.

"Okay, okay," Stephen said, raising his hands. "Let's choose who's going and who's staying."

"Don't take long," Sam suggested.

"Yes, be as quick about it as you can," Galen said.

"We will," Stephen promised.

When the dust settled, Galen and Sam were accompanied down the stairs by Stephen, Thomas, Cloris, and seven others whose names Galen knew barely or not at all. All were armed to the teeth. Galen carried a fusion torch and several pistols, knives, and grenades; as if that weren't enough, he also had an energy rifle slung over his back. Befitting his cyborg strength, Sam carried a shrapnel gun and a rocket launcher. The others were similarly encumbered.

The stairwell zigged and zagged downward for three flights, ending at a plain metal door.

"This is the moment of truth, I guess," Stephen said.

"It's not too late to go back," Sam told him.

"Yes, it is," Thomas said, clutching the fusion torch he carried.

Sam laughed nervously, and Galen asked, "What is it?"

"I remember an old sinny image. These military men were standing outside a door just like this one, preparing to open it. Behind it, they supposed, was a creature from another world."

"That's an *old* sinny," Galen marveled.

"So what happened?" asked one of the others.

"They opened the door and the alien *was* right there on the other side. When it lunged at them, they closed the door so quickly that they cut off its arm." Sam frowned, trying to extract all of the memory trace. "He was a kind of vegetable, so I guess that's why his arm came off so easily."

"Well, get ready for a killer carrot," Galen said, reaching out with his right hand. He paused a second, then hit the entry patch and the door hissed open.

Someone or something was standing just inside.

"GOOD DAY, GENTLEMEN," THE SIMULACRUM WITH ALVES'S face said pleasantly. Something intended to pass for a smile lifted up the corners of its mouth.

"Good day, Luis," Galen replied. "I'm taking the liberty of calling your stand-in here by your first name for two reasons. First, wherever the real you is, you're family. The second reason is simpler: As the man who will find you and kill you, I don't believe I should hide behind formalities."

"How confident you are, Galen," the simulacrum marveled. "I like that in an opponent. As for killing me . . . well, perhaps. It is possible that Sam or one of these other gentlemen will kill me. Or—dare I say it—I might kill you all."

"I have two questions," Sam told the simulacrum.

"Yes?"

"Why didn't you seek help when you realized you were beginning to lose your grip on reality? The days when someone has to hide psychological disfunctionality are long gone."

"What is your second question?"

"It's related to the first," Sam explained. "Having concealed your illness from even those closest to you, when did you realize that you had delayed treatment to the point where it was too late?"

"My goodness," the simulacrum said in a shocked voice. "What remarkably rude questions!"

"I think that's all the answer we're going to get from this nutcase," Sam told Galen.

"Nutcase?" Galen hadn't heard the term before.

"Just one of a plethora of derisive words people used to describe the mentally ill. You know, from the 'bad old days.' "

"Do you remember those times, Mr. Houston?" the simulacrum asked.

"Not really," Sam admitted. "Occasionally I recover bits and pieces of my life before. Nothing more than scraps."

"Would a filecube containing your detailed history be of any interest to you, Mr. Houston?" it asked. The simulacrum immediately emitted a short, barking laugh and added, "Or should I say, Mr. . . . " Sam's eyes widened and he unconsciously leaned forward to hear the name Alves tantalizingly threatened to reveal. Sam stared at the simulacrum as though he was in a trance.

Having paused so dramatically, the simulacrum declined to say any more. Instead, cocking its head at Sam like a metallic praying mantis, it said, "No, sorry. I can't reveal your true identity at his time. I'm too much the businessman to give that information away for nothing."

Looking first at his shaken partner and then at the simulacrum, Galen demanded, "What's your price?"

"Sam and I shall talk more about this later," the simulacrum said, beginning to back away.

"Stop," Galen ordered.

"Goodbye."

"Goodbye, my ass!" Sam shouted, breaking out of his trance. He threw down his rocket launcher and grabbed the fusion torch out of Galen's hands.

"Sam, don't!"

Sam caught up to the retreating simulacrum and raised the fusion torch. Futilely throwing up its arms to ward off the blow, the simulacrum could do nothing as the torch cut through its left hand and then sliced the top of its metallic skull off.

Sam angrily kicked at the sticklike figure of the semidecapitated simulacrum. "Bastard, lying bastard!"

After allowing Sam to calm down, Galen said casually, "You think Alves was lying?"

"Of course. Don't you?"

Galen shook his head. "No."

Sam sighed and admitted, "Me neither. Not really."

Galen laid a hand on his friend's shoulder, saying nothing.

"Come on," said Stephen as the Empyreans rejoined Sam and Galen. "We've got to find the real Luis Alves."

"Then what?" Galen wanted to know.

Stephen's eyes were hard as he replied, "Then we do the same thing to him as Sam did to this walking, talking piece of metal and plastic." He kicked the remains of the simulacrum with the toe of his boot.

"Hey," protested Sam. "I'm a walking, talking piece of metal and plastic."

Now it was Stephen's turn to lay a reassuring hand on Sam's shoulder. "No, my friend, you are not. You are a human being."

* * *

"Sonofabitch!" exclaimed Galen.

"Ditto," said Sam.

They had found and entered a large, brightly lighted room with a score of zero-degree-Celsius tanks and a half-dozen sophisticated surgical tables. It had the antiseptic smell and look of any hospital. Or morgue—there were several bodies lying faceup on the tables, tubes and wires trailing from their arms and skulls. Their eyes were open but unseeing. They seemed suspended between life and death.

"What is this place?" asked Cloris. Her eyes darting nervously about the room, she avoided looking at the bodies.

"Victor Frankenstein's laboratory," Thomas said, having recently read Mary Shelley's novel.

"With more than one monster," Stephen added, pointing to the seemingly lifeless bodies lying on the tables.

Galen warily approached one of the bodies and prodded it with the barrel of his energy rifle, half-expecting its eyes to swivel toward him or for it to leap off the table, its hands reaching for his neck.

Galen's eyes narrowed as he stared intently at the motionless body's face. Then his jaw dropped and he exclaimed, "Well, paint me blue and call me a turnip!"

Accommodating him, Sam said, "You're a turnip. Now, you want to tell us what roodied your kazoo?"

"I know this . . . person," Galen stammered. "We all do."

"We do?" someone said.

"Galen's right," Thomas said, coming over and staring down at the body's relaxed visage. "This is Consul Wilcox."

"Or a cyborg impostor," Galen said between clenched teeth.

"What about the others?" Cloris asked.

The others, excepting two of the unresponsive bodies, were all consuls or highly placed Principate bureaucrats. Those two were special in their own way.

"Hello, Sam," Stephen said, staring down at the two bodies.

"What?"

Sam and the others joined him at the sides of the two cyborgs.

Sam gulped. There, lying faceup on two tables, their golden eyes staring sightlessly at the ceiling, were identical copies of Sam. They were even clad in copies of his blue jumpsuit. They were indistinguishable from Sam.

"My God!"

As Sam contemplated his mirror images, his doppelgangers, one of the Empyreans, keeping an eye out for unwelcome visitors, pressed a section of wall and watched, amazed, as it moved back a meter.

"Hey, over here!"

Everyone clutched his or her weapon tightly and responded to the awed summons.

"What is it?" asked Thomas.

"A corridor. There's a corridor back here." The man pointed. There was indeed a corridor, and it made a ninety-degree turn to the left at the end of its ten-meter length.

When Sam and Galen stepped forward, Stephen raised his rifle and blocked their passage. "Hold it." He nodded at Cloris and a red-haired man. "Saul and Cloris, you two take a look at what's around that corner. And be careful."

Following Stephen's orders and advice, the two ventured to the end of the hallway and slowly peeked around the corner. "Looks okay," Saul said.

The others quickly hurried after them, making the turn and finding themselves staring at a series of elevators and lift/drop tubes. They went in only one direction: up.

"Uh-oh," Galen said. "Decision time."

"I agree," Thomas said. "But whatever we decide to do can wait."

"For what?" asked Sam.

"For us to finish our business down here first."

"And what's that?"

"We must destroy those abominations we discovered in that madman's laboratory."

"Destroy them?" asked Galen, sounding as if the idea hadn't already occurred to him. Looking at the others' faces, he guessed that they'd all considered the possibility. The *necessity*, perhaps.

"Yes, destroy them."

"But, we can't!" Sam heard himself say.

"And why not?" demanded Cloris.

"They may be people like me," he said, putting a hand to his chest. "They may be cryo-sleepers whose personalities and brain patterns have been preserved and successfully transplanted into a host body, into the body of an android."

"Or they may be unstable killers like the 'borg that tried to murder Fedalf and take his place," Galen said quietly.

"But . . ." Sam threw up his hands; he knew his partner might be correct. *<Am I letting my emotions overrule my intellect?>* he asked Galen.

<No one can blame you for reacting like that.>

<That means yes.>

<Yes.>

Unaware of Galen and Sam's internal dialogue, Thomas leveled his rocket launcher at Sam and said quietly but with authority, "We will do what we must. If we are forced to choose between the safety of our families or destroying these new body-snatchers, it is no contest. Our families come first." He smiled, but his eyes were hard. "You are a brave man, Sam Houston. Don't force us to destroy you as well."

Quietly, unobtrusively, several Empyreans pointed their weapons in Sam's direction. Sam stared at the grim-faced Thomas for a long time, neither man wishing to be the one to avert his gaze first.

Finally, Sam looked at Galen and then at the floor. "Destroy them," he said quietly. "I won't try to stop you."

The tension slowly melted away, and the Empyreans lowered their weapons.

"Come, let's do it," Stephen said, retracing their steps.

Returning to the sterile laboratory, they quickly surrounded the first table. Everyone's eyes stared at the unconscious form lying there.

"He looks so real, so alive," marveled Cloris, finally forcing herself to confront the quiescent cyborgs.

"He is," Sam said softly.

"How shall we do this?" asked Saul.

Licking his lips, Galen said, "Take one of the fusion torches and cut off the top of his . . . er, its . . . skull."

Taking a fusion torch from one of the others, Stephen said, "I will do it." Following Galen's instructions, he destroyed the cyborg's brain with one swipe of the sun-core-hot fusion torch's flame.

"The second one's always easier," Galen told him encouragingly as they moved to another table.

"Let me," insisted Thomas, taking the torch from Stephen. Stephen didn't resist.

"Now me," said Saul.

Galen appreciated the wisdom of the Empyreans, each generously assuming a share of the guilt so that no one had to bear the brunt of it alone.

The executions continued until . . .

"By my father's grave!" exclaimed Saul.

"What is—Ohmygod!"

The two duplicate Sams were gone.

II

Whether by chance or by some stroke of luck—good or bad—Galen selected a pathway that led directly to the sixth floor. While Galen chose a nonstop elevator, Sam took a lift/drop tube that ended one floor below the sixth.

Both were deposited on levels that announced their strangeness from the beginning. Galen found himself facing a series of corridors that radiated out from his arrival point; the walls of each corridor were an electric blue.

The fifth-floor level that Sam found himself on was a maze of red brick walls. Unsure whether or not to believe his eyes, Sam reached out, expecting to touch a rough brick surface. Instead, his fingertips encountered a completely smooth surface. "I'll be damned," he murmured. The bricks were an illusion, most likely the result of hidden holo projectors.

"Toto, I don't think we're in Kansas anymore," Sam said, patting the shrapnel gun he carried.

On the sixth floor, and feeling very lonely and vulnerable, Galen mulled over which corridor to choose. "Does it matter?" he asked himself. Shrugging, he headed down the corridor directly in front of him, all the time telling himself he was probably doing just what Alves wanted him to do.

At the end of the corridor was a closed door. "Oh, no, not again," he moaned. Turning his head, he looked back the way he had come, something telling him he ought to retrace his steps. *And then what?* he asked himself. Sooner or later he was going to come to another door; sooner or later he had to open one of them.

"Sam, where are you?" he asked out loud; then, readying the energy pistol he clutched in his right hand, he reached out with his left and hit the glowing entry square.

The door hissed open, revealing . . . Sam.

"Sam! Am I glad to see you! What happened to you?"

"I ended up on another floor," his friend told him. "Fortunately, it didn't take me long to find a way up to this level."

"What's down that way?" Galen asked, pointing over Sam's shoulder.

"C'mon, I'll show you."

"Great."

"Go ahead," Sam told him. "I'll watch our backs."

<*Galen.*> Sam's transmitted voice was harsh and weak, like a transcontinental caller on the archaic telephone system that once carried voice communication across the seas.

<*Yeah, what is it?*>

<*What is it?*> Sam asked, sounding puzzled. <*Where the hell are you?*>

Galen turned and glanced over his shoulder. Sam smiled back at him and gave him the thumbs-up sigh. <*Ah . . . aren't you right behind me?*>

<*Are you crazy? Of course not. I—Jesus jumping Christ, Galen, that's one of Alves's cyborgs!*> he shouted before their link was broken.

* * *

Sam felt frustrated. Galen was in trouble and he could do nothing. Still, he had to try. <*Galen . . .*> he called. When he got no response, he called again. <*Galen. Can you hear me, Galen?*> Again there was no response.

Don't panic, Sam told himself. *There are a couple of reasons he's not responding, including being shielded or moving too far away from me*. There were other reasons for Galen's nonresponsiveness, as well, but Sam did not permit himself to consider them.

He followed the maze *faux* brick walls, turning this way and that. To take his mind off Galen, Sam thought about their antagonist. It was beginning to look more and more like Luis Jorge Alves was a textcube case of monomaniacal madness. This whole structure, with its hidden rooms and elevators, was proof of the man's insane compulsions. Sam wondered how long he'd been degenerating into the madman he'd become. Years, he supposed.

The corridor came to a huge red brick block and bifurcated around it. Sam chose the right side. Halfway down the length of the block was another corridor, split off at a right angle. Ignoring it for a moment, he proceeded around the block. The original corridor continued on straight ahead. He backtracked along the opposite side of the block, and wasn't especially surprised to find that a corridor split off from that side as well. Sighing, he went down it.

Returning to his musings, he decided that Alves's compulsions and paranoia were probably behind the poorly conceived efforts to kidnap him to see what made him tick. The attacks on the Voorhees family compound and on the Foundation didn't make a lot of sense if one considered that there were better—not to mention less drastic and risky—ways to get the data.

The corridor ended abruptly; it was a dead end. Sam was about to retrace his steps when he muttered, "Dead end, my ass!" He began feeling the walls with his sensitive fingertips.

Having found nothing after five minutes, he was about to give up when he sensed the merest hint of a crack. It was less than the thickness of a human hair, but it was there. Once he found it, he was quickly able to trace its outline. The rectangular shape implied a door.

Every door needs a knob or an entry square—something, he thought, his fingertips now moving across the supposed door's surface. Nothing. *Dammit, it has to be here! It—*

He found a slight indentation, the size of a thumbnail. "Eureka!" Readying himself, he pressed the indentation. At first nothing happened; then the rectangle moved backwards.

Unsure what to expect, Sam moved cautiously in and around the two-meter-high rectangle and toward a faint glow.

III

"Well, we meet again," Luis Alves said, pushing back his chair and getting up from behind his communications console.

"Excuse me if I don't shake your hand, cousin Luis," Galen told him, rubbing the back of his neck.

"Oh, I'm sorry about that," Alves said. "But 'Sam' here anticipated your attempt to ignite your fusion torch. Forced by your hostile intent to prevent his own destruction, he struck you rather forcefully."

"That's one way of putting it."

"You're lucky I didn't kill you," the cyborg told him. "You flesh-and-blooders are so fragile."

"Keep thinking that, superman," Galen told the cyborg. "Pride goeth before a fall."

"Tell me," Alves said. "How did you know Sam-one here was not the real thing?"

Galen made a come-here gesture with his index finger. When Alves leaned toward him, Galen whispered conspiratorially, "It has bad breath."

Alves blinked several times, threw his head back, and laughed uproariously. When his shoulders stopped shaking with laughter, he leaned forward again and slapped Galen hard across the face, splitting his lip and sending a thin stream of blood flying to spatter against a wooden cabinet.

"How I hate you and all you stand for, little rich boy!" Alves hissed, his face contorted by anger. "You've had everything in your life handed to you on a silver platter!"

"It was gold, actually," Galen said, unable to stop himself from taking Sam's role as the smartmouth. "We're from South Africa, remember."

"Oh, yes, I nearly forgot."

"You're part of the family now, so what's the big deal, Luis?" He felt his lip swelling; fortunately, the blood flow seemed to be slowing.

"Part of the family now?" Alves closed his eyes as if remembering something unpleasant.

"Through your marriage to Ghannee."

"Yes, Ghannee," Alves said in a strangled voice, looking at Galen strangely.

"And you seem to have Aunt Kitrina in your back pocket."

Alves took a deep breath, unable or unwilling to say anything.

"What's the matter?" Galen asked. "What have I said?"

"Your aunt is dead. She was becoming unreasonable; she wished to abrogate our arrangement. It was necessary that she die in order to be reborn as a cyborg like Sam-one here."

"You killed Aunt Kitrina?"

"Yes. Unfortunately, there's more."

"Ghannee?"

Alves nodded. "The new Kitrina proved to be . . . unstable. When confronted by Ghannee's accusations that she was not her mother, the cyborg went berserk and . . ." He stopped, swallowing several times. Composing himself, he continued. "It killed her before anyone could stop it."

"My God! You *are* mad!"

Alves struck him openhanded once again. "The cyborg killed her, I didn't!"

"My mistake," Galen said. "That's a big difference. Never mind, that makes all the difference."

"I never wanted to kill you," Alves said.

"But you'll swallow your qualms and do it anyway."

"I must say, you are making it easier and easier for me."

"Where is the other one?" the cyborg asked. "The one that looks like me."

"It's the other way round, actually," Galen corrected. He flinched when the cyborg took a threatening step toward him. "What is this, slap a helpless person day?"

"You are quite calm for one facing death," Alves informed him.

"We've been 'facing death' since we arrived on this stinking planet," Galen told him. "Do you expect me to start wetting my pants now?"

"Perhaps you will feel differently once I have your friend under my control."

"You have to find him first."

"Don't worry, I will. And when I do . . ."

"Yeah?"

"When I do, he will do whatever I ask of him."

"And why is that?"

"Because of this." Alves withdrew the filecube from its hiding place.

"What's that?" Galen demanded.

"It's a biographical report on Sam Houston." He grinned. "Or should I say on the person who became Sam Houston?"

Galen stared at the filecube.

* * *

"Is that you, Kitrina?" Sam asked the plain-faced woman standing before him.

"Of course it's me, Mr. Houston."

"How did you get here?"

"My daughter is here."

"Ghannee?" he said. Then, "Yes, I suppose she would be." He looked around the small room, noting that it was essentially featureless.

Seeing his examination of the room, the cyborg explained, "I was just on my way to see if I might find Ghannee. The two of us want very much to leave this place of death and madness."

"I can't blame you there," Sam told her, unable to put his finger on what it was about her that bothered him. "You say you're looking for Ghannee?"

"Yes, have you seen her?"

"No. If I had, I would have her with me."

"Of course."

"What's back that way?" Sam asked, pointing over her shoulder.

"That way?" She seemed surprised by the question.

"Yes, that way," he repeated.

"Come, let me show you," she told him.

Shrugging, Sam followed her to the door and waited while she pressed the entry square. After the door hissed open, she stepped aside and said, "After you."

The room, the first of what appeared to be a suite of interconnected rooms, was clearly meant to be a sitting room. Plushly carpeted, it contained a couch, several chairs and tables, and a real wood-burning fireplace, complete with a flickering fire.

"Allow me to fix you something," she told him, directing

him to the sofa. He put the rocket launcher down, but rested the shrapnel gun on his knee.

"You know I don't drink except as a courtesy," he told her. "Besides, I have to find Galen; he's in danger." Looking down at himself, as if he were suddenly outside his body and seeing it clearly for the first time, he said, "Wait a minute. What the hell am I doing here?"

When he started to get up, Kitrina crossed over to him, her right arm hidden behind her body. Without warning, she brought her arm out from behind her body and swung a heavy polysteel poker at him.

Even catlike as his reflexes were, Sam was almost caught off guard by the sudden attack. Almost, but not completely; he twisted and the poker, meant to crush his skull, struck him where his neck and shoulder met. Given the Kitrina-cyborg's strength, it was an immensely powerful blow and it sent Sam and the couch over backwards.

The cyborg was on him in an instant, battering him savagely with the poker. Realizing that he couldn't be hurt any more by a frontal assault than he was being already, Sam reached up and grabbed hold of his attacker's plain black dress and pulled "her" down on top on him.

As they rolled about the floor, the cyborg's fingers sought his eye sockets. Sam found the cyborg's hands and closed around them, capturing them like two small wild animals. Slowly, powerfully, he drove them down alongside the cyborg's body.

"I'll kill you! I'll kill you!" the cyborg screamed.

"That'll be the day," Sam grunted, methodically forcing the composite creature's arms behind its back. Panicked by Sam's superior strength, the cyborg resorted to desperate measures.

Screaming obscenities, the cyborg drove its forehead into Sam's with as much force as it could muster. Since Sam's skull was the recipient of the blow, it was driven backwards, rebounding off the hard, wooden floor. The dual impacts momentarily stunned Sam, allowing the cyborg to escape his grasp.

His vision clearing, Sam had enough presence of mind to roll to his knees and scrabble for a weapon. Locating the shrapnel gun, he snatched it up—only to find himself staring down the barrel of the rocket launcher.

"Don't shoot!" Sam implored the cyborg.

"The great Sam Houston is begging for mercy?" the cyborg asked.

"Not at all," Sam said, getting to his feet. "I'd just like to point out that if you fire that thing in here, we'll both be blown apart by the warhead's detonation."

"Hm-m-m," mused the Kitrina-cyborg, "you have a point." It risked a quick look behind it, spotting the still-open doorway they'd passed through. The cyborg quickly grasped that if it backed into the next room and fired the rocket from there, most—if not all—of the explosion would be contained in this room.

Sam figured out the cyborg's plan and smiled grimly. He had a chance; it was a huge risk, but he could see no alternative. He continued to smile as the cyborg backpedaled into the other room.

Raising the rocket launcher, it said, "Goodbye."

Sam watched the cyborg's finger. When it tightened on the firing mechanism, he fired his own weapon, unleashing a stream of shrapnel. The shards of metal met the rocket just as it emerged form the launcher's firing tube and caused the warhead to explode instantly.

A blast of flame and hot gases erupted into the room, picked Sam up, and hurled him through the wall behind him into the bedroom where he landed on the bed.

He lay there for a long time, then laughed semihysterically. "Sam," he admonished himself, "this is no time to be a slug-a-bed. You've got to get up and go find Galen."

He sobered up immediately. Yes, he had to find Galen.

"But where are you, partner?"

21

"WHY HAVE YOU BROUGHT ME BACK HERE?" GALEN ASKED Alves as Sam-one hustled him out of the elevator and out onto the factory floor.

"Everyone's either looking for us upstairs or down," Alves said. "I figure we have a good chance to find sufficient numbers of my loyal mercenaries to escort us safely out of here. We can commandeer a vehicle from one of the maintenance sheds and find safety with one of my neighbors."

"What about Sam? I thought that's what so much of this was about."

"I can acquire Sam Houston anytime," Alves told him. "I've got this"—he held up the filecube—"and I've got you. Either of you is enough to get his attention; together, you're irresistible."

"Be careful what you wish for," Galen told Alves. "Sam'll come after us, sure enough. And then he'll kill you."

Alves shook his head. "Not if he wants this badly enough."

"What's to stop him from killing you and taking the damn filecube?"

"It's linked to a biofunction key implanted in my skull. If my life functions cease, the filecube will be irretrievably erased."

"That's bullshit."

"If you think I'm bluffing, there's only one way to find

out, isn't there? And if I'm not, there goes Sam Houston's opportunity to discover his true identity."

"You bastard!"

Alves took a bow. "Come, we must be going."

* * *

Cloris, Thomas, and three others had managed to find their way from the fourth floor to the fifth. After rejoicing over their success, they realized that they had to begin all over again at square one to find a way up to the sixth floor.

"These red brick passages all look alike!" moaned Thomas, pulling at his brown beard in frustration. "This level is a maze, an impenetrable maze."

"A maze, yes. Impenetrable? No."

"Why don't we just keep turning right?" one of the others suggested, a ruddy-complexioned man named Edward.

Cloris looked at Thomas, who just shrugged. "Sure, why not?" she said. "It's as good a strategy as any."

After passing through a dozen doorways, they found themselves in a short corridor that looked suspiciously familiar.

"I think we've been going in circles," Thomas said.

"Let's go right for the next two doors, then try turning left," Edward offered.

"All right," Cloris said. "But let's leave a marker." She ignited the fusion torch she carried and made an "X" on the right wall. "If we come this way again, at least we'll know for sure that we've been here already."

After two right turns, the group left. As they were about to go through yet another doorway, Cloris groaned and clutched her abdomen.

"What is it?" a concerned Thomas asked.

"Cramps," Cloris said through clenched teeth.

"Will you be all right?"

"I have some medication in my kit," she told him. "I'll get some water out, take the pills, and everything'll be fine in a few minutes."

"Hey, this looks promising," Edward said, examining the door.

"Why don't you four go check it out," Cloris told them. "As soon as I take my medication, I'll catch up to you."

"All right," Thomas decided. "Don't be long."

"I won't. Don't get too far ahead."

"Just through here and maybe the door beyond," Edward promised. With that, they left her behind.

They found their way into the ruined suite where Sam had outdueled the fake Kitrina. It was badly damaged, and all that was left of the dead cyborg was a polysteel viviplastic leg, the foot wearing a severe black shoe.

They walked through the suite into the empty bedroom. "Wow, a really deadly confrontation occurred here!" one of the Empyreans said, whistling.

"I wonder who won?" Thomas mused.

"I did," said a voice from the sitting room.

They raised their weapons, then lowered them almost immediately.

"Oh, it's you," Edward said.

"Hi, Sam," Thomas greeted the cyborg.

"You wanna hear something really funny?" Sam-two asked as it stepped into the bedroom.

"Yeah, what?"

"I'm not Sam Houston."

"Huh?"

The cyborg opened fire with the automatic slug-thrower it carried, killing all four men with several short bursts. Even though the cyborg could see that they were dead, it continued pumping slug after slug into the bodies.

Cloris gulped down three capsules and felt better almost immediately. Some of it was just the idea that she'd taken something for the pain, she realized. But whatever worked, worked. She wasn't about to try to convince her roiling innards that they ought to still be sending out those hot, stabbing sensations.

Holding the fusion torch out in front of her, she hurried to catch up to the others. After she'd gone through the first door, a shiver ran down her spine and she reacted by igniting the torch.

Moving slowly and cautiously now, she saw that the door in front of her was not quite closed. She pushed it open gingerly and eased through. She picked her way silently across the sitting room. Suddenly, the distinctive cough of an automatic slug-thrower came from ahead of her.

Someone was standing just inside the next room firing a

slug-thrower, his back to her. In one horrifying instant the scene resolved itself before her eyes and she saw Sam Houston pumping round after round into her friends' bodies.

"Goddamn you!" she shrieked, raising the fusion torch high.

The cyborg was just turning when the hot stream of energy sliced down through his head and on through his torso, cutting him in half.

"You bastard! You dirty, rotten bastard!" Cloris screamed over and over.

II

"Going somewhere?" Sam asked, stepping out of the shadows.

"Hi, Sam," Galen said to his friend.

"Hello, Mr. Houston," Alves said. "You know, it's difficult for me to remember to call you by that name. It's difficult because I know your real name."

"Yeah, what is it?" Sam asked, uneasily shifting his attention back and forth between Alves, an energy pistol held to Galen's head, and his doppelganger, the false Sam-one.

"You must pay the price first."

"And what might that be?"

"You could put down that formidable weapon you are carrying," Alves said, nodding at Sam's shrapnel gun, "and kill cousin Galen, using something less likely to injure me as well."

"Sorry, can't do that."

"What happened to the rocket launcher?" Galen wanted to know.

"Aunt Kitrina borrowed it."

"Ah, you encountered my cyborg mother-in-law, did you?" Alves asked.

"We chatted."

"I suppose I needn't ask who won the confrontation, since you are here and she is not."

"You killed her?" Galen asked.

"You heard the man—she was a cyborg. Alves killed the real Kitrina, copied her as a cyborg, and then the cyborg ran amok and killed Ghannee."

"I know," Galen said softly.

"I guess I didn't really expect you to eliminate cousin Galen for me," Alves said. "But you can still earn the right to see what's inside your filecube if you simply put down your weapons and walk away from all this. You needn't play the part of 'the pale companion' for the rest of your existence. If you just walk away, the 'cube's yours."

"Sorry, I can't agree to that one, either."

"You are being very tiresome, Mr. Houston."

"Sam," Galen told him. "If you kill this fruitcake, the filecube will be erased—at least that what he says."

"It doesn't matter," Sam told them both.

"Maybe this matters," Alves said. He released Galen and gave him a strong shove. Galen stumbled forward several meters or so and was turning around when Alves shot him through the back.

A bloody mist erupted from the right side of Galen's chest and he exclaimed, "Well, fuck me! I've been shot!" He crumpled to the ground.

"No!" screamed Sam, rushing toward the fallen Galen.

At a signal from Alves, Sam-one intercepted Sam, clamping his hands around his neck. As Sam knocked the cyborg's arms akimbo and punched it in the face—his face—Alves said, "You boys fight it out," and turned to walk away.

Laughing, he keyed in a series of numerals and letters which would unlock a molecular-steel door leading to an underground emergency exit tunnel.

Hearing something behind him, Alves turned and—

—Everett Hanks, the left side of his lab coat caked with dried blood, plunged a vibroblade into his tormentor's throat.

Alves gurgled, trying to say something, then stumbled forward a few meters, his arms outstretched. Dropping the filecube, Alves collapsed, bright arterial blood pumping from the wound in his neck. Then the flow slowed, and finally stopped.

Luis Jorge Alves was dead.

The dropped filecube hissed and sputtered, a foul black smoke pouring from its interior. The history of John Patrick O'Brian disappeared, evaporating with the last few wisps of smoke.

* * *

"You're good, very good," Sam told his opposite, having just parried a furious series of blows from the other's length of polysteel pipe. "But, then, you should be, shouldn't you? I mean, you're me."

"Yeah, I'm you," the cyborg replied. "I'm better than you, though."

"How do you figure that?"

"Because I don't have feelings; you have feelings."

"You're right about that," Sam said, stepping forward and lashing out with a well-placed kick that knocked the cyborg back into a pile of empty oil drums. In an instant, he was standing over the evil machine that wore his face, trying his best to smash in its skull.

As skilled as Sam, the cyborg rolled out of harm's way and regained its feet, all the time fending off Sam's blows, powerful blows that rang sharply off its own polymetal pipe.

They were evenly matched; too evenly matched for either cyborg to gain an advantage. Sam could see no end to their deadly contest.

Galen opened his eyes. He remembered being shot, but he could feel no pain. He looked down at the scarlet ribbons spreading across his chest and flowing onto the floor.

With the clarity of insight of a condemned man, he knew two things. The first was that if he didn't get help soon, he was going to die. The second was that he had several precious minutes, perhaps only sixty seconds, in which to act before he lapsed into unconsciousness and, in all probability, died.

Somehow, he managed to get to his feet. Now he had to find a weapon. *Please, God*, he thought. *When I went looking for you in hyperspace, I found only emptiness. True emptiness would be a universe without Sam. Help me to save him. I need a weapon.*

Several Empyreans showed up from nowhere and were shocked by his appearance. Refusing their offers of assistance, he made one of them give him the rocket launcher he carried. Then, like a walking corpse, he stumbled across the factory, looking for Sam and the cyborg with Sam's face.

They both saw him out of the corners of their eyes at the same time. "Jesus Christ!" they chorused.

"Hi, Sams," Galen said thickly. He could sense his time running out.

When they moved toward him, he said, "Stop," and raised

the rocket launcher. Pointing in the general direction of the two cyborgs, the weapon wavered unsteadily.

"Shoot the other one, Galen," the Sam on the right said. "I'm Sam, the real Sam."

"I'm the real Sam," the one on the left insisted.

"Shut up," Galen said, blood frothing on his lips. "I'm gonna ask one question, and I want a good, smartass answer."

"Sure," the Sam on the right said.

"What did the elephant do to you?"

The Sam on the right said, "He stomped me, he kneeled on me, he pulled me apart."

"Good answer," Galen said. "What about you?"

"He truncated me."

"Better answer." Galen swung the rocket launcher to the right and fired. The head and shoulders of the *faux* Sam disappeared in a fiery blast.

Sam rushed over to catch Galen before he could hit the floor. "Goodbye, Sam," Galen told him. "I'm gonna die now."

"The hell you are, you bastard!" Sam shouted. Then he calmed himself. Saying, "I don't suppose you could get much more limp and muscle-relaxed than you already are," Sam whispered "Rogue elephant ears" into Galen's right ear.

Just then Stephen rushed up and, seeing that Galen was not breathing, asked, "Is he dead?"

"I don't know."

ADRIANNA HELD HIS HAND. SHE HELD HIS HAND AND TALKED to him. And although no one could say that he could hear her, neither could they say that he couldn't.

The trance that had saved Galen Yeager's life had turned into a coma. Faced with the possibility that he might never reawaken, Adrianna nonetheless showed up every day to hold his hand and to talk to him. She didn't know why she did either.

That wasn't true, she told herself. She did it because she still loved him. If anything could bring him back, she thought, it was love.

<<Hello, Galen.>>

<Hello, Alfie.>

<<How are you, Galen?>>

<I'm fine, I guess. Why?>

<<They want you to go back, Galen.>>

<They?>

<<Adrianna and Sam. And Hashem Fedalf. And your family. But Adrianna and Sam more than anyone else.>>

<Adrianna and Sam? Why?>

<<They love you.>>

<But it's so peaceful out here. I can stay as long as I want, you know.>

<<Yes, I know.>>

<What should I do, Alfie?>

<<Do not ask me,>> Alfie told him. *<<Ask your heart.>>*

<My heart?>

<<Yes.>>

Galen's senses reached out to what surrounded—or didn't surround—him. His ordeal on the starship seemed to exist in another lifetime. When he had gazed into hyperspace seeking the meaning of life, he had seen nothing—no God, no eternal truth, no all-encompassing force or presence that permeated every subatomic particle of the universe.

Galen knew now that he had been oblivious to what even a blind man with love in his heart could see: that as long as a living creature loved and was loved in return, the universe was filled with life and meaning. Only those who failed to reach out and accept the love of family or friends saw nothing but a yawning void. That was the real Hell, he realized—not a place of fire and brimstone, but a cold, empty abyss devoid of friendship and love.

Alfie saw Galen "smile" and disappear. Smiling himself, Alfie went to find his friends.

Sobbing into Sam's shoulder, Adrianna said, "He's never coming back, is he? I mean, it's been six weeks now."

"That's not such a long time," Sam said, comforting her as best he could.

"You're right," she said, wiping her eyes. "I'm being weak. I have to do whatever it takes."

Galen's eyelids fluttered, and he opened his eyes to see Adrianna being consoled by Sam. "Hey, what's going on here?" he demanded. "My best friend and my wife are cheating on me."

"Galen!" shrieked Adrianna.

"Ex-wife," Sam said with a smile as Adrianna covered Galen's face with kisses.

"I can rectify that."

"Oh, Galen, I love you so," Adrianna told him.

"And I love you, too."

"Welcome home, partner," Sam said.

"Thanks. It's good to be back."